WARSPITE

WARSPITE

CHRISTOPHER G. NUTTALL

http://www.chrishanger.net
http://chrishanger.wordpress.com/
http://www.facebook.com/ChristopherGNuttall

Cover by Justin Adams
http://www.variastudios.com/

All Comments Welcome!

Text copyright © 2014 Christopher G Nuttall
All rights reserved.
Printed in the United States of America.

ISBN: 1505400767
ISBN 13: 9781505400762

AUTHOR'S NOTE

It will probably surprise most readers to see a fourth book of *Ark Royal*, as the titular ship died quite spectacularly at the end of *The Trafalgar Gambit*. *Warspite* is set in the era immediately following the First Interstellar War, which was detailed in the first three *Ark Royal* books. I've done my best to allow new readers to jump right into the series without actually needing to read the first three, but I would recommend reading them first to gain an understanding of the background.

As always, I am indebted to my beta readers, to whom this book is dedicated.

Thanks for reading!
Chris

PROLOGUE

Published In *British Space Review,* 2207

Sir.

Although Commodore Biotin and Admiral Fredrik raise excellent points concerning the philosophical implications of other forms of intelligent life (aside from us and the Tadpoles), they are hardly the prime subject of interest to the readers of *British Space Review.* Not to put too fine a point on it, we are concerned with the outcome of the First Interstellar War and its implications for the future development of both the Royal Navy and the United Kingdom.

Prior to the Battle of Vera Cruz, naval thinkers anticipated facing a human enemy, rather than an outside context villain. The Royal Navy was shaped in line with lessons learnt through studying American-Chinese skirmishes and war games conducted by the major spacefaring powers. However, when we were actually faced with a serious war, our doctrine proved to be largely insufficient. The disaster at New Russia, if nothing else, proved that our imagination when it came to alien threats was definitely inadequate. Indeed, were it not for the freak circumstances that kept *Ark Royal* in service, we would have lost the war. As it was, *Ark Royal* was able to buy us time to react to the new threat.

However, the outcome of the war leaves us with a multitude of urgent questions, all concerning the government and defence of the human race. It is not my place to speculate on any of the proposals to turn the Earth Defence Organisation into a real government, but I must note that history suggests that any attempt to embrace a single government for much of the human race is doomed to failure. The Troubles – and the Age of Unrest – were largely *caused* by such attempts. Therefore, we must assume that the Royal Navy, while working closely with allies such as the Americans and French, will have to prepare for the future alone. This will not be an easy task.

We started the First Interstellar War with fifteen fleet carriers, not including *Ark Royal*. Ten of those carriers, a significant proportion of our budget, were lost in the fighting, along with forty-seven smaller warships and an undisclosed number of support and replenishment vessels. The Royal Navy has refused to declassify the precise number of starfighters and their pilots lost in the war, but outside observers have concluded that eighty percent of the pre-war establishment died in the first year of the war. These loss figures, which are comparable with those suffered by the other major spacefaring powers, are truly horrific.

This leaves us with a major problem. We must rebuild the fleet, at the same time as recovering from the damage inflicted on our country by the Battle of Earth and mustering as many freighters as possible to transfer settlers from Earth to Britannia. Failing to do so, despite the hideous costs involved, will merely render us weak and vulnerable, against both a recurrence of the war and conflict against our fellow humans. I hardly need remind the reader that many nations have suffered badly as a result of the war and some of them blame the whole conflict on us. Indeed, the troubles suffered by the Russians in regaining control of New Russia, following the Tadpole withdrawal from the system, suggest that a whole new series of inter-human conflicts may be about to begin.

And there is a further threat. Prior to the Battle of Vera Cruz, we believed ourselves to be unique in the universe, the sole intelligent race. This belief has been resoundingly shattered by the war. We cannot afford to rule out the possibility that other races may be out there in the darkness – and that some of them will pose a threat. Or, for that matter, that we will be hemmed in by alien-occupied stars and find ourselves with no further space for expansion.

Therefore, sirs, we must turn our attention to the task of rebuilding the Royal Navy, integrating Tadpole-derived technology and ensuring the security of the United Kingdom of Great Britain and Britannia.

Yours
Admiral Sir Joseph Porter (Ret.)

———

"Mary," Lieutenant Higgins said, as he entered the compartment. "We have completed our latest transit along the tramlines."

Mary turned to the handsome young officer and beamed. "Thank you, Joe," she said, warmly. "It's always good to know when we can relax."

Seated at the opposite side of the compartment, Gillian McDougal sighed. Mary was five years younger than herself, a beautiful girl fresh out of university who had married her husband just days before he had departed on the Cromwell Mission. They'd thought – just as Gillian and her husband had thought – that they would be separated for less than a month before the secondary personnel were allowed to board ship for the distant colony world. But then the war had begun and a month-long separation had swelled into four *years*. Mary hadn't wasted time finding a new lover to warm her bed.

Not that I could really blame her, Gillian thought, as Higgins led the dark-haired girl out of the compartment. *She barely knew her husband before she tied the knot.*

It had seemed an adventure, once upon a time. They would move from Earth to Cromwell; a whole new world, a human-compatible planet utterly untouched by any mortal hands. There, they would set up their own farms or businesses, which – because they would be in on the ground floor – would lead rapidly to wealth and power. Not a few new scions of the aristocracy had been created after the settlement of Britannia, Gillian's husband had noted when they'd put their names down for the colony mission. Success on Cromwell would ensure that his children had a chance to truly make something of themselves. It was why he had insisted on leaving first, even if it meant leaving his wife and daughters behind for a month or two. He had been adamant it was the only way to ensure they staked a proper claim.

But a month had become two months, and then a year, and then several years...

Mary had asked, more than once, why Gillian had remained loyal to her husband. It was the 23rd Century, after all, and marriages rarely lasted longer than it took for the children to grow to adulthood and flee the nest. And her husband was literally thousands of light years away, growing plants on a distant world. Gillian had considered it, then pointed out sharply that she genuinely loved her husband, even if they were apart. They'd made memories together...

She shook her head at the thought, then turned her attention to the datapad in front of her, barely reading the words. After so long, they were practically engraved in her mind; the complete records of the first survey party to visit Cromwell and certify the world safe for human habitation. Cromwell was everything Earth was not, even now; a safe environment, free of higher-order forms of life...and two-legged predators who would chase after her daughters, even before they entered their teens. It was a chance to build a new home, she knew, even though it *would* mean a great deal of hard work. But a doctor trained in emergency and colonial medicine could practically write her own ticket.

A dull quiver ran through the ship and she looked up, startled. *Vesper* was a large colonist-carrier, not a warship. The passage had been smooth, save for the uncomfortable sensation of passing through the tramlines. There had been nothing save for an endless thrumming from the ship's drives since they'd boarded the vessel. For it to quiver...

"Your attention please," the captain said. "Please return to your quarters and strap yourselves down. I say again, please return to your quarters and strap yourselves down."

The hatch opened, revealing a surprised-looking Mary in a dishevelled state. "What's happening?"

"Your lips are swollen," Gillian said, bitchily. It helped override her growing alarm. "What are you going to do when Brian" – her husband – "finds out about your affairs?"

Mary glared at her. "And who is going to tell him?"

"Every last person on the secondary lists knows you've been fucking around," Gillian pointed out, as sweetly as she could. "There's nowhere to go on Cromwell..."

Another quiver ran through the ship, followed by a *bang* that shook the bulkheads. Alarms started to sound moments later; Gillian had barely stood when the emergency airlocks slammed down, sealing the relaxation compartment off from the rest of the ship. It took her a long moment to realise that it was the hull breach alarm, warning that – somehow, somewhere – there was a gash in the hull. The ship's atmosphere was pouring out into interstellar space.

Mary screamed. "What…what was that?"

"Remain calm," Gillian ordered. The maps she'd seen of the tramline network were not encouraging. They were an unimaginable distance from anyone who might have been able and willing to help them. "Panic is the enemy right now."

"Your attention please," the captain's voice said. "This vessel is about to be boarded."

Gillian felt her mouth drop open. Boarded? Boarded by whom? Space pirates existed in dull entertainment programs, not real life. And which nation would risk war with the United Kingdom by attacking one of its colony ships? But they were so far from Earth, she realised dully, that it was quite likely that the ship's ultimate fate would never be known.

"Remain calm," the captain ordered. "There is no immediate danger."

Gillian gritted her teeth. Mary looked at her, sharply.

"What do we do?"

"We pray," Gillian said. "There's nothing else we can do."

Mary looked disbelieving, but Gillian only nodded. They had no weapons, save for a handful of hunting rifles stowed in the hold. Even if the crew had been able to get them out in time before the pirates – or whoever they were – boarded the ship, they would not be able to offer any meaningful resistance. *Vesper* couldn't hope to outrun or outfight even a small warship.

She cursed under her breath, then returned to her seat. All she could do was wait and see what happened…and pray that her daughters survived. Unless a miracle happened, she knew they were unlikely to see Cromwell, ever again. And her husband…

Closing her eyes, she settled down to wait.

CHAPTER
ONE

London wasn't what it used to be.

Captain John Naiser stood in Trafalgar Square and looked towards the War Memorial, placed below Nelson's ever-watchful eye. It was nothing more than a piece of the *Ark Royal's* hull, salvaged from the wreckage of the once-mighty ship, but it had a special meaning for the men and women of the Royal Navy. He took a step closer, ignoring the handful of children clustered around the memorials, until he could see the faint edges of the names engraved into the metal. There were far too many names listed of those who had died during the war.

He looked for a specific name, but it wasn't visible. The Royal Navy had lost over ten thousand officers and men in the war, a loss that had crippled the post-war navy. Each of the names were too small to make out with the naked eye, carved out of the metal by cutting lasers guided by computers carefully programmed to include each and every known casualty of the war. There was no point in looking for the names of those who had served on HMS *Canopus*, still less his friend and lover. He took one final look, then forced himself to turn away. There was no point in dwelling on the past.

The children headed back towards the teacher standing at the edge of the square, their faces pinched and worn compared to the children he remembered from his own childhood. They knew what it was like to be hungry, he knew, and what it was like to lose everything in one afternoon. God alone knew how many of them were war orphans, fostered out to whoever was willing to take in a child after their parents had been killed, or how many had seen nightmares as they struggled for survival. Three years after the end of the First Interstellar War, large parts of the population were still traumatised.

He drew in a breath, then started to walk down towards the Ministry of Defence. Most of the once-white buildings looked torn and faded, damaged badly by the giant waves and endless rainfall that had swept over London. Even crossing the Thames was an adventure these days, after the waves had knocked down all the bridges. The Royal Marines had established pontoon bridges in the early days of the recovery, and the Royal Engineers had added a handful of more solid structures, but there was nothing as reassuring as the bridges he'd once known. It would be years before the city recovered from the attack on Earth – and decades, perhaps, before the population recovered from the war.

A line of young men, wearing the muddy-brown overalls of the Civil Reconstruction Corps, marched past him, swinging their tools in a manner that reminded him of soldiers carrying rifles. They'd been lucky – or unlucky, depending – to escape military conscription in the years following the war, instead being detailed to work on civil recovery projects. John felt a moment of envy for their simple lives, even though he knew they had little true freedom. But then, everyone in Britain was required to play a role in rebuilding the country. The reserves of manpower represented by the civilian population could not be allowed to go untapped.

He smiled to himself as the workers were followed by a handful of young women, old enough to be out on the streets on their own, but young enough to escape their own conscription into the CRC. Half of them already looked pregnant, having worked out that pregnancy was the one sure way to avoid being subsumed into serving their country. They hadn't realised, the cynical side of his mind noted, that they were also serving Great Britain by providing children – or, for that matter, that raising a child would take far more than two years of compulsory service in the CRC. But it might not matter. If they were reluctant to raise the children, after giving birth, the children could be passed to foster parents for adoption.

"Hey, spacer," one of the girls called. "You want to go for a drink?"

John shook his head. Colin and he had often hit the bars of Soho, chatting up young men and trying to take one or more of them home for the night, back when they'd been young and foolish and the very concept of alien life nothing more than a figment of human imagination. And now Colin was dead and there were days when John found it hard to raise his head from the pillow and do his duty.

The thought made him scowl, bitterly. He wasn't the only one to be badly affected by the war. Two weeks ago, he'd heard that one of his old classmates – it bothered him profusely that he didn't remember the man's *name* – had put a gun in his mouth and killed himself, blowing his brains over the compartment. He wasn't the only ex-military officer to kill himself in the wake of the war, either through survivor's guilt or the simple realisation that nothing would ever be the same again.

He sighed as he turned the corner and walked up to the line of armed soldiers on duty. The sight of soldiers in the capital, wearing battledress uniforms rather than ceremonial garb, had once been an unpleasant surprise. Now, with Britain practically under martial law, it was depressingly common. The Royal Horse Guards had been a firm and highly-visible presence on the streets since the Battle of Earth. There were days when John wondered if anything would be the same again.

Of course it won't, he told himself, sharply. *We're no longer alone.*

Five years ago, the human race had known it was alone in the universe. A hundred Earth-like planets had been discovered, with none of them possessing any life forms larger or more interesting than a dog. Earth had seemed unique in giving birth to an intelligent race…

…And then humanity had encountered the Tadpoles. And, if a single elderly carrier had been scrapped, the Tadpoles would have won the war. Instead, they'd been held, barely. And then, when the peace talks had finally concluded, the human race had looked out on a universe that was fundamentally different. They were no longer alone in the universe and, perhaps, it was only a matter of time until they encountered a third intelligent race.

And who knows, he asked himself, *what will happen then?*

The guard stepped forward as John reached the security fence. He didn't *quite* point his rifle at John's chest, but the threat was clearly there.

London had learned hard lessons about security in the days following the attack on Earth. The food riots and outright panic had made the task of recovery far harder.

"Papers, please, *sir*," the guard said.

John reached into his uniform jacket and produced his ID card, then the printed letter inviting him to the Ministry of Defence. The letter had been short and to the point, but he had been unable to avoid a thrill of excitement after two weeks on Earth. Paper letters were rarely sent unless he was being summoned for promotion, a new command – or disciplinary action. And he knew he'd done nothing to warrant being hauled up in front of the First Space Lord for a bollocking. That would be the task of his immediate superior.

"You'll be met inside the building by a guide," the guard said, after scrutinising the papers and checking with the building's datanet. "Remember not to stray from the path, sir."

"I know," John said. Being arrested by the military police and spending the night in the guardhouse wouldn't be fun. "Are there any problems I should know about?"

"Couple of reports of bandits in the Restricted Zones, but nothing too serious," the guard said. He stepped backwards and waved John into the building. "Good luck, sir."

John smiled, then stepped though the gate into the Ministry of Defence. It was the largest military building in London, apart from the barracks serving the army regiments based in the capital, now that command and control facilities had been moved to secret locations or Nelson Base, hanging in high orbit over the city. Inside, it was decorated with giant paintings showing scenes from British military history, culminating in a painting entitled *The Last Flight of Ark Royal*. It was surprisingly good, compared to some of the others.

"Captain Naiser," a female voice said. "I'm Commander Stephanie Underwood. If you will come with me...?"

John nodded, then allowed the young woman to lead him through a network of corridors. Outside the entry lobby, it was surprisingly bare, as if the walls had been stripped of paintings and all other forms of decoration. It was political, he guessed, as Commander Underwood paused in front of a large pair of doors. The Ministry of Defence couldn't afford to be living it up when a fifth of the British population was still living in shoddy prefabricated accommodation scattered around the countryside.

"The First Space Lord," Commander Underwood said.

"Sir," John said, stepping into the office. It was as barren as the rest of the building, save for a large holographic display floating over the Admiral's desk. "Reporting as ordered."

"Take a seat, Captain," Admiral Percy Finnegan said. He returned John's salute with one of his own. "It's been a while."

John sat, resting his hands in his lap. Finnegan had commanded HMS *Victorious* during the war, where he'd had the dubious pleasure of saving John's life when his carrier had responded to the report of an attack on Bluebell. John had met him twice, once for a debriefing and once for a transfer from starfighter piloting to mainline command track. Both meetings had been short, formal and largely unemotional.

"I was reading through your file," Finnegan said, as he sat down and placed his elbows on his desk. The show of informality didn't help John to relax. "It's quite an interesting read."

"Thank you, sir," John said.

"Born twenty-three years ago, in London," Finnegan continued. "Parents largely absentee; you were practically brought up in boarding school. Joined the Cadet Corps at fourteen, then switched to the Space Cadets at fifteen. Your instructor spoke highly of you and cleared the way for you to enter the Starfighter Training Centre at eighteen. You were involved in an…*incident* the week before graduation and were accordingly assigned to HMS *Canopus*, rather than a posting on a fleet carrier."

John stiffened. The…*incident*…had seemed a good idea at the time.

"You served on *Canopus* for five months before the Battle of Bluebell, where you were the sole survivor. Your heroics during the battle won you the Victoria Cross. You were asked to return to the Training Centre to share your experience, but instead you requested a switch to command track. May I ask why?"

There was no point, John knew, in pretending to be mystified by the question.

5

"Colin and I were...close," he said. "We were wingmates, sir. When he died, I decided not to fly starfighters anymore."

"Indeed," Finnegan said. He took a long breath. "You were appointed First Lieutenant on HMS *Rosemount*, as she required a CAG at short notice. I might add that you weren't expected to keep that position indefinitely. Captain Preston, however, chose you to succeed Commander Beasley when he was promoted to take command of HMS *Jackson*. You served as his XO until you were transferred to HMS *Spartan*. Again, you were quite young for the post."

"Yes, sir," John said.

"But you would be far from the only officer to be promoted rapidly," Finnegan concluded, shortly. He met John's eyes. "Your failure to follow a conventional career path would, under other circumstances, limit your chances of advancement. As it happens, however, we have a posting for you."

John kept his face expressionless with an effort. The Royal Navy needed all the trained manpower it could get, after so many officers and men had been killed in the war. In truth, he'd expected to be assigned to the Luna Academy or the Starfighter Training Centre years ago. He would have hated it, but it might be the best place for him to go. The recruits needed someone with genuine experience to ensure they knew what they needed to know.

"This isn't an easy time for the Navy," Finnegan continued. "We no longer have enough hulls to meet our commitments, even without having to refit a number of pre-war designs with alien-derived technology. Worse, several second-rank human powers are now in a position to challenge us, because they didn't take such a beating in the war – and then there's the threat of renewed conflict with the Tadpoles. Accordingly, we're having to rush a stopgap design of starship into service."

John felt a sudden burst of hope as the First Space Lord tapped his console and a holographic image of a starship appeared in front of him. She was larger than a frigate, he noted, although she would still be dwarfed by a fleet carrier. Oddly, she looked smoother and sleeker than the more mundane craft the Royal Navy deployed. He couldn't help being reminded of some of the alien ships he'd seen during the war.

"The *Warspite* class is a hodgepodge of human and alien technology," Finnegan informed him. "They're armed with a mixture of weaponry, carry alien-grade jump drives and are generally faster and more manoeuvrable than any previous design. On the other hand, the mixture of technology has already led to teething troubles and kinks in the design, which we don't have time to work out before pressing the ships into deployment. We're *that* short of hulls. Unfortunately, they also require non-standard commanders."

That made sense, John was sure. The starship's combination of human and alien technology might daunt a commander with more experience of human starships. *He'd* have less to unlearn than someone who followed the standard command track to high rank. And besides, if the data at the bottom of the display was accurate, the starship would handle more like a starfighter than any pre-war starship. He was sure, now, that he would assume command of one of the new ships. The thought of the challenge made him smile.

Finnegan shrugged. "They have considerably more range than a frigate," he explained, as the holographic display twisted to show the starship's interior. "Thanks to some of the alien technology, she can even draw fuel from a gas giant if necessary, although she lacks the machine shops and other onboard replenishment systems of a carrier. In short, she should be ideal for both escort missions, showing the flag and coping with limited problems without needing a major fleet deployment.

"You will assume command of HMS *Warspite*," he concluded. "We already have a task for her, Captain. You will not have a proper period to settle in to your new command."

John nodded, unsurprised. The meeting wouldn't have been organised so rapidly if the Royal Navy hadn't needed to get *Warspite* into operational service as quickly as possible. It was likely to be a major headache if the ship was as untested as the First Space Lord was suggesting, if only because of the risk of failing components. There had to be a reason for the haste.

But he would assume command! It didn't matter what Finnegan wanted him to do. All that mattered was that he would be commander of a starship, master under God. It would be the peak of his post-war career.

"We've been probing through the new tramlines," the First Space Lord said, unaware of John's inner thoughts. "We've had some successes in locating newer ways to travel through human space which will, I suspect, cause a major economic boom once the technology is commonly available. Two months ago, however, a survey ship located a star system on the edge of explored space that possesses no less than *seven* tramlines, three of them alien-grade. One of them is directly linked to the Cromwell Colony."

"Founded just before the war, if I remember correctly," John said, slowly. There had been a political argument over the British claim to the world, with several second-rank powers asserting that it should be *theirs*, damn it! Britain already had one major star system and several minor ones. "They were untouched by the fighting, I take it?"

"They weren't touched directly," the First Space Lord confirmed, "but there were delays in getting supplies and new colonists out to them. They're not our concern, though. You will take your ship and a small flotilla of starships to Pegasus, the newly-discovered system, and lay claim to it in the name of the British Crown. Someone else might try to get there first."

"Possession being nine-tenths of the law," John commented. There were endless arguments over who should claim systems with life-bearing worlds, but systems with several tramlines could be equally important. Control over shipping lanes would give the system's owner a fair source of revenue in its own right – assuming, of course, they could make their will felt. "I assume the system hasn't been formally claimed?"

"It won't be, until we have an established presence there," the First Space Lord warned. "I would prefer to avoid a challenge from one of the other powers over ownership."

He stood up. "Your formal orders are here," he said, holding out a datachip. "You will travel to *Warspite* and assume command at once. I expect you and the flotilla to be ready to leave within the week, barring accidents. You will not find it an easy task."

"I will not let you down," John assured him, as he took the datachip. There would be more than just his formal orders on the chip, he was sure.

He could expect details of everything from his new command to her crew roster. "Thank you, sir."

"Thank me when you come back," Finnegan said. His voice hardened as he rose to his feet and held out his hand. "Not before."

CHAPTER
TWO

"Lots of ships flying through local space right now," the shuttle pilot observed, in a strong cockney accent. "You know how hard it was to get a permit to fly you to Hamilton?"

John snorted. "Devilishly easy?"

The pilot laughed. "Just about," he said. "But it wasn't *easy*, you know."

"Tell me," John said. "Does anyone actually fall for that line?"

"Depends who I'm flying," the pilot admitted. "Experienced spacers snigger, while inexperienced dirty-feet worry about colliding with an asteroid."

John made a show of rolling his eyes. Space was *vast*. He had a greater chance of winning the lottery - without actually entering - than accidentally hitting an asteroid. The entire Royal Navy could fly through the asteroid belt in tight formation without running a serious risk of striking an asteroid. It only ever happened in bad movies and worse television shows. But then, he had to admit, so much that would have been deemed impossible had happened in the last few years. Humanity had gone to war with an alien race, for one. Why not an asteroid impact?

He looked at the pilot and smiled. "Reservist?"

"Used to drive cabs in London for a living," the pilot confirmed. "Then I was called back to the war, because the last shuttle driver had to go fly starfighters for a living. My wife says it keeps me away from the camps."

"Probably a good thing," John agreed. "Is she *staying* in the camps?"

"Nah," the pilot said. "She's got a place in Doncaster now, thankfully. My oldest son was in a Reconstruction Brigade, while my daughter and younger son are at boarding school on Luna. I think they both want to follow me into space."

John nodded, then turned his attention to the near-space display. Earth was surrounded by orbital defence stations, shipyards and settled asteroids, while hundreds of starships made their way to and from humanity's homeworld. Two-thirds of the ships, he saw, were colonist-carriers, transporting as many humans from Earth to various colony worlds as possible. Earth had been bombarded during the war and millions of humans had died. No one wanted to risk losing so much of the human race again.

"I've been on one of those ships," the pilot observed. "I wouldn't go on one again for love or money."

"The colonist-carriers?" John asked. "Why?"

"They cut corners," the pilot said. "Lots of corners. I think the Chinese actually lost a couple last month, if you believe all the rumours. The ships just aren't safe."

"Risk is our business," John said, quoting the motto of the British Survey Service. "If we took no risks, we'd still be stuck on Earth."

"There's a difference between taking calculated risks and taking stupid risks," the pilot countered, with a wink. "Sooner or later, one of the corners they cut is going to catch up with them and a colonist-carrier will be lost. And then all hell will break loose."

He was right, John knew. Civilian settlers hadn't signed up to take risks. There were always uncertainties surrounding space transport - all the more so now that humanity knew that hostile aliens existed - but the risks should be cut as much as possible. But he also knew there was no alternative. The colony worlds needed to be expanded as much as possible before humanity ran into the next threat. Or started fighting amongst itself again.

Which isn't entirely impossible, he thought, coldly. *The bombardment did a great deal of damage to our planetary security net.*

"The Indians are building their own carriers now," the pilot added, as they headed further away from Earth. "I hear tell that they learned from our experiences."

"They probably did," John agreed. Learning from someone else's mistakes was cheaper than learning from your own. "Armoured hulls, plasma weapons and mass drivers?"

"Looks that way," the pilot added. "But then, everyone is also saying that the carrier has had her day."

"People say a lot of things," John said. It was an old debate, sharpened by the outcome of the war. Did the development of rapid-fire plasma weapons ensure that starfighters were no longer relevant...or would other advances make them harder to target in future? There was no way to know until the human race went back to war. "But not all of them are right."

He leaned forward, studying the display. The Indians weren't the only ones pouring resources into rebuilding their naval power. Near-Earth space was *crammed* with shipyards: American, French, Chinese and even Russian, as well as the British installations. Newer shipyards were springing up too as second-rank powers, seeing an opportunity to join the first-rank powers, worked frantically to build up their own fleets. It was a good thing, he told himself, even though he worried about the future. If humanity hadn't invested so much money and resources into its pre-war build-up, the war would have been over very quickly and the human race would have lost.

"I suppose not," the pilot said. "Time will tell, won't it?"

"Yeah," John agreed. "It always does."

Slowly, HMS *Hamilton* came into visual range. As always, it looked like a handful of half-built starships, surrounded by pods and industrial modules, but it was clear, just from a glance, that the shipbuilding tempo was increasing rapidly. A dozen carriers hovered in the midst of the shipyard, their skeletal hulls illuminated by spotlights mounted on the industrial pods. It would be at least another two years, John knew, before they were completed, then put through their paces and declared ready for deployment. Until then, the Royal Navy would be dangerously weak.

So are the other human powers, he reminded himself, firmly. *We're all weak.*

A pair of starfighters flashed past as they approached the shipyard, weapons at the ready. John watched them go, feeling a hint of wistfulness. It had been years since he'd flown a starfighter and he knew it was unlikely he would ever fly one again, unless he managed to take command of a carrier. Starfighter pilots enjoyed freedoms unknown to the rest of the Navy, although they came with a price. Over eighty percent of the Royal Navy's pilots had died in the war.

"Show-offs," the pilot grumbled. "They could have stayed safely away while they checked our IFF codes."

John shrugged. Starfighter pilots *loved* to show off. Besides, it was much easier to perform a visual check at close range.

"Don't worry about it," he said. "The Navy wouldn't have assigned careless bastards to here, of all places."

"Ruddy cheek," the pilot said. "Do they think we're terrorists?"

"I doubt it," John said. "But they do have to be careful."

He winced at the thought. International terrorism had been sharply reduced towards the end of the Age of Unrest, although some cynics claimed that levels of terrorist activity were still higher than they'd been before the Troubles. But terrorist activity had been on the rise since the Battle of Earth, as the homeless or the dispossessed lashed out at those they blamed for their torments. Most of it had been small-scale, more like pinpricks than anything else, but it could easily grow worse. A terrorist taking control of an orbital freighter and crashing it into the planet below was everyone's worst nightmare.

"And here we are," the pilot announced. He put on a more formal tone as HMS *Warspite* came into view. "Your new command, sir."

John leaned forward, drinking in the sight. *Warspite* was definitely sleeker than the pre-war frigates and cruisers the human navies had used to picket systems and escort the giant fleet carriers, but her dark hull was studded with weapons and sensor blisters. She looked almost like a flattened arrowhead, he decided, her dark armour providing protection against everything short of heavy plasma cannons or laser warheads. Or a direct nuclear hit.

"I can take us around her, if you like," the pilot offered. "Let you see her from prow to stern."

"Please," John said.

He pressed his face against the porthole as the pilot took them on a gentle circle of the starship's hull. Her prow was a weapon, he noted; they'd placed a heavy plasma cannon there, right at the tip of the arrowhead. Two Marine shuttles were docked below her hull, half-shielded by armour plates. The designers had clearly expected that the ship would need to deploy her Marines as rapidly as possible. At the rear, her drive nodes looked bigger and more powerful than anything he would have expected on a ship of her class. But then, they were built with alien technology, he reminded himself. They might not look like standard human designs.

"Take us to the shuttlebay," he said, finally. "And tell them that I don't want a greeting party."

"Aye, sir," the pilot said. The shuttle yawed slightly, then headed right for the gaping hatch in the vessel's hull. "But they may alert the XO anyway."

John had to smile. He'd been told, once, that the way to see if the XO was popular among the crew was to order them *not* to alert the XO that the captain was boarding - and see if someone alerted her anyway. At the time, he hadn't been sure what to make of it. Now, with years of experience as an XO under his belt, he thought he understood. The Captain was meant to be unapproachable, but the XO was there to take care of the crew.

"It doesn't matter," he said. "I just don't want to waste everyone's time by forcing them to greet me."

A dull tremor ran through the shuttle as *Warspite's* gravity field asserted itself over the shuttle's onboard generator. John braced himself as the shuttle came to a halt, then settled down on the deck and landed with a dull thump. He felt dizzy, just for a second, a sensation that faded away so quickly it was easy to believe he'd imagined it. The boffins swore blind that it *was* imaginary, but nine out of ten spacers reported it regularly.

"Good luck, sir," the pilot said. "Come back safely."

John threw him a sharp glance, then picked up his duffle, slung it over his shoulder and stepped out of the hatch. Warm air struck his face at once, carrying with it the fresh smell of a starship newly out of the yards. It wouldn't be long before the presence of two hundred crewmen altered the ship's smell, but for the moment it smelt clean. He took a long breath, then turned to face the flags painted on the bulkhead. The Union Jack, as always, reminded him of home.

He saluted, then turned to face the airlock as it hissed open, revealing two people. One of them was surprisingly young for her rank, wearing a commander's uniform with an alarming lack of service pips; the other was older and darker, wearing an engineer's overall. John was surprised to realise that he recognised him; Mike Johnston had served as Chief Engineer on HMS *Rosemount* before being reassigned to the Next Generation Weapons program on Britannia.

"Captain," the commander said. She hesitated, then saluted imperfectly. "I'm Commander Juliet Watson, your XO. Welcome onboard HMS *Warspite*."

John felt an icy chill of suspicion - directed at the First Space Lord - as he studied Juliet Watson. She was young, around twenty-five, and her salute wasn't the only imperfect thing about her. Her dark hair was far too long to suit regulations, her uniform looked as if she didn't quite know how to dress herself and the lack of service pips suggested that *Warspite* was her first operational deployment. It made no sense. *He'd* had to fight a promotions board all the way to become a line officer, even after the Battle of Bluebell. Had someone seen fit to promote Commander Watson because she had links to the aristocracy? It was possible, but he honestly couldn't recall *any* aristocratic family with that name - or anything closely related to it.

"Thank you, Commander," he said, finally. Maybe appearances were deceiving. "And you, Mike. You're looking well."

Was it his imagination, he asked himself, or did Johnston look relieved to see him? The burly engineer had a reputation for working hard, then drinking and fighting hard; thankfully, he'd never been enough of a drunkard to appear on duty still worse for wear. Some people, like the late lamented Admiral Smith, might have been able to get away with it. An engineering officer who turned up for duty drunk would be lucky if his commander didn't shove him out of the nearest airlock and swear blind it had been a terrible accident.

"Thank you, sir," Johnston said. "It's good to see you again."

Juliet looked from one to the other. "You know each other?"

"Served together on *Rosemount*," Johnston said, immediately. "It was an exciting deployment."

"Very exciting," John agreed, carefully. Something was *definitely* not right. "Please would you show me round the ship, then I will formally assume command."

Juliet beamed. "It will be my pleasure," she said. She nodded to Johnston, then turned to lead the way through the airlock. "If you'll come with me…?"

John followed her, glancing from side to side as they entered a long passageway. Half of the inspection hatches were open, revealing various components; a dozen engineering crewmen, some of them obviously borrowed from the shipyard, were working to install dozens of other components before the ship left the yard for good. Juliet moved with easy confidence through the passageway, then stopped in front of a large hatch. It hissed open, revealing a giant engineering compartment.

"This is Main Engineering," Juliet said, cheerfully. "As you can see, we actually have three fusion reactors powering the ship, although we could operate quite effectively on just one of them. The third reactor is intended to power our weapons array; naturally, if necessary, we can switch from reactor to reactor, should we require additional power. Our drive fields are actually more sophisticated than anything else known to exist, giving us a speed advantage of twenty percent over the next-fastest human ship. I think we will stack up well against alien technology too, should we meet a Tadpole starship."

John frowned. "Do you think they won't be advancing too?"

"I imagine they will be trying to figure out how to mix and match their technology with ours, just as we are doing with theirs," Juliet said. She waved a hand towards a large control panel, then smiled at him. "However, we have an advantage, I believe. Our R&D efforts were given quite a jolt when they showed up, while they enjoyed their technological superiority for far too long."

She took a breath, then continued. "Of course, the *real* objects of interest are the modified Puller Drives," she said. "Right now, we can access the longer tramlines without worrying about blowing the drive systems, but I believe that is only the tip of the iceberg. Imagine being able to jump from system to system *without* a tramline. *That's* the promise of our research, Captain. We might be able to banish the tramlines once and for all."

"It would be great, if it were possible," John mused.

"Theoretically, it *is* possible," Juliet assured him. "And one day, it will be practically possible too."

John couldn't help a sinking feeling in his stomach as Juliet led him on a tour of the rest of the ship. The crew seemed calm and professional, but Juliet herself was *far* from professional. He was starting to have a feeling that the First Space Lord had had motivations of his own for assigning John to *Warspite*. A non-standard commander, he'd said. Maybe it was because the crew was non-standard too. John had met officers who would summarily have relieved Juliet of duty by now, just for forgetting to call them *sir*.

He pushed the thought to one side as they stepped onto the bridge. Like the rest of the ship, it exuded a sense of *newness*, of just having come out of the yard. The consoles looked shiny, the command chair looked as if no one had sat in it since it had been installed and the deck plates were shiny. He took a step forward, then glanced back at the rear bulkhead, where the ship's dedication plaque was placed. *Warspite's* motto - *belli dura despicio* - was clearly written below the list of officers who had attended the ship's formal commissioning.

"I despise the hard knocks of war," he muttered.

"We have to be careful not to be hit," Juliet said, suddenly serious. "A single mass driver strike could smash us, no matter how much armour we nail to the hull."

John nodded. Once, mass drivers had been practically outlawed by international agreement. Now, everyone was building mass drivers, after seeing just how effective they had been against the Tadpoles. A single kinetic strike would be enough to wreck almost *any* starship, save for a giant armoured carrier. And even a carrier would require years of work before she could return to duty.

He sat down in his command chair, then drew the sheet of paper the First Space Lord had given him from his jacket. "Now hear this," he said. "From the First Space Lord to Captain John Naiser, VC. You are ordered to take command of HMS *Warspite…*"

"I stand relieved," Juliet said, when he had finished.

She didn't seem annoyed at losing command, something that bothered John more than he cared to admit. He'd never known an officer who hadn't been a *little* irked at losing command, save perhaps for young midshipmen who'd been plunged into the fire. No one reached command rank without being ambitious *and* confident in his abilities. But Juliet had shown no reaction at all.

"Continue as you were," John ordered. It was high time he got to the bottom of this, before he tripped over an unexpected surprise. "I need to speak to Engineer Johnston in my cabin, then go through the ship's files."

"Of course, sir," Juliet said.

CHAPTER
THREE

"CO wants to see you, Percy," Captain Kimball said. "You been up to anything I don't know about?"

Corporal Percy Schneider shook himself awake. "I don't think so, sir," he said, as he hastily checked his uniform. "What does he think I did?"

"I don't know," Kimball said. "But you'd better hurry. He didn't look to be in a good mood."

He's never in a good mood, Percy thought, as he swung his legs over the side of the cot and stood. Colonel Hawkins - his men called him the Hawk when they thought he wasn't listening - wasn't a bad sort, but he had grown stricter in the years since the Battle of Earth, when he'd lost his wife and two small children. Percy, who'd lost both of his parents to the war, found it hard to blame him. There were days when he wished he had died instead of his father or mother.

He checked his appearance, then strode out of the barracks and down towards the CO's office. Quite why the higher-ups had thought to put 47 Commando in Redford Barracks, Edinburgh, mystified him, although he had to admit it was good for leave. Wearing a Royal Marine uniform was a guarantee that one didn't have to spend the night alone, even if a third of the country wore one uniform or another. The CO was based in a large redbrick building, guarded by a pair of armed soldiers. They nodded to Percy as he approached, then stepped aside to allow him to enter. Thanks to his father, he was the most recognisable soldier on the base.

Colonel Hawkins didn't hold with luxury, Percy noted with approval as he was shown into the office. A simple folding table, a field-grade terminal and a pistol were the only things in the room, save for a small drinks machine. Percy came to a halt in front of the desk, then saluted. Hawkins looked up, then returned the salute.

"At ease," he said. He looked Percy up and down, then sighed. "Is that *At Ease* for you, Corporal?"

"Yes, sir," Percy said, stiffly.

Hawkins shrugged. "Your father's heroics ensured you could apply for a place in the Academy, if you wanted," he said. "Instead, you joined the Royal Marines. Was there a reason for that, Corporal?"

"I wanted to prove myself, sir," Percy said.

It was more than that, he knew. He'd been drafted into a disaster recovery unit shortly after the aliens had attacked Earth, where he'd seen Royal Marines spearheading the effort to save as many people from floods and tidal waves as they could. The Marines had impressed him in a way his father, the starfighter pilot, never had. And so, when the time had come to apply for military service, he'd volunteered for the Royal Marines.

"And so you have," Hawkins said. "You came second in your class, then you spent six months on Mars, two months on wet-navy duty and four more months here. Which one did you find most interesting?"

"Mars, sir," Percy said. "It was a fascinating environment."

"Glad to hear it," Hawkins said. "You know Corporal Tailor? He came down with a particularly nasty stomach flu only two days ago. I was hoping it would respond to medical treatment, but…well, the doctors say it will be several weeks before he's fit for duty once again."

Percy frowned. "Something *biological*, sir?"

"It could be, although the medics think otherwise," Hawkins said. "He probably just went out on the town and ate something unhealthy before returning to base. Or he picked it up in one of the reclamation zones."

"Perhaps, sir," Percy said. The bombardment had left thousands of festering dead bodies in its wake. Disease had swiftly followed, despite modern medical treatment. "I'm sure he will recover."

"So am I," Hawkins said. "However, it leaves me with a problem. Tailor was assigned to *Warspite*, the latest cruiser. She was intended to take two sections of Royal Marines on her deployment. Naturally, Tailor will be unable to make her departure date."

"Yes, sir," Percy said. There were strict procedures in place for handling injuries or illnesses among the Royal Marines. The affected Marine would be taken off the duty roster until fully recovered, then slotted in wherever possible. It wasn't something he cared to think about, not really. Leaving his mates behind wouldn't be easy. "I'm sorry to hear that."

"Not as sorry as you will be," Hawkins predicted. "I'd like to assign you to cover the slot."

Percy blinked. "Me, sir?"

"You," Hawkins confirmed. "You have the right qualifications for the role. Lieutenant Darryl Hadfield has overall command, with Hastings as CO of Section 1. You'll take Section 2. I don't think I need to tell you, Corporal, that this could make your career."

"No, sir," Percy said.

He considered it, briefly. Serving on a starship, even as third-in-command of the Marine detachment, would put his name to the top of the list for further deployments. It wouldn't be quite the same as serving on the ground, but…but it would be fun. Besides, he wasn't blind to the hidden implications either. If he refused the assignment, it was unlikely he'd be offered another one.

"You'll catch a shuttle from Turnstile Spaceport tomorrow," Hawkins said. He tapped his terminal, removed a datachip and passed it to Percy. "Report to the RAF hanger at 1300 for your flight, taking with you a standard deployment bag. Everything else is already on the ship, waiting for you. Tailor's personal possessions can be stored until his return to active service."

He smiled. "Get your stuff out of the barracks, then consider yourself on leave until 1300 tomorrow," he added. "I'm afraid we can't offer the standard week of intercourse and intoxication, but this did happen at short notice."

"I understand, sir," Percy said. "And thank you."

"We shall see," Hawkins said. "Have a good one."

Percy saluted, then turned and strode out of the office, unsure if he'd been given a stroke of good fortune or bad. On one hand, as he'd noted, there would be certain promotion if he didn't screw up, but on the other hand it would bring him closer to his father. And, in truth, he wasn't sure if he could handle it. His father had been a hero. How could Percy hope to live up to Kurt Schneider?

He walked back into the barracks and opened the drawer under his cot, removing a spare set of clothes, a handful of pictures of his family and his spare pistol. It wasn't entirely permitted to keep a spare weapon - all weapons had to be accounted for - but the old sweats had taught him it was a wise precaution. They'd served in hellholes like North Africa or the Middle East, where a situation could go from peaceful to extremely dangerous in the wink of an eye, and having a spare weapon often made the difference between life and death. Placing them all in his duffle bag, he took one last look around the barracks and smiled to himself. He would miss it.

The communications lounge was right next door, crammed with videophones, computers and privacy shields, just to give the talkers the illusion that no one could hear a word they were saying. Percy sat down in front of the nearest computer, then linked into the datanet and entered a planetary contact code. There was a long pause, then his sister's face appeared in front of him.

"Percy," she said. "Are you alright?"

"Penny," Percy said. "I've been reassigned."

"To Antarctica?" Penny asked. "Was that because of my expose of someone pinching supplies from the refugee camps?"

"I don't think so," Percy said. He honestly didn't understand why his sister had chosen to become a reporter, rather than something *useful*, but he respected her choice. "I've been assigned to a starship. I won't be back for several months, at least."

"Shit," Penny said. "You'll miss your birthday."

"I'll just have a party when we get back," Percy said. He hadn't been looking forward to his birthday, but it was the least of his concerns right now. "I hope you'll be alright while I'm gone."

Penny stuck out her tongue. "I'm old enough to take care of myself," she reminded him, snidely. "Worry about Nora. Or Jane. Or Alisa. Or... what was the name of the last girl you were dating?"

"Those were *last* year," Percy said, embarrassed. "I'm dating Canella now. And I think Jane thought I was going to inherit a bucket-load of money."

"Gold-digger," Penny muttered. They'd been paid compensation for their father's death - and they were the sole beneficiaries of his life insurance policy - but money was worth less now than it had been five years ago. "Take care of yourself, all right?"

"I will," Percy assured her. It had been three years since they'd fled their home, ahead of a tidal wave of water, but the memory still chilled him to the bone. They'd come close to being killed more than once, first by the aliens and then by their fellow humans. "And you too, Penny."

He closed the connection, then tapped another contact code into the computer. There was a long pause, then a pretty brown-skinned face appeared in the display. "Percy!"

"Canella," Percy said. They'd been dating, on and off, for three months, but he wasn't sure that either of them were serious. "Can you take the afternoon off work?"

"I can ask my manager," Canella said. "Is this important?"

"Yes," Percy said. "It's very important."

He waited for her to ask her manager and get back to him, knowing that she had no choice. There were few jobs available these days, at least for people without practical skills, and Canella - she'd studied sociology in university - had been lucky to get the one she had. If her boss said no, she'd have to turn Percy down. The risk of losing her job and being reassigned to a labour battalion was too great.

"He says yes, but I won't be paid for it," Canella said, when she returned. "Where do you want to meet?"

"Lombardi's," Percy said. "I know it's expensive, but I can pay."

They exchanged goodbyes, then he closed the connection and walked out of the building, down towards the gates. They were guarded by armed soldiers - there had been shootings near other barracks, although Edinburgh was largely peaceful - who glanced sharply at him as he signed himself out, then took one last look at the barracks before starting the walk into town. After running up and down Brecon as part of his training, he was hardly likely to wait for a bus into the centre of Edinburgh. It wasn't *that* long a walk.

Edinburgh had been lucky, he reminded himself, as he approached the centre of the city. It had been shielded from the tidal waves, which had spared the city the damage inflicted on London, Glasgow, Cardiff and many others. But the rainstorms had inflicted considerable damage of their own, flooding vast parts of the city while the population looked for shelter or tried to steer the water away from their homes. Princess Street Gardens had become a loch once again, while the castle looked decidedly weather-beaten, even under the bright sunlight. And, like everywhere else, teams of labour units were struggling to cope with the damage.

But at least they didn't abandon the city, he thought, remembering Cardiff. The city had been effectively deemed unsalvageable and abandoned. *Edinburgh will return to her glory soon enough.*

He smiled as he saw Canella, standing outside Lombardi's and waiting for him. She waved to him, then kissed him as soon as he was close enough to kiss. Percy kissed her back, feeling like a heel. There was no way to escape the fact that he was going to tell her that he was leaving, that he wouldn't be back for months. Stronger relationships than theirs had been torn apart by the demands of deployments. He knew, all too well, that his parents had been on the verge of splitting up before the aliens attacked and his mother had been lost. His father had died shortly afterwards.

"Percy," she said. Her eyes narrowed for a split second when she saw his duffle. "You're looking good."

"It's the uniform," Percy said. "It makes me look taller. And you're looking beautiful."

Canella smiled as he looked her up and down. Her dark brown skin, dark hair and long brown legs contrasted oddly with her uniform, but she still looked gorgeous. He tried not to think about the night he'd carefully unbuttoned her blouse, the night they'd made love for the first time. Penny would have laughed - she knew he'd gone through a dozen girlfriends - but there was something about Canella that made her more than just a one night stand. It was why he had gone out with her, again and again and again.

The waiter showed them both to a booth in the far corner, then waited until they ordered pizza and drinks. Percy declined the offer of wine, choosing instead to stick with fresh orange and lemonade. Canella eyed him in surprise - Percy might never have been a boozer, yet he'd always taken alcohol before - but said nothing. She'd admitted, once, that she'd seen too many people drunk out of their minds.

"Well," she said. "This is a surprise, isn't it?"

Percy nodded, looking down at the table. "I didn't know I would be free this afternoon," he said, finally. He'd faced people shooting at him with greater aplomb. "There's something I have to tell you."

Canella frowned. "What?"

"I've been reassigned," Percy said, softly. "I'm going to be on a starship for the next six months, at least. Probably longer. I may not even be able to return to Edinburgh."

"I…see," Canella said. Her face was impassive, but her lower lip was wobbling. "You won't be seeing me again?"

"I don't know," Percy warned. "Shipboard duty isn't the same as duty on the ground. Here, I had a night off each week; on ship, there won't be any nights off until we return to Earth. It may be a long time until you see me again."

He swallowed. "If you don't want to wait for me," he added, "you don't have to wait."

"I knew it might happen," Canella said. "But I didn't think it would be this soon."

"Me neither," Percy said. "I wasn't given a choice."

"I think you would have taken it even if you *had* been offered a choice," Canella said, flatly. "No matter how much you deny it, there's a part of you that wants to just get stuck in and…well, get on with your job. I always liked that about you."

The waiter returned, carrying a steaming plate of pizza, before Percy could think of a reply. Instead, he cut up the pizza, passed Canella a piece, then dug into his own slice. It tasted far better than the rations he'd been fed at the barracks, although he had to admit, if he were being honest, that he'd tasted better pizza. Lombardi's seemed to get by on social cachet rather than quality. The chicken tasted plain, the tomato was thin and the cheese barely there.

Canella finished her piece of pizza, then looked up and held his eyes. "Do you *want* to see me again?"

"I would like to," Percy said, honestly. "But I would understand…"

"If I find someone else in the meantime, I will tell you," Canella said. "And you do the same."

She sighed, then changed the subject. "My manager is planning to hire a couple of new girls," she added. "I guess he got tired of harassing the last two hires."

Percy winced. "Are you going to warn them?"

"They'll need the jobs," Canella said, bitterly. "These days, anyone who bitches or complains can expect to leave employment for good, shortly afterwards. I don't think I want to spend the rest of my working life picking up shit from the ground."

"I understand," Percy said. He worried, sometimes, about his sister. Would she be harassed by *her* superiors? Or told she had a choice between sleeping with her boss or losing her job? But then, Penny *did* have connections. A wise leech would go hassle someone else. "But you deserve better."

"I used to think I had a good job waiting for me," Canella said. "I should have gone into psychology. Lots of demand for psychologists these days. The entire country has been traumatised."

"Tell me about it," Percy said. The tidal waves had been bad, but the refugee camp had been worse. Law and order had broken down completely. "We're still having nightmares of the day we were forced to run for our lives."

They finished the pizza, then Canella led him back to her flat and grabbed him as soon as the door was closed. "I don't want to think about the future now," she breathed, as she started to undo his uniform trousers. "And I don't want you to think about the future either."

"I won't," Percy promised. He pulled open her blouse, allowing her breasts to bobble free and dance invitingly in front of him. His tongue seemed to slip out of his mouth of its own accord, licking at her dangling nipple. "I'll just make love to you."

They spent the rest of the day in bed together, then went out to eat dinner before returning to bed and sleeping until early morning. Percy climbed out of bed at 0600 - life in the Royal Marines had taught him when to rise - poured two cups of coffee and then carried one of them back to Canella. She thanked him for it, sleepily, then closed her eyes again. Percy looked down at her for a long moment, then showered and dressed. She was still fast asleep when he returned.

Feeling like a bastard, he kissed her on the cheek and then left, closing the door carefully behind him.

CHAPTER
FOUR

"Thank you for coming to see me, Mike," John said.

"I was under the impression I didn't have a choice," Johnston said. The Chief Engineer settled down into a chair, facing John's desk. "You are my commanding officer, sir."

John couldn't disagree. A request from a starship's commander was an order, however phrased. Mike Johnston and he might have served together before - he was counting on that, for the discussion they had to have - but he was still *Warspite's* commanding officer. He couldn't afford to get too close to the crew.

He waited until Midshipwoman Jodie Powell had poured them both tea, then retreated into a side compartment, before leaning forward and fixing the older man with a gimlet stare.

"I need you to be frank, Mike," he said, flatly. "This discussion is completely off the record."

"Yes, sir," Johnston said.

"The XO," John said. "How did she get the job? Because I can't believe we're *that* short of experienced officers who could take the post."

Johnston sighed. "Permission to speak freely, sir?"

"Already granted," John said, irritated.

"Politics," Johnston said. "And technical expertise."

He sighed and sipped his tea. "I was assigned to the NGW program shortly after you left *Rosemount*," he said. "Commander Watson was the departmental head of one of the program's subdivisions. And, to be fair, she is an absolute genius. Not many people can look at human technology, then alien technology, and see how they might be made to work together. Commander Watson can and does. Indeed, I believe she was behind the modifications made to *Ark Royal* that allowed her to launch Operation Nelson."

"That's very good for her," John said. "But how did she wind up as XO of a starship?"

"Politics, again," Johnston said. "Commander Watson was assigned to the *Warspite* program before it had a proper name. She did most of the early design work; my contribution was largely turning it into practical hardware. Admiral Soskice - the overall head of NGW - gave her a formal rank because otherwise the shipyard staff wouldn't listen to her. You know what bastards they can be, at times."

"I know," John said. "But XO…?"

"I'm getting to that," Johnston said. "She remained in place as they put the ship together, allowing her to solve new problems as they cropped up. Eventually, when *Warspite* was formally commissioned, Admiral Soskice ensured she would be the vessel's XO, despite not having any formal military experience. I don't think anyone in the Second Space Lord's office thought this was inappropriate, at least until it was too late. Admiral Soskice would probably react badly if his selection was removed without due cause."

"Fuck," John said. "She's inexperienced. And everyone will *know* she's inexperienced."

"Yes, sir," Johnston said.

John fought down the temptation to put his head in his hands. "Let me guess," he said, crossly. "There have been problems already."

"Some," Johnston admitted. "Myself and Howard - Lieutenant-Commander Howard - took care of them. Mostly, she's liked by the crew, which is fortunate. She's a very poor disciplinarian."

"Lucky for her," John said. He didn't know many people who would have willingly tangled with Johnston. "A non-standard commander, he said. A commander who was willing to do the work of an XO, he meant."

"Sir?"

"Never mind," John said. "Give it to me, now. What are the other problems with the ship?"

"Mostly, some minor teething problems," Johnston said. "However, I do have concerns about the integration of human and alien technology. It has a nasty habit of setting up power curves that could cause real problems, if allowed to run on for too long. And then there's the prospect of accidentally overwhelming the compensators if we push the drives too hard…"

"Turning us into strawberry jam before we know we're in trouble," John said. He'd seen recordings of what happened to a starship's crew when the compensators failed. "Is that likely to happen?"

"I wish I knew," Johnston said. He looked down at his hands. "Frankly, sir, the whole project is moving forward much too fast. Apart from a handful of people like Commander Watson, we don't really understand what we're doing."

"Hardly anyone understands how a drive field works," John pointed out.

"I do," Johnston said. "But I don't understand precisely how the alien tech integrates with human tech. And that's what bothers me."

He shook his head, then looked up. "There are other issues," he said. "Our main gun is a long-range plasma cannon, an experimental model. It works fine in simulations and live-fire drills, but it's never been tested in combat conditions. I have a feeling that any half-way competent sensor crew will see us taking aim before we fire. Then there's the missile tubes, which have been redesigned twice to accommodate the other changes, and the short-range plasma weapons, which have a tendency to overheat and explode."

"Shit," John said. "And our armour?"

"Improved, but still nowhere near as strong as I would like," Johnston said. "I don't think we will be able to stand up to a hit from a comparable plasma weapon."

"Understood," John said. "One final question, then. Are we likely to meet our departure date?"

"Almost certainly," Johnston said. "Commander Watson *is* good at sorting out minor hiccups, as long as they don't involve dealing with personnel. The real test, of course, will come when we jump through the tramline and see what happens."

"Wonderful," John said, sardonically. "Do you have any other concerns I should know?"

"Not as yet," Johnston said. He smiled. "My complaints aside, sir, *Warspite* is a good little ship. Once we manage to sort out the teething problems, we should be fine."

"I hope you're right," John said. "You will inform me if there are any problems with Commander Watson?"

"Yes, sir," Johnston said, although he looked uncomfortable. Asking a junior officer to spy on a senior rarely ended well for anyone. "I would advise you to read through the official notes, but also the additions Commander Watson and I have been making. Trying to ensure that every change was documented wasn't an easy job either."

"It never is," John agreed. "I shall be hosting a dinner for the crew in two days, I think. You will be attending?"

"Of course I will, sir," Johnston said. "Unless the ship blows up first, in which case I shall be eating dinner in heaven instead."

John snorted. "Are there any other issues?"

"Some grumbling about reduced shore leave," Johnston said. "The departure date was pushed up twice, sir. Crewmen who were planning holidays had to cancel them at short notice."

"Odd," John mused. "The First Space Lord only gave me the command a few hours ago."

"They may have intended to give you more time to come to grips with the ship." Johnston said. "Or maybe they're just jerking us around for the hell of it."

"Sounds plausible," John said. "I'll organise a couple of shuttle flights to Sin City II at the end of the week, I think. It will give the crew a chance to blow off some steam before the shit hits the fan."

"Seems like a good idea," Johnston said. "Mind you, I don't think Sin City II is quite as good as Sin City I."

"But more moral," John said. "And besides, half of the spacers won't know the difference."

He smiled at the thought. Sin City had been destroyed by the Tadpoles during their attack on Earth, earning them the undying hatred of almost every spacer in the system. The new Sin City was owned and operated by a consortium of the major spacefaring powers, taking advantage of the situation to close the loopholes that had allowed Sin City to exist. It still held beer, prostitutes and VR chambers, but most of the more problematic entertainments had been removed.

"True, I suppose," Johnston said. "Did you have fun in Soho?"

"It's not what it used to be," John admitted. "Most of the bars are closed now, sadly. I think quite a few of the community moved out to an asteroid, where they will be safer from alien attacks."

He shook his head as he recalled some of the times Colin and he had shared in Soho, then dismissed the memory. Colin was dead. There was no point in dwelling on a dead man.

"Safe is relative," Johnston said. "I heard that several ships were sent out to establish a new human homeworld. How safe do you think they are?"

"Safer than here, I expect," John said.

He smiled, then finished his tea. "Are you still dating Sofia?"

"She decided she preferred to stay with a pretty boy from Luna One," Johnston said, without heat. "I can live without her."

"Quite right," John said. "We'll speak later, I think."

Johnston nodded, then rose to his feet, saluted and walked out the compartment. John watched him go, then looked around his cabin-office. It was larger than the space he'd been assigned on his last shipboard berth, although *that* was saying nothing. HMS *Spartan* had been a frigate, with most of her hull volume occupied by engines and weapons. The crew had had barely enough room to swing a cat. *Warspite* was over three times her size, yet even the CO got little more than an office, a bedroom and a tiny washroom. The only decoration was an oil painting of HMS Warspite, the superdreadnaught that had served in the Second World War, firing her guns towards an unseen threat. But, on the plus side, his cabin *was* right next to the bridge.

Midshipwoman Powell tapped on the hatch, then opened it and peered in. "Would you like some more tea, sir?"

"Yes, please," John said. "And a ration bar or two, if you could manage it."

He chewed on the bar as he opened his terminal and started to read through the endless series of notes, incident reports and screeds written by various designers to the Admiralty. John had never actually *served* in the Admiralty, but he'd been an XO long enough to understand when several Admirals were actually fighting a private war over funding, pet projects and - at base - their vision of the Royal Navy's future. Commander Watson might have no inkling of the titanic power struggles her superior had been fighting, but that hadn't stopped her being at the centre of one of them. No wonder she had been left in a slot she was manifestly unsuited to handle…and no wonder the First Space Lord, sensing trouble, had arranged for *Warspite* to receive a commanding officer who wouldn't make a fuss, just quietly handle her XO duties as well as his own.

"I need a bloody secretary," he muttered. Paperwork was normally the XO's responsibility, although the Captain had a fair share of it himself. "And possibly a stiff drink."

Cursing under his breath, he checked the personnel files. Lieutenant-Commander Paul Howard had a good record, although he'd been a Midshipman during the war and only been promoted in its aftermath. Unfortunately, the tactical department would require his full attention, so he couldn't be given some of Commander Watson's duties and a promise of early promotion. He briefly considered letting some of the paperwork slide, but he knew it would only cause more trouble later on. The bureaucrats would whinge and moan and complain loudly to their superiors, who would demand explanations from John and his crew.

You haven't filled out Form 644, Paragraph 7, he thought, ruefully. *What is your explanation for this?*

I was bored, his own thoughts answered him. *Should I report for execution now or later?*

His console chimed. "Captain, this is Hemminge in Communications," a voice said. "The First Space Lord is calling you on a priority link."

"Put him through," John ordered.

He turned his attention to his terminal, as the First Space Lord's face appeared in front of him.

"Admiral," he said, neutrally.

"Captain," Admiral Finnegan said. "I trust you are impressed with your new command?"

"Nothing I can't handle," John said, biting down several responses that came to mind, all of which would probably have earned him a court martial. "I may be requesting additional personnel, sir, but I can handle the ship."

"That's good to hear," Admiral Finnegan said. "The other ships in your squadron are being assigned now. I shall expect you to meet with their commanding officers once the formation is assembled."

"Yes, sir," John said, wondering just when he was meant to do it. He wasn't sure he trusted Commander Watson to handle the ship in his absence. "Sir, with all due respect, I do wonder at some of the personal assignments that have already been made."

"Politics," Admiral Finnegan said, bluntly. "You'll just have to live with it, Captain. I don't have much room to manoeuvre."

John sighed, wondering if Johnston and the First Space Lord had coordinated their conversations. "Yes, sir," he said. "I can handle the ship."

"That's good to hear," Admiral Finnegan said. "And, for what it's worth, I'm sorry for the problems you're going to face."

His image vanished. John scowled at the console, then turned back to his datapad and hunted for a particular set of personnel files. When they popped up in front of him, he was gratified to see that two of his first choices had not been assigned anywhere outside the personnel pool. They were on leave at the moment, but the Royal Navy could recall anyone who wasn't actually retired, if it saw fit. John keyed in a request to the Personnel Office, requesting that one of his two selections be recalled and reassigned to *Warspite*, then rose to his feet and stalked out onto the bridge. Two officers were bent over the tactical console, running an exercise. They turned around, then jumped to attention when they saw him.

"Captain," one of them said. "I'm Lieutenant-Commander Howard. Welcome onboard."

John looked him up and down, then nodded in approval. Howard *looked* like a naval officer; he didn't have a single button out of place, while he wore two service pips and a campaign ribbon on his jacket. His short brown hair was cut close to his scalp, like most spacers chose to wear their hair. Long hair just got in the way on a starship.

"Pleased to meet you," he said. "What sort of exercise are you running?"

"Us against an alien battlecruiser," Howard explained. "We might actually have an advantage, but there are tactical problems in bringing the heavy plasma cannon to bear on any target."

"We actually have to line up the whole ship to take aim," John noted. "And just powering up the cannon sends out telltale bursts of radiation."

"It does," Howard confirmed. "So far, the only tactical doctrine we have for using it, sir, involves not powering the cannon up until we're already engaging the enemy. But that takes half of our firepower off the board before we've even started the fight. The enemy might notice our weakness and close with us."

"So we could only use it to get the first shot if we weren't trying to hide," John said. He sat down in the command chair and keyed a switch, bringing up the tactical display. "And if we were trying to sneak up on someone, our first broadside would be lame."

"Yes, sir," Howard said.

John frowned. It was starting to look as though *Warspite* could either beat or outrun anything else in space. The plasma cannon was a great idea, in theory, yet Howard and Johnston had already outlined some of the problems of using it in real life. On the other hand, there were some definite possibilities...

"We could still use it," he said. One idea had already occurred to him. "Set up the tactical simulators for 1900, Mr. Howard. We'll start playing through some possibilities tonight."

"Aye, sir," Howard said.

John rose, then walked out of the hatch and through the ship, inspecting each and every compartment. Most of them looked unfinished, although it was clear that all of the essential gear had already been installed and that *Warspite* shouldn't have any problems in meeting her scheduled departure date. The real problem lay in the fact that most of the crew were inexperienced, despite the recent war. But he was starting to get the impression that using crewmen who had served on more conventional starships to crew *Warspite* was asking for trouble.

"Doctor Thomas Stewart," a grim-faced man said, when he entered sickbay. "I hope I will be seeing you soon for your physical."

John groaned. "I think you add half the steps to torture people," he said. It was evident he wasn't going to be developing a personal relationship with his ship's doctor. "And I did have a physical before I returned to Earth."

"Never trust doctors who just want to verify you can return to Earth," the doctor said, firmly. "I shall expect to see you here before we depart, sir."

"As you wish," John said, with a sigh. "Any problems in your department?"

"Half my staff hasn't arrived, but other than that everything is fine," Stewart said. "A couple of crewmen tried to malinger, so I sent them back to duty with a few well-chosen words and threats. If you're trying to fake an illness, you might as well do something that isn't easily verifiable."

John frowned. "Is that a major problem?"

"It certainly wasn't during the war," Stewart said. "I blame it on all the enhanced training programs we had after New Russia fell. Lots of spacers out there who never had the full battery of tests, let alone the exhaustive training program we put together after years of experience. Some of them really don't want to be here, but don't want to join a reconstruction battalion either."

Or maybe it's a form of protest, John thought. Not, in the end, that it would have made any difference. Military personnel weren't allowed to strike. *It will have to be dealt with.*

"Thank you, doctor," he said, out loud. "I'm sure things will get better once we're on a proper training and exercise roster."

CHAPTER
FIVE

It had been years since Percy had last visited Turnstile - Edinburgh - Spaceport. It had been important then, as one of the gateways to the stars, but it had only expanded rapidly since the war. Hundreds of thousands of people, emigrants heading to Britannia or one of the other settled worlds, waited patiently for the shuttles that would take them to the orbiting colonist-carriers, while work crews struggled desperately to expand the facilities to cope with the growing exodus. Thousands of cars and other vehicles were parked outside and abandoned, being sifted through and towed away by reclamation squads. Their former owners no longer needed them.

He showed his ID card at the desk, passed through a biometric screening and was then pointed into the military waiting compartment. In stark contrast to the civilian departure lounges, it was almost empty; the handful of personnel chatting quietly to one another or trying to catch up on much-needed sleep. Percy checked his terminal and noted the shuttle's departure time, then sat down on a chair and closed his eyes. He'd spent too long making love to his girlfriend, he noted ruefully as sleep overcame him, instead of catching up with his rest. But then, it was unlikely there would be any chance to make love on *Warspite*.

It felt like bare seconds before someone shook him, gently. Percy snapped awake, one hand grabbing for the concealed pistol, before he remembered where and when he was. An older man was standing next to him, peering down at him with concerned grey eyes. Percy couldn't help being reminded of his father, even though his father had never looked so…dignified. There was something about the newcomer that practically *shouted* father.

"The shuttle is loading now, Corporal," the newcomer said. "You and I are the only passengers, I'm afraid."

Percy stood and grabbed his duffle. "Coming, sir," he said. The newcomer wasn't wearing any rank insignia, but he had an air of authority that pervaded his voice. "You're assigned to *Warspite* too?"

"Damned strange thing," the newcomer said. "One moment, I'm on leave; the next, someone calls me and tells me to get my ass up to *Warspite* pretty damn quick. And to think I thought I wouldn't be flying more than a desk for the foreseeable future."

He turned and strode towards the departure gate. Percy followed him, noting absently that several of the soldiers had gone, while others had taken their place. Perhaps there had been a slew of reassignments, he told himself, as they walked onto the tarmac. The military only seemed efficient when compared to civilian life. One officer falling sick at the wrong time could throw the entire schedule out of whack.

"I'm Philip," the newcomer said. He had to shout to be heard over the sound of a shuttle taking off and vanishing into the overcast sky. "Philip Richards."

"Percy Schneider," Percy said. "Yes, he *was* my father, thank you for asking."

"There are worse fathers to have," Richards said. He didn't seem impressed at all, much to Percy's relief. "Mine wanted me to become a corporate rumour-monger and marry into aristocracy. Then he overdosed on something and died horribly. Or so I was told."

A young female MP, standing outside the shuttle, checked their ID cards and then waved them into the boxy craft. Percy wasn't surprised to discover that half of the seats had been taken out, nor that the space cleared by removing the seats had been filled with storage pallets, all destined for *Warspite*. The military would hardly have wasted a shuttle flight on the pair of them, even if they *did* have to get to their destination as swiftly as possible. Someone had probably noted that the shuttle was available to carry supplies and promptly delivered the supplies to the spaceport.

"Pick a seat, any seat," Richards said. "I don't think there's much choice."

"And not much chance of a hot stewardess either," Percy said, as he stuffed his duffle into an overhead compartment, then sat down beside the porthole. As always, the seat was at least one size too small. "Why were you assigned to *Warspite*?"

"Good question," Richards said. "And I would be much happier if I knew the answer."

Percy raised his eyebrows. "You don't know?"

"I was merely told that I was being reassigned," Richards said. "That's the military life for you, son. Love it or jump out an airlock."

"I don't know if I will re-up when my time expires," Percy admitted. It wasn't an easy thing to say. Richards was clearly a natural lifer, a man who would stay in the Navy until it was time for mandatory retirement, while Percy had his doubts. "I could find a patch of land on Britannia and settle down to farm."

"They won't run out of land in a hurry," Richards said. "But do you really want to farm?"

Percy shrugged. His father had been a investment banker when he hadn't been flying starfighters, but Percy had never cared for the life. It hadn't done his mother any favours, he saw now in the cold light of hindsight, while Penny hadn't really handled it well either. There was definitely something to be said for the simple life, even if it did mean hours of backbreaking labour on a farm. Britannia was booming and those who got in on the ground floor, he'd been told, were certain to make a packet in later life. *And* have something worthwhile to pass down to their children.

"I see doubts," Richards said. "Just make sure you know what you want before you commit yourself."

"Thank you for your advice," Percy said, waspishly. "What did you do before someone sentenced you to fly a desk?"

"Senior Chief Crewman on *Illustrious*," Richards said. "I survive the war and they up and throw a desk at me. It wasn't fun, let me tell you."

Percy blinked. "*Warspite* needs a Senior Chief?"

"I have no idea," Richards said.

They looked up as a young man wearing a pilot's uniform stepped into the compartment and frowned at them. "If I could have your attention please," he said, "I will commence the safety briefing."

"Don't drink, don't smoke, don't turn on the lights, don't do anything I wouldn't do and don't do half the things I would do either," Richards said, loudly. "Did I miss anything?"

The young man scowled, then went through a long safety lecture. Percy tried to pay attention, but after the third repetition it grew harder to keep his mind fixed on the speaker's droning voice. One thing he had learned, in the Royal Marines, was that if something went wrong on a shuttle, it would probably be completely fatal. There was no point in worrying about what to do if the shit hit the fan.

"If you're not close to life support gear," his instructor had said, years ago, "bend over and kiss your ass goodbye."

"Thank you for listening," the co-pilot said finally. "I hope you have a pleasant flight."

"Definitely not a hot stewardess," Richards said, once the co-pilot had left. "How disappointing."

Percy shrugged. "I don't think the military assigns pilots based on their hotness," he said, although he had his doubts. Penny had told him that their father had brought a pretty young pilot to the camp, after the Battle of Earth. Percy wondered, sometimes, if their father had been having an affair. "And besides, what hot pilot would want to fly an Earth-based shuttle?"

Richards smirked, then launched into a long and complicated story involving ten hot pilots, nine stewardesses and a dozen Royal Marines, all of whom had been trying to find out just how many people could fit into a shuttle. It took Percy several moments to realise that Richards was trying to distract him from the shuttle's takeoff, something that was hardly necessary. But, as a Senior Chief Crewman, Richards would no doubt have supervised hundreds of young crewmen taking their first steps off-world. Keeping them distracted from everything that could go wrong was part of his job.

"It sounds like a porn movie," he said, when Richards finally came to an end. "I think I might have seen it, once."

"Everyone's seen it," Richards agreed. "Do you know how many copies I had to confiscate while I was on duty?"

Percy snorted. The Royal Marines weren't supposed to store porn on their military-issue terminals, but he'd yet to meet a Marine who actually obeyed that injunction. Porn was one way to while away the time while on deployment, after all. He still recalled the lecture his unit had received, during their first deployment, when one of the bootnecks had been careless about his giant porn stash. The Sergeant had insisted, sharply, that nothing like that was ever to be left lying around where the senior officers had to take notice of it. They might understand - they were bootnecks too - but they had to uphold standards.

"Hundreds," he guessed. It was amusing to know the regular crewmen had the same problem. "Or thousands?"

"Around that," Richards said. "The war, at least, got people focused on our true reason for existence."

Percy nodded, then turned his head and peered out of the porthole. Earth was gone, replaced by a field of unblinking stars. It had surprised him, once upon a time, to see the stars burning steadily in the inky darkness of space, but there was no atmosphere to produce the twinkling effect. Now, he couldn't help but realise just how tiny he was compared to the immense universe. Even humanity's growing domains covered only a tiny fraction of the galaxy.

And there are dangers out there, he thought, recalling his father's final battle. He still didn't know the full story - he knew no one who did, because the files had been carefully sealed - but he knew his father had died a hero. *Aliens out there, waiting to fight us.*

He shuddered. Five years ago, no one had believed in aliens. Humanity had discovered over thirty Earth-like worlds and none of them had evolved anything more complex than a small dog-analogue. Earth had seemed a lucky accident, the sole world to develop an intelligent race. No one had seriously believed that there might be others, scattered across the stars, not until Vera Cruz. And then the human race had been plunged into war.

"There might be other threats out there," he mused. "Other aliens with bad intentions."

"There might," Richards agreed.

Percy jumped. He hadn't realised he'd spoken aloud.

"We can't really say for sure *what* we will encounter," Richards offered, gently. "All we can really do is make sure we're ready for anything."

"Which might boil down to being ready for nothing," Percy said, crossly. It had been years since a thoroughly embarrassing exercise in the Bristol Reclamation Zone had taught him and his fellow recruits to watch for *all* possible angles of attack. They'd anticipated a land offensive and had been taken by surprise when the aggressor force dropped from the skies. "I don't think we can prepare for *all* possibilities."

"True," Richards agreed. "We might run into the Bat Ships tomorrow and get blown into tiny pieces."

"Oh," Percy said. "Do you believe the rumours?"

Richards shrugged. "Spacers see all sorts of crazy things out in the darkness," he said, simply. "The Tadpoles were real, so the Bats might be real too."

Percy had heard the story, but he also had his doubts. Years ago, a starship exploring a newly-discovered star system had reported sighting a giant bat-like starship, hovering over a deserted world. There had been no sensor recordings, not even visual images, and so most people had dismissed the whole encounter as a hoax cooked up by bored survey crewmen. But a handful of other reports had come out of the woodwork since then, all sharing the same basic elements. A bat-shaped ship, visible only to the naked eye.

"Rumours," he said. "Maybe it's just another UFO craze."

"Maybe," Richards said. "But who believed in aliens before the Tadpoles arrived?"

They fell into a companionable silence as the shuttle raced towards its destination. Percy reached into his duffle, found his terminal and glanced through - again - the set of orders he'd been issued by the CO. Report to Lieutenant Darryl Hadfield, HMS *Warspite*. Assume command of 2 Section. Follow orders from superior authority. As always, the orders were vague; the person on the spot was expected to handle the situation using his own initiative, rather than await orders from higher up the food chain. Percy wasn't too surprised. If someone had seen fit to assign twenty-one

Royal Marines to *Warspite*, when they were needed on Earth, it suggested they expected trouble.

Or that we will be going far from civilised space, he thought, grimly. *Who knows what we might encounter so far down the tramlines?*

"There she blows," Richards said, suddenly. "Take a look."

Percy looked up. The shuttle was approaching a starship - a cruiser, judging by the size - and heading towards a docking port. *Warspite* was larger than he'd expected, her hull bristling with weapons and sensor blisters. A unit number was blazed across her dark hull, with her name written underneath. He sucked in his breath as the hull loomed closer, then braced himself. A dull *clang* ran through the shuttle as it locked on to the airlock, followed by a hiss as the airlock opened.

"Come along," Richards said, as the gravity field shimmered around them. "We don't want to be late."

Percy nodded his thanks to the two pilots as he walked past them and through the airlock, into the ship. A small work crew was already forming up outside the airlock, evidently ready to start moving supplies from the shuttle into the hold. Beyond them, there was a young man wearing a Royal Marine battledress, optimised for starship deployment. Percy walked past the work crews, stopped in front of the young man and saluted, smartly.

"Corporal Percy Schneider, reporting," he said.

"Lieutenant Darryl Hadfield," the young man said. His voice was largely unaccented, but Percy had enough experience to be fairly sure Hadfield was from Wales. Blue eyes flickered over Percy's face and uniform, leaving him wishing he'd had time to freshen up. "Come with me."

He turned and marched down the corridor. Percy followed him, quietly assessing his new commanding officer. Hadfield was young, strong and clearly experienced, although he probably hadn't expected sole command of a deployment so early in his career. But then, one habit the Royal Marines had eventually copied from the USMC was to have everyone start out as a groundpounder, then have promising young men turned into officers after they gained some real experience. Hadfield was young, but he was still old enough to have seen *real* combat in the war.

"This is Marine Country," Hadfield said, as they stepped through a hatch. "You've served before, so I won't bother to go over the specifics. We follow standard procedures, save for the absence of a guard on the hatch. I don't have anyone to spare for the post."

"Yes, sir," Percy said.

"Nor do we have separate accommodation." Hadfield continued. "We have one barracks for all of us, one office for us to do our paperwork and one training compartment. And we have to share exercise facilities with the crew, I'm afraid. They're as pleased about it as we are."

Percy smiled as Hadfield led him into the office. Starship crewmen and Royal Marines tended to keep themselves to themselves, even though they were both cooped up in the same starship. The idea of sharing an exercise compartment with crewmen was irritating, although he knew it was hardly the end of the world. There might be arguments, disagreements and fights, but it wouldn't be the worst thing he'd experienced. The deployment on Mars would be hard to beat.

"We're running constant training exercises, in and out of the ship," Hadfield continued, as he sat down on one side of a metal table. "You'll take command of 2 Section at once, then bring them up to speed. I'm not anticipating any need for a deployment, but I'm damned if we will be caught unprepared."

"Yes, sir," Percy agreed. Taking command of a section he barely knew - he hadn't had time to do more than glance at the personnel files - would be a challenge. "I won't let you down."

Hadfield keyed his terminal. "Sergeant Peerce, report to my office," he ordered. "Danny has been in command of 2 Section until you arrived. You'll find him very helpful."

Percy nodded, although he wasn't as sanguine as he tried to appear. There were always tensions when one commanding officer was relieved by another, even when it had been planned in advance. Sergeant Peerce might resent being replaced by someone fresh off the shuttle from Earth, even though Percy knew he'd earned his rank. But then, one of the best pieces of advice he'd been given, back when he'd had the stripe pinned on his dress uniform, had been to listen to the senior NCOs. They had forgotten more about making the unit work than he'd ever learned.

The hatch opened, revealing a short man with a stern face. Not someone to cross, Percy realised, recalling the sergeant he'd met on the Royal Marine Insight Day. The man had looked like a gym teacher from hell; short, bald and terrifyingly loud. Peerce had the same attitude, but smoother. It took Percy a moment to remember that Peerce didn't have to deal with raw recruits.

"Lieutenant," Peerce said.

"This is 2 Section's new CO," Hadfield said. "Take him, get him sorted out, then start exercising. I want 2 Section up to speed by the time we leave."

"Yes, sir," Peerce said. He turned to look at Percy. "Coming, Corporal?"

Percy nodded, then picked up his duffle and followed Peerce out of the tiny compartment.

CHAPTER
SIX

"Captain," Midshipwoman Powell said. "Mr. Richards is here to see you."

John barely glanced up from his terminal. "Show him in," he ordered. "Then bring us both tea and a snack. He must be hungry."

"You want something," a familiar voice said. "Should I be worried?"

"Not yet," John said, as he rose. "It's good to see you again, Philip."

"And you, sir," Philip Richards said. "I was *very* surprised to be reassigned. The Royal Navy had me flying a desk for the foreseeable future."

John shook his hand, then motioned Richards into a seat. "I need someone with your...unique skill set," he said, as he sat down behind the desk. "In a fit of desperation, I chose to ask for you."

"You must have been desperate," Richards said. He glanced up as Midshipwoman Powell entered the office, carrying a tray of tea and biscuits. "Thank you, love."

John waited until Midshipwoman Powell had retreated, then leaned forward. "I need an assistant, Phil," he said. "Someone's set me up the bomb."

"That sounds bad," Richards said. "And, in the interests of great justice, you sent for me?"

"My XO is brilliant, but doesn't have the slightest idea how to command respect," John said. He picked up the datapad and waved it at Richards, meaningfully. "I don't think I have to tell you just how many things remain undone, or unaccounted for, or...well, you know how easily things can go wrong when someone doesn't do their work. There are enough hiccups here to cause real trouble when we're well away from Earth."

"Shit," Richards said. "They've been getting away with too much."

"Tell me about it," John said. He put down the datapad and took a sip of tea. "I want you to serve as my...well, my assistant."

"You want me to do everything your XO can't," Richards said. "Without, I might add, the rank to actually *do* it."

"In one," John said. "The Admiralty will allow me to give you a rank without a formal approval procedure, as long as we both understand it's strictly temporary. You won't be allowed to retire as a Lieutenant-Commander."

"I wouldn't *want* to retire as a Lieutenant-Commander," Richards said, dryly. "Very well. I accept."

John smirked. "And to think I had a ten thousand word speech planned out to tell you *why* you should take the job."

"You can save it for your next attempt at hijacking an underling," Richards said. He drained his teacup, then placed it to one side. "What would you like me to tackle first, sir?"

"Everything," John said. He picked up another datapad, glanced down at it and then passed it to Richards. "I hate paperwork as much as the next line officer, but half of these papers haven't been done properly and it could prove a major headache, further down the line."

"I should coco," Richards said, as he studied the datapad. "When were half these components replaced?"

John sighed. Military-grade components were ultra-reliable, but the Royal Navy insisted on replacing them regularly anyway, just in case the ship needed to go to war tomorrow. It wasn't something he grudged the beancounters - for once, the bureaucrats had a point - but he understood the temptation some crewmen would face to skip the paperwork. Replacing a single component could take minutes, while filling in the paperwork could take hours. And most of his crewmen *knew* it was a pointless endeavour, right up until the moment it wasn't.

"I don't know," John said. "Which is the problem, isn't it?"

"You could have a rat onboard too," Richards offered. "You know how much naval components are worth on the civilian market."

"Yeah," John said. He leaned forward. "If there is a rat onboard, I expect you to find him and bring him to Captain's Mast. But if it's just laziness, I want them beaten into shape before they can cause a real disaster."

"Yes, sir," Richards said. "I'll get to work at once."

John nodded, then returned to his paperwork as Richards left the office. It wasn't a good thing to call in outside help - it would reflect badly on Commander Watson - but he didn't think he had a choice. Richards would clear the decks, he was sure; there were very few crewmen who would cross him once, let alone twice. And if there were any bad apples in the bunch, Richards would smoke them out before they managed to infest the rest of the crew.

His intercom chimed. "Captain," Midshipwomen Powell said, "it's about time for the dinner to begin."

"Joy," John said. He glanced at the chronometer and swore under his breath. He'd been reading and marking paperwork for hours. "Have the other commanders arrived?"

"Yes, sir," Midshipwomen Powell said. She'd taken over responsibility for organising the dinner, something else that should have been handled by the XO. "They're on their way to the Officer's Mess."

"Then I'm on my way too," John said. Thankfully, he'd specified informal wear, although he suspected that a couple of the officers would wear dress uniforms anyway. "Tell them I'll be there in a couple of minutes."

He checked his appearance in the mirror, then hastened out of the hatch and strode down towards the Officer's Mess. Midshipwomen Powell was standing outside, showing another commanding officer to his seat. John nodded to her, then stepped into the room and looked around. It was small, barely large enough to hold all of his officers at once, but it was tolerable. Unwritten rules dictated, after all, that any starship larger than a frigate had to have separate eating spaces for the officers and enlisted crewmen.

"Thank you for coming," he said, as he took his seat at the head of the table. "I apologise for the short notice."

"Everything about this mission is short notice," Captain Heath Meeks grumbled. "I don't get paid enough to be jerked here and there."

"That's what you pay for signing up with the Royal Fleet Auxiliary," Captain Glen Larne reminded him. "They paid half the cost of your starship in exchange for your service when they needed it."

John motioned for them to sit, trying to keep his expression under control. The Royal Fleet Auxiliary were torn between being civilians and being military; the Royal Navy had invested in their ships, in exchange for having first call on their services if a sudden emergency developed in interstellar space. He couldn't blame Meeks for being a little annoyed - the Colony Support Vessel he commanded was a licence to print money, if he based himself in the right system - but he *had* signed the contract. The Royal Navy would be happy to repossess his vessel and place a prize crew on her if he refused to uphold his end of the bargain.

Besides, he thought dryly. *The RFA is a suitable place for officers and men who want to remain close to the navy, without actually being in the navy.*

"My cook has taken the liberty of preparing a simple meal," he said, "using ingredients sourced from Earth. There won't be another one like this for months, I'm afraid."

He had to smile at their expressions. Only the very largest starships carried enough supplies to be able to offer their crews fresh food every day. Everyone else got ration bars, reprocessed foods and algae-based meals. They might taste nice, once the cook added some flavouring, but they became monotonous very rapidly. It was one of the reasons why fresh fruit and vegetables were always included in care packages from home.

"Six months of deployment," Meeks moaned. "Do you know how much I could earn in a different system?"

"The Royal Navy is paying you well enough," John said, patiently. "And besides, there may be opportunity. You never know."

He cleared his throat as Midshipwoman Powell entered, pushing a trolley loaded with bowls of carrot and coriander soup. "There will be time to discuss the mission afterwards," he added, firmly. "Until then, let us eat and chat about nothing."

The ship's cook had definitely excelled himself, John decided, as they ate their way through a three-course meal. He allowed himself to relax slightly at the chatter, listening to stories of life in the post-war RFA, while silently envying some of their freedoms. The Royal Navy didn't allow him or anyone else wearing the uniform anything like the same amount of freedom, although he knew it came with a cost. Meeks was right, in a way; the RFA demanded attention, often at the cost of long-term financial security.

He knew it when he made the deal, he reminded himself, as the dinner came to an end. *And he can't complain now.*

"I would like to be brief," he said, once Midshipwoman Powell had cleared away the plates and retreated into the galley. "But I don't think I can be."

He smiled at them all, then keyed a switch, activating the holographic projector. "Our destination is Pegasus, the star system here," he said, nodding towards a blinking icon. "As you can see, Pegasus plays host to a number of tramlines, thus ensuring that whoever controls the system will be able to control those tramlines. Our mission is to proceed to Pegasus and establish a base on Clarke III, a moon orbiting a gas giant. Once the base and cloudscoop is established, we will formally lay claim to the entire system."

"And make sure no one else can tap the gas giant for fuel," Meeks commented, sourly. "I like it."

"I'm glad to hear it," John said. "And I'm sure there will be long-term opportunities here."

He shrugged. Meeks was right, again. Ownership of the sole economical source of HE3 in the system would ensure that Britain maintained a controlling interest, even if other powers managed to establish their own outposts. International treaties forbade such blatant theft, but there were loopholes. Pegasus didn't have any Earth-like planets to claim, so *someone* could easily try to argue that the treaty didn't apply to that system.

"And once we have the base established, we proceed to Wells?" Captain Jerry Samisen asked. "Or do we leave that world for later?"

"I believe our long-term plans call for a slow terraforming program," John said. "It isn't as if anyone is interested in investing the resources for a least-time effort. Wells isn't Mars."

"True," Meeks agreed. "There are several Earth-like worlds within one or two jumps of Pegasus."

John nodded. Mars had been force-terraformed, a project that had started well before the first tramlines had been discovered. The various nations that had established settlements on Mars had dumped millions of tons of water into the atmosphere, followed by producing genetically-engineered seeds and orbiting mirrors to heat the planet. Mars's original ecosystem, such as it was, had been utterly destroyed, replaced by a fragile world that could support human life. There were people who still hinted that there might have once been life on Mars, but the terraforming program had obliterated it. Until the Tadpoles had arrived, speculation that Mars had once possessed *intelligent* life had been among the most popular conspiracy theories in human existence.

But Mars had also cost the various nations a great deal of money. And the colonists hadn't been entirely grateful. It wasn't something that would be repeated in a hurry.

"We will depart in three days, barring accidents," he said. "Will your ships be ready to depart by then?"

"We could have left last week," Meeks said. "I think the real delay came out of Nelson Base."

"Probably," John agreed. It didn't take much imagination to see how the political struggle had delayed the colonisation mission. "We can leave on the scheduled date, though?"

"Yes," Meeks said, flatly. The other commanders echoed him. "Do you anticipate running into trouble?"

"I would prefer to be prepared," John said. "The Tadpoles might be on the other side of human space, but there might be other threats out there. That's another good reason to secure Pegasus as soon as possible, I think. There could be *anything* out there, waiting for us."

"Yes, Captain," Samisen agreed.

"*Warspite* will take point," John continued. "*Canberra*" - an escort carrier - "will bring up the rear. We will maintain a watchful eye on our surroundings at all times, including a CSP of no less than four starfighters. I trust such a tempo will not prove too challenging?"

Captain Jonny Minion shrugged. "We've been practicing heavy deployments regularly, ever since the war," he said. "Keeping a mere four starfighters on station at all times will not prove to be a challenge, at least not for the moment. I'd be happier with more, of course…"

John nodded as Minion's voice tailed off. Escort carriers were nothing more than converted bulk freighters, lacking the weapons, sensors and armoured hulls - such as they were - of fleet carriers. The Royal Navy had seen no choice, but to deploy the modified starships, knowing that they would take hideous losses. And they had; by the time the war had come to an end, thirty-seven escort carriers had been lost, along with over five hundred pilots. John had served on one himself and knew, beyond a shadow of a doubt, just how lucky he had been to survive.

And Colin died, he thought, morbidly. *I could never fly a starfighter after that, could I?*

He pushed the thought aside as he rose to his feet. "We can affix a couple of starfighters to *Warspite's* hull, if necessary," he said. "It would give us some additional striking power, if we do run into trouble."

"Let us hope not," Meeks said. "Danger will only delay proceedings."

"Tell me about it," John muttered. He walked around the table and stopped in front of the display. "Do any of you have any concerns about our proposed route?"

There was a long pause. "I would prefer not to go through Terra Nova," Captain William Hunter said, when it was clear that no one else was going to speak. "The system is not entirely safe."

"Nowhere is *safe*," Minion snapped.

"Terra Nova is having a major civil war," Hunter said, ignoring the unsubtle jab at him. "And some of the fighting has spread to outer space. I would prefer not to take the squadron through the system if it could be avoided."

"I don't think any of the out-system powers are likely to court a war by attacking us," Minion sneered. "And the locals don't have the firepower to take on the entire squadron."

"It would also add two weeks to our journey time if we avoided Terra Nova," John said, quietly. He understood the concerns, but he also knew there was no time to lose. "We will avoid the settled parts of the system as much as possible, I think. It should be enough to prevent an encounter with the locals."

"Something ought to be done about Terra Nova," Meeks grumbled. "Right now, the entire system is falling apart."

"Like what?" Minion demanded. "Put an army on the ground and kill anyone who even looks at us funny? That never worked out very well during the Age of Unrest."

John sighed. It had been a semi-serious debate before the First Interstellar War, when Terra Nova had merely been unstable. Now, with a full-scale civil war on the planet's surface, there were people calling for armed intervention. But how could the problem be actually *solved*? The only real solution, he suspected, was for anyone with half a brain to flee the planet, which was what they were doing. They wanted to live somewhere where there was not only a demand for skilled labour, but a chance to keep their earnings without having them stolen, or their sons conscripted into a militia, or their daughters raped by whatever force happened to occupy their hometown *this* week.

He shook his head. They were getting away from the subject at hand.

"Leaving Terra Nova aside," he said, "does anyone have any other concerns?"

There was a long pause. This time, no one spoke.

"Then we will leave on our scheduled departure date," John said. "Please let me know if you have any concerns, prior to departure. I will be sending some crewmen to Sin City for a brief period of leave; you may do the same, if you make sure they know to report back twenty-four hours prior to departure. Anyone who isn't back by then can explain themselves to the Shore Patrol and the Military Police. And yes, that includes RFA personnel."

"Yes, sir," Meeks said, without argument. "My crew will be glad of a short break."

"Just remind them not to take out any loans," John said, ruefully. He had, as a junior pilot, and he'd regretted it ever since. "If they run out of hard cash, they can make their way straight back to the ship."

Meeks smiled. "I'll make sure they know," he said. "It's always the young ones who get into trouble, isn't it?"

John nodded. "My officers need their Mess back," he said. The others rose. "Next time we meet in person, it will be in the Pegasus System."

He watched them file out of the room, then turned and walked through the door into the galley. Not entirely to his surprise, there were signs that the cook had saved some of the dinner for himself and Midshipwoman Powell, a tradition that was technically forbidden, but winked at by almost all senior officers. Powell herself was sitting at the table, reading a datapad and waiting for the call. John cleared his throat and she jumped.

"Sir," she said, rising. "I…"

"Thank you for your service," John said. "It was very good."

Midshipwoman Powell coloured. "Thank you, sir."

"You can clear away the rest of the dishes now," John continued. "Make sure that the remains of the dessert are handed round in the Crew Mess. And tell the cook to save some of the supplies for later. You never know when we might need a fresh dinner."

"Yes, sir," Powell said.

John smiled, then walked back to his office. There was still no shortage of work to do.

CHAPTER
SEVEN

"They're coming around our flank, Corporal."

"I see them," Percy said. 1 Section was attacking, while 2 Section was defending. He'd distributed his men carefully around the airlock, but he knew the dangers of trying to be strong everywhere. "Keep your head down."

He gritted his teeth as he crawled forward. There were worse places to fight, he was sure, than the hull of a starship, but he couldn't think of any. Hardly any cover, apart from weapons emplacements and sensor blisters, and no way of digging a protective foxhole to conceal his men. He hated to think of what the Captain would say if he actually *did* manage to cut a hole into the hull, releasing the atmosphere out into interplanetary space…

The enemy appeared, wearing the same light combat suits as his own men. Percy levelled his rifle at the nearest enemy soldier and opened fire, sending flickering bursts of laser light across the hull and into their target. The enemy soldier jerked, then made a show of lying there dead as his comrades scattered, then advanced, throwing grenades towards Percy's position. Red lights flashed up in front of him and he cursed as his suit locked up.

"You're dead, Corporal," Sergeant Danny Peerce said.

"I noticed," Percy said. He'd blundered badly and his men were about to pay the price. 1 Section advanced into the gap they'd created, then secured the airlock and drove the remnants of 2 Section away. They'd still have to board and storm the entire ship, but command of the airlocks would ensure they could bring in as many reinforcements as they wanted. "And we lost."

"Indeed you did," Hadfield said. "Exercise terminated; I say again, exercise terminated."

Percy pushed himself to his feet as his suit unlocked, then looked around as the other Marines made their way towards the airlock and safety. As always, his head swam when he contemplated that he was standing on the hull of a starship, where it wasn't actually clear which way was *up* and which way was *down*. He forced himself to look back at the deck, cursing under his breath. It had been too long since his last stint of shipboard duty.

He stepped through the airlock, then joined the other Marines in clambering out of the suits and checking them, before hanging them back on the hooks for later use. Taking care of his equipment was important, he knew; it had been hammered into his head, time and time again, that taking care of his equipment was the only way to make sure it would take care of him.

"Back to the barracks," Hadfield ordered, as soon as the suits were checked. "We need to go over the exercise."

Percy groaned, inwardly. Two days of constant exercises had left him tired, sore and cranky, but he knew he couldn't avoid the aftermath. At least he'd done better in the simulated ground environments, thankfully. No one seriously expected the Royal Marines to have to fight off boarders in this day and age, although it *had* happened during the war. It was one of the reasons why every crewman was required to carry a personal weapon at all times, despite the risks.

"2 Section misread the enemy's intentions," Hadfield said, once they were back in the cramped barracks. *Warspite* had no briefing compartment for her Marines. "They also missed a chance to launch a counterattack by sending half the section around the ship and ramming their rifles up the enemy's butt. Once this mistake had shown itself, it was too late to recover."

Percy nodded, ruefully. It had been his mistake.

"We will try again, of course," Hadfield said. "And again, and again. Get some sleep, then return here for the next exercise at 1700. Schneider, Peerce, you're with me."

"Yes, sir," Percy said.

"You lugs get plenty of sleep," Peerce said, addressing the Marines. "You'll need it."

Percy nodded, then followed Hadfield out into the corridor, then into the small office. "I'm sorry, sir," he said. "That was my fuck up."

"Yes, it was," Hadfield said. There was a grim note to his voice that made Percy quail inwardly. "Luckily, it wasn't real. You get to try it again."

And then discover there's more than one way to fuck up, Percy thought. He'd thought training at Lympstone was bad, but it never really ended. *There's no shortage of ways to fuck up and get people killed.*

"I have to report to the Captain," Hadfield said. "I'm supposed to be terribly subtle about finding a way to get you two to bond, but I really can't be arsed. There's cheap whiskey in the cabinet, the hatch will be locked and I've blocked your terminals. Sit down and bond. Or I can find a less friendly environment for you to do your bonding thing."

Percy stared at Peerce in astonishment as Hadfield strode out of the compartment, closing the hatch behind him. "Sergeant...?"

"Perils of taking over a Section without spending weeks of quality time training together first," Peerce said. He stood up and walked over to the cabinet, opening it to reveal a bottle of amber liquid. "Do you know how many regulations prohibit drinking on duty?"

"Yes, Sergeant," Percy said.

"But we're not on duty now," Peerce said. He opened the bottle, sniffed it suspiciously, then poured two glasses. "He wasn't kidding about the whiskey being cheap either. I've had better brews made by Military Moonshine, Inc."

"For people who want to know why we're in such a vile temper all the time," Percy said, recalling the adverts. They had brought a certain amount of amusement into the camps, even if half the manufacturer's claims were bunk. "But why would he spend half of his salary on a bottle of expensive whiskey?"

He took the glass Peerce offered him, then sipped it carefully. "Are we on the two-pint rule?"

"The one-glass rule, here," Peerce said. He returned to the seat and sat down. "So...we're meant to bond, aren't we?"

Percy scowled. "I don't know how to bond," he said. He paused, thinking. "How did you become a bootneck, Sergeant?"

"Runs in the family," Peerce said. "My father was a bootneck, *his* father was a bootneck...I think the very first Royal Marine in the family lived during the Napoleonic Wars. Got quite a few medals by the time he retired too. My mother rolls her eyes every time my father starts talking about his career, but she's very proud of him."

"Rupert Peerce," Percy said, placing the name. "Right?"

"Big hero of Tripoli," Peerce confirmed. "Jumped in to recover a pack of idiot hostages from the teeth of a bunch of wogs, then called in a kinetic strike that flattened the remains of the city after the hostages were dragged back to Britain. Fucking miserable place, my father said, and he was right. It didn't improve any since then, sir, and I know that because I served there too, twenty years after dad."

Percy nodded, slowly. Parts of the world had gone to the stars, claiming the endless resources of interstellar space for themselves, while others had declined into chaos and endless anarchy. They had nothing the spacefaring powers wanted, so they were generally left to kill each other to their heart's content...unless they impinged, somehow, on one of the great powers. And then military raids or kinetic strikes were used, once again, to remind the savages that no one had any patience for their antics. It was no longer the era where a few oil sheikhs could hold the entire planet hostage.

"It was largely their fault," Peerce said. "The hostages, I mean. You know what they wanted to do? Start their own society on Mars. But...big *but* here...it turns out that Mars needs women. So they have the bright idea of recruiting women from refugee camps on the grounds they would be grateful enough to be rescued that they wouldn't complain about being used as breeding stock."

"Arseholes," Percy commented.

"Yes, sir," Peerce conformed. "And when you think about just how many youngsters were willing, even then, to leave Earth behind for good, you realise that their motives were very far from *pure*."

He sighed, then took another sip of cheap whiskey. "Not that things got much better for the refugees, in any case," he added. "The tidal waves only made it far worse."

"I know," Percy said.

"So tell me," Peerce said. "Why did *you* join the Royal Marines? I know there was a slot held for you at the Naval Academy."

Percy looked down at his glass. Whiskey had never been his favourite drink; hell, he'd never really liked drinking at all. His mother had used to start the most terrible rows whenever she'd seen his father drinking…and, now his mother was gone, he didn't really want to disgrace her memory by becoming a drunkard.

"My father," he confessed. "I didn't want to live in his shadow."

"I always honoured my father," Peerce said. "The old buzzard moved to Britannia, where he's terrorising the wildlife and building a farm. Why didn't you want to honour yours?"

Percy hesitated, unsure of what to say.

"My father died a hero," he said. "I don't know how many people outside the Royal Marines knows your father's name, but *everyone* knows mine, even if they don't know the exact details of his death. Even after we were…adopted…we still carried the family name."

"Odd," Peerce observed. "I would understand if you were called Quisling, or Morrison, or even Gallows, but not *Schneider*. Your father died a hero."

"Yes, but everyone expected me to follow in his footsteps," Percy said. "If I had gone into starfighters, I would have been pushed through the Academy on the strength of my name. I think the same would have happened if I'd become a line officer, rather than a pilot. My name would have opened doors for me, rather than my accomplishments. Does that make sense?"

"It does," Peerce said. "And the Royal Marines treated you as just another recruit."

Percy nodded. "There's no other part of the service where the aristocracy doesn't have a huge amount of influence," he said. "I could stand or fall on my own merits."

"And you won the Green Beret," Peerce said. "You have a great deal to be proud of, Corporal."

"Thank you," Percy said. He gave his nominal subordinate a long look. "How many other junior officers have you kicked into shape?"

"Too many," Peerce said. "It helps that most of them have combat experience, so they know what's really important, but it's sometimes hard to separate them from the bootneck they were before they were promoted. I imagine you should have been sent to Officer Training - and you would have been, if there had been a chance. As it is, you will just have to learn on the fly."

He smiled. "And I think your father will understand," he added. "He was a reservist, wasn't he?"

"Yes," Percy said. "Sergeant…why haven't they disclosed everything about his death?"

Peerce considered it. "You do know," he asked finally, "that closed-casket funerals are not uncommon in Special Forces? Or that the truth behind some of our combat losses will not be publically known for over a hundred years, when everyone involved is dead?"

"He wasn't a soldier," Percy protested. "He was a pilot. Nothing more than a pilot."

Peerce looked down at his empty glass, then put it on the table. "There is a story, which I am *not* going to tell you, about a starship that sneaked into the Waco System during the Chinese-American Confrontation. That starship stealthily monitored shipping in the system and reported home to its base, then prepared itself to intervene if the two sides came to blows."

"But they didn't," Percy reminded him.

"No, they didn't," Peerce agreed. "The ship withdrew as quietly as it came…and there will be no formal public acknowledgement that the mission even took place, not for another fifty years."

"If that's true," Percy asked, "how do *you* know about it?"

"I was on the ship," Peerce said.

He shrugged. "Point is, sometimes a veil of secrecy is drawn over an affair to avoid causing diplomatic upsets," he said. "And sometimes the truth is hidden because it upsets those in power. I've heard enough rumours about the last flight of *Ark Royal* to think that *something* happened, something bad enough for *everyone* to want to cover up the details."

"Helped by everyone being dead," Percy muttered.

"Quite," Peerce said. "There were only a handful of survivors from *Ark Royal* and none of them are talking. But you know what?"

He reached out and clapped Percy on the shoulder. "You wanted to build your own destiny, sir," he said. "So stop worrying about what happened to your father and concentrate instead on becoming the best damned bootneck in the history of the Royal Marines."

"Thank you, Sergeant," Percy said. He drained the last of his glass, then put it down on the table. "Is that enough bonding now or do we have to talk about something else?"

"You've had a couple of days with your Section," Peerce said. "Do you have any observations?"

Percy hesitated, thinking hard. "The two Johns have each other's back, half the time," he said. "They're good at watching out for each other."

"We're surrounded by Johns," Peerce said. "I think there's twelve people on the ship called John, including the Captain."

"I was surprised they were together," Percy said. It was far from uncommon for naval personnel to share the same first name, but it could cause problems. "Doesn't it cause confusion?"

"I just call them by their surnames, even in combat," Peerce said. "They got here together, so there's no precedence for which one should be called John. Besides, they do work together well, so why break up a successful team?"

He smiled, thinly. "Anything else?"

"Matt is very much the baby of the team," Percy said, after a moment. "He did well at the training camp, but this is his first real deployment and it's clear he's a little unsure of his place."

"Some proper experience will put paid to that," Peerce assured him. "Or weren't you unsure when you spent your first night in the barracks?"

Percy nodded, although he knew he'd had an easier time than most. Thanks to the tidal waves and the refugee camps, he was used to having very little to his name. Besides, as uncomfortable as they were, the Royal Marine Barracks were far more pleasant than the refugee camps…and the company was better too. But not all of the recruits had endured such a life before joining the Marines. Homesickness had affected quite a few of them before they'd either got used to it or quit.

"And Ron is worried about his girlfriend," he concluded. He'd overheard enough whining to understand the problem, even though Ronald

Fisherman hadn't spoken to him about it directly. "He thinks the poor bitch will leave him."

"Not an uncommon problem," Peerce said. "Young men and women may pledge themselves to one another in person, but absence makes the heart grow colder and start looking for comfort elsewhere. You may wish to keep an eye on him, once we leave the system. He won't be able to get many messages from home until the mail packets arrive."

"And one of them might be a Dear John letter," Percy said. "I've found someone else, so goodbye and thanks for all the fish."

"Might be," Peerce said. "You may, of course, review all such messages before they are forwarded to their recipients. However, I would caution you that such reviewing could cause problems with the troops."

Percy winced. He'd never actually reviewed, let alone censored, letters from the outside world to Marines on active duty, but he'd heard rumours. Everything from nude photographs to wifely nagging and 'Dear John' letters had passed through the censors, back during the war. There had even been a major scandal when one of the censors had started copying the most interesting photographs and putting them on the datanet. Percy wouldn't have given a rusty penny for the man's chances once the husbands found out.

"I know," he said.

"It could be worse," Peerce said. "You know what happened during the war?"

He went on before Percy could answer. "Someone in Public Relations had the bright idea of getting young girls to write to soldiers on deployment," he added. "It worked reasonably well, for a few months, then we got a howler of complaint from someone's mother. The squaddie her daughter had been writing to had written back, asking for naked photographs and videos."

"Oh, God," Percy said. "Do I want to know what happened?"

"I believe the young man in question was bawled out by his superior, then his superior's superior, then several other officers," Peerce said. "Luckily, it didn't stop the program. I believe several post-war relationships grew out of such exchanges."

"Perhaps including nude photographs," Percy mused. "No one offered to send *me* any."

"The program was discontinued after the war," Peerce said. "But it might be worth trying to restart it at some point."

"The CO can worry about that," Percy said. "What should I do about the situation?"

"Keep an eye on Ronald and be prepared to give him some counselling if necessary," Peerce advised. "Deployments are never easy."

"I know," Percy said.

The hatch opened, revealing Hadfield. "I trust you two have managed to bond?"

"Yes, sir," Peerce said, before Percy could say a word. "We know each other a little better now."

"Good," Hadfield said. He made a show of looking at his watch. "Go get some rest, both of you. I intend to kick off the next exercise as soon as possible."

"Yes, sir," Percy said.

CHAPTER
EIGHT

"All systems are online, sir," Commander Juliet Watson reported.

"Thank you, Commander," John said, with the private thought that Richards must have found some time to advise the XO on how best to handle the Captain. "Helm…take us out of the shipyard."

A dull quiver ran through *Warspite* as her drive field came to life. John braced himself, feeling an odd mixture of anticipation and fear. To command a starship was to be Master Under God, sole voice of authority on his ship, but also to bear the burden of being responsible for the entire ship and her crew. If something went wrong and his ship were to be lost, it would rest with him, not with anyone else. Even if he hadn't known what was going wrong until it was too late, the Admiralty would assert he certainly *should* have known.

He watched, grimly, as *Warspite* slowly detached herself from the shipyard's nodes and made her way out of the shipyard, passing a number of automated weapons platforms. They saluted the new starship briefly, flickering their running lights at her, before returning to their silent contemplation of interstellar space. John studied the display for a long moment, then turned his attention to the updates from all decks. Everything seemed to be working at peak capacity, although he was expecting some glitches. Very few starships powered up without discovering that something - anything - wasn't quite right.

Maybe the shipyard did it perfectly this time, he thought. It was unlikely - human error crept into the damndest places - but he could still dream.

"Report," he ordered.

"All systems are functioning as predicted," Commander Watson said. "Drive field is active within nominal parameters. Sensors are active and calibrating now."

John nodded. *Warspite* would be blind without her sensors, both active and passive. The specs he'd read had told him that the Royal Navy had vastly improved their sensor suites in the wake of the war - and encountering alien stealth technology - but no one had deployed the new systems in combat. He would almost have preferred to rely upon tried and tested technology, but he knew that would be dangerous - and stupid. Even if Britain refused to move forward, the rest of the human race - and the Tadpoles - certainly would.

"Passive sensors are functioning at predicted levels, sir," Lieutenant-Commander Paul Howard said. *Warspite* had no dedicated sensor officer, unlike a fleet carrier. "Active sensors are functioning at seventy percent of predicted levels."

John swallowed a curse. "I see," he said. "Why?"

"One of the sensor blisters failed when we tried to power it up," Howard reported. He sounded irked - and well he might. This failure could be laid at his door, if his commander decided he wanted someone to blame. "I've earmarked it for replacement."

John glanced at his terminal. "Have it replaced now," he ordered. An engineering team could go EVA and replace the sensor blister now, while the ships of the squadron gathered around *Warspite*. "And then run checks to make sure the rest of the network is fully functional."

"Aye, sir," Howard said.

"The remaining blisters can pick up the strain, if necessary," Commander Watson said. "I designed a considerable degree of redundancy into the system."

John scowled, inwardly. Clearly, Richards's lessons hadn't gone very far.

"I prefer to have everything in working order," he said, tightly. Didn't Commander Watson know it was unwise to question her commander on his own bridge? John had disagreed with *his* CO, from time to time, but he'd always done it in private. In public, in front of the junior officers and crew, the Captain and his XO had to provide a united front. "And besides, we won't be departing for another hour."

He settled back in his chair as department after department checked in, reporting that almost all of their systems were functioning within acceptable parameters. John ordered a handful of systems replaced, then checked again. Even if they'd been assigned to Home Fleet and kept within the Sol System, he would have insisted the systems be replaced. War could come at any moment, he had learned, and it was much harder to make repairs while under fire. He'd even read reports that speculated the First Battle of New Russia wouldn't have gone so badly if the human ships had been at full readiness.

But it wouldn't have made any difference, he told himself, as the endless checks went on and on. *The Tadpoles had us bang to rights the moment they jumped into the system.*

"Captain," Lieutenant Gillian Forbes said. "The squadron is transmitting its readiness details to you."

"Transfer it to my terminal," John ordered. "And then inform the commanding officers that we will leave on schedule."

"Aye, sir," Gillian said.

John smiled to himself. He wasn't sure he approved of keeping the communications officer, when a sensor officer might be more useful if they ran into trouble, but he knew the Admiralty's thinking. Three years ago, the prospect of running into aliens had seemed a pipe dream, at best. No one thought that now. Opening communications with aliens as fast as possible was a priority, before another war broke out over a misunderstanding. The last thing humanity needed was to be pushed to the wall - again.

He checked the reports, one by one. Captain Minion - he smirked at the name, even though he knew it was unfair of him - had reported with military efficiency, while the other four commanders had been considerably more lax. John wasn't surprised - they were merchant skippers, rather than military officers - but it was annoying. All five commanders reported that they were ready to move on his command, then follow *Warspite* through the tramline to Terra Nova.

And then they will want to go home, he thought, ruefully. RFA *Argus* might be designed as a giant Colony Support Vessel, intended to transport and then assist the settlers as they carved out a new home, but the other three were nothing more than glorified freighters. They would reach Pegasus, unload their cargo, and then find themselves surplus to requirements. Their commanders would want to go home and find themselves a more rewarding contract shipping goods from Sol to one of the better-established colonies.

He smiled, sardonically. Anyone would think they were ungrateful for the Royal Navy's contribution to the running costs of their ships.

"Captain," Commander Watson said, breaking into John's thoughts. "All systems are fully functional."

There was a hint of annoyance in her voice. John understood, but it was still bad for discipline. He took a moment to check the reports for himself - the EVA crews had plenty of experience in replacing or repairing damaged components on the ship's hull - then smiled, tiredly. The ship had barely left the shipyard and he was already feeling the strain.

Maybe I should have stuck with starfighters after all, he thought, mournfully. *But without Colin, it wouldn't have been the same.*

"Lieutenant Forbes, record," John said. He waited for the communications officer to give him the thumbs up, then continued. "From Captain John Naiser, CO HMS *Warspite*, to Admiral Percy Finnegan, First Space Lord. Sir. I certify that HMS *Warspite* is ready to depart the Sol System on schedule. We will commence our mission to Pegasus immediately and pass through the tramline in two hours, forty minutes from this message. God save the King."

He drew a finger across his throat. Lieutenant Forbes stopped recording and looked at him, expectantly. He couldn't help thinking that she looked too young and too inexperienced to be an officer, but that seemed to be par for the course on *Warspite*. The experienced officers would simply have to carry the load themselves until their newer comrades were brought up to speed. But Gillian Forbes...if her file hadn't stated she was twenty-three, he would have wondered if the Admiralty had resorted to conscripting Secondary School-age children. He wouldn't have placed her as any older than seventeen.

"Encrypt the message, then transmit it to Nelson Base," he ordered, silently calculating the time it would take for the message to reach the First

Space Lord. It was unlikely the mission would be scrubbed on short notice, but the First Space Lord would have barely an hour to respond before it was too late. "And then signal the other ships to assume formation."

"Aye, sir," Lieutenant Forbes said.

John sighed, inwardly. On Earth, the speed of light - and radio transmissions - was effectively immediate. There was no time delay in sending an email or v-mail from London to Kuala Lumpur, from one side of the world to the other. But spacers knew the speed of light was far from infinite. It took seconds to signal from Earth to the Moon, minutes to signal Mars at closest approach and hours to send a signal to Jupiter and the planets beyond. And even *that* didn't include sending messages through the tramlines. It could take weeks to send a message from Earth to Britannia, even longer to Vera Cruz or Heinlein. During the war, entire fleets had gone to the wrong destinations because their orders had changed after their departure, but their commanders hadn't known until it was too late.

The boffins keep promising FTL communications, he thought. *But I'll believe it when I see it.*

"The squadron has responded," Lieutenant Forbes said. "They're standing by."

John rose to his feet, his eyes fixed on the holographic display. "Mr. Armstrong, set course for Tramline One," he ordered. "Best possible squadron speed."

"Aye, sir," Lieutenant Carlos Armstrong said. He tapped a switch on his console. The course would have been laid in as soon as *Warspite* cleared the shipyard. Moments later, the background noise of the ship's drives grew louder, an omnipresent thrumming echoing through the entire ship. "ETA Tramline One; two hours, thirty-nine minutes."

John smiled to himself as he sat down, then monitored the readings from the ship's drives. Everything seemed to be fine, much to his relief. Johnston wouldn't let matters get out of hand, he was sure, but *Warspite* was new, utterly untested. The tactical department ran tracking exercise after tracking exercise, locking the ship's sensors on the other starships in the squadron, then asteroid miners and transport ships some distance from the small convoy.

"Fools," Howard muttered, as his sensors locked - briefly - onto *Message Bearer*. "They don't have a hope."

"The technology is solid," Commander Watson disagreed. "But it is *slow*."

John smiled, inwardly. *Message Bearer* had been built before the tramlines, a giant starship intended to crawl from Sol to the nearest system with life-bearing worlds. The consortium of libertarians who'd built the ship had declared their intention to leave Earth and her many governments behind altogether...mere years before the first tramline had been discovered. And at that point, they'd abandoned their planned starship and moved *en masse* to one of the newly discovered systems. *Message Bearer* had been left, utterly abandoned, until the war, where her current owners had hastily readied her for departure. There *were* systems that were free of tramlines, after all, systems where some remnant of the human race could survive.

But we survived the war, he thought. *And yet they're launching the mission anyway.*

He pushed the thought aside, then turned his attention to the next set of reports from various intelligence departments. The Indians, Turks and Brazilians were all showing interest in the worlds near Pegasus - and Cromwell. They would have to be crazy to risk challenging the pre-war Royal Navy, but post-war he knew the odds were a great deal more even. Besides, the newer powers had learned from the war...and the mistakes made by the older spacefaring powers. *And* they could build a modern fleet without worrying about hulls that had been modern only twenty years ago.

And they're signed up to the Solar Treaty, he reminded himself. *They could send more of their fleet out of the Sol System than we could countenance.*

"Captain," Lieutenant Forbes said. "The Admiralty has acknowledged our message and sends us its best wishes. They've also included an encrypted packet for you."

"Good," John said. "Transfer it to my console, then dump it into the secure data store."

"Aye, sir," Lieutenant Forbes said.

John pressed his hand against the scanner, allowing it to read the implant buried in his palm and check it against the secure database. Moments later, the message decompressed itself and demanded a second security check. John snorted, inwardly, at the cloak and dagger precautions, but complied without argument. Every year, it seemed the intelligence officers came up with a new and unbreakable code…and, every following year, enemy intelligence services succeeded in breaking it. There were times when John felt it would make more sense to agree that everyone would send messages in the clear, but he knew it would never happen. Even a delay of a few short days between receiving the message and cracking it through brute force decryption could mean the difference between victory or defeat.

And we assume the Tadpoles are still watching us, he reminded himself tartly. *We might go back to war with them one day - and this time, we won't have Ark Royal.*

The message unfolded itself in front of him, divided into three sections. One was a précis on known human activity in the region - the diplomats would have to come up with a name for the entire region, John thought - while the second was a warning that two starships had been reported lost by their insurers. Both were old, dating from the early days of tramline exploration, which suggested there was nothing particularly sinister about their disappearance, but the Admiralty would prefer to know what, if anything, had happened to them. They weren't British ships, John noted, yet that hardly mattered. Spacers in distress were spacers in distress, regardless of their nationality.

But the search would be futile, John suspected. Space was incomprehensibly vast. A powered-down starship was almost completely invisible, unless it happened to drift close to a planet or another starship using active sensors. By now, months had passed before the owners had requested the insurance companies pay up - and the companies, unsurprisingly, were dragging their heels about payment. After all, it *could* be part of a scam…

He shrugged, then moved to the third section - and froze. It was written permission to relieve Commander Watson of duty, if he felt it necessary, and promote either Howard or Richards to take her place. John wasn't blind to the politics behind the appointment - or the political risk the First Space Lord had taken by sending him the message. Commander Watson herself might not complain if she was relieved of duty - John suspected she wasn't keen on the position - but her patrons definitely would. There would be hard questions to be answered when they returned, with Richards or Howard inspected closely for signs of undue influence over their commander. It might well ensure they never saw another promotion for the rest of their careers.

Damn it, he thought, darkly.

"Captain," Armstrong said, suddenly. "We are approaching the tramline."

"Signal the squadron," John ordered. "We will proceed through the tramline in the order discussed."

He looked up at the holographic display, noting the green line that marked the location of the tramline. There was nothing to see, at least not with the naked eye; it took finely-tuned gravimetric sensors to pick out the corridor of gravity linking one star to another. Some reports suggested there were greater quantities of space dust within the tramline, as if the gravity field was slowly drawing tiny particles into its grip, but it didn't seem to be a consistent pattern. But then, there was a great deal about the tramlines that no one, human or Tadpole, truly understood.

A shame we can't establish battlestations along the tramline, he thought, as *Warspite* moved closer to the tramline. *But the enemy could jump out anywhere and leave the defenders to wither on the vine.*

"The squadron has responded, sir," Forbes said. "They're standing by."

John sucked in a breath. "Then take us through the tramline," he ordered.

"Aye, sir," Armstrong said. "Reducing speed. Transit in ten seconds... nine..."

John braced himself as the countdown reached zero. Only a desperate fool would try to jump through the tramline at high speed, knowing it would have half of his crew throwing up on the deck. A faint shudder ran through the ship, followed by sensation of indescribable *wrongness*, then the display snapped out of existence and hastily rebooted itself, sucking in data from the Terra Nova system. It wasn't anything like Earth.

"Transit complete, sir," Armstrong reported.

"The Puller Drive was poorly tuned," Commander Watson said. "Unfortunately, we could not calibrate properly without making a jump,"

"Then I suggest you recalibrate the drive now," John said, harshly. He hadn't thrown up, but his head hurt. Was it a problem caused by poor calibration, he wondered, or the attempt to merge human and alien technology into a single unit. Did the Tadpoles suffer from jumping through tramlines? No one actually knew. "Did we make it through without serious problems?"

"Yes, sir," Commander Watson said. "Our drives and other systems are undamaged."

"Then set course for Tramline Seven," John ordered. "The sooner we are out of this system, the better."

"Aye, sir," Armstrong said.

John rubbed the side of his head, feeling the pain slowly fading into a dull throbbing that didn't seem disposed to disappear anytime soon. He was tempted to reach for a painkiller, but he knew he didn't dare use any kind of drug in front of the crew. Instead, he watched as the reports came in from all over the ship. Headaches, it seemed, were very common. It had to be a problem with the drive.

And we need to fix it, he told himself, firmly. *Because if we're going to fight, we can't afford to be distracted.*

CHAPTER
NINE

"They say we're going to be fighting there, one day," Sergeant Peerce said. "What do you make of that?"

Percy winced, inwardly. "Not much," he said. "Terra Nova is a mess."

He rubbed the side of his head, cursing the Puller Drive under his breath. A third of the Marines had reported headaches, while - from what he'd heard - nearly half the ship's crew had had the same problem. There was nothing to separate the affected Marines from the unaffected Marines, as far as he could tell. It didn't seem to matter if they'd spent years in space or if this was their first deployment; the headaches seemed totally random. And he had one himself.

"How true," Peerce agreed. "I hear tell that the shore-leave facilities on the planet are nothing more than armed fortresses, with hardly any locals permitted to enter."

He shrugged. "But if you had to intervene," he added, "how would you go about it?"

Percy gritted his teeth and tried to think. Peerce seemed to like tossing questions at him, forcing Percy to consider everything from an enemy boarding party to a crash-landing on a hostile planet. He'd done his best to answer, but he couldn't help feeling as though he'd let the older man down more than once. Peerce had a long enough career to deserve respect, even if he had stayed a Sergeant for longer than Percy cared to contemplate. The Royal Marines had found a round peg for a round hole and had no intention of sending Peerce anywhere else.

"I would try to separate the warring factions," he said, finally. His experience on Earth had showed that the only way to end factional warfare was to separate the two sides, but the political will to intervene so boldly had been lacking ever since the Troubles - and the move into space. "But I would need much more manpower."

"True," Peerce said. "The entire complement on this ship would vanish without trace on Terra Nova. And if you were forced to intervene with the forces at your disposal?"

Percy considered it, slowly. "Assassinate the leaders," he said, knowing it was an unsatisfactory answer. It seemed good enough - brilliant, even - until one considered the dangers involved in killing the only people who could surrender. Killing their foot soldiers was much less kind - he'd seen enough armies in the Third World to know that most of their manpower was composed of hapless conscripts - but there was little choice. "Kill the ones who refuse to make peace until their replacements start giving peace a chance."

"But that might cause more problems," Peerce pointed out. "Their factions might fragment."

"I know, Sergeant," Percy said. "But what else could I do?"

Peerce gave him a long look. "You could go back to your superiors and point out that the task is impossible with the resources they dedicated to it," he said. "Most of Britain's greatest military disasters resulted from the resources being utterly insufficient for the job at hand."

He shrugged. "Sometimes, courage is more than just charging the enemy strongpoint, rifle in hand," he added. "Sometimes, courage is telling your superiors that the job is impossible."

"I see," Percy mused. "But..."

He broke off as his wristcom bleeped an alert. "Time to go back to drilling?"

Peerce smirked. "So it would seem, Corporal," he said. "Just remember: these drills might save your life one day."

———

"So," John said. They sat together in his office, drinking tea. "What happened?"

Commander Watson and Johnston exchanged glances. "Basically, sir," Commander Watson said, finally, "the harmonics produced by the modified drive created interference patterns that disrupted…"

John held up a hand. "English, please," he said.

Johnston cleared his throat. "We didn't tune the modified drive properly, because the simulations didn't account for rogue gravity fluxes within the tramline," he said. "The jump was thus rather less gentle than we had assumed."

"And *I* assume it will get worse if we have to jump at high speed," John snapped. "Half the crew had headaches for hours after the jump. The doctor is already warning me that our supply of painkillers has been severely depleted. *Already*! Can we fix this problem or should we resign ourselves to no longer being combat-capable when we jump?"

He scowled at them both. The whole problem was outrageous. There were times, true, when a fleet would jump through the tramline and then take hours before it engaged the enemy, but there were other times when combat would start almost immediately. The thought of having to fight with half his crew effectively incapacitated was horrific.

"I believe we can make use of the readings we took during the jump to retune the drive," Commander Watson said, finally. *She* hadn't had a headache. "However, I am unable to determine *why* so many crewmen suffered an adverse physical reaction."

"There is no defining factor, as far as I can tell," Richards said. "Experienced crew got headaches; inexperienced crew got headaches. Men got headaches; women got headaches. Old officers got headaches; young crew got headaches. There is a slight preponderance of men affected by the jump, but that could easily be a reflection of the crew's makeup. Men outnumber the women two to one."

"This isn't the first time humans have used a modified drive," John mused. "Did *Ark Royal* ever encounter the same problem?"

"If she did, it was never listed in the logs," Commander Watson said. She sounded intensely disapproving. "Chief Engineer Anderson was in charge of supervising the refit, Captain, but his log entries left something to be desired. I believe he would have been penalised for insufficient data if *Ark Royal* hadn't been unique."

"I don't think that either Admiral Smith or Admiral Fitzwilliam would have left such a detail out of their logs," John mused. He took a sip of tea, thoughtfully. "And the ship's doctor would definitely have recorded such an incident, wouldn't she?"

"Yes, sir," Johnston said. "There would have been multiple reports of people suffering from using the drive. I do not believe that such reports were ever made."

Richards leaned forward. "So," he said. "What's different about *our* drive?"

Commander Watson coloured, slightly. "Previous attempts to use alien technology effectively consisted of bolting the alien tech to the hull and praying for the best," she said, tartly. "There was no time to refit multiple carriers and frigates with modified drive systems, given there was a war on. Our drive, however, represents the first attempt to marry human and alien technology within a hull. Clearly, our models were insufficient to predict issues caused by the marriage."

"The Tadpoles might have used the same kind of technology as ourselves," Johnston added, "but they had some different ideas about how the universe worked."

"Stuff and nonsense," Commander Watson snapped. "The laws of science are identical, wherever one goes. Maybe the aliens can do something that looks inexplicable, but we will understand it, one day. There's no such thing as different laws of science for different races."

She glared down at the deck. "Imagine this ship being tossed back in time to the early days of space flight," she said. "Imagine Yuri Gagarin coming face to face with *Warspite*, or a carrier like *Illustrious*. He'd think the ship did the impossible, but it is merely an application of technology. It would take years, perhaps, for the humans of that era to come to grips with our technology, but they could do it."

"They would have to reinvent a great many technologies," Johnston mused. "Even our standard reaction drives would be several steps ahead of them."

"It could be done," Commander Watson insisted. "Knowing that something is possible is half the battle."

John cleared his throat, loudly. "As fascinating as this debate is," he said, "we are getting away from the point. Can the drive be modified to prevent future headaches?"

"Yes," Commander Watson said. "I have recalibrated the systems personally. Once we upload the refitted drive matrix, we should have a smoother transit through the known tramlines. However…"

John felt his blood run cold. "However?"

"The early days of tramline exploration concentrated on lines of gravimetric flux we knew were solid," Commander Watson said. "In many ways, there was no need to chart the subtle gravity fluxes that made up the majority of the tramline. Our drives effectively made their way through using brute force. Now, however, we are more dependent on monitoring the tiny gravity fluxes, because they can cause problems for us."

"We've used Tramline One for over a hundred years," Richards said, doubtfully. "I don't think we ever had such problems before."

"We didn't have the modified drive system either," Commander Watson said. "I suspect we may have problems every time we try to use an unexplored tramline."

John winced. "Can we solve this problem?"

"I believe we can reconfigure the drive as we approach the tramline," Commander Watson said. "But we would have to do that in something of a hurry."

"I see," John said. "Make the calibrations, then write up a full report for transmission to the naval station in this system. They can take the message home if we don't return."

Commander Watson leaned forward. "Shouldn't we take the message back ourselves?"

John frowned, considering the thought. It would take a brave or foolhardy commanding officer to take it upon himself to rewrite orders from the Admiralty, particularly given the urgency of their mission. But Commander Watson had a point. Transmitting the message to the naval base near Terra Nova ran the risk of having the message intercepted, then decrypted by other human powers. They'd get a leg-up on their own advanced drive programs.

But it was a risk they needed to take. "We'll transmit the message," he said, firmly. "Inform me when you have the messages prepared."

Commander Watson nodded, drank the rest of her tea and rose. "Thank you," she said. "I will start right away."

"With your permission, sir, I will go with her," Johnston said. "I need to monitor every last aspect of the drive recalibration."

"Make it so," John said.

"I think he likes her, sir," Richards said, once the hatch had hissed closed behind him. "They do spend a lot of time together."

John groaned. Whatever was tolerated on *Hamilton* - and he knew shipyard crews had plenty of leeway for getting into trouble, just like starfighter pilots - he knew he couldn't tolerate such a relationship on his ship. Commander Watson was Johnston's direct superior; if they developed a relationship, it would result in a court martial. They'd be lucky to keep from being busted down to midshipmen when the board was finished with them. But Commander Watson was deemed *important*... perhaps the board would choose to overlook the affair, which would be bad for discipline...

Or maybe I'm making a fuss about nothing, he thought.

"Let me know if they seem to be doing more than meeting minds," he said, instead. "But close relationships between engineers aren't exactly uncommon, even if they're rarely sexual."

"Of course, sir," Richards said.

John nodded. "And the crew?"

"A little stunned by the headaches, sir, but recovering nicely," Richards said. He'd already started to form ties with the crew, something John couldn't do and Commander Watson *wouldn't* do. In some ways, a posturing blowhard would be preferable. "Some muttering about the shortage of shore leave, but given what happened to the last crewmen who went for shore leave on Terra Nova, the muttering was very muted."

"Good," John said. People who wandered outside the secure zones on Terra Nova tended to come to short and gristly ends. "We will certainly try to organise something when we call in at a colony world."

"If we do," Richards agreed. "I don't think anyone would want shore leave on Clarke III. At best, it's another Titan."

"And Titan helped power us to the stars," John said. "Clarke III may do the same for the entire sector."

He smiled at the memory of lessons he'd absorbed as a young man. Titan had been the objective of Britain's first large interplanetary mission, one that had ensured that the British Space Program would remain prominent for decades to come. Water from Titan had helped the terraforming of Mars, as well as providing fuel and support to spacecraft heading out into the further reaches of the Solar System. Maybe Britain had made a smaller contribution to Mars than the Americans, Russians, Chinese or Japanese, but it didn't matter. Britain had controlled a major source of resources that had boosted the space program to the stars.

"Let us hope so, sir," Richards agreed. "With your permission, Captain, I will resume my rounds."

John nodded, then turned his attention to the latest set of reports as Richards left the cabin and Midshipwoman Powell cleared up the cups and saucers. The situation on Terra Nova hadn't improved in the weeks since he'd last looked at the Naval Update; the locals were still killing each other in job lots, hundreds of experienced personnel were fleeing to space and outside powers were still colonising the outer edge of the system, despite protests from Terra Nova's various factions. Brazil and India had even opened naval bases of their own, running regular patrols though the system. John had a suspicion that the Indians, at least, weren't just posturing. There was a sizable population of Indian settlers on the planet's surface.

It was nearly four hours before he was called to the bridge, where the XO was waiting for him. "The message is ready, sir," she said, holding out a datapad. "I have described the problem and my method of solving it in great detail."

John took the datapad and studied it, carefully. Technobabble had always irritated him - it had always seemed a way for engineers and computer programmers to put one over their superiors, who didn't have the slightest idea what they were talking about - but Commander Watson had thoughtfully included a summery at the beginning. He approved it for transmission, added a short note of his own for the First Space Lord, then uploaded the entire message to the communications console.

"Encrypt the message using Level Forty-Two protocols, then send it via laser to the naval station," he ordered. "Repeat the message twice, then inform them we require an acknowledgement."

"Aye, sir," Lieutenant Forbes said.

John nodded, then sat back in his command chair and studied the tactical display. The squadron had dog-legged around the inhabited parts of the system, although it was clear that a handful of new asteroid settlements had sprung into existence since the last time the Royal Navy had tried to perform a census of the system. Most of them were tiny, perhaps manned by a single family; others looked large enough to hold a few hundred engineers. It was like the early days of space exploitation, he considered, only worse. Terra Nova wasn't the safest place to live and raise a family.

His eyes narrowed as he saw the number of patrolling starships in the system. None of them belonged to Terra Nova itself, unsurprisingly; they belonged to various human spacefaring powers, apart from one ship making its way to Tramline Five. The Tadpole starship was clearly visible on the display, not even trying to hide. They'd sent another mission to Earth, John recalled; perhaps the ship making its way back home was their transport. And probably doing some spying at the same time. Officially, John knew, human starships visiting alien space didn't spy on the aliens. He would have been very surprised, he told himself, if anyone actually believed it. Spying on one's former enemy was a very good idea.

After all, the war could break out again, he thought. *And we have to be ready.*

It was a haunting thought. The squadron could travel to Pegasus, putting itself out of contact for several months…during which time the war could start again, with him and his men completely unknowing until they returned to more settled worlds. And then…he shook his head at the thought. No matter the modifications to her design, *Warspite* was not intended to cruise indefinitely. She would rapidly decay into uselessness without access to spare parts and a shipyard.

A carrier might be able to either escape or launch a final vengeful attack on the alien homeworld, he thought. *But we might not be able to make it.*

"Captain," Forbes said. "We have received an acknowledgement from the naval station."

"Excellent," John said. He turned to face Armstrong. "Take us through the tramline as soon as we reach it."

"Aye, sir," Armstrong said. "Transit in ten minutes."

John nodded, then keyed his console. "Now hear this," he said, his voice echoing through the ship. "Transit in ten minutes. I say again, transit in ten minutes."

"Everyone is going to be nervous, sir," Richards muttered, too quietly for anyone but John to hear. "It may take a few safer jumps before the tension wears off."

"It isn't as if we're jumping right into the unknown," John muttered back. He'd considered survey work, when it had become clear he no longer wanted to be a pilot. "But we might as well be, with the new drive."

He forced himself to relax as the countdown reached zero. No matter how nervous he felt, he couldn't show it, not to the crew. A panicking commander would almost certainly cause the crew to panic too. Rumour had it that a couple of Russian commanders at New Russia had panicked, when the Multinational Fleet was cut to ribbons. They'd been practically unable to mount any kind of defence when the aliens moved in on their planet.

And they could have wiped out most of the Russian population from orbit, if they'd seen fit, John thought. *If they'd been bent on slaughter…*

"Jump in ten seconds," Armstrong announced. "Ten…nine…eight…"

The entire ship shook, violently. And then the bridge was plunged into darkness.

CHAPTER
TEN

"What the fuck?"

"As you were," Peerce bellowed. The Marines had been in their barracks, bracing for the jump, when the lights went out. "Sound out, by numbers!"

Percy listened, grimly, as the Marines called out their numbers, one by one. Everyone seemed alive, at least; this time, there hadn't been any headaches. But the darkness was almost worse. On Earth, it had rarely been truly dark; in space, the darkness was absolute. It was easy, chillingly so, to imagine that *anything* could be lurking in the shadows, just waiting for them.

He reached for the flashlight at his belt and switched it on. To his relief, the light worked perfectly, allowing him to see twenty faces staring back at him. The other Marines rapidly grabbed their own flashlights, then freed themselves from their bunks. A moment later, the gravity failed, sending them drifting into the air. Percy cursed as he floated over to the hatch and forced it open. Thankfully, the loss of power had also disabled the lock.

"Section 1 will make its way towards the bridge," Lieutenant Darryl Hadfield said, crisply. "Section 2 will head down towards Main Engineering. Corporal Hastings and two men will remain here, ready to coordinate our response."

"Aye, sir," Hastings said.

Percy shivered as he floated out into the corridor. If main power was offline, everything from sensors to life support would *also* be offline. An asteroid colony would have bioengineered grass serving as carpets, ensuring a fresh supply of air whatever happened, but the grass would have been a liability onboard ship. Without life support, the crew would eventually run out of air and suffocate in a largely unexplored system.

His radio buzzed. "Corporal Schneider, respond," Corporal Hastings said. "I say again, respond."

"This is Schneider, responding," Percy said. Their radios worked too, which was a definite relief. Internal communication would also be down, at least until the engineers managed to rig up a separate system. Wristcom units were dependent on the ship's internal network to work, he recalled, an oversight that might prove lethal. "I confirm receipt, over."

"Proceed to Main Engineering," Hadfield said. "Remain in touch - and stay low. The gravity might come back at any moment."

Percy gritted his teeth as he pulled himself down the corridor, towards a hatch that remained firmly closed. He'd had training in zero-gee - it was a must for anyone who wanted to serve in the Royal Marines - but there was no escaping the fact that it was one of the most awkward environments to handle. A single breath could send someone tumbling head over heels, or straight up into the ceiling. And space-sickness was also a very real threat.

"The hatch is depowered," Peerce reported. He opened a panel and peered inside. "I'm going to have to disconnect the system from the main power network and try to power it directly from my battery pack."

"Do it," Percy ordered. He motioned the section to take up positions as Peerce worked on the hatch, his mind frantically reminding him that they weren't on a hostile vessel. "Let me know when the hatch is about to open…"

"Now, I think," Peerce said, cutting Percy off. "I just connected it to the battery…"

There was a hiss from the hatch, which opened to reveal a darkened corridor and a handful of crewmen, working on the hatch at the far end. They spun around, then looked relieved when they saw the Marines. Percy pulled himself forward, located the senior crewman, and briefly compared notes. The crew, uncertain of just what had happened, were also trying to make their way to engineering.

"Proceed with them," Hadfield ordered, when Percy reported the meeting. "But take care at all times."

Percy nodded. He'd explored *Warspite* thoroughly since he'd assumed command of 2 Section, both on his own and with his men, and he knew the ship like the back of his hand, but that hadn't been in the dark. Corridors looked dark and sinister in the shadows; he nearly grabbed for his weapon and loosed a round when he saw a scary face in the darkness, only to realise, as his flashlight shone brighter, that it was a depiction of a weeping angel someone had stencilled on a hatch leading into a set of crew quarters. Cursing in the privacy of his own mind, he pulled himself past the picture and down the corridor. Yet another sealed hatch lay at the far end…

This could take a while, he told himself. *But it has to be done.*

———

"Report," John snapped, as half of the consoles shimmered back to life. The emergency lighting activated a second later, bathing the bridge in eerie shimmering light. "What happened?"

"I'm not sure," Commander Watson said. She sounded dispassionate, even when the gravity failed. "Main power collapsed, just after we made it through the tramline. Half of our monitoring systems are down."

John cursed under his breath. The designers had anticipated losing power, but losing all three fusion reactors at once was disastrous. He doubted the ship's batteries could power even the emergency systems for more than an hour before they too ran out of power. And life support, too, would be offline. The crew was at very real risk of suffocation.

"Right," he said. "Do we have a link to engineering?"

"No, sir," Forbes said. "Internal communications are down right across the board."

Then we should have insisted on including separate communicators, John thought. Hindsight was such a wonderful thing. He'd do it, once they survived the disaster and restored main power. *And then something else will happen we didn't anticipate…*

"Get a crew down to the storage pods and recover away team gear," he ordered. There was no time for recriminations. "Pick up radios and flashlights, then get them back here. We'll decide what to do next once we see what we have on hand."

"Aye, sir," Richards said. "Do you want a second team to start making their way through the tubes?"

John shook his head. The internal tubes would be sealed and breaking through the hatches, one by one, would take hours, perhaps more time than the ship had. Instead, the team would have to go EVA and walk over the hull to the airlock closest to Main Engineering. It would still be a challenge, he knew, but there was no alternative.

"There are other stations with radios," Howard offered. "We might be able to raise them."

"Good thought," John agreed. "Lieutenant Forbes, do we have any links with the rest of the squadron?"

"Yes, sir," Forbes said. "Captain Minion is attempting to raise us. The others seem unsure of what to do."

Civilians, John thought. Even so, he was disappointed. Merchant skippers would have seen their fair share of emergencies in space. But at least he and his crew weren't trying to cope with the disaster on their own.

He pushed the thought to one side and leaned forward. "Tell Captain Minion I want him to put together an away team with radios, oxygen cylinders and space suits," he said. "They are to prepare themselves to deploy to our hull."

"Aye, sir," Forbes said.

Richards and his team forced open the hatch and headed down towards the store at the far end of Officer Country. John wasn't sure why anyone would place the store there, but it was lucky for them that it *was* there. Moments later, Richards returned, carrying a handful of radio sets and a pair of emergency spacesuits. Forbes took one of the radios and began to cycle through the frequencies.

"Captain," she said. "I have Major Hadfield for you."

John took the radio, smiling inwardly. The senior Marine on a starship was given a courtesy promotion to *Major*, as the senior Marine was almost always a Captain and there could only ever be one Captain on a starship. But Hadfield was a *Lieutenant*, not a Captain. What did he think of being jumped several ranks at once? It wasn't as if he needed the courtesy...

"Major," he said, dismissing the thought. "Report."

"I have one section making its way towards the bridge and another heading down to Main Engineering," Hadfield reported. "The crewmen we have encountered have been assisting us in opening hatches, but it's still a slow process."

"Understood," John said. "I'm sending two of my officers EVA. They can link up with your Marines in Main Engineering."

He looked up at Richards, then Commander Watson. "Take the suits and go over the hull to Main Engineering," he ordered. "And take at least two of the radios with you, just in case."

"Aye, sir," Richards said. "Commander?"

Commander Watson was already donning her suit. "We'll sort this out, somehow," she promised. "The problem may be very simple."

John gritted his teeth. They'd recalibrated the drive shortly before the jump - and, moments after the jump, main power had been lost. That could *not* be a coincidence. Something had gone badly wrong and, he knew from bitter experience, that it might be impossible to fix without a shipyard. And if they *did* need a shipyard, getting back to Earth would be tricky.

"I hope so," he said, tersely.

He turned back to Forbes as Watson and Richards left the bridge, heading for the nearest airlock. "Is the away team ready?"

"Yes, sir," Forbes said. "Captain Minion has shuttles ready to go too."

"Then tell him to send them over as quickly as possible," John ordered. "We need to put the communications back together before we can start repairing the damage."

He pulled himself back to the command chair and sat down, buckling himself in. He'd never had to buckle himself in before, not even during a battle. The memory made him think dark thoughts as he waited, knowing there was nothing else he could do. Once, he could have reached out his hand, tapped his console and linked to any part of the ship. Now, he was practically isolated on his own bridge, powerless to affect whatever was happening on the lower decks. His crew was slowly suffocating to death and there was nothing he could do about it.

There has to be something I can do to make it better, he thought. But all he could do was wait and pray.

"Captain," Forbes said. "The XO has just reached the airlock to Main Engineering."

"Good," John said, although he had his doubts. Had Commander Watson, quite by accident, laid the groundwork for the disaster? "Keep me informed."

––––––

Main Engineering wasn't dark, Percy discovered, as the Marines forced their way through the hatch. The Chief Engineer had ordered his men to rig up emergency lighting, then had started grappling with the problem at once. For Percy, who had been anticipating everything from a destroyed engineering section to the death of everyone assigned to the compartment, it was something of a relief.

"We're here to help," he said, as the Chief Engineer turned to look at him. "What can we do?"

"You have radios, I assume," the Chief Engineer said. "Pass me one so I can call the bridge."

"Aye, sir," Percy said, and passed the officer his headset. "Just key it with your hand to speak."

The Chief Engineer nodded, impatiently. "Captain, this is Johnston," he said. "We had a major failure in the power nodes, sir; technically, a cascade of failures. The fusion reactors automatically shut down to prevent further damage to the ship."

There was a pause as the Captain answered. Percy couldn't hear the reply; the headset was designed to prevent anyone apart from the wearer hearing anything. They tended to be hard to use in combat zones, if only because it was far too easy to get distracted, but they were reliable. Perhaps, he thought, as he looked around the darkened compartment, using largely untested cutting edge technology on an important mission hadn't been the best idea anyone ever had.

"We're replacing the damaged components now, sir," the Chief Engineer said. "Yes, I'm putting them aside for later inspection. I'd buy one failure, sir, but not four in quick succession. The components are rated for much greater power surges than they had to handle, Captain. Someone deliberately sabotaged the ship."

Percy felt his blood run cold. Sabotage was something every starship crewman feared, if only because it could be very hard to catch before it was too late. And that wasn't the worst problem. Starship crews had to trust one another to survive - and, if someone was believed untrustworthy, it could tear the crew apart. A witch-hunt would put morale in the drain and nothing, perhaps not even a major victory, could repair it.

And if someone is believed to have sabotaged the ship, he thought numbly, *it will be us who will have to track him down.*

"I'll keep you informed, sir," the Chief Engineer said. He looked up as two new people floated into the compartment. "The XO has just arrived."

He passed the headset to Percy, then pulled himself over to the XO and motioned her towards the rear section of the compartment. Percy waited, unsure of what to do, until an engineering crewwoman called him over and asked the Marines to help float ruined components into a side room. It was interesting to see some of the starship's innards, Percy decided, even though he didn't really understand what he was seeing. He could strip down a BAR-56 in less than a minute, but handling the inner workings of a starship was beyond him. All he could really do was transfer the burned components into the side room and hope the engineers could make head or tails of whatever had happened to them.

"Corporal," Richards said, after speaking with the Chief Engineer. He was all business, now there was a serious problem at hand. "Detail two men to guard the components at all times. I don't want them left unguarded for even a second or two."

"Yes, sir," Percy said. He wasn't entirely sure if Richards could give him orders, but he understood the logic behind them. If someone had sabotaged the components, the only way to find out who had carried it out was to study the components and see who had planted them there. The bastard might try to destroy them before they could be studied. "I'll keep the door sealed at all times."

"I think we have it," the Chief Engineer called. "If we do this…"

A low hum spread through the compartment. Percy watched, feeling a flicker of awe, as darkened consoles came to life, followed by the main lights. He blinked, hard, as his eyes started to water, then forced himself to look around Main Engineering. No one looked suspicious, but he didn't really have the training to tell. He hoped Sergeant Peerce or Lieutenant Hadfield knew how to interrogate suspects, because *he* didn't. The closest thing he'd done along those lines was the dreaded Conduct After Capture course, which had included everything from drugs to sleep deprivation and outright torture.

"Now hear this," the Chief Engineer said, his voice echoing through the ship as the internal communications system came back online. "Gravity will resume in five minutes; I say again, gravity will resume in five minutes. Get down to the floor and brace yourself."

Percy obeyed as the engineer counted down the seconds to zero. Moments later, gravity slowly began to reassert itself; he heard a number of crashes in the distance as objects, which had been floating freely in the air, hit the deck. He wondered, absently, who would clean up the mess as the gravity field stabilised, then stood up as soon as it was Earth-normal. The remainder of his Marines and the engineering crew did likewise.

"Lieutenant," he said, keying his radio. "I've had to detail two men to serve as guards, sir, but the remainder of the section is intact. Do you have any orders for us?"

"Search the lower decks for wounded personnel," Hadfield said. "There have already been some injuries reported. If you find any, provide basic medical attention and contact sickbay."

"Aye, sir," Percy said. It wasn't as glamorous as fighting the enemies of the British Crown, but it was necessary. His father, he suspected, would have approved. "We're on our way."

———

Two hours later, John stood in sickbay, feeling a wave of bitter helplessness as he looked at the handful of wounded crewmen. One officer had been trapped in his cabin and nearly run out of atmosphere before the life support came back online; a handful of crewmen and women had been injured when the gravity reasserted itself. One woman in particular had been *very* unlucky. An object, sent floating up to the ceiling, had fallen on her head when gravity had suddenly pulled it back down to the deck.

"They will survive," Doctor Thomas Stewart said. "I had to perform emergency surgery on a couple of crewmen, but they will all survive."

"Thank God," John said. He'd lost comrades before - his last memory of Colin drifted in front of his eyes, mocking him - but it was worse when he was in command. "Do any of them require emergency transport to a naval base?"

"Probably not," Stewart assured him. "There's nothing they can do for them that I haven't already done. A couple probably should be transferred to *Argus* for long-term care, but the others will be ready to return to duty within the week."

"I'll let the Senior Chief know," John said. It was another duty Commander Watson had shirked. Richards would have to handle the duty roster for her. "And thank you, Doctor."

"You're welcome," Stewart said, dryly. "Just try to avoid a repeat of that disaster, Captain."

John scowled. "I'll do my best," he said. He took one last look at the sleeping forms, then looked back at Stewart. "And you may be needed, Doctor, when we have someone to blame."

He nodded to the older man, then turned and strode out of the compartment. Whatever else happened, he resolved, he was going to find the person responsible for damaging his ship and wounding his crew. It had been sheer luck, he knew all too well, that no one had actually been killed.

Next time, it might be different.

CHAPTER
ELEVEN

"Tell me some good news," John said, as he stepped into the briefing room. "Do we have someone to blame yet?"

"I think so," Johnston said. There was a bitter tone to his voice. "But the person who should have caught it was me."

John glowered at him. "Explain."

"In layman's terms, the power conduits failed," Johnston said. "The drive recalibration needed additional power from the fusion reactors to handle the transit down the tramline, which overloaded the conduits. As the first one failed, the emergency systems activated and demanded power from the other conduits, which triggered a catastrophic series of failures and left most of the ship powerless."

"I see," John said, darkly. "And why did this happen?"

"The power conduit routers are supposed to be replaced on a regular basis, because they wear out quickly," Johnston explained. "In this case, sir, the power conduits were certified as having been replaced, but in reality the old components remained firmly in place. The net result was that they eventually proved unable to handle the burden placed on them and crashed."

"Shit," John said.

He allowed his voice to harden. "I'm no engineering officer," he added, "but aren't these subsections supposed to be checked and checked again?"

"They are," Johnston said. "The fault was mine."

John forced himself to reign in the urge to bite his engineer's head off. There were commanding officers, he knew from bitter experience, who wouldn't hesitate to shout and scream at the offender, no matter their rank. But Johnston was a good man and, if he had overlooked something, it hadn't been deliberate. He'd just have to learn from his mistakes, like everyone else.

"Did you refuse to check them," he asked finally, "or did you put your trust in the wrong person?"

"The wrong people," Johnston said. "I checked the records, once we had identified the offending components. Engineering Officer Frank Cole and Engineering Officer Lillian Turner were responsible for replacing the components and verifying that the task had been handled properly. Three of the four failed components had their signatures on the task record, sir. The fourth, the final one to fail, probably couldn't have handled the sudden power surge even if it was fresh out of the factory."

John glared down at the deck, furiously. "And they did this…why?"

"I checked the records," Johnston repeated. "The components they claimed to have inserted into the systems are not onboard ship. I assume they took the components and sold them, probably to one of the civilian factors visiting *Hamilton*, while asserting that the old components were, in fact, the new components. Given that we were originally scheduled to leave later in the year, sir, they may have assumed that there would be time to replace the older components with newer ones before a general inspection."

John cursed under his breath. The Royal Navy was a brotherhood, one where everyone onboard ship had to rely on their fellows. To be betrayed was bad enough, but to be sold out was worse. The two engineering officers might have earned millions of pounds by selling military-grade hardware, yet they had also risked an entire starship and the lives of two hundred crew. They'd be lucky not to be lynched by their former comrades when the truth came out.

Johnston rose to his feet. "Sir," he said, "I trusted them when I shouldn't have. The fault was mine."

"Sit down," John said, before Johnston could start a melodramatic offer of resignation. "We have to assume our crewmen are honest, because otherwise we will go mad."

He scowled as his Chief Engineer sat down. No matter what happened next, he knew, the damage had been done. Everyone was going to be watching everyone else carefully, for signs of sabotage or treason. There could be no trust among different departments when two engineers, the people responsible for maintaining the ship, had sold out the crew. It was going to turn into a nightmare.

"Two things," he said, holding up a hand. "I want you to organise a full check of each and every component on the ship. Jumble up the normal work teams, then get them checking units they were not personally involved in installing."

"That will be tricky, sir," Johnston warned. "*Warspite* isn't a fleet carrier. We don't have engineering sections devoted to separate parts of the ship."

"Do the best you can," John said. "If nothing else, make sure you disrupt any pre-deployment relationships and teams. Second, I want you to check our spare part situation, starting with pallets our two suspects verified. If we're short on spare components, we may have to return to Earth before something else fails."

"Aye, sir," Johnston said. He sounded bitter. Thanks to two bad apples, months of work would have to be checked, rechecked and, if necessary, redone. The mission would be badly delayed. "I assume you will be taking steps to arrest our two bastards?"

John turned to Lieutenant Hadfield. "Take your Marines and arrest the pair of them, then transfer the bastards to the brig," he ordered. "Once they're in the brig, you can start interrogating them."

"Yes, sir," Hadfield said, standing. "I shall see to it at once."

"And tell your men that I wish to gather evidence for a Captain's Mast," John added. "They will have to be tried onboard ship."

Richards cleared his throat. "Captain," he said. "I must point out that regulations…"

"The crew needs to see justice done," John said, shortly. It was true that regulations frowned on holding courts onboard ship, at least when the death penalty was a very real possibility, but it was within his legal rights. "You'll act as their defender, should they request one."

"Yes, sir," Richards said. He didn't sound pleased, but John could hardly blame him. Being a defender, when the case was open and shut, was a good way to wind up feeling frustrated and powerless, even if the culprits were guilty as sin. "I will, of course, require time to visit my clients."

"Let me arrest them first," Hadfield said. "Then you can talk with them, once we have completed the interrogation."

"Very good," John said. "Dismissed."

Richards and Hadfield left; Commander Watson remained, looking cross.

"Captain," she said. "I never...I never knew this could happen."

"People aren't machines," John said, curtly. He thought, briefly, of the letter from the First Space Lord. Relieving Commander Watson of her duties as XO would allow her to spend most of her time in Main Engineering, assisting the Chief Engineer. "They can do stupid things for money, or because they have some ideological motive, or because they're scared, or because they're just stupid. You have to watch people closely."

"It isn't logical," Commander Watson insisted. "They could have killed everyone on the ship and set the program back several years."

John took a closer look at his XO. A pair of pointed ears, like some of the odder settlers on asteroid colonies, might suit her. She definitely had the face and body for it.

"People are rarely logical," he said. "Logic might have urged us to surrender after the Battle of New Russia; human stubbornness kept us fighting until we had a chance for victory."

He sighed. "We can go over it later," he added. "For the moment, we have to concentrate on getting the ship back into fighting trim."

Commander Watson nodded, then rose. "I shall be in Main Engineering," she said. "It should be another few hours before we have verified all of the replacement components."

She left, leaving John alone.

"Damn it," he muttered, staring down at his hands. Betrayal was always the worst, even if it had been motivated by money rather than allegiance to a foreign power. "What the hell do we do now?"

Impatiently, he rose, walked through the hatch and out onto the bridge. The main display, right in front of him, was showing the squadron as it waited, patiently, for the most modern starship in the Royal Navy to complete its repairs. John ground his teeth in bitter frustration, then sat down in the command chair and checked the reports. At least they'd managed to distribute radios, flashlights and other emergency supplies to the various departments. If the power failed again, they would be far better prepared to handle it.

We should have anticipated the problem, he thought, grimly. Hindsight was *such* a wonderful thing. Whatever happened at the Captain's Mast, there would be a Board of Inquiry as soon as *Warspite* returned home. The Admiralty would be less than impressed, both with the disaster and his crew's response to it. *But we didn't and we suffered for it.*

"Captain," Howard said. "Main Engineering reports they've installed additional power links between the fusion reactors and the ship's power distribution network. A second set of failure cascades is unlikely."

"Let us hope so," John said. "And the rest of the ship?"

"There was no damage, outside Main Engineering," Howard reminded him. "The tactical department is functioning normally."

And if we lose power when we're going to war, John thought morbidly, *we will die before we even know we're under attack.*

"Run a handful of tracking exercises," he said. "We may as well put the time to good use."

"Yes, sir," Howard said.

John sat back in his chair and studied the system display. It had only recently been discovered, as it was only reachable through an alien-grade tramline, and there were no settlers, save for a single independent mining colony. The colonists hadn't noticed the squadron's arrival, which was something of a relief. It would have been embarrassing to have to admit that they'd lost power as soon as they'd emerged from the tramline. John wondered, absently, if the colonists intended to ally themselves with one of the spacefaring powers or try to remain independent, although it would be hard for them to make their independence stick. The Space Treaty might concede a life-bearing system to the nation that first discovered it, but systems without habitable worlds couldn't be claimed. It might not be long before other settlers arrived in the system.

Particularly if it seems a more attractive place to live than Terra Nova, he thought. *But then, Hell would seem a more attractive place than Terra Nova.*

He smirked at the thought, then frowned as his wristcom bleeped. "Yes?"

"Captain," Hadfield said. "We have the two miscreants in custody."

"I'm on my way," John said. He rose, then looked at Howard. "You have the bridge, Commander."

"Yes, sir," Howard said. "I have the bridge."

John stepped through the hatch, then walked down the long corridor to the brig, situated just past the hatch leading out of Officer Country. It always surprised civilians to discover that military starships had their own prisons, but they were necessary. Crewmen could get drunk, or rowdy... and there had to be somewhere to put them until they cooled down, even if they hadn't committed any serious crimes. Besides, there were brigs on passenger liners too, John knew. Civilians could do the damndest things in space and sometimes had to be restrained for their own good.

Hadfield met him at the hatch. "Sir," he said, holding out a datapad. "We have reviewed their personnel files."

"Thank you," John said.

He took the datapad and skimmed it quickly. Engineering Officer Frank Cole was in his early fifties, really too old for his rank. A quick check revealed that he had several notes inserted into his record that meant promotion was extremely unlikely; indeed, if the Royal Navy hadn't been so short of experienced personnel, he would probably not have been permitted to reenlist when his contract expired. John sighed inwardly, knowing that Cole would be a bitter man. To be denied promotion for so long had to sting, even if he acknowledged he deserved it. But John had to admit that was unlikely. Very few people blamed themselves for their own misfortunes.

Engineering Officer Lillian Turner, by contrast, was young, young enough to be Cole's daughter. John frowned down at her image - Royal Navy personnel files always made their subjects look stupid, criminal, dead or some combination of the three - then checked her record. She'd graduated from the Academy just before the end of the war and served on two frigates before being assigned to the NGW program. There hadn't been any complaints about her, as far as he could tell. But there were some issues that were never written down.

"I see," he said. "Let me see them."

Hadfield nodded, then pressed his hand against the scanner and opened the hatch. The brig was tiny, only four cells: cramped, sound-proofed and effectively escape-proof. One hatch was open, revealing an empty cell; the other three were closed, two marked occupied. The Marine standing in front of the cells, as if they needed to be guarded, keyed a switch, activating the internal monitor. Cole was seated on the bunk, his hands cuffed behind his back, his face flushed with helpless rage. In the other cell, Lillian Turner, also cuffed, looked as though she was crying. She also looked too young for her uniform.

"We're ready to begin the interrogation," Hadfield said. "I was think-ing we'd start with Cole, then move on to Turner. He's probably the ring-leader in the affair."

John looked at the weeping girl, then nodded. If Johnston was right and profit was the motive, Cole would have the contacts to sell military-grade hardware to the highest bidder, which left Lillian as his assistant. But he knew he could be wrong; it would be dangerous to assume that Cole was in charge, even though he was the older and probably the most cunning of the pair. Lillian might have seduced him, then bent him to her will.

"Do so," he said. "I will watch from the observation section."

The interrogation chamber was slightly larger than the cell, sepa-rated into two sections. One held the suspect and his interrogators, a pair of burly Marines; the other held space for a handful of observers to watch, without being observed themselves. John stood in the chamber and watched, dispassionately, as Cole was hauled into the interrogation chamber and cuffed firmly to the chair. The Engineering Officer didn't stop fighting until it was completely pointless, even though his hands were cuffed and his feet were shackled. Somehow, John wasn't too surprised. If Cole was found guilty, the death penalty was a very real possibility.

"Interrogation Session *Warspite* 001 begins," Hadfield said, for the benefit of the recording systems. Everything would be recorded for the inevitable Board of Inquiry. "Suspect; Frank Cole. Interrogators; Lieutenant Hadfield, Royal Marines. Sergeant Peerce, Royal Marines. Field Medic Seymour Chalmers, Royal Marines. Charges against the suspect are detailed in the attached files, including - but not limited to - falsification of documents, deliberate sabotage of HMS *Warspite* and injuries to nine crewmen, caused by said sabotage."

He turned to look down at Cole. "Under the Military Justice Act, revised in 2190, I am authorised to conduct this interrogation with the aid of a lie detector and, if necessary, truth drugs. Should you refuse to cooperate, or lie repeatedly, these drugs will be used. In the event of you disclosing evidence of other crimes, this evidence may be used against you at the Captain's Mast. Do you understand what I have told you?"

Cole glowered at him. "Go to hell, you stupid green-skinned bastard!"

John sighed, inwardly. Civilians would see a Captain's Mast as an inherently unfair trial - and they might be right. There was no protection against self-incrimination, nor was there any appeal; indeed, the ship's commander was the judge. But it also helped to prove to the rest of the crew that justice *would* be served, whatever the situation. There would be no room for lawyers to have the case abolished on a technicality.

Hadfield didn't show any anger at the insults. "Do you understand what I have told you?"

"Yes," Cole said.

"Good," Hadfield said. "We begin."

He picked up a datapad and glanced at it, then looked back at Cole. "On 23rd June, 2209, you entered a statement in the engineering log that component #3762, a power conduit router, was replaced with a new component drawn from ship's stores. Is that correct?"

"I don't remember," Cole said, sullenly. "I change many components each week."

"However, you didn't replace this component," Hadfield said. "By checking the serial numbers against the log, we confirmed that the original component was actually left in place, while its replacement vanished from the stores. What happened to the replacement component?"

Cole glared at him, furiously. "I don't remember..."

"You're lying," Hadfield said, without apparent emotion. "What happened to the replacement component?"

"I…I took it to Luna City," Cole said, reluctantly.

"True," Hadfield observed. "And did you have official permission to take the component to Luna City?"

There was a long pause. "Yes," Cole said.

"Another lie," Hadfield said. "Medic?"

"No, please," Cole pleaded. "You can't drug me!"

John watched, as dispassionately as he could, while the medic pressed an injector against Cole's arm. The man fought frantically, bruising himself against the cuffs, until the drug took effect, whereupon he collapsed into a daze. Hadfield waited until the medic gave the all-clear, then resumed the interrogation. This time, there was no attempt to obstruct the truth.

"He was selling the components to civilian suppliers," Hadfield said, once the interrogation was finally over. "He wasn't spying on us, thank goodness."

"That would have made life difficult," John agreed. "And Turner?"

"He forced her into assisting him," Hadfield said. He sounded disgusted, unsurprisingly. "But we will have to verify that for ourselves."

"We'll hold the Captain's Mast tomorrow," John decided. He knew it would be nothing more than a formality, now that Cole had - reluctantly - confessed. "Check Turner, then we can decide her fate tomorrow too."

"Aye, Captain," Hadfield said.

CHAPTER

TWELVE

"This is a travesty of justice," Cole moaned, as he waited in the tiny compartment. "You shouldn't be doing this to me."

"The prisoner will be silent," Percy said, without looking at Cole. The man was pathetic; easily old enough to be Percy's father, he'd wasted his career and dragged down a young and impressionable crewwoman. "The prisoner will have a chance to plead his case before the commanding officer."

He scowled, inwardly, as Cole subsided into dark mutterings. The Royal Marines might serve as the navy's police, at least onboard ship, but it wasn't a role he enjoyed. Breaking up fist fights among the crew was one thing; marching a crewman to face his commanding officer and an almost-certain death penalty was quite another. But who else was there to do the job? Besides, he'd seen the transcripts from the interrogations. Frank Cole was as guilty as sin.

His radio bleeped. "Bring the prisoner into the court," Hadfield ordered.

"Yes, sir," Percy said.

He nodded to Private Hardesty, standing on the other side of Cole, and took Cole's arm. Hardesty took the other one and together they frogmarched Cole through the hatch and into the wardroom. Cole moaned as they entered the compartment, perhaps realising for the first time that his life was about to come to an end. The Captain was sitting at the far end of the room, flanked by his XO and a Lieutenant-Commander Percy didn't recognise, while a handful of crewmen - witnesses - were seated to one side. Philip Richards was standing next to the prisoner's chair, which stood alone in the centre of the room. Percy nodded politely to him, then forced Cole to sit and cuffed him to the chair. Once the task was done, he withdrew to the rear of the compartment.

"This Captain's Mast is now in session," the Captain said. "Lieutenant-Commander Howard will read the charges, then detail the evidence against the suspect."

The Lieutenant-Commander rose to his feet. "Engineering Officer Frank Cole is charged with theft of military supplies, falsification of main-tenance reports, corruption of a junior officer, directly sabotaging HMS *Warspite* and indirectly causing injuries to nine crewmen, including two that may result in said crewmen being permanently beached."

He took a breath, then continued. "Frank Cole recorded a number of components as having been replaced on schedule, when - in reality - the older components were left in place while the newer components were sold to civilian shipping interests. His name on the maintenance reports was enough to warrant an investigation, which turned up further evidence of his activities. Frank Cole, during the nine months he was assigned to HMS *Warspite*, sold over five hundred thousand pounds worth of mil-itary-grade equipment. In doing so, he was directly responsible for the power failure we suffered a day ago."

There was a long pause. "Mr. Richards," the Captain said. "Does your client wish to enter a plea?"

Percy winced, inwardly. He was no legal expert, but it was clear that the whole case was open and shut. Cole's evidence alone, given under the influence of truth drugs, was more than enough to convict him. And, given the disaster he had caused, the Captain had ample grounds to hang him in front of his former comrades. Indeed, the more he thought about it, the more he wondered if there was any point in holding the Captain's Mast.

"My client does not wish to enter a plea," Richards said.

No surprises there, Percy thought. *What would be the point?*

He looked at Cole's head, feeling an odd burst of pity. What could Cole say that could do anything more than annoy the Captain, who was standing in judgement? This was no harmless prank that had gotten out of hand, no case of spacers drinking themselves into a stupor when they were off-duty...there could be no excuse that justified Cole's actions. He hadn't been blackmailed into submission, or forced to hand over the components on pain of death, or anything else that might serve as an excuse. He'd just wanted money.

My father was always loyal to the Navy, he thought. *Even when the Navy beached him, he was loyal to it and remained a reservist. And in the end, he died for it.*

"All rise," the Captain said, after a brief conversation with the XO. "Mr. Cole. This court finds you guilty. You will be taken from this place and hung in front of your former comrades, the men and women you betrayed, unless you wish to choose another form of execution. And may God have mercy on your soul."

Hadfield cleared his throat. "Remove the prisoner," he ordered.

Percy stepped forward, released Cole from the restraints and man-handled him towards the hatch. The condemned man seemed in shock, unable to believe he'd just been sentenced to death; Percy couldn't help wondering just how he'd thought he'd be able to escape justice, let alone punishment. He'd signed a lie into the maintenance logs, using his own name. There was no way he could have escaped detection indefinitely.

Perhaps he planned to jump ship before we met our original departure date, Percy thought, ruefully. *Plenty of people got lost on Earth after the bombs fell.*

He shoved Cole into the small cell, then turned and walked to the second holding compartment. Lillian Turner was sitting inside, her hands cuffed behind her back and her pale face streaked with tears. She wasn't much older than Penny, Percy saw, and she was staring down the barrel of a death sentence. He couldn't help feeling a flicker of pity, even though it was something he knew he should avoid. Pretty girls had been used to smuggle IEDs up to British soldiers in the past, relying on the troops being reluctant to shoot at young ladies or children. It had worked too, he recalled. The Sergeants who'd supervised their first live-fire exercise had told them that such tactics had dissuaded the West from doing anything more than punitive strikes in the Third World.

"Bring in the second prisoner," Hadfield ordered.

"Aye, sir," Percy said.

He helped Lillian Turner to her feet, then escorted her down the corridor and into the wardroom.

———

John studied Lillian Turner as she was cuffed to the chair, thinking hard. She was a victim as much as a victimiser, used and manipulated by Frank Cole to ensure his little deception lasted longer than the time it would take for his work to be rechecked. What should have been a decent working relationship had become something darker, something *poisonous...* whatever else could be said about Cole, he decided, he'd been a master manipulator.

But Lillian Turner couldn't be allowed to get away with everything, either.

Poor bitch, he thought, as the Marine retreated to the rear of the room. It was easy to condemn someone like her for being weak-minded, yet he knew it was often hard to blend into the crew. *What are we going to do with her?*

"Lieutenant-Commander Howard will read the charges," he said. "Begin."

Howard rose to his feet. "Engineering Officer Lillian Turner is charged with theft of military supplies, falsification of maintenance reports, directly sabotaging HMS *Warspite* and indirectly causing injuries to nine crewmen, including two that may result in said crewmen being permanently beached."

Almost the exact same charges we threw at Cole, John thought.

He leaned forward as Howard sat down. "Mr. Richards," he said. "Does your client wish to enter a plea?"

"My client does," Richards said. He'd spent more time with Lillian Turner than with Cole, although John couldn't blame him. Cole stood condemned out of his own mouth. "My client, inexperienced in the ways of the world, allowed her superior, Frank Cole, to manipulate her into a compromising position, then blackmail her into submission. She believed, from the very bottom of her heart, that any attempt to reveal her situation would destroy her life. It did not seem as though there was any way to escape."

He paused, dramatically. "My client acknowledges that she made mistakes and became involved in criminal activities," he added. "However, she is also determined to make up for her mistakes and serve the Royal Navy well in the future."

John considered it. Legally, he didn't *have* to condemn Lillian Turner to death. It might be questioned, when the Board of Inquiry was finally held, but it wouldn't be held against him. She was young, she had had a good record before Cole had managed to lure her into his clutches…and she did have promise. But, on the other hand, justice had to be seen to be done. Lillian Turner would certainly have no future on *Warspite*. Even if someone didn't stick a knife in her, she would never be trusted again.

He rose to his feet, carefully formulating his words. "Lillian Turner," he said. "The charges against you are serious. You could be executed for your crimes. Do you understand me?"

Lillian Turner nodded, once. She didn't say a word.

"However, you have also been a victim," John continued. "Accordingly, we will offer you a choice. You will be held in the brig until we reach our destination, whereupon you will be transferred to Clarke III to serve as the Colony Governor sees fit. You will be, to all intents and purposes, an indentured labourer. Your future status will depend upon how hard you work; no matter what happens, you may never be allowed to leave the colony.

"Alternatively, you will be held in the brig until we return to Earth, whereupon you will be transferred to Colchester Military Detention Centre for a period of not less than ten years," he added. "Once you have completed your sentence, you will be dishonourably discharged from the Royal Navy, with a black mark on your record that will ensure you will no longer find work in space. Your future will no longer be our problem."

He studied her for a long moment. Life on a newborn colony would be hard, particularly a colony on such an inhospitable world. But it would be better than life in the Colchester Glasshouse. It was considered one of the least pleasant prisons in the world, certainly for its guests who were long-term residents. Only the Luna Penal Facility, on the dark side of the moon, was regarded as tougher and thoroughly escape-proof.

"You will be held in the brig until we reach Clarke III," he concluded. "You will be provided with reading materials concerning the planet and future colony plans. At that moment, you will have to decide where you want to go. I suggest you think carefully about your future, then make up your mind."

He looked at the Marines. "Remove the prisoner," he ordered. "The court is now dismissed."

Lillian Turner was marched out of the cell, her face dripping with fresh tears. John watched as she left, then turned his attention to Richards. The older officer was looking down at the deck, his face pale and wan. John understood, although it wasn't something he could say in public. Being a defender was never fun, particularly when there was no chance of actually winning the case. The role was nothing more than a meaningless formality, intended more for the Board of Inquiry than anything else.

"Please inform me of how Mr. Cole would like to meet his maker," John said, once everyone else had left the room.

"Old age, probably," Richards said. He smiled, humourlessly. "There are drugs that simulate the aging process, sir, if one takes them with proper medical attention."

"Perhaps not something anyone wants to think about," John said, ruefully. There was no shortage of treatments for extending one's life - several asteroid colonies had even pioneered genetically-engineered children they swore would live for over a thousand years - but he'd never heard of anyone wanting to speed up their aging. "Are you all right?"

"I have been better, sir," Richards said. "You went out on a limb for Lillian Turner, I noted."

"Yes," John said, flatly.

The Board of Inquiry would question his decision, he knew. It was what they did. If he'd been willing to execute one of his crew, they would ask, why hadn't he been willing to execute his partner-in-crime? But, in the end, Lillian Turner had been seduced, lured to the dark side so carefully that she hadn't realised the danger until it was far too late. John sometimes wondered what he would have done, if he'd been manipulated into a compromising position. It was easy to *say* he would go to his superiors and confess, but in reality it was never so easy to do the right thing.

And my superiors would have been looking for someone to blame, he thought. *They might blame me too, even though I confessed.*

"I think she deserves a chance," he said, firmly. "Besides, being on Clarke isn't going to be *that* different from being in the Glasshouse."

"Worse food," Richards said, at once. "I dare say you can't feed prisoners on the slop colonists get to eat, during their first months on the hellhole."

John smiled. "True," he said. "Let me know about Mr. Cole. I'll be in my office."

He walked back to his cabin, called for a cup of tea from Midshipwoman Powell, then started to write out the formal report while the whole affair was still fresh in his mind. The Board of Inquiry would be interested in his immediate reactions, as well as his later reflections. He was midway through the report when there was a chime at the hatch. When it opened, Richards stepped into the cabin.

"Captain," he said. "Mr. Cole has requested that he be executed by being spaced."

John blinked. "Are you sure?"

"Yes, sir," Richards said. He held up a datapad. "I have his signed request here."

"I see," John said. Spacers were superstitions, sometimes, about having their bodies left in space. Being killed on active service, their bodies blown to bits or completely vaporised, was one thing, and being buried in space was quite another, but deliberately choosing to dive into the darkness of space to die was something else. "Did he have any other last requests?"

"He recorded a pair of messages for his closest relatives," Richards informed him. "But I don't think there was anything else."

John glanced at the chronometer hanging on the bulkhead. "The sentence will be carried out in one hour," he said, finally. Thankfully, repairing the damage Cole had caused hadn't taken as long as he'd feared. "We'll get underway immediately afterwards."

"Yes, sir," Richards said.

"If he's religious, see if there's someone who shares his faith who will spend the last hour with him," John said. Fleet carriers carried a dedicated chaplain, but *Warspite* was too small to carry unnecessary crewmen. "And then do what you can to prepare him for death."

"Aye, sir," Richards said.

John couldn't help wondering, as the minutes ticked down to the moment of execution, why Cole had chosen to die in space. Was it a final act of love for the interplanetary void or a gesture of pointless defiance, aimed at John and the rest of the crew? Spacing wasn't the only method of execution he could have chosen, but it was the only one with superstitious connotations. In a way, it was a form of suicide, the abandonment of everything that kept humanity alive in the interstellar void.

He could have overruled Cole, he knew. Regulations allowed him considerable leeway. He could have ordered him hung, or executed through lethal injection. But it was well to honour Cole's last request.

When the time came, he walked down to the main airlock and stood by the hatch as Cole was marched down, his hands bound behind his back, and pushed into the small chamber. His eyes were flickering from face to face, as if he'd expected a last-minute reprieve, but John knew there would be none. There was no way to excuse Cole's actions without undermining shipboard discipline - and, unlike Lillian Turner, Cole couldn't be dumped on Clarke. He was too manipulative a bastard to be let loose among the colonists.

Behind him, Lillian Turner stood, her face pale. John felt a flicker of pity, which he savagely suppressed. She needed to see Frank Cole die, both as a warning and proof she'd finally escaped his grip. But watching him die wouldn't be easy for her. She stood between two Marines, looking tiny compared to them, and watched.

Poor bitch, John thought, again.

"Frank Cole," he said, once the Marines had stepped backwards. "You have been found guilty of the charges laid against you. For those charges, you are sentenced to death. Do you have anything you wish to say before sentence is carried out?"

Cole glared at him, but said nothing.

John reached for the control panel and tapped his override into the system, then closed the hatch. It rolled closed slowly, cutting off his view of the older man as he stood there. John wondered, in a moment of insight, if Cole had *intended* to force John to execute him personally, rather than leave it to the Marines. But in the end, it hardly mattered.

"May God have mercy on your soul," John said.

He keyed the panel. The outer airlock opened. The outrush of air picked up Cole's body and tossed it out into the vacuum of space. John watched it vanish into the darkness, then turned to face Lillian Turner.

"Remember this," he said, then looked at the Marines. "Take her back to her cell."

He walked back to the bridge, keeping his thoughts to himself. Frank Cole's body would eventually fall into the primary star and be consumed, his atoms returned to the universe. Until then, he was doomed to wander forever in interstellar darkness...

Shaking his head, he sat down in the command chair and gave the order.

"Take us out of here," he said. "And inform the squadron to follow us, best practical speed."

"Aye, sir," Armstrong said.

CHAPTER
THIRTEEN

John couldn't help feeling nervous as *Warspite* passed through the third tramline, but nothing happened, apart from the normal feeling of brief disorientation. After an hour to check all the systems for unexpected problems, *Warspite* resumed her course towards Pegasus, passing through three more tramlines in quick succession. By the time they finally jumped through the final tramline, John was starting to relax, slightly. The bugs seemed to have been worked out of his ship.

"Jump completed, sir," Armstrong said, formally. "We have arrived in the Pegasus System."

"Good," John said. "Are there any signs that anyone else has visited the system?"

"No, sir," Howard said. "The only sign of intelligent life is the survey beacon left behind when the system was first discovered."

And that, John knew, proved nothing. An entire settlement could be hidden somewhere in the Pegasus System, completely undetectable as long as its owners were careful to avoid emitting any betraying signature. But it was unlikely that an independent settlement would matter, in the great scheme of things, while a settlement landed by another nation would cause legal problems for them on Earth. They would have noted the presence of the beacon and chosen to ignore it.

"Set course for Clarke," he ordered. "Engage."

He smiled to himself, knowing it wouldn't be long before they were free of the squadron, able to explore the surrounding systems without being forced to crawl from tramline to tramline, held back by the slow RFA starships. The First Space Lord had been right, he decided, as more and more data popped up in the holographic display. Pegasus might not have a life-bearing world, which would probably cause disputes later, but the presence of seven tramlines - three of them alien-grade - was well worth the risk of ordering *Warspite* to her duty station before her final checks had been completed. Seven tramlines…the British Crown would be able to charge a fee to anyone who wanted to use them. It would ensure the colony would pay for itself within a very short space of time.

Assuming the sector takes off, he reminded himself. *The war did a lot of damage to our economy.*

But he was sure it would. The gas giant - Clarke - would provide cheap fuel, while there was a giant asteroid belt, a Mars-like world and five moons orbiting the gas giant. Given a couple of decades, the system would probably host a small industrial empire and thousands of settlers. They'd need extra incentives to live on Wells, he knew, but the government could offer them. Being on the ground floor of a system as economically important as Pegasus could make thousands of millionaires.

"The gas giant has a surprising amount of space junk in low orbit," Armstrong commented, as they drew closer to their destination. "I'd say one of the moons shattered, a few thousand years ago."

"Interesting," John said. "But why did it shatter?"

"We may never know," Armstrong said.

"Alien mining," Howard suggested. "Didn't there used to be a plan to blow up Mercury for ease of access?"

John nodded. It had been seriously considered, he recalled, around fifty years after a joint Chinese-Russian colony had been established on the surface of the rocky world. They'd pointed out that shattering the planet would make it much easier to mine the debris field for rare minerals. The plan had floundered, in the end, when even the Russians hadn't been able to devise a bomb big enough to shatter the planet…and strong objections from the other spacefaring powers. They hadn't liked the thought of tossing so much debris into interplanetary space.

"If it happened only a mere thousand years ago," Armstrong said, "wouldn't we have run into the aliens by now?"

"They might have evolved into something far beyond us," Commander Watson offered. "We already have ways to transcribe ourselves into computer databanks. Arguably, they might have continued the process and become beings of pure energy."

John shrugged. Alien life *was* a very real possibility - but, just like Armstrong, he had his doubts. The Tadpoles hadn't been able to blow up entire planets - and, even if someone else could, why would they bother? It wasn't as if there was a shortage of raw material floating in orbit around Pegasus, or any of a hundred systems within a few short jumps. They didn't need to waste the energy...

Unless it was a war, of course, he thought, darkly. *And one side resorted to blowing up entire planets to exterminate the other side.*

He ignored the discussion as Clarke slowly grew larger on the display. Armstrong was right, he saw; there was a considerable amount of debris in low orbit. It would be a problem for the cloudscoop specialists, he suspected, although they would probably be able to handle it, perhaps by using a large asteroid as an anchor for the scoop itself. Or they could simply start pushing pieces of debris into the gas giant until they had cleared enough space to ensure they could operate the cloudscoop safely.

"Sir," Forbes said. "We just picked up an IFF demand from the beacon."

"Transmit our IFF back, then copy its files to us," John ordered, coolly. In theory, if anyone had visited the system between the survey team and *Warspite*, the beacon should have noted and logged their presence. But, in practice, it was far too likely that any intruders had escaped detection. "And inform me if anything shows up."

"Aye, sir," Forbes said. There was a long pause as her signal raced across the void to the beacon, then was returned. "Nothing visited the system until we arrived."

"Let us hope that is actually true," John said. "Lieutenant Armstrong?"

"Yes, sir?"

"Take us to Clarke III," John ordered. "The remainder of the squadron can wait here while we survey the planet."

He couldn't help being reminded of Bluebell as the gas giant grew larger on the display, but he knew it wasn't the same. Clarke was larger and simply more useful - and there was no dispute over settlement rights.

No aliens prowling around either, he reminded himself, and shivered. Colin had died at Bluebell, along with everyone else on HMS *Canopus*, save John himself. Even now, he wasn't sure if anyone had gone back to the system to recover what was left of the bodies.

The Canny Man deserved better, he thought. *And so did her crew.*

"That's a very useful world," Commander Watson observed, as the display refocused on Clarke III. "We could do a great deal of work here."

John concealed his amusement with an effort. Clarke III - he supposed they'd have to come up with a better name, once the settlement was firmly established - looked beautiful, an icy white sphere of light shining against the darkness, reflecting the blue light of the gas giant. But, to someone like Commander Watson, natural beauty was worthless, while the majesty of engineering was all too important. He found himself torn between the two attitudes; Clarke III was beautiful, yes, but so was engineering.

"Launch probes," he ordered, as *Warspite* entered orbit. "And then prepare to deploy the landing pods."

"Aye, sir," Howard said. The probes dropped into the moon's atmosphere and vanished from sight, under the clouds. "Live telemetry established, sir."

"Make sure you copy it to the squadron," John ordered, as he watched the images flicker up in front of him, one by one. "Let them all see where they're going."

Clarke III was deceptive, he noted, as the probes skimmed through the planet's atmosphere. Parts of the landscape looked almost like Scotland, under a layer of snow, but he knew it was very inhospitable. The seas were liquid water and ammonia, while the atmosphere held vast quantities of nitrogen and methane. But it also contained trace levels of hydrogen cyanide, perhaps just enough to poison any human who stepped out without protection.

But that would be the least of their problems, he thought. *The atmosphere just isn't breathable.*

"I've located a handful of volcanoes just under the water, sir," Howard said. "They must be keeping the planet warm, despite the ice."

"I believe the colony intends to tap them for power," Commander Watson said. She turned to face John. "Captain, we should deploy the landing pods now."

"Do so," John ordered. "Have you isolated the planned landing site?"

"Yes," Commander Watson said. "The survey team seem to have done a good job, but we will need results from the landing pods before we can confirm it."

John nodded, then turned his attention back to the endless stream of data. The planet's gravity was slightly stronger than Luna's, around one-fourth of Earth's gravity field. It would be easy to use mass drivers to launch water and other supplies into orbit, he noted, but the colonists would require special genetic treatments to ensure their children didn't suffer from the low gravity. They'd probably also want treatments to allow their kids to breathe the planet's atmosphere, but John doubted it was possible. The planned Titan Genetic Modifications had never quite produced a human who could live on the surface without life support gear.

"It would be fun to ski on that mountain," Armstrong commented. "And we could set up a flying dome over there…"

"Someone could probably fly under their own power, if they had wings," Howard suggested. "The spacesuit would be a problem, but the pressure levels would keep them from needing heavy armour or other equipment. One day, people might get around the colony on wings, as easily as people in Cambridge get around on bikes."

"Settlement first," Commander Watson said, firmly. "Entertainment later."

It was another hour before the first set of results came in from the landed pods. John breathed a sigh of relief as the survey team's report was confirmed. The designated landing zone could be used, without the settlers having to go and search for another. They wouldn't also have to worry about finding a better location for the mass driver. Placing it along the planet's equator made it easier to shoot capsules into space.

"Contact Captain Minion," John ordered. "He is to bring the remainder of the squadron here and then start preparing the landing."

"Aye, sir," Forbes said.

"Commander Watson, you will take this opportunity to work with the Chief Engineer and check our drive systems, *thoroughly*," John ordered. "Howard, you have the bridge."

"Aye, sir," Howard said.

John rose, then motioned Commander Watson to lead the way off the bridge. He nodded politely to her when they reached the edge of Officer Country, then turned to walk into the brig. The Marine on duty saluted smartly, then stepped aside as John checked the cell monitors. Lillian Turner had remained in the brig for the two weeks the rest of the trip had taken, doing very little beyond using her terminal and copies of books and movies John had ordered sent to her.

He opened the hatch, then stepped into the cell. It smelled vaguely unpleasant, as if the occupant hadn't been able to do more than rub herself with a sponge. The toilet was nothing more than an open seat, in the rear of the compartment. And yet, it was still a better place to live than a junior officer's quarters on a frigate. Prisoners had rights junior officers had surrendered, in order to join the Royal Navy.

"Captain," Lillian Turner said. Her voice was hushed as she sat upright. Someone had given her an orange prison uniform, then wrapped a security bracelet around her wrist. It would knock her out if she stepped out of the brig without permission. "What can I do for you?"

John studied her for a long moment. She looked as if she hadn't been sleeping properly; there were dark marks around her eyes, while her movements were slow and deliberate. John couldn't blame her for nightmares, if she was having them. In hindsight, maybe it had been too cruel to force her to watch as Frank Cole was ejected into space. But the lesson had to be learned, if not by her then by the rest of the crew. Crimes against the Royal Navy could not be allowed to go unpunished.

"We have reached Clarke III," he said. "I have…talked to Governor Brown, the colony commander. He is willing to add you to his team, if you wish to accept semi-permanent exile. If not, you will remain here until we return to Earth, whereupon you will be handed over to the Military Police and transferred to Colchester. I'm afraid I have to ask for your choice now."

"My parents are going to be so disappointed," Lillian Turner said. "I wanted to make them proud."

"I know," John said. "But why did you think your activities would remain undiscovered indefinitely?"

Lillian Turner flushed. "I didn't think," she said. She looked down at the deck. "What is life in Colchester like?"

"Unpleasant," John said, flatly. "You wouldn't like it."

Indeed, he wasn't sure she would *survive*. Lillian Turner wouldn't see the barracks where minor offenders were kept, or the educational facilities where some detainees were prepared for a return to civilian life. She would spend her days in a cell, running through a daily routine of cleaning her cell, exercising and carrying out make-work prescribed by the CO, while her every move was supervised and she was searched or interrogated at the drop of a hat. And while the guards were supposed to be disciplined, there had always been dark rumours about how the long-term prisoners were treated.

And, after the bombardment, few people would give a damn if the prisoners were abused, he thought, bitterly. Something had been lost in the bombardment, if it hadn't been worn away to a nub by the Troubles. A certain basic decency, perhaps. *She might find herself forced into whoring to survive.*

He sighed, then shrugged. There was nothing else he could do for her, not now. She'd been charged, the charges had been proven…she had to be punished. And regulations offered little room for leeway.

"I will go to Clarke," Lillian Turner said. "Thank you, Captain."

John tapped the hatch. The Marine opened it and peered inside, one hand on the butt of his weapon. John wasn't sure if he'd really thought Lillian Turner could overpower her commanding officer, but it was well to take precautions. It would have been drummed into him, right from the start, that even the most harmless-looking person could be very dangerous, at least with the right training.

"Call Lieutenant Forbes," John ordered. "When she arrives, she is to ensure that Lillian Turner is showered and dressed in something suitable for transfer to RFA *Argus*. Once she is ready, have her duffle picked up" - fortunately, Lillian Turner hadn't had a chance to amass more than a handful of personal possessions - "and then take her to the shuttlebay. A shuttle can pick her up once she's ready to leave."

"Yes, sir," the Marine said. "Should she be cuffed?"

"I don't think so," John said. He spoke loudly, knowing that Lillian Turner would overhear. "But if she causes trouble, return her to the cell."

John turned his head to take one last look at Lillian Turner, then strode out of the brig. It should have been Commander Watson's job, he knew, but he couldn't rely on the XO to handle the prisoner transfer. Not that Lillian Turner was *precisely* a prisoner any longer…he shook his head, tiredly. There had been hundreds of plans to use prisoners as brute labour on colony worlds, but they'd all amounted to very little in the end. The logistics of shipping prisoners to Luna, let alone Britannia, were daunting. And besides, with so many innocent refugees ready to ship out for a colony world, who would need convicts?

"Captain," Lieutenant Forbes said. The Communications Officer looked surprised at her summons. "I don't know how to handle prisoners."

"Watch her while she showers and dresses, then walk with her to the shuttlebay and wait for the shuttle," John ordered, bluntly. He couldn't leave Lillian Turner alone - and she had enough problems without being openly watched by male spacers. Privacy was a rare thing in the Royal Navy, but the crew tended to cling to what they had. "If she causes trouble, the Marine can take her back to the cell and she can go to Colchester."

"Aye, sir," Lieutenant Forbes said, doubtfully.

John nodded, then turned and walked away. The Royal Marines wouldn't have had a problem with the prisoner, but the Royal Marines were all male, even now. A company-sized detachment would probably have included a handful of female supporting personnel, yet it had been hard enough to get two sections of Marines for *Warspite*. Like so many others, Lieutenant Forbes would just have to grin and bear it, even if she wasn't trained for her new task.

He keyed his wristcom once he was back in Officer Country. "Raise Governor Brown and inform him that he can pick up his new crewmember as soon as possible," he said, curtly. "And then he can begin the landings when he's ready to move."

"Aye, sir," Howard said.

"And inform me once the shuttle has departed," John added. He needed to finish the report for his superiors, who would probably accept Lillian Turner's exile, but ask him some very hard questions when he returned home. "I'll be in my office."

He stepped through the hatch, called for a cup of tea, then sat down at his desk. The first part of the mission was complete, but the second part was just about to begin. And, once the colonists were settled, *Warspite* could start probing the nearby tramlines. Who knew what they would find?

God, he thought. The survey ships had barely probed past Cromwell before the war began. Anything could be lurking out there, anything at all, from aliens to isolated independent human colonies.

John smiled. He couldn't wait.

CHAPTER
FOURTEEN

"This is one very big step for the Royal Marines," Percy said, as he stepped out of the shuttle and onto the planet's surface. "And one even bigger step for me."

He stopped, dead, as he took in the landscape. He'd seen Mars, a year ago, but Clarke III was very different. The skies were an eerie dark blue, glowing faintly with flickers of electrical discharges in the upper atmosphere, while the ground was covered in what looked like white snow. But he knew, from warning icons popping up in his suit's HUD, that it was poisonous, rather than water ice. He took a step forward, staring towards the mountains in the distance, looming up against the dark sky. It was meant to be the middle of the day, as far as Clarke was concerned, but it might as well be twilight. He'd never stood anywhere so eerie, not even the remains of the Cardiff Reclamation Zone.

"Move along, Corporal," Peerce said, dryly.

Percy flushed, then lowered his eyes and walked forward, away from the shuttle. It wasn't easy to compensate for the lowered gravity; every step he took seemed to threaten to throw him into the air, like he'd done on a school trip to the moon. Behind him, the rest of 2 Section filed out of the shuttle, their suits hastily adapting to the new world. Percy turned and looked towards the ocean, shaking his head in awe at the wonders of the universe. The ocean looked like a thin layer of slush, slowly rising and falling as the gas giant exerted its influence on the tides.

There could be life under there, he thought. There were some small creatures on Titan, he knew, although nothing larger than a small fish. *Clinging to the volcanic vents, struggling to remain in the warm zone...*

He turned and looked towards the growing colony. A week of hard work had culminated in the establishment of a handful of tent-like buildings, each one prefabricated on Earth and crammed into the freighters for transhipment to Clarke. They didn't look very impressive, not compared to some of the structures he'd seen on Mars, but they were liveable. The crews no longer needed to return to the shuttles each night to rest, before going back to work the following morning. Beside them, a large drill bored its way into the ground, probing down towards a volcanic vent. Geothermal power would keep the system going if the fusion plant happened to fail.

"Shit!"

Percy spun around, weapon in hand, just in time to see Private Fisherman slip and fall to the ground. Several of the Marines snickered, not unkindly, as Fisherman's suit tore into the icy ground, before its wearer regained control and clambered back to his feet. Percy wasn't too surprised *someone* had fallen; Royal Marines were meant to have hundreds of hours in the suits by the time they graduated, but suits had been in short supply since the war. The Tadpoles had destroyed far too many during Operation Nelson.

And it isn't as if we had a large supply anyway, he thought, ruefully. *Each suit costs twice as much as a Falklands-class tank.*

"Have a care, Fisherman," Peerce said, tartly. "You don't want to go ice-skating here, that's for sure."

"No, Sergeant," Fisherman said.

Percy cleared his throat. "All right," he said. "It's time to start jogging. Follow me."

He turned and started to jog away from the colony, heading towards the shore. The Marines followed him, keeping pace easily. Percy smiled to himself - it felt so good to be off the ship, even if they had to wear the suits - and led them on a long march around the shore, then up towards the nearest mountain. It looked like something out of a fairy tale, he decided, as they reached the lowermost slopes and paused for breath. He'd climbed a dozen mountains as part of his training, but none of them had looked as inhospitable as the mountain before him. The mountain rose up to the clouds, its peak hidden in the dark blue atmosphere. His suit reported heavy discharges in the upper levels. It would definitely not be safe to climb.

"I hereby claim this mountain in the name of Janet Oakley, my sister," Private Oakley announced, mischievously. "Does anyone have a bottle we can use to dedicate it?"

"You only get to name landmarks if you happen to stay here permanently," Peerce pointed out, sarcastically. "But if you chat up the Governor a little, I'm *sure* he will consider naming the mountain after your relatives."

Percy had to smile. Terra Nova had suffered, badly, from bureaucrats on Earth trying to name everything from mountains to oceans, all the while trying to avoid something - anything - that someone could construe as offensive. None of the names had lasted, he recalled, while later colonists going to other worlds had insisted on the right to name landmarks themselves. Unsurprisingly, there were places on Britannia that had ended up with names no one dared write down. But the Governor would probably have vetoed them if they'd been *too* offensive.

He took one last look at the mountain, then led the way towards the Exercise Ground. It was a flat plain - or as close as anywhere came to *flat* on Clarke - which would serve as an ideal route for a hostile force to approach the colony. A handful of men in armoured combat suits could pass through it quickly, he noted as the Marines came to a halt, but it would be harder to get wheeled or tracked vehicles through the gap. It would depend, he decided finally, on just how aggressive the enemy was determined to be. Clarke Colony - or whatever they ended up calling it - wouldn't have any real defences for years to come.

"They're going to come from the north," he said. 1 Section had already landed, he was sure; they would have shook themselves down by now, easily. "We can meet them here..."

"Yes, Corporal," Peerce said.

Percy thought hard. Peerce would follow orders, but he wouldn't offer suggestions, not now. The exercise was as much a test of Percy's tactical skills as it was anything else; he had to set up the ambush himself, or risk being marked down by his CO. He looked from side to side, silently evaluating the position, then sorted out a plan.

"You three, dig foxholes here, here and here," he said, using his HUD to mark out three separate locations. There was no need for entrenching tools when the suits could dig into the ground with ease. "You three, lay wires from here to here, then place the active sensors to the rear. You three, set up the mortars over here."

Peerce turned to face him as the Marines hurried to work. "Wires, *Corporal*?"

"Wires," Percy said. He tried very hard not to smirk. "I've got a cunning plan."

"Just don't pull a Baldrick," Peerce said. *Baldrick* had entered the military lexicon to symbolise an officer who became so impressed with his own cleverness that he missed the basic flaw in his plans. "Wires will make it harder for you to move your troops."

"I know, Sergeant," Percy said.

He smiled to himself as he started to dig one of the foxholes himself. Armoured combat suits had been hailed as the be-all and end-all of military technology, at least until they'd actually entered service. It was true that even a light suit of powered combat armour could resist bullets, or even protect its wearer from IED blasts, but they had their limitations. And one particular limitation was a major problem on a world without a standard atmosphere. They needed radios to communicate with their fellows.

And radio pulses can be detected, Percy thought. There wasn't any quicker way to get oneself killed on the battlefield than by radiating a signal that might as well say 'come kill me now.' He'd seen it happen during hundreds of exercises, when they'd been allowed to make mistake after mistake, just so they could see the consequences without anyone actually having to be hurt. *The CO will deploy passive sensors for sure, looking for us.*

But, by using wires, the suits wouldn't need to radiate anything.

"You've also put the active sensors to the rear," Peerce added. "You *do* know they will be detected?"

"I'm counting on it," Percy said. If he was lucky, Lieutenant Hadfield would assume that the active sensors were placed next to his men. He might be suspicious if he picked up *no* traces of radio emissions. "But we will see."

He frowned as a red icon popped up in his HUD. The exercise was about to begin.

"Places," he ordered, sharply. The foxholes were ready; he clambered into one, then carefully dug through the icy soil until he had an excellent view of the plain. "Here we go."

The waiting was always the hardest part, he reminded himself, as the minutes seemed to stretch into hours. There was always the temptation to declare the exercise a failure, or to suspect the enemy had cheated and attacked the colony through a different angle of attack, or even to leave one's position and start scouting forward. He kept his eyes peeled on the landscape as a snowstorm blew up in the distance, sweeping towards them threateningly. The weather seemed to be largely unpredictable, as far as he could tell. It would probably be years before the weather service managed to come to grips with Clarke III's weather and start making accurate predictions.

"I'm picking up a drone," Private Oakley warned. He'd been placed in charge of the section's ECM. "They're probing us."

"Bollocks," Percy said, slowly. He was impressed they'd managed to fly the drone in the planet's atmosphere. It had been designed for Earth-like environments, not Clarke III. "Take it down if it gets close enough to get us on visual…"

"Contact," Peerce said, sharply. "Incoming suits!"

Percy swung around and peered towards the enemy troops. There were only three of them, wearing the same armoured suits as his own men. They were advancing in sequence, one man moving forward while the other two covered him, then moving forward themselves. He wasn't surprised to note that their chameleon units were active, even though they drained power at a staggering rate. It was nearly impossible to pick them out from their surroundings when they were still.

But where, he asked himself, *are the others?*

He risked a glance at his suit's passive sensors. There were no radio pulses being exchanged between the point men and the rest of their section, as far as he could tell, and it didn't look as though they were dragging wires behind them. Peerce had been right; wires were useful, when a section was locked in position, but actively dangerous if the troops had to move in a hurry. And the drone was practically hovering over the incoming soldiers…

It struck him in a single flash of insight. "They're using laser links to the drone to communicate," he said. He'd heard of the possibility, but he'd never seen anyone use it in an exercise, let alone a battlefield. There were just too many ways it could go wrong…yet, here, it allowed Hadfield to control his men without emitting any betraying emissions that would get them killed. "Oakley, target the drone. Mortars…I want spread fire to the rear. Rifles, target the incoming point men. On my command, fire."

"That will be costly, Corporal," Peerce pointed out.

"Do it anyway," Percy said. There was a pause. "Fire!"

He pulled his own trigger at the same moment. The hapless point men, caught in fire from several different positions, fell to the ground as their suits locked up, leaving them out of the fight. Percy smiled, then checked his HUD. The drone had shut down at the same moment, while the mortars had laid down heavy fire where he thought the rest of the enemy force had to be. There was a pause, then mortar fire came screaming back at them, aimed at his own mortars. They'd been waiting, he realised as he waited to see the outcome, for him to open fire, revealing the location of his own support weapons.

"Incoming," Peerce snapped. Four men appeared in front of them, crawling towards the foxholes with terrifying speed. "Corporal?"

"Take them out," Percy ordered, sharply. Two of his three mortars had managed to move before the enemy shells took them out, but the third was dead and gone. "And then alter position…"

A second salvo of mortar shells landed around them. There was a long pause, then the electronic umpires decided that none of his men had been hurt. He smiled in relief, then keyed in a command to his remaining mortars. A shell fell among the advancing troops, locking up their armour. They were out of the fight.

"Fire Team One, with me," he ordered. He jumped out of the foxhole as the mortars fired another barrage, taking the risk of being caught in the air. A suit might be a hard target to see and take out on the ground, but in the air it was an easy target. "Quickly!"

He boosted his suit as he led the charge forward, hunting for the remaining enemy targets. The CO wouldn't have put himself at the front, but he wouldn't have put himself at the rear either, not when he might have needed to take direct command. For a moment, a sudden flurry of snow almost blinded him, then he saw a handful of armoured troops advancing forward. He hurled a set of grenades from his suit's inbuilt launcher, then opened fire as his men followed him. Two minutes later, it was all over.

"Exercise complete," a dispassionate computer-generated voice said. "I say again, exercise complete."

"And 1 Section is buying the beer," Oakley said, as the 'dead' Marines rose to their feet and headed towards the foxholes. "We kicked serious ass."

"So we did," Peerce said. "Well done, Corporal."

Percy beamed. "Thank you, Sergeant."

"Definitely very well done," Hadfield said, as his suit loomed out of the gloom. "Leading the charge yourself was reckless, but by then you probably had the victory in the bag anyway."

"I only lost two men," Percy said. He hadn't even noticed the second man 'killed' until scanning the after-action report from the automated monitors. Private Hardesty had joined him in the final mad charge. "But it would have been bad if there had been more of you out there."

"Good thinking," Hadfield said. He raised his voice. "Back to the nearest shuttle now, if you please. The storm is getting closer."

Percy mulled it over as the Marines started the walk back to the colony. He'd started the battle with eleven men, counting himself and Sergeant Peerce. Losing two men didn't seem like a lot, but most of the battles the Royal Marines had fought in the past century had been against superior numbers, sometimes vastly superior numbers. Only better training and advanced technology had prevented complete disaster, at times. It was quite possible they'd fight someone who could afford to trade a hundred men for each Royal Marine and come out ahead…

And the Tadpoles upset all of our calculations, he thought, looking down at the BAR-47 he carried in one hand. The plasma rifle could burn through a suit as easily as it could burn through bare skin; worse, the plasma blast inflicted horrific internal injuries on anyone it struck. Death was almost instant, in most cases. The suit was designed to seal itself and help keep its wearer alive, but the Tadpole weapons had made that almost impossible. *Their weapons could do us real damage, if they got into the wrong hands.*

The storm was pressing on their heels by the time they reached the shuttle, positioned neatly to one side of the colony. Percy opened the hatch, then waited for the remainder of the Marines to enter before following them in and closing the hatch behind him. The shuttle felt warm and welcoming compared to the outside world, even if it was cramped and smelled of too many young men in close proximity. He sighed, then cracked open his suit anyway.

"Take a break," Hadfield ordered his men. "It may be some time before we can take off and return to the ship."

And pick up your shuttle, Percy thought, as the snowstorm swept over the shuttle. He peered out of the porthole and saw snowflakes brushing against the hull. It looked beautiful, but he knew it would be lethal if he went out in the storm without a suit. *This place might make a good resort one day, if it can be terraformed.*

He sighed inwardly as he picked up a datapad, then pulled up the records and started to work his way through the brief battle. It was easy, in hindsight, to see his mistakes, although he had managed to adapt, react and overcome his errors. The CO had launched a conventional attack too, he noted; if it had been real, the CO might have looked for another way to attack the colony, instead of impaling himself on the defences. There were several other prospective routes if he'd been willing to march around Percy's position.

"We'll go over it in great detail later," Hadfield promised, as he looked at Percy's datapad. "You'll have a chance to redo the battle yourself, too."

And see if I can sneak around the defences, Percy thought. The thought made him smile, darkly. *Or would that be considered cheating?*

He shrugged, a moment later. If one wasn't cheating, his instructors had insisted, years ago, one wasn't trying. War wasn't fair, not really, nor was it romantic. All that really mattered was making the other poor bastard die for his country.

CHAPTER

FIFTEEN

"They seem to have done a considerable amount of work," John said, as the shuttle flew over the colony. "I didn't realise they could expand so fast."

"The colony planners did a good job," Commander Watson assured him. "And they didn't run into any unexpected snags."

John nodded. One month of boredom in space, running endless tactical exercises and surveys of the inner system, hadn't been anything like as boring for the colonists on the ground. The freighters had lowered the dumpsters into the atmosphere, dropping them neatly beside the special environment tents that made up the majority of the first colony. Once the dumpsters had landed, the colonists had started to unpack them, then put the prefabricated buildings together and fix them securely to the ground. The colony had expanded rapidly after that, with mining equipment being decanted and used to dig tunnels deep underground. It looked very much like the first lunar colonies.

"That's good," he said. "The next flood of colonists will have ready-made homes."

He looked down at a farming module as the shuttle dropped towards the ground. It would be several months before it was ready to go, but once it *was* ready it would produce enough foodstuffs to keep the entire colony fed for years. The British Colonisation Service always over-engineered its systems, just to make sure they could handle an unanticipated demand, if necessary. Ironically, for a service intent on getting as many people away from Earth as possible, its paranoia had helped to feed millions of refugees after the Tadpoles had struck Earth.

The shuttle touched down with a bump, the gravity field fading seconds later. John unbuckled himself, then stood, careful to move slowly in the low gravity. Commander Watson didn't seem to have any problems at all, he noted with a hint of amusement; to her, gravity was just another factor for engineers to take into account. He nodded politely to the pilot, then stepped up to the airlock and waited until the docking tube was secure. The hatch hissed open once the checks had been made, revealing a tube leading to the colony. John smiled to himself, then stepped through the airlock and into a whole new world.

"Captain," Governor Brown said. "Welcome to Clarke."

John smiled and shook hands, firmly. Governor Brown hardly seemed to deserve the title, not when Clarke's population was no more than four hundred people, but it gave him authority he could use, if necessary. He was a middle-aged man, an engineer and colony support officer by trade, which made him more qualified to serve than the last Governor John had met, a couple of years ago. *That* man had been nothing more than a bureaucrat who'd obtained his post as payment for services rendered.

"Thank you," he said. He couldn't help noticing that Brown was attractive; he looked mature, yet young enough to be frisky. "It's good to be here."

"I'm afraid we don't have a band yet to welcome you properly," Brown said, as he turned to lead the way into the colony. "Most of my people are still very busy. But you are welcome."

"I don't mind," John assured him. "I never had much patience for formalities."

"Me neither," Brown said. "They always seemed to get in the way of my work."

He led them on a short tour of the colony, covering the places they could visit without a spacesuit. Most of the prefabricated buildings, put together by the numbers, were empty, waiting for the next set of colonists to arrive from Earth, but a handful were already filled with people. Two large barracks held most of the colonists, while smaller sleeping quarters were allocated by lottery. Even Governor Brown slept in the male barracks, rather than claiming one of the private bedrooms for himself. John was mildly impressed.

The colonists themselves looked busy, he decided, as they passed through a growing machine shop. Most of them were young and very well-trained; it was quite possible they would move on, once the colony was firmly established. Others would probably remain indefinitely, including Lillian Turner. John caught sight of her, working on a piece of machinery, as they turned to leave the machine shop. She didn't look back at them.

"She's been a good worker," Governor Brown said, once they left the chamber. "I didn't tell anyone what happened, back when she was serving under you. She deserves a fair chance to shine, here with the rest of us exiles."

"You'll be going back to Earth in five years, I believe," John said. "She will be here indefinitely."

"I may stay," Brown said. He shrugged. "There's no shortage of interesting problems to solve here, Captain, and the landscape is remarkable. And I wouldn't encounter any idiots here too."

"There are idiots everywhere," John said, crossly. "Even in the Royal Navy."

"They don't tend to survive out here," Brown said. "Stupidity is a capital crime, punished by the universe. A single mistake can take someone out of the gene pool...and thank heaven for that, I say."

John frowned. It wasn't an uncommon attitude, not among asteroid dwellers. They lived in an environment that was unrelentingly hostile, where a simple mistake could be utterly lethal...and where no one, not even a child, could be isolated from the dangers. The asteroid dwellers were objectivists in the strongest possible sense, the men and women who couldn't allow themselves any form of wishful thinking. But, at the same time, it struck him as a dangerous attitude. Dreamers had taken the human race far.

They want to weed out the stupid, he thought. *But how can they separate the truly stupid from the ones who make simple mistakes?*

"I understand you're working on the mass driver," Commander Watson said. "Have you managed to solve the problem of anchoring it to the ground?"

"We've established the colony on rock, once we blasted away the snow," Governor Brown said, pulling his terminal off his belt. "As you can see" - he tapped the screen several times - "we managed to anchor the mass driver pretty solidly. It may still be problematic to shoot capsules into space, but we will have plenty of time to calibrate the system before we start planning our settlement on Wells."

John nodded. *Warspite* had entered Wells orbit, a week after the first landing on Clarke III, and dropped a shuttle to the surface to plant the British flag. A handful of geologists had confirmed the results of the first survey; Wells would take years to terraform, even with the latest developments in bioengineered systems. But the process would be relatively cheap, once it got underway. The bacteria that would convert the planet's atmosphere to oxygen would reproduce itself.

"We have also located sources of everything we need to feed ourselves," the Governor added, as they stepped into another prefabricated section. "There won't be any difficulty supporting the colony."

"That's good to hear," John said. "I don't think the Admiralty would be pleased at having to ship food out here."

"No, probably not," the Governor said. "We'll definitely have a market for luxury foods, I believe, even something as simple as beef or pork, but we won't be dependent on foodstuffs from Earth or Cromwell."

He led them into a refectory, then turned to smile at them. "Behold, the wonders of governorship," he said. "Crystal decanters of sherry, wooden tables, expensive foods, maids in skimpy uniforms…"

John laughed. The tables were plastic, the food was nothing more than ration bars, there was only water or tea to drink and there were no maids or waitresses. Indeed, the entire room was empty. He followed the Governor over to the nearest table, then sat where he was told and picked up the ration bar without enthusiasm. The military might be allowed flavoured ration bars, but colonists were expected to eat the bland-tasting kind. It was, he'd been told, meant to encourage them to grow their own food or, at least, produce their own flavourings.

"I'll be mother," the Governor said. He poured them each a glass of water, then sat down facing them. "This water comes directly from the ocean."

Commander Watson eyed it doubtfully. "It's safe to drink?"

"We ran it through the filters," Governor Brown assured her. "You can drink it, or use it to wash, or…well, whatever else you use water for. It's perfectly safe."

"I'm glad to hear that," John said, as he sipped his water. He'd half-expected it to taste strange, but it tasted as bland as the water onboard ship. "What else have you done with it?"

"Set up a bath, a swimming pool and a sauna," Governor Brown said. "If you happen to have crewmen who want a bath, you can rent our facilities at the low price of fifty pounds a shot."

John snorted. There were crewmen who would probably take the Governor up on his offer, even if it was hideously over-priced. *Warspite*, like all starships smaller than fleet carriers, rationed water strictly, while the colony had an infinite supply in the nearby ocean. It would be the height of luxury to relax in a hot bath for an hour or two, even if it did cost an arm and a leg. Indeed, he was tempted himself.

"Not much to spend money on here," Commander Watson observed. "Or do you charge your own people to use the bath?"

"There's a rota for the bath and sauna," Governor Brown said. "The swimming pool is first come, first served. It's good for morale to have somewhere everyone can just relax and have fun."

He shrugged. "Everyone's salary is held in trust for them on Earth," he added. "It will either be transferred out here, once we set up a monetary economy, or they can collect it once they return to the home-world. There's no point in trying to charge for the bare necessities of life here."

John nodded. Some of the early colonies on Luna and Mars *had* tried to charge for oxygen and water, but it hadn't worked out very well. At least one colony had suffered an uprising that had shattered the dome and killed everyone. Eventually, once bioengineered grass had been worked into the settlements as carpets, the whole idea had been abandoned. Clarke III would hardly follow such a destructive path, certainly when there was no need to follow it.

"I can offer tea too," the Governor added. "They packed millions of teabags into the ship."

"There would be riots if they hadn't," John commented. "The Royal Navy *runs* on tea."

"So do us colonials," the Governor agreed. He stood, walked over to the rear table and picked up three china mugs. "I brought these with me, but someone will probably set up their own mug-producing system soon enough, I predict."

John nodded. Newly-founded British colonies had almost no regulations or taxes, at least in their first decade. Anyone who wanted to set up their own company could do so, without hassle, and trust to the free market to make their company work - or not. There were limits to what planners could do, after all, particularly once the colony grew large enough to require money. By the time the government finally started taxing the colonists, there should be hundreds of local businesses helping to provide jobs, services and other benefits for the newly-settled world.

As long as we don't wind up refighting the American Revolution, he thought. A number of hard lessons had been learned from the American War of Independence, but it was still hard to escape the conviction that the colonials should pay for their own upkeep. Several independent planetary development corporations had failed when it came to working out how their investment would be repaid. *What will happen when they decide they don't want to be taxed by Britain after all?*

He took the mug of tea, sniffed it carefully, then took a sip. It tasted of powdered milk and sugar, but he drank it anyway. Commander Watson didn't seem to notice the taste; like most engineers, she didn't seem to care what she ate and drank, as long as her body remained charged with energy. It was an attitude John wished he shared. He'd spent much of his adult life in the Royal Navy, yet he still appreciated good food and drink.

Or perhaps you're just fussy, he thought, remembering his mother's words. The strict woman had never approved of any of his tastes, from food and drink to boyfriends. *You were always the one to cut the fat off the meat.*

"We are planning to start our own survey work soon," he said, after he'd finished his ration bar. "Do you have any objections to us leaving within the week?"

"I believe that some of the freighter commanders may have objections," Governor Brown said. "But I have none, now we have our complement of shuttles on the ground. I assume *Canberra* is going to stay with us?"

"Yes," John said, flatly. "The Admiralty would prefer not to leave you completely defenceless."

"Far be it from me to disagree," Governor Brown said. "This world would be an excellent target for raiders."

John sighed. Pirates - independent pirates - were the stuff of bad fiction, not reality. It would be immensely difficult for any pirate faction to get its hands on a small warship, or even a combat-capable freighter, and then maintain it while raiding poor colonies at the edge of human space. They might make great villains for pro-Navy propaganda, particularly as the Foreign Office frowned on branding any merely human power a potential enemy, but they never really existed in reality. The closest humans had come to producing pirates in space had been during the Rock Wars, before the tramlines had been discovered.

But there was always the prospect of another power secretly sponsoring an attack on Clarke, aimed at removing the colony by force…

"It would be," he agreed. "We'll survey the nearest systems while the remainder of the freighters are emptied, then we can escort the three cargo ships back home. They'd be glad to get away from here, I expect."

"Probably," Governor Brown agreed. "I think their crews want more shore leave facilities than we have."

"But you have a *bath*," John protested, dryly. "And a *swimming pool*!"

"That isn't enough for them," Governor Brown said.

John snorted. The freighter crews would want bars, whores, games and beds, perhaps not in that order. Even Britannia or a mid-size colony would have a red light district, crammed with hundreds of places ready and willing to take as much money from spacers as they could. It hadn't been *that* long since John - and Colin - had sampled both Sin City and the red light districts surrounding a dozen military bases. The thought made him smile, then frown. He was supposed to be a responsible adult now.

And you had to drag people out of the bars, when you were an XO, his own thoughts reminded him. *There was no time to enjoy yourself after you were promoted.*

"They'll be due at least two weeks on Earth," he said. "And they will be paid a colossal bonus for their time."

"It never looks large from hundreds of light years away," Governor Brown said. He looked up as several colonists entered the room, looking tired and worn. "People are always more focused on the matter at hand, rather than the matter in the future."

"True," John said. He finished his tea, then glanced at Commander Watson. "Are you going to show us the rest of the colony?"

"Most of the rest is undeveloped," Governor Brown said, as he rose to his feet. "I'm nervous about the prospect of serious injury for my people, Captain. Our medical facilities are quite limited, compared to a starship or a proper hospital."

"And *Canberra* doesn't have a proper sickbay," John finished. The escort carrier hadn't been designed, originally, as a warship. Sometimes, that worked in her favour, but not always. A poor sickbay was the least of her problems. "We can probably lift someone to orbit…"

"While you're here," Governor Brown said. He led them through the hatch, then down a bland prefabricated corridor. "What happens when you're not?"

John hesitated. He knew that the colonists knew the risks, just as he'd known the dangers when he'd enlisted in the Royal Navy. But that would be no consolation if someone was seriously injured, perhaps even crippled, by something that could have been cured effortlessly in a proper hospital. There would be hostile news reports, public inquests, questions in Parliament and pressure for the BCS to change its ways. And it would make it harder for Britain to settle more colonies in a time of uncertainty.

"We can only do our best," he said. "I'm sure there will be more warships heading through this system, particularly once the cloudscoop is established. They'll want cheap fuel."

"True," the Governor said. "But I still worry."

John kept his thoughts to himself as the Governor showed them the remaining sections, then took them down into the underground tunnels. They looked to have been hacked out by pickaxes, although they had to have been carved by lasers, John decided; it would be years before the walls were smoothed out, then covered with something to hide the scars.

By then, there would probably be children growing up in the colony too. Quite a few of the colonists had been selected because they were young married couples.

And they will have less room to stray here, he thought, sardonically. *No one can keep a secret in a place like this.*

His wristcom buzzed. "Captain, this is Richards," Richards said. "An unknown starship has just entered the system through the Cromwell Tramline. One of our long-range probes picked it up."

John frowned. The Cromwell Tramline was alien-grade. A Tadpole ship? Another human ship from one of the major powers? Or what?

"Understood," he said, shortly. "We're on our way."

CHAPTER
SIXTEEN

"Report," John ordered, as he strode onto the bridge. "Do we have an ID yet?"

"Yes, sir," Richards said. He rose from the command chair, then nodded to the main display, where a blue icon was steadily approaching Clarke. "She's the *Larry Niven*, sir."

John felt his eyes narrow as he sat down. He knew the story; everyone did. The *Larry Niven* had been built by a commercial shipyard just before the war, then a salvaged alien drive had been bolted to her hull and she'd served as a transport during the latter part of the war. And then her CO and his crew had repaid their loan from the Admiralty, thanks to salvage monies, and taken their ship - and her alien drive - into civilian life. There had been people insisting the ship ought to be seized, John recalled. Common sense, thankfully, had intervened before snatching a ship without any real cause destroyed what remained of the interstellar economy.

"Ping her," he ordered. The *Larry Niven* was no threat - even if she had weapons mounted, she would be no match for a genuine warship - but *something* had made her travel the tramline from Cromwell to Pegasus. "Request she send us an update."

"Aye, sir," Forbes said. It would be nearly forty minutes before there was a reply, assuming it was sent back at once. "Message sent."

"Set up a tracking exercise," John ordered, as he prepared himself to wait. "We may as well learn *something* from her presence."

It was nearly fifty minutes before *Larry Niven* replied. "Captain," Forbes said. "They're requesting a meeting with you."

"Helm, take us out to meet them," John said. "Lieutenant Forbes, inform them that we are on our way, then contact *Canberra* and inform Captain Minion that we will be leaving him behind."

"Aye, sir," Armstrong said. A dull shiver ran through *Warspite* as her drive engaged, propelling her out of orbit. "ETA fifty-seven minutes."

"Message sent, sir," Lieutenant Forbes added.

John nodded, then sat down, thinking hard. What had happened to bring *Larry Niven* to Pegasus? Had they been exploring a new tramline, assuming they hadn't realised that Pegasus had been earmarked for British settlement, or had they expected to run into help? But there was no point in worrying, not now. All he could do was wait.

An hour later, Captain Peterson was welcomed onboard *Warspite* and shown into John's cabin. He was accompanied by his daughter, a fifteen-year-old girl who looked around with undisguised fascination, which the crew returned with interest. John sighed, inwardly, as Midshipwoman Powell poured them all tea, then retreated into her compartment. He had a feeling this discussion was not going to be pleasant.

"I'm surprised to see you, Captain," Peterson said. He was a tall thin man, his head shaved to the scalp. It wasn't uncommon among spacers, John knew; Peterson's daughter had only a thin fuzz of hair covering her head. "I was expecting to have to run all the way to Terra Nova."

"We only just started to settle the system," John said, shortly. He ran through the maths in his head. Assuming Peterson had intended to go to Terra Nova, it was quicker to use the alien tramlines rather than go the long way home. "I wasn't expecting to see you either."

Peterson settled back in his chair, then frowned. "I shall be blunt, Captain," he said. "We've been making our way around some of the newer colonies in this sector, including Cromwell. I don't know if you know, Captain, but the colony is in pretty dire circumstances."

"I didn't know," John said. Cromwell had been isolated by the war, he'd been told; it had only been a few short months since new colonists had finally been dispatched to the isolated world. "What happened, Captain?"

"From what I heard, the river burst its banks and drowned a number of farms," Peterson said, grimly. "And the new colonists, including a number of wives and children, have not arrived on the planet. The settlers are mutinous, sir. We were actually advised not to land by the Governor, once he had established that we weren't transporting families."

John frowned. "And did you land?"

"We thought about it, but decided it would be better to head straight for a settled world and request assistance for the colonists," Peterson said. "We weren't expecting to meet you."

"No," John agreed. He keyed his wristcom. "Mr. Armstrong, Mr. Richards, prepare the ship for immediate departure. We're going to Cromwell."

Peterson's daughter blinked. "You're going to help the colonists?"

"If we can," John said. He hastily ran through a mental checklist of what supplies remained onboard the freighters, but there wasn't anything that would be helpful on Cromwell. "I can't sit on my butt when civilians are in trouble."

"Thank you," Peterson said, before his daughter could say another word. "Do you want us to continue to Terra Nova?"

"Earth, if you can," John said. He reached into his desk, then produced a secure datapad and pressed his thumb against the scanner. "I'll write you an authorisation to draw on military supplies to refuel your ship, Captain. Is there anything else you might reasonably need?"

"I suppose there's a hidden charge here," Peterson's daughter said. "What do you want in exchange?"

John concealed his amusement with an effort. It wasn't an uncommon attitude; military forces had always been concerned about starships in civilian hands, particularly independent starships. They preferred to keep the ships firmly tied to the bigger corporations or shipping consortiums, even though independent traders helped keep shipping costs low. And Peterson had something just about every corporation would want, a starship capable of traversing the alien tramlines. They'd be happy to do whatever it took to lure him into their clutches.

"I will give you a copy of my report," he said. He wrote out the authorisation, then stuck a datachip into the datapad and copied it over. "If you deliver it to Nelson Base, Captain, I will consider it quits."

"That will be sufficient," Peterson said. "I take it there are no shore leave facilities in this system?"

"Only if you want a bath or a swim," John said. He smiled at their expressions, then shrugged. "I would prefer you to leave as soon as possible, though. You might be able to draw some new movies and audio tracks from the database before you go, if you wish."

Peterson's daughter looked up. "Do you have the latest album by Joan, Jane and Janice?"

"...Maybe," John said. "I'd have to check the database. There are millions of songs loaded into the core."

The thought made him smile. He had the distinct feeling that her father would prefer the answer to be a resounding *no*. Joan, Jane and Janice were best known for producing songs that were used as part of the Conduct After Capture course, before someone had pointed out that actually torturing the recruits was Not Allowed. Or so the joke went. John had heard enough of their music to believe the story, even though it was unlikely.

"You can wait until you get home, Sally," Peterson said. His voice hardened. "And Dave can wait for the latest *Green-Skinned Space Babes* too."

John tapped his terminal. Midshipwoman Powell entered the compartment, a moment later.

"Please help these two check to see if we have any new entertainment in the database," John said. If Peterson had been away from Earth for the last year, there was probably quite a few songs and movies he hadn't seen. "Then escort them back to their shuttle and inform me when they've departed."

He looked at Peterson as the older man rose. "I'll have copies of my logs prepared for you and delivered to your shuttle," he said. "Please hand them to Nelson Base, for the attention of the First Space Lord."

"Of course," Peterson said. "And I look forward to cashing in your datachip."

John nodded in understanding. HE3 was cheap, in star systems where a cloudscoop had been established, but it could be extremely expensive elsewhere. Peterson wouldn't have the chance to make additional money if he had to go back to Earth, so the authorisation John had given him might make the difference between going into debt or returning to the outer worlds, utterly unscathed. And Peterson would sooner crash his ship into an asteroid, John suspected, than go into debt.

He watched them leave his cabin, then keyed his terminal. "Commander Watson, Mr. Richards, Major Hadfield, meet me in my cabin immediately," he ordered. Thankfully, the Marines had returned from their latest exercise on Clarke III. "We have a problem."

The hatch hissed open two minutes later, revealing Commander Watson and Richards. Major Hadfield joined them a moment later, rubbing sweat off his face. He'd been in the simulator, John realised, feeling a flicker of guilt. Some people - even hardened Marines - had been known to throw up after being yanked out of the simulator without proper precautions. But there was no point in trying to commiserate. Hadfield wouldn't thank him for drawing attention to his problems.

"Cromwell has suffered a major disaster," John said, and outlined what Peterson had told him. "We will proceed immediately to the system to render what aid and support we can."

"Flooding," Hadfield said, when John had finished. "It's something we do have a considerable amount of experience in handling."

"True," John agreed. "But you only have a handful of Marines."

"I would prefer to evaluate the situation once we arrive, sir," Hadfield said. "Then we can determine where best to commit our support."

He paused, significantly. "I must warn you, however, that our ability to make an impact may be very limited," he added. "I was on the ground when the Tadpoles hit Earth. All of 47 Commando and a dozen regular units couldn't make much of a difference after the waves washed over the west coast, sir. The best we could do was get thousands of people out of the area before even the strongest buildings started to collapse. Cromwell is a great deal smaller than Cardiff, but we may not be able to do as much as you might hope."

"We'd be reassuring the colonists that they haven't been forgotten," Richards pointed out, thoughtfully. "If they're genuinely convinced they've been abandoned…"

"That might not help," Hadfield said, cutting him off. "You know 48 Commando lost the Deputy Prime Minister?"

John frowned. He'd known the Deputy Prime Minister had died in the bombardment, but he hadn't known how. At the time, he'd just assumed the man had been unlucky, like millions of others. Tidal waves were no respecters of persons, let alone rank and status. He could have been drowned, his body swept out to sea or lost somewhere in the reclamation zones dotted along the coast.

But if 48 Commando had *lost* him...

"No," he said. "What happened?"

"About a day after the bombardment, 48 Commando manages to set a refugee camp up on high ground," Hadfield said. "It looks like a detention camp, complete with barbed wire, armed guards and awful rations. They have to separate male and female refugees after a couple of unfortunate incidents, which really doesn't help civilian morale. The rain is pouring down like God's dumping buckets of water on our heads, their clothing is soaked to the skin and even the military-grade tents are leaking. No one is very happy at all.

"And then, along comes the Deputy Prime Minister, right into the midst of the camp," Hadfield continued. "A couple of the lads from 48 Commando have close-protection duty; they think it's too much, but the arsehole insists on going into the camp. And then, looking like a man who's never missed a meal in his life to people who have lost everything they ever owned, he starts wittering on about how they haven't been forgotten and how the government will help them, if they vote for him when the next election comes around."

He paused, dramatically. "And they lynched him."

"Shit," John said. "It was all covered up?"

"More or less," Hadfield said. "There were rumours, of course, but there are always rumours about what happened to missing people after the bombardment. The lads on close-protection were sharply reprimanded, I believe, but nothing else was said. I think the PM was probably glad to be rid of a liability."

"Probably," John agreed. Politics had never quite recovered from portable video cameras, worked into mobile phones or wristcoms. A recording of the Deputy Prime Minister suggesting that refugees should vote for him to receive help would practically hand the election to the Opposition. "And you think something similar will happen on Cromwell?"

"I think we need to be very careful," Hadfield said. "And we also need to avoid any suggestions that the colonists will go into debt because of a natural disaster. People with nothing to lose, sir, make the most dangerous enemies."

"I understand," John said. "Prepare your Marines for duty on the planet's surface, Major, and continue to monitor the situation. If you have doubts about sending them down, let me know and we can change our plans."

"Yes, sir," Hadfield said.

John turned to Richards and quirked his eyebrows. "I believe we can spare about forty to fifty crewmen, if necessary," Richards said. "Maybe more, if we are remaining in orbit around Cromwell, rather than exploring the system."

"Peterson said they lost a freighter," John said, slowly. Now he'd had a moment to think, he recalled the First Space Lord saying that shipping to Cromwell had resumed before he'd been assigned to *Warspite*. He'd have to check the records, which would be two months out of date, but he was sure the freighter had been dispatched. "And this freighter was meant to carry their families."

"Then they will be very pissed," Hadfield said, grimly. "How long have they been separated already?"

"Five years," John said, quietly. "It was meant to be five *months*."

He looked down at his hands, thinking hard. Naval service always meant long separation from one's loved ones - he'd been lucky; Colin had been assigned to *Canopus* beside him - and it could tear marriages and relationships apart with chilling ease. If a naval rating could lose his wife over a few brief months of being apart, he hated to think of what could have happened after five years of separation. Somehow, no matter how hard the Royal Navy tried, long voyages always ended with one or two crewmen being told that their partner had found someone else. It rarely ended well.

We ought to penalise the civilian partner, he thought. He'd had to talk one of his crewmen out of killing himself, back when he'd been an XO.

The poor bastard had come home to discover that his wife had not only divorced him, but remarried…and taken the kids with her. He had even been denied access to his kids, on the grounds that long separations from their father weren't good for them. *But it can be hard to make them suffer without hurting any children too.*

"Well, shit," Hadfield said.

John nodded. "Get your men ready," he said. "Mr. Richards, get work crews ready and start considering what they might need that can be drawn from ship's stores. If worst comes to worst, we'll bring in a couple of medics from Clarke."

"The Governor will love *that*, sir," Richards observed, bluntly.

"There's no choice," John said. "There's nowhere else we can beg for assistance."

He sighed, running through the calculations once again. It would take *Larry Niven* at least three weeks to make it to Earth, assuming nothing happened *en route*. If the Royal Navy managed to mount a rescue mission at once, which was somewhat unlikely, it would still take another month to get the ships to Cromwell, unless they used the alien tramlines. And even if they did, it would only shave a week off their journey.

"There's Boston," Commander Watson said, surprising John. "The Americans will help, won't they?"

"Boston is a small colony," Richards reminded her. "We can ask, but I doubt they have much to spare. And how would we get any supplies to Cromwell?"

John grinned, although he knew Richards was right. Boston was only a month or two older than Cromwell. The Americans would help, if asked - they had the same obligations as the other spacefaring powers - but they might not be able to do more than provide a handful of trained personnel. But he would worry about that problem when he confronted it.

"We *do* have three freighters with increasingly bored crews," he pointed out. "I'll order them to tranship supplies until one of the ships is empty, then it can be sent after us."

His wristcom bleeped. "Captain," Midshipwoman Powell said, "Captain Peterson and his daughter have left the ship."

"Good," John said. He closed the connection, then called the bridge. "Mr. Armstrong, set course for Cromwell and take us there, best possible speed."

"Aye, sir," Armstrong said.

John dismissed the others, then keyed his terminal to record a message. "Governor Brown," he said. "The *Larry Niven* has informed us of a major crisis on Cromwell. I intend to investigate and render assistance. Captain Minion will remain in command of the squadron until my return. Please empty one of the freighters - I leave which one to your discretion - and have it follow us as soon as possible. I will report back to Clarke before heading elsewhere."

He tapped the terminal again, sending the message. There was no point in trying to hold a normal conversation, not at this distance from Clarke. Besides, he needed time to think. If a freighter had gone missing, what did it mean? The long-predicted disaster the shuttle pilot had warned about, or something worse? There were too many possibilities and nowhere near enough evidence to speculate.

"Captain," Armstrong said, through the intercom. "We are underway and will pass through the tramline in thirty minutes. All systems appear nominal."

"Understood," John said. They'd tested and retested everything while they'd been lurking around Clarke, but they hadn't jumped through a tramline for weeks. "I'll be on the bridge when we jump."

CHAPTER

SEVENTEEN

"Jump completed, sir."

"Very good, Mr. Armstrong," John said. "I barely felt it."

"Thank you, sir," Armstrong said. "I was able to take Captain Peterson's records and use them to ensure a safer transit."

"Good thinking," John said, approvingly. "Take us to Cromwell, best possible speed."

He learned back in his command chair as *Warspite* swept away from the tramline. Long-range passive sensors revealed no sign of human presence in the system, save for the automated beacon orbiting Cromwell itself. Originally, the files had stated, Cromwell would have been provided with an orbiting station and probably some asteroid miners by now, but even then it had seemed unlikely the schedule would be kept. Cromwell sat on the end of a chain of tramlines; pre-war, everyone had thought the system only had one. And then the war had shaken up everything.

Poor bastards, he thought.

He shuddered at the thought. The colonists wouldn't have known a thing about the war until a freighter came calling, after the truce. They might have been surprised, one day, by alien ships appearing in their sky and dropping bombs, or they might have regressed to barbarism when it became clear they'd been forgotten. And there wouldn't have been enough of a balanced population to ensure their survival. Men outnumbered women by at least ten to one.

"Lieutenant Forbes, transmit our IFF to the orbiting satellite," he ordered, shortly. "Inform them that we will enter orbit in three hours and request a sit-rep."

"Aye, sir," Lieutenant Forbes said.

It would be at least an hour, John knew, before they received a reply. He forced himself to wait, studying the system as more and more of it appeared in the display. No one would have considered Cromwell a major find, were it not for the presence of a life-bearing world in the correct location. There were four other planets in the system, but they were all rocky: one comparable to Mercury, the other three comparable to Mars. Maybe there *would* be good grounds for blowing up one of the outermost worlds, he told himself, remembering the shattered moon orbiting Clarke. The Cromwell System had no asteroid belt and only a handful of comets, orbiting at a safe distance from the local star. Its economic development would always be hampered, at least when the colonists started moving into space.

But they also have the tramline to Pegasus, he thought, dispassionately. *They could earn a transit fee on every ship that passes through the system, while purchasing their fuel from Clarke.*

"I have the latest efficiency reports," Richards murmured in his ear. "Do you want to review them now?"

John had to laugh. Trust Richards to find a way to distract him from his worries.

"They can wait," he said. *Warspite* hadn't lost *too* much of her efficiency while she'd been trapped in the Pegasus System, thanks to endless drills he'd ordered to keep the crew sharp and alert. The internal shore leave rota might have been slimmer than anyone wanted, but it also ensured that everyone managed to get at least a few hours of downtime every week. "I don't have time to review them properly."

Richards nodded, then looked up at the display. Cromwell was growing closer, a blue-green sphere hanging against the darkness of interplanetary space. She looked very much like Earth, John thought, without the slender towers reaching up from the surface to low orbit, or any other sign of human occupancy. Most of Cromwell's surface was completely empty, at least of any higher-order life forms. The first settlers hadn't had time to expand before the war cut off any supplies from Earth.

They can eat the local animals, at least, he reminded himself. One of the reports had speculated that Cromwell's economy might be boosted by selling meats from native animals, although it wouldn't last. Someone would obtain live samples and start a cloning program, if the meats really took off. *They weren't at any real risk of starvation.*

"Captain," Lieutenant Forbes said. "I'm picking up a signal from the planet. The Governor is requesting you visit him as soon as we enter orbit."

"Good," John said. "Did he include a sit-rep?"

"No, sir," Lieutenant Forbes said.

John frowned. It was possible that the Governor was still trying to put one together - he couldn't have anticipated Peterson finding help so fast - but it was odd. Most colonies maintained a standard sit-rep for transmission to incoming starships, although he did have to admit that Cromwell's settlers had had other things to think about. He considered sending a demand for one anyway, then pushed the thought aside. There would be time to see the situation for himself as they entered orbit.

"Captain," Richards said, quietly. "We know nothing about the situation on the ground."

"I know," John said. He also knew what Richards was *really* trying to say. John was *Warspite's* commanding officer. He shouldn't leave her bridge, let alone go down to the planet, when the situation was so unclear. But he couldn't allow Commander Watson to go in his place, while anyone lesser would be considered an insult to the Governor. "I don't think I have a choice."

He keyed his terminal. "Major Hadfield, please access the live feed from the sensors as we enter orbit," he said. "I want your impressions."

"Aye, Captain," Hadfield said.

John forced himself to remain calm as *Warspite* drifted into high orbit, floating over the colony. It had been established by the side of a river - the River Fairfax, according to the map Howard placed over the images - which had quite clearly burst its banks. Large sections of farmland were covered in water, while buildings that had been noted the last time the Royal Navy had surveyed the system were gone. It was far smaller than the devastation along the Thames or several other rivers in Britain, when rainfall and tidal waves had made *them* burst their banks, but proportionally it was far worse. Large tracts of farmland had been completely obliterated.

"It might have been a mistake to build so close to the river, sir," Richards observed.

"You don't say," John said, dryly.

Offhand, he couldn't help wondering precisely *why* someone had built so much of the colony so close to a river. It was close to the sea and there *were* a handful of boats, clearly visible on the waters; maybe the original planners had intended the colony to grow into a harbour, as well as a farming settlement. But the rising waters had done immense damage to the small town. John had the nasty feeling that it was no longer a viable settlement.

His console buzzed. "Captain, this is Hadfield," the Marine said. "I don't think we can do much in the way of SAR, not now. This disaster happened months ago."

"It does look that way," John agreed. He thought rapidly. "I want you and a handful of Marines to escort me down to the surface. If there's something we can do to help, we can figure out what down there and do it."

"Yes, sir," Hadfield said. "Do you want to use a Marine shuttle?"

John concealed his amusement. Marine shuttles were piloted by daredevils, at least when compared to normal shuttle pilots. They had to be daring; they flew shuttles through incoming flak from the ground, dropped their Marines in landing zones that could turn hot at any second, then returned to their ships through another hail of incoming fire. But he'd been a starfighter pilot, back before the Battle of Bluebell. He had no fear of Marine shuttle pilots.

"I think so, yes," he said. He closed the connection, then turned to Commander Watson. "Once we get a list of supplies they need, organise them for immediate dispatch to the surface."

"Aye, Captain," Commander Watson said.

John nodded. In some ways, Commander Watson was the ideal disaster relief officer. She didn't allow emotions or political demands to get in the way of saving as many people as she could, even when she had to make hard decisions about abandoning some people to save others.

The post-war evaluation of the disaster recovery efforts in Britain had noted that too many officers had made the emotional choice, rather than the pragmatic choice. But it was never easy to condemn people to death, knowing that they might have a chance to survive with a little assistance. That way, madness lurked.

And how many of those officers, he asked himself, *committed suicide after the war?*

"Lieutenant-Commander Howard, you have the bridge," he said, as he rose. "Remain in contact with the away team at all times; in the event of something going wrong, take whatever action you deem fit, in consultation with Mr. Richards."

"Aye, sir," Howard said.

John took one last look at the orbital display, then walked down to the shuttle hatch. Hadfield and three other Marines, wearing rural combat battledress, were waiting for him, their faces under very tight control. John smiled, knowing they were anticipating watching a starship officer panic as the shuttle dropped through the planet's atmosphere, then opened the hatch and led the way into the shuttle. It was cruder than he remembered, but no one designed assault shuttles for elegance. They tended to be considered expendable by their commanding officers.

The shuttle disengaged from *Warspite*, then dropped rapidly towards the planet. John felt the hull shake violently as the craft hit the upper edge of the planet's atmosphere, then closed his eyes, concentrating on the sensations. The shuttle rocked from side to side, as if it had been slapped by an angry god, then plunged again, deeper into the planet's atmosphere. John smiled to himself, knowing that far too many officers would be trying to avoid throwing up by now. The shuttle pilot had the craft under complete control, but it sure as hell didn't feel like it. There was a final series of violent manoeuvres, one dull *thud* that echoed through the entire shuttle, then nothing. John opened his eyes and peered out of the porthole. They'd landed at the colony in record time.

"Excellent flight, Major," he said, as he unbuckled himself from the seat. "My compliments to the pilot."

"Thank you, sir," Hadfield said. He sounded astonished, much to John's private amusement. "I'll pass your words on to him."

John smirked, then stepped up to the hatch and out into the planet's atmosphere. The air smelled of brine, he noticed at once; it was cool enough, despite the water droplets hanging in the air, for him to smell the brine clearly. The bright sunlight illuminated a landing pad that had clearly seen better days, even though regulations insisted that colony spaceports had to be kept open at all times. But to dignify the complex surrounding him as a spaceport seemed an unthinkable exaggeration. It was really nothing more than a hanger, made from rotting wood, and a small metal fuel tank on the other side of the field.

"I've been in worse places," Hadfield said, as a handful of figures appeared in the distance and started to walk towards the shuttle. "And some of them were actively threatening."

John nodded as the figures came into view. He recognised two of them from the files - Governor Jim Baxter and Deputy Governor Murray Gamble - but the other three were unknown to him. One was a harassed-looking woman who seemed to have aged a decade in less than a month; the other two were older men, their hair rapidly shading to white. From the way one of them was limping, it looked as though he had broken his leg and had it set very badly. The colony had to be short of medical supplies by now.

"Captain," Governor Baxter said. "Welcome to Cromwell."

"Thank you," John said. He took a moment to study the Governor. His file had stated that he had experience on a dozen colony worlds, but he'd always been a subordinate. Cromwell was his first real command. "We would have come sooner, if we had known."

"I'm glad to hear that," the Governor said. "But tell me…was there really a war?"

His deputy snorted. "With *aliens*?"

"Yes," John said, quietly. "There was a war against an alien race."

There had been people, he recalled, who had frozen themselves in hopes that their terminal diseases could be cured, with the proper application of nanotechnology. Some of them had been woken up, just after the war, and hadn't believed in the Tadpoles until they'd met the aliens, face to face. He couldn't blame the Governor and his staff for having the same reaction. Aliens hadn't been part of the human experience until a mere five years ago. It wasn't surprising the Governor had taken the reports with a pinch of salt.

"That's...bad to hear," the Governor said, quietly. "If you will come with us, Captain, we can show you the city."

Cromwell City - it was really more of a large town - didn't deserve the name, John decided, after five minutes of walking. Most of the town was composed of wooden buildings, which had suffered badly in the wake of the flood. A number had fallen down, while others were clearly on their last legs. The handful of prefabricated buildings - and the modified dumpsters - at the centre of the city had held up better, but even they were streaked with rust and other signs of decay. If *he'd* been in sole charge, he thought, he would have moved the colonists to higher ground and abandoned the city until the planet was firmly under control.

"I meant to ask," he said, as they entered one of the dumpsters. The air inside stank, but no one seemed to notice. "Why did you build the colony so close to the river?"

"It was a compromise," the Governor said. "We managed to convince a number of folk from the outer islands to immigrate here. They would only come if we guaranteed them a harbour and somewhere to sell their fish. And we didn't have the resources to do both."

Fuck, John thought. A decision, made in the hopes of saving money, had managed to wreck most of the colony before the next wave of settlers arrived. *No wonder everyone's mad.*

"I shall be blunt," he said, once they were in the Governor's office. "We have one ship, a modified cruiser. How may we be of assistance to you?"

The Governor and his Deputy exchanged glances. "We need medical support, if possible," the Governor said, finally. "Most of the material that could be recovered from the flooded zone has been recovered. We may need help in moving it to higher ground, but that would take time to organise. How long can you spare?"

"And can you search for the missing colonists?" The Deputy added. "They should have arrived by now."

"They departed on time," John agreed. He knew they would have to search, once he had ensured Cromwell was going to survive, but he knew the odds of finding any of the missing colonists were very low. "But if they didn't make it here, something must have happened along the way."

"We would also appreciate a show of force," the Deputy Governor said, sharply. "There have been…rumours of trouble from the farmers, Captain. I would prefer to cow them before it's too late."

"That will do," the Governor said. "We can't blame the farmers for being worried, not now."

John understood. The farmers would owe debts to the colonial development consortium, debts that wouldn't be repaid unless they made a success of their farms. If the farms were now wrecked, the farmers would be faced with spending a lifetime in hock to the consortium or trying to repair the damage in the midst of a known flood zone. And most of their wives and children, who had been separated from them for the past five years, had vanished somewhere in interstellar space. It was a recipe for trouble.

But it's also a recipe for a long-term commitment, he thought. He couldn't spare his Marines - and even if he could, he doubted there were enough of them to keep the colonists under control. *We need another solution.*

"You may need to talk to the consortium and sort out a revised payment plan," he said, thoughtfully. "I don't think they will want to lose the investment completely, which is what will happen if the colony collapses."

"My superiors will not be happy," the Deputy Governor said. "Their investments have already been placed at risk."

So you're the one working for them, John thought. It wasn't really a surprise. The British Government might insist on appointing the Governor, but the consortium in charge of founding the planet had a considerable amount of influence. *But do you really want to lose your masters everything?*

He sighed, inwardly. Only one human colony had failed outright - even Terra Nova had successfully established a major human population on the surface - and it had failed through mismanagement by bureaucrats back on Earth. Even then, when the settlement rights had been sold to someone else, the planet had eventually become a success. But it remained economically poor…

"Send us your doctors, if you can, and manpower," the Governor said, breaking into John's thoughts. "We will use them as best as we can."

"I will," John said. Perhaps, if they made a determined effort to help, they could head off trouble before there was any need for violence. He could send a note home, requesting the Admiralty use its influence with the consortium. British security would be threatened if farmers were penalised for problems that weren't their fault. "And, once we are secure here, we will start looking for the missing ship."

The Governor's face darkened. "Good luck," he said. His voice was very grim. "But we all know the odds."

Poor bitches, John thought. *But we have to try.*

CHAPTER

EIGHTEEN

"What a mess," Percy commented.

The landscape below him reminded him of flying over the Forth River in Scotland, except there were no human settlements on either side of the river. Indeed, the only sign of human life was a sailing ship that had glided up the river, probably hunting for freshwater fish. It was beautiful, in a way, and yet there was something about it that bothered him. Few humans had set foot on the ground so far from the colony.

"There's the cause of the downfall, or I'm a moron," the pilot said, calling their attention forward. "There must have been some extra rainfall and the lake just overflowed its bounds."

Percy sucked in his breath as the shuttle circled the giant lake. The source of the mighty river was huge, larger than Loch Ness or any of the other lakes they'd used as training zones; indeed, it was easy to mistake it for an inland sea. But it was clear that the lake had overflowed six months ago, crumbling a natural dam and sending a tidal wave of water rushing down towards the sea, sweeping away anything in its path. Earth had suffered worse, Percy knew, but Earth had also had more resources to cope with the disaster. The colonists had very little.

"You could swim in this lake," the pilot observed. "Or set up an entire boating industry."

"I dare say someone will, once the colony is back on its feet," Peerce muttered. "Are you planning to settle here?"

"No, Sergeant," the pilot said. "But it might be nice to go for a holiday."

Percy shrugged. Ex-military personnel, particularly personnel who had seen real action, were in great demand on the colonies. If he chose not to renew his contract, it wouldn't be hard to find a colony world willing to take him, even pay a considerable salary if he wanted to work as a policeman or colonial marshal. But he wasn't sure he would want to live on Cromwell indefinitely. He enjoyed walking in the wilderness, climbing mountains and dozens of other outdoor sports, but he also liked the finer things in life. Cromwell was so primitive, in many ways, that it was unlikely it would develop an industrial economy any time soon.

"Take us back to the settlement," he ordered, pushing his thoughts aside. He had fifteen years to go, unless he managed to get himself discharged ahead of time. "We have work to do there."

His heart sank as the shuttle turned and rocketed back towards the nearest settlement. It was almost completely destroyed, with only a handful of buildings still standing. Even they were too badly damaged to be considered habitable; most of the settlers, he knew, had headed downriver to Cromwell City. Only a handful had remained at the settlement, doing what they could to rebuild.

The shuttle touched down, gently. Percy checked his weapons and equipment, then opened the hatch and stepped out onto the damp soil. It felt soggy beneath his feet, even though the flood had abated weeks ago. Months of hard work preparing the soil for farmland had been wasted, he suspected, from what little he recalled of geography class in school. A dull crashing sound caught his attention and he looked up, sharply, just in time to see one of the buildings collapsing into a pile of rubble. Beyond it, a pair of men in leather overalls barely looked up from their work.

"You'll need to ask them where to put the emergency supplies," Peerce murmured in Percy's ear. "If there's anything we can do for the people here."

Percy nodded, then walked towards the men as quickly as he could. Up close, he could see a handful of others, doing what they could to recover their possessions from the mud. Seven of them were men, he noted; only one of them was a woman, her face as tired and worn as her male counterparts. He'd known that most of the settlers were men, but it

154

was still strange to look at it in reality. Most colonies tried to balance the sexes evenly.

They did try to balance the sexes evenly, he reminded himself, sternly. *They just didn't have time to send out the women before the war began.*

"Sir," he said. "Where do you want us to put the supplies?"

The older man sighed. "Wherever you want to put them, son," he said. "We don't mind."

Percy sighed too, inwardly. He'd seen people like it before, back during the floods and tidal waves on Earth. They were too stunned to care about the future, their minds unable to comprehend what had happened to them. The settlers had endured the flood only a few scant months ago, yet even they had problems coming to grips with it. Just how much, Percy asked himself, as he looked towards the pathetic piles of debris, half-buried in the mud, had they lost?

"We're here to help," Peerce said, quietly. "I would suggest moving activities to higher ground."

"I'm sure you *would* suggest it," the other man said, nastily. "Where were you the night the flood came?"

"We're here now," Peerce said, his voice hardening. "How may we be of assistance?"

"Help us dig up the remains of the infrastructure and move them up there," the older man said. He nodded upland, towards a place that should be safe from the river breaking its banks. "And put any bodies you find over there."

Percy followed his pointing finger and saw a handful of bodies, all young men, lying on the ground. They'd need to be buried, sooner rather than later, but no one seemed inclined to dig a pit for the bodies. Perhaps they should be burned instead, he thought - in disaster zones, there was no time to do anything more than cremate the bodies as quickly as possible - but it would depend on what the locals wanted to do. They'd all have the full set of immunisation shots, making it harder for them to get infected with anything.

"We will," he said. "And we'll put the emergency supplies upland too."

The next few hours turned into a grim nightmare. There was no enemy to fight; the waters had already come and gone as the river burst its banks.

All they could do was recover what they could from the mud, then carry it up towards the nearest safe zone. Percy had his doubts about half of the wooden planks they recovered, but he had to admit they would make great firewood once they dried, if nothing else. Another team arrived and started cutting more planks out of the nearby forest, then massing them together to use as construction material. It looked as though the colonists hadn't given up completely...

...And yet, they looked *beaten*.

Percy had seen such looks before, on the faces of countless refugees on Earth. Indeed, if he hadn't been conscripted into relief missions, he might have wound up like the walking dead, the zombies who were unable to cope. But there was something about the colonists that was worse, almost. They hadn't just lost their homes; they'd lost their families and their hopes for the future. In a way, he would almost have preferred sullen anger. Anger was a dangerous emotion, he'd been taught, but it could galvanise a person into action. Apathy was far - far - worse.

"I think that's everyone who was unaccounted for," the older man, who had finally introduced himself as Greg, said. They stood together and looked at the fifteen bodies, lying on the ground. "There were a couple of others reported missing, but they turned up at the settlement down the river."

"That's lucky," Percy said. He would have expected some bodies to be washed all the way out to sea. "How do you want to bury them?"

"We don't have a priest," Greg said. "Perhaps if we dig a grave just above the waterline, we can place them there to return to the soil. We can mark the spot and hold a formal ceremony later."

Percy nodded, then issued orders to a couple of Marines. They hastily dug a pit, then carefully carried the bodies - one by one - up to the grave and lowered them into the ground, leaving them lying at the bottom of the pit. Percy couldn't help noticing that three of the dead bodies were younger than himself, while two others were the same age. Their lives had come to a sudden end, in the midst of the night. The others looked old enough to be their fathers.

He wanted to say something - anything - but he honestly didn't know what to say. All he could do was pick up a spade, then start shovelling earth back into the pit. The others joined in, burying the dead men below the soil. As soon as the earth had been patted down, a small stone marker was placed on top of the makeshift grave. The dead would remain there until they either rotted or they were dug up, then reburied in separate graves.

"They were good people," Greg said. He took a bag from one of his fellows, then produced an unmarked bottle. "They deserved better than such an unpleasant death."

Percy swallowed. Millions of people - perhaps billions - had died on Earth, after the bombardment. Britain had been lucky, in so many ways; other countries, more exposed than the United Kingdom, had been hit badly. To lose fifteen men from one tiny settlement seemed like nothing… and yet, proportionally, the settlement had lost more of its population than Earth. It might well destroy the colony completely, if law and order came apart at the seams.

"To the dead," Greg said. He opened the bottle, then took a long swig. "And to the living."

He passed the bottle to Percy. Percy sniffed it suspiciously - it smelled worse than military moonshine, which he hadn't believed possible - and then took a sip. It burned his throat as it went down and pooled in his stomach. He passed the bottle to Peerce as quickly as possible, fighting the urge to gag. Drinking had never been part of his life, not after his father had hit the roof after he'd been caught with a bottle of alcoholic juice at the age of thirteen. He still winced every time he remembered the lecture, and the hangover he'd suffered the morning after. He'd rarely touched alcohol since that day.

"Thank you for your help," Greg said, once everyone had taken a swig. The dregs of the bottle were poured over the grave, then the bottle itself was returned to the bag. "But I don't think you can do much more here."

"I know," Percy said. He looked over at Peerce, who shrugged. "We'll go down to the next settlement, but don't hesitate to call if you need us."

"We won't," Greg said. "And thank you."

Percy nodded, then motioned the Marines back to the shuttle. They hadn't done much, he knew, for all the time they'd spent at the unnamed settlement. But then, the settlement would be abandoned, left to rot away into nothingness. He hoped the new settlement would do better, even if the land wasn't quite as good for farming as the previous site. And yet…he shook his head. He'd heard too many mutterings from some of the farmers about help only arriving when it was far too late to make a difference. Cromwell needed more than *Warspite* could provide, and soon.

"I'll write up a report for the Lieutenant," he said, once they were back on the shuttle. "Please would you review it, once I'm done, and see if there's anything I should add?"

"Of course, Corporal," Peerce said. "But these people really need more settlers."

"I know, Sergeant," Percy said. He knew how to handle himself in a fight, either as a simple bootneck or local group leader. But he didn't know how to handle a natural disaster. "After this, how many new settlers will be coming from Earth?"

The sergeant shrugged, expressively. There was no way to know.

Percy had his doubts. Cromwell was quite some distance from Earth, even using the newly-discovered tramlines. It might be years before any new settlers arrived…and the Cromwell Development Consortium might have to make very extensive promises before it managed to lure thousands of newcomers to Cromwell, rather than Britannia or Oz or even Nova Scotia.

"They might recruit from Terra Nova," he said, thoughtfully. "How many people want to leave that shithole of a planet?"

"All of them," Peerce said. "But they won't get any government grants if they do try to recruit from Terra Nova. The government wants to get people off Earth, not Terra Nova."

Percy swore. He was right.

The next settlement was almost completely identical to the first settlement, right down to the dead bodies and the handful of survivors struggling to pull the remains of their possessions from the mud. Once the Marines joined them, the remaining bodies were discovered and recorded, then buried in another grave. The settlers themselves were planning to join the first settlement or head down to the city, whichever one seemed the better idea at the time. Percy encouraged them to join up with the first settlers, although it didn't look as though the settlers were listening. They'd lost almost everything in the floods.

"They're going to demand the government takes care of them," Peerce said. "And, when the government fails to do anything of the sort, there's going to be trouble. Make sure you put that in your report."

Percy nodded. Cromwell had no police, save for a handful of colonial marshals, and no emergency assistance service. There was no fire brigade or ambulance service; local problems had to be handled on the spot, while anyone who suffered a serious injury had to be moved from their settlement to Cromwell City before the doctors could have a look at them. He'd expected the settlers to be self-reliant - indeed, their training had been almost as intensive as military training - but none of them had planned for such a colossal shock to the system. It was hard to blame some of the settlers for wanting to give up.

And they're armed, he thought. Some of the local wildlife was dangerous - and had developed a taste for human flesh. *They could cause real trouble if they decided to fight.*

He frowned as the third settlement came into view. The sun was slowly sinking beyond the horizon, casting the planet into twilight, but he still couldn't see anyone within the settlement, or coming out into the open when they heard the approaching shuttle. He reached for his night-vision gear as the shuttle touched down, then stepped out, followed by four of his Marines. The settlement, as ruined as the first two, was as dark and silent as the grave.

"Remain with the shuttle," he ordered the remaining Marines. Something was badly wrong; he could feel it. "If we run into trouble, be prepared to render assistance."

The sensation that something was wrong grew stronger as they made their way into the settlement. Night was falling rapidly now - Cromwell had no moon to reflect light from the local star - and it was growing harder to see, but he couldn't retreat back to the shuttle. He switched on his UV lamp, knowing it would help him to see while leaving any potential enemies in the dark, and peered into the nearest building. It was a flooded wreck, and utterly deserted. Someone had stripped out everything from the building and then vanished into the countryside.

"They could have gone to a new settlement," Peerce suggested, as the Marines headed to the next building. "Only a fool would want to stay here after dark."

CHRISTOPHER G. NUTTALL

"True," Percy agreed. He peered into the next building…and froze. A handful of bodies lay on the ground, utterly unmoving. His NVGs insisted they had no body heat at all. "They're dead, Sergeant."

Peerce leaned down, examining the bodies. "Poison, I think," he said, as he switched on his flashlight. There were seven bodies lying there, some clearly having died in agony. "Note the discoloration of the lips. They took poison and died together…"

"There," Percy said. One of the bodies was holding a plastic bottle of liquid. A glance at the label told him it was poisonous, normally used for clearing away unwanted plant life. "They came here and killed themselves."

"A suicide pact," Peerce agreed. He looked up at Percy, his face grim. "There's nothing more we can do for them here, Corporal. We'll have to come back in daylight and bury them properly."

"We will," Percy said. He'd thought the apathetic settlers had given up, but this was worse. Far worse. Seven young men had taken their lives, rather than face the future. "Back to the shuttle, I think."

Outside, darkness had fallen over the abandoned settlement like a shroud. Percy couldn't help a shiver as they walked back to the shuttle, looking up at the night sky. It glowed with life, twinkling stars looking down on the hapless human race. There was no such sight on Earth, he knew, not when humanity had built so many cities of light. But here… there was something about the stars that cheered and chilled him at the same time.

He pushed the thought aside as they boarded the shuttle, then started the flight back to *Warspite*. There would be a chance to rest, then return to work the following morning. And perhaps they could make a difference, after all. They had managed to help some settlers, after all, even if it had been on a small scale. There was hope for the planet's future.

But it didn't seem that way, he knew. And others would definitely feel the same way.

CHAPTER

NINETEEN

Just stay still, Hamish McDougal thought, as the Dog-Thing came into view. *Just stay still and let it come to you.*

He braced himself as the Dog-Thing came closer, took careful aim and pulled the trigger. The Dog-Thing jerked, then fell to the ground. Hamish stepped forward, keeping his rifle pointed at the creature's head, just to make sure it actually *was* dead. He'd been surprised before, after encountering Cromwell's wildlife for the first time. The Dog-Things might *look* like dogs, hence the name, but their internal structure was very different. But, as he poked the body gingerly, it became clear it was definitely dead.

Good, he thought, as he hefted the Dog-Thing off the ground and slung it over his shoulder, then turned to walk back to the city. *There's good eating on these things.*

He hadn't intended to become a hunter, when he'd moved to Cromwell. He'd managed to get himself a nice little farm, along the riverbank, with a promise from the CDC of more land later, if he turned his first farm into a viable enterprise. And he'd worked and worked and worked, waiting all the time for his wife, until the river had broken its banks. Five years of work had been destroyed overnight, pushing him all the way back to square one. It galled him to know he'd wasted his time, but the thought of being in debt was much worse. The CDC was unlikely to give a damn about *how* he'd failed, only that he had.

And Gillian will be lucky if she gets her farmhouse after all, he thought. Once, the settlers had worked together to raise farmhouses, barns and shelters for their farms. Now, the colony's society had been badly undermined. *If she ever arrives, that is.*

The thought nagged at his mind as he walked back to the city. He'd left Cromwell City as soon as he could, when he first arrived; he'd only returned rarely, desperate for news from Earth. Now, the handful of wooden and metal buildings were surrounded by makeshift refugee camps, where hundreds of young men waited for the Governor to do something - anything - to give them a future once again. Hamish found it hard to blame them, even though the part of him that refused to give up hated their attitude. They'd been kicked so hard they wanted to be sure there were no further kicks before they returned to work.

But that's the one thing the Governor can't promise them, Hamish recalled bitterly, as he strode towards the cooking tent. *The CDC has yet to rule on where our debts stand.*

He cursed under his breath as he pushed the flap aside, then stepped into the tent. The cook - an older man who'd lost his farm in the floods too - took the Dog-Thing, then started to cut it apart for meat with practiced ease. Hamish had a feeling the cook wouldn't go back to his farm, even if all debts were cancelled. He'd lost too much to consider returning to the backbreaking labour that defined farming.

Poor bastard, he thought. *And poor all of us.*

"Not bad meat," the cook assured him. "You'll be eating the stew tonight?"

"Of course," Hamish said. It was lucky the countryside around Cromwell City teemed with game, or the refugees would have had nothing to eat. "Did you get your hands on any spices?"

"Only a handful of promising-looking seeds," the cook said. "But the doctors refused to clear them, so they may have to wait."

Hamish nodded, disappointed. He couldn't blame the doctors, though. Only a tiny percentage of the planet's native life had been checked and verified as safe for human consumption - and even some of the items regarded as safe could cause problems, if one ate too much of them. He still recalled a night of stomach cramps with horror, after eating something he hadn't prepared properly. He'd never been able to eat those fruits again.

"Brian was looking for you," the cook added. "Go see him, if you can."

"I'll go now," Hamish said. "Have fun with your Dog-Thing."

The cook gave him a one-fingered gesture, then returned to his work. Hamish grinned and walked out of the tent, passing the handful of cooking fires being laid for the evening dinner by the cook's assistants. Firewood wasn't a problem either, although it did have to be dried before it could be burned in the fire. He couldn't help wondering what would happen once they depleted the nearby countryside, but he doubted it would be a major problem. It would take years to cut down all the trees within easy walking distance.

Brian was standing outside a tent, addressing a small group of younger settlers. Hamish rather liked the younger man, although he had a feeling that Brian was more capable of acting impulsively than anyone would care to admit. On one hand, Brian had the determination to make something of himself that so many others lacked; on the other, Brian was reluctant to ever admit that anything could be his fault. And his wife, too, was missing. She should have been at the colony a bare three months after the first wave landed.

And God alone knows what's happened to Gillian, Hamish thought, as he nodded to Brian. *She was ready to follow us...and then nothing.*

There had been a war, he'd been told. Some of the colonists believed it, but others found the whole story impossible to believe. Aliens? Yeah, right; there was no such thing as aliens. A hundred and fifty years spent exploring the tramlines had turned up nothing larger than a cow, certainly nothing *intelligent*. Humanity was the one and only intelligent race in the universe, they insisted, with clear title to every star and planet it discovered. There were no such things as aliens. It was an excuse, a pathetic excuse, to hide the fact that the CDC had dropped the ball.

But Hamish wasn't so sure. He'd been born the youngest of seven children and he'd seen, all too often, just how easy it was to try to use an unbelievable lie. But they were simply never convincing; dogs didn't eat homework, not in real life. It was far easier to be believed if one kept the lie simple...and the corporate executives of the CDC would know that, wouldn't they? Why come up with a big lie concerning aliens when it would be far simpler to come up with a smaller one? There could have been a crisis that diverted shipping to somewhere else in the human sphere…

"You've all heard what *Gamble* said," Brian said, lacing the name with as much contempt as possible. "We will not have any of our debts settled; instead, we will be forced back to work as corporate slaves."

Hamish winced. Deputy Governor Murray Gamble was easily the most hated man in the colony, the CDC's representative charged with looking after the consortium's interests. It was something of a mystery why he'd got the job in the first place; there were days when Hamish wondered if he'd managed to offend someone higher up the corporate ranks, who'd sent him into permanent exile. But stopping all shipping to Cromwell seemed a bit excessive to get rid of a single man, no matter how annoying.

The crowd muttered their anger as Brian continued. "They've already told us a bunch of lies," he said, "and now they've brought the Royal Marines to force us back in line. I don't know about you, but I am not going to stand for it! None of us can be blamed for the flood, can we? How was it *our* fault?"

He was right, Hamish knew. The first anyone had known about the problem was when the river had started rising rapidly, breaking its banks and flooding the farms. It was, in the purest possible sense, an Act of God. But the CDC wouldn't see it that way. Every problem had to have someone to take the blame, particularly when large sums of money were at stake, and while Cromwell's settlers were poor, the CDC itself was rich. It would be a great deal easier to insist the settlers continue to pay their debts, rather than accept the loss of the money.

Bastards, he thought. *And Gamble sure as hell won't hesitate to make us pay, now he thinks he has armed support.*

"He's planning to use the Marines to ship us back to the farms," Brian continued, "even though the farms are drenched and useless. Once we are there, we will be separate and weak, unable to resist demands for payment. And they will even withhold our wives until we submit to them!"

Hamish sighed, inwardly. Brian had married just before the colony ship departed, to a woman too young to settle down. Hamish had taken her measure and knew the relationship wouldn't last, not on Earth. Five years…it was quite possible that Brian's wife had decided to abandon the colony mission, even if the stories of alien attack were untrue. She might not be on the ship when it arrived at Cromwell...

The thought caused him a bitter pang. *His* wife might not be on the ship, when it arrived.

But Brian had put his finger on a very sore spot. The colonists had been *chosen*, at least in part, because they were married. They had been told that married men and women would give the colony's early years a degree of stability, particularly as there would be fewer risks of men and women straying from their partners on Cromwell. Some of the colonists had even married quickly, just to ensure they were selected to go. But they had been separated from their wives, unable even to receive letters, for five *years*. Even the strongest marriage would have problems surviving such a long separation.

"We have weapons," Brian said. "Together, we outnumber the marshals ten to one. We can go to the Governor and demand a clear statement, right here right now. He has the authority to force the CDC to see reason, if necessary. We just have to give him a reason to use it!"

"At gunpoint?" Hamish asked. "Would that be legal?"

Brian snorted. "Do you want to spend the rest of your life a legal slave?"

Hamish shuddered. Brian was right. The original debts should have been easy to pay off - and would have been, if the river hadn't broken its banks. Now, if the contracts remained in force, it was unlikely any of them would be able to earn enough to either repay the loan or escape crippling penalty charges. By the time Gillian arrived - if she ever did arrive - he might never be able to get out of hock. And why bother struggling to build a life when he could leave nothing to his children?

"Then we go now," Brian snapped. He pulled his rifle from his back and held it up. "Who's with me?"

Hamish hesitated, then followed Brian and a line of armed colonists through the streets, heading directly for the Governor's office. The handful of people on the streets stared at them, then called out questions. When Brian explained what they were doing, the people either joined the growing crowd or retreated rapidly into their homes. Hamish couldn't help thinking of a riot he'd seen on a university campus once, years ago. There was an air of unmistakable violence in the air.

Two marshals stood outside Government House, eying the crowd with some alarm. Both of them had genuine military experience, Hamish knew, but they were also decent men - and they too had debts to pay off. Who knew which way they would jump?

"We're here to see the Governor," Brian said. "Please let us in."

The marshals exchanged glances. They carried weapons, both stunners and rifles, but they were heavily outnumbered and outgunned by the crowd. Hamish hoped - prayed - that they would do the smart thing and step aside. It was the only way to prevent bloodshed...

"The Governor isn't seeing anyone at the moment," one of the marshals said. He lifted an arm to block Brian's path. "He's trying to organise support..."

Brian punched him, hard. The marshal staggered backwards, then hit the ground like a sack of potatoes. His partner grabbed his weapon, but failed to draw it before the crowd roared in anger and lunged forward. He was rapidly overpowered, disarmed and left bleeding on the ground, as the crowd surged into Government House. The interior was darker than Hamish had expected - clearly, the Governor had sent his backup power generators where they were needed - but the crowd still had no difficulty in finding the Governor's staff. Three young women and two young men, all appointed by the CDC, were hauled out of their offices and dragged along by the crowd.

"Rape the bitches now," someone called, hidden within the crowd. "They deserve it."

"No," Hamish snapped. It was bad enough that two people had already been hurt. He was damned if he was going to allow five innocent people to be raped, then murdered. "We have to live with ourselves afterwards."

He glared a couple of protesters into silence, then followed Brian into the Governor's office, where Governor Baxter was seated in front of his desk. To Hamish's mixed disappointment and relief, there was no sign of the Deputy Governor. The bastard had probably heard the crowd coming and wisely scarpered, he decided, tartly. If *he* had fallen into the crowd's hands, it was unlikely he would have been allowed to survive.

And that would definitely have poisoned our relationship with the CDC, he thought. *They can't accept having their people murdered.*

"Well," the Governor said, into the silence. "What can I do for you?"

Brian's face purpled. "We want you to cancel all of our debts, produce our wives and send Gamble back to Earth," he said. "And get the Royal Marines off our planet."

There was a long pause.

"I can't do any of those," the Governor said. "They would all have to be cleared through the Colonial Office and the CDC."

"You have the authority," Brian snapped. "We didn't make the river flood and we're damned if we're paying for it!"

"That will be considered," the Governor said. "However, I do not have the authority to cancel all your debts unilaterally…"

"Yes, you do," Brian insisted. He slammed his fist down on the table, making a handful of people jump. "We are *not* going to lose our freedom because of your tight-fisted masters."

"We need hope," Hamish said, before Brian could shoot the Governor or do something else that would burn their bridges behind them. "Your Excellency, the situation we face, right now, is not of our making. We need you to make sure we are not asked to pay for having suffered a disaster."

"The agreement was that you would produce functioning farms," the Governor said, coolly. "If they are delayed…"

"The contract specifically states that there are penalty clauses for failing to produce a functioning farm on time," Brian snapped. "We cannot repair the destroyed farmland, nor can we afford to replace the equipment we lost in the floods. None of us have a hope of meeting the contract's deadline, *Governor.*"

"There's no hope right now," Hamish put in.

"And your fucking deputy is threatening us with the Marines," Brian added. "We're British citizens, not some tribe of wankers in Arabia who have taken hostages and are threatening to kill them…"

"You *have* taken hostages," the Governor pointed out. He held up a hand before Brian could say a word. "I understand that you have problems and yes, I understand that none of them were your fault. And *yes*, I will try to make sure you are not held to account for them. But - and this is a big issue - I cannot be seen to be bowing to force. Leave now and I will do my best to ensure that the contracts are either scrapped or extended to cover the disaster."

"That isn't good enough," Brian hissed. "Do you really think we would accept your word?"

The Governor met his eyes. "I have nothing else to offer," he said. "My authority is very weak planetside and non-existent outside the atmosphere. What do you want from me?"

"I told you," Brian shouted. His voice was breaking with frustrated rage. "We want the contracts torn up! We want our wives back! We want our freedom!"

The crowd roared its approval. Hamish watched one of the office girls start to cry and winced inwardly, cursing himself and the crowd under his breath. She was barely out of her teens, on her first posting; she was young enough to be his damned daughter. And now she was scared out of her wits by the crowd - and the threat to rape her. It wouldn't happen, he tried to reassure her with his eyes, but it didn't seem to work. How could it?

"And I can't give you those," the Governor said. "I don't know what happened to the freighter with your wives...the Royal Navy is going to search for them..."

"Then consider yourself removed from office," Brian snapped. He pointed his gun at the Governor's face. "We're taking over!"

The Governor rose to his feet with icy dignity. "Good luck," he said, as he was motioned around the desk. "And I hope you do better than I did."

Brian glared at him, then turned to Hamish. "Take the bastards into a side room and tie them up," he ordered. "They're our hostages."

Hamish stared at him. "Brian, if we do this, we're committed..."

"We were committed the moment we lost our farms," Brian snapped. "Win or lose, Hamish, at least we'll go down fighting."

CHAPTER
TWENTY

"Captain," Richards said. "We have a situation."

John cursed under his breath. The first time he managed to get a good night's sleep, after three days in orbit, and it had to be interrupted. He checked the chronometer and swore under his breath, then cursed again as he realised it was mid-afternoon on Cromwell. It might have been a mistake, in hindsight, not to set the ship's onboard time to match the planet's.

"I see," he said, as he sat upright. "What sort of situation?"

"A hostage situation," Richards said. "Deputy Governor Gamble is calling it a rebellion, but it looks more like a mere hostage situation to me."

Shit, John thought. He swung his legs over the bed and stood. Midshipwoman Powell had already entered his sleeping quarters, carrying a large mug of coffee. He gave her a thankful look, then took the mug and placed it by the side of his bed. There would be time to drink it once he had a handle on the situation.

"Details," he said. "What happened, precisely?"

"As far as we can tell, a crowd of colonists stormed Government House, such as it is, and demanded satisfaction from the Governor," Richards said. "When they failed to obtain it, they took the Governor and his staff hostage. Deputy Governor Gamble was at the Marine CP when the situation began and is currently safe."

What a pity, part of John's mind whispered. He'd met Gamble twice, since the first meeting, and the man had failed to impress him. Gamble was a corporate beancounter, not a visionary or even someone committed to the success of the colony. It was something of a surprise that he'd managed to last five years, with the colonists increasingly convinced they'd been abandoned, without suffering a horrible accident. Colony beancounters had been assassinated before. Terra Nova alone had accounted for dozens of them.

"Get Hadfield to give me a situation report, once I reach the briefing room," John ordered. He took a long swig of his coffee, looked longingly at the shower, then reluctantly pulled his trousers and jacket over his underclothes. His duty shift wasn't meant to start for another three hours; normally, he would have had plenty of time to shit, shower and eat a healthy breakfast before stepping onto the bridge. "What about our personnel?"

"Everyone is safe, as far as we can tell, but I've taken the precaution of calling them back to the CP," Richards said. "Better safe than sorry."

"Better safe than sorry," John agreed. Hostage situations were tricky enough at the best of times. They tended to be far harder to handle if there was an emotional connection between the hostages and those negotiating with their captors. "I'm on my way."

He splashed cold water on his face, then strode out of the cabin and into the briefing room. Richards was already waiting for him, while Major Hadfield's holographic face floated in the middle of the table. The Marine had refused to attempt to coordinate recovery operations from the ship, something that hadn't really surprised anyone. Marines hated the thought of remaining cooped up onboard ship when they could be out and about on the ground.

"Captain," Richards said. "Howard has the bridge."

"Good," John said. The last thing they needed was Commander Watson assuming command during a tricky situation. "Major. Report."

Hadfield nodded. "Sir," he said. "We sneaked a handful of bugs into Government House. There are currently eight hostages, including the Governor himself. They have all been tied up, then stowed in one of the storage rooms. So far, none of them appear to have been hurt, save for a handful of bruises. That may change, however, if negotiations go badly."

He paused. "I think there's a hint that some of their captors may actually be trying to protect the hostages from some of the other captors," he added. "But I can't be sure."

"Shit," John muttered. "And the captors themselves?"

"There's forty-two of them, mostly crammed into Government House," Hadfield said. "A handful are on patrol outside the building, with a handful of others taking up sniper positions in nearby buildings. I don't think they appreciate just how sophisticated our surveillance technology is, sir."

"It certainly looks that way," John agreed. "Now...what do they actually *want*?"

"We don't know," Hadfield said. "The Deputy Governor" - his face twisted in disdain - "believes they want the colony itself, that this is their first bid in an attempt to secure independence from Great Britain and the CDC. It might be true, for all we know; the hostage-takers have only said one thing, when they called the Deputy Governor."

John leaned forward. "And that was?"

"They want to talk to someone empowered to make decisions," Hadfield said. "The Deputy Governor flatly refused to talk to them, sir; indeed, he declared martial law."

Which he is entirely incapable of enforcing, John thought. Cromwell only had twenty colonial marshals, who would be heavily outnumbered by armed colonists. The Royal Marines from *Warspite* were more flexible, but even they would be outnumbered, if not outgunned. *On the other hand, most of the rebels are gathered in one place.*

"I see," he said. "Major, tell me: can you recover the hostages without losing them?"

Hadfield shook his head. "I wouldn't care to guarantee anything, Captain," he said. "They may be amateurs, but they haven't made any serious mistakes. I can guarantee to kill or capture all of the rebels, sir, yet they would have time to massacre the hostages before we could save them."

"Then we can't countenance a frontal attack," John mused. "There would be too much risk of losing everyone."

"Yes, sir," Hadfield said.

John thought, rapidly. The hostage-takers might not *want* to start hurting their hostages, but they would, if they felt themselves pushed against the wall. They'd committed themselves the moment they took hostages. Even if the Governor had been inclined to overlook the colonists forcing their way into his office, he couldn't afford to ignore the hostages. He'd wind up looking both weak and stupid.

And the bastards want to talk to someone with authority, he thought. *Someone who might be able to grant them what they want.*

He smiled, thinly. "I will talk to them personally," he said. "Have a shuttle prepared."

Richards and Hadfield both opened their mouths to protest. Richards won.

"Sir," he said. "I must remind you that regulations clearly state that the commanding officer of a Royal Navy starship may not deliberately place himself in danger."

"And we couldn't guarantee your safety either," Hadfield added, sharply. "They might take you hostage too."

John took a breath. "Can you suggest any alternative?"

"We can wait," Richards said. "They can't have been *planning* an uprising, no matter what the Deputy Governor believes. There's little food in Government House."

"I know," John said. "They will start to starve, which will make them only more desperate, more willing to harm the hostages. Or, if we allow this situation to go on, there will be other uprisings in the rest of the colony. And if we launch an attack, the hostages and many of their captors would be killed. Do you disagree with my assessment?"

"No, sir," Hadfield said.

"Damn," John commented. He looked at Richards. "If this wasn't a planned uprising, they might be as shocked as we are. There should be some room to talk before we have to consider force."

"I hope so, sir," Richards said. "But having you walk into their hands may encourage them to demand more."

"Risk is our business," John said, firmly. "I don't think Cromwell can afford a bloodbath."

He met Richards's eyes. "Mr. Richards," he said, formally. "You are to take the sealed orders from the wardroom safe and hold them in readiness. If they capture or kill me, you are to open the orders and declare yourself Captain. Major Hadfield and his men will back you up, if necessary. Do whatever you see fit to resolve the crisis, then return to Clarke and send a full report back with the freighters."

"Aye, sir," Richards said.

John scowled, inwardly. Commander Watson might not protest at having Richards jump ahead of her - he'd already taken over most of her duties - but Howard and Armstrong would certainly object, if they were given a chance. The First Space Lord's solution to his political dilemma involved subverting the chain of command; Commander Watson might not have been suited for her position, but she *had* it. And Howard and Armstrong were third and fourth in line respectively. Howard would make a good CO, John was sure, if he were given time, yet would he have the nerve to relieve Commander Watson?

This could get them all facing a court martial, John thought. Whatever the merits of the case, they would rapidly be buried beneath a morass of accusations and counter-accusations. *And they might even wind up in Colchester.*

"If you must do this, sir," Hadfield said, "I advise you not to go armed."

"I understand," John said. "I'll get on the shuttle in a few moments, Major. Until I arrive, picket the area, but do not make any hostile moves. And don't let the Deputy Governor do anything stupid either."

"He's already been trying to issue orders to my men," Hadfield said. "I had to speak to him quite sharply."

John groaned. No doubt the Deputy Governor would complain to his superiors, who would complain - in turn - to the First Space Lord. Or there would be questions asked in Parliament, which would cause problems for the Prime Minister…he shook his head, then rose. There was no point in worrying about it now.

"I'm on my way," he said. Hadfield had good reason to be irked. Issuing orders to someone else's men was a severe breach of military etiquette. "Hold the line until I arrive."

"Good luck, sir," Richards said. He rose, then snapped a salute. "Permission to speak freely, Captain?"

John's eyes narrowed. "Granted, Mr. Richards."

"Sir," Richards said slowly, "do you have a death wish? You could wind up giving them a much more important hostage than a planetary governor."

"No," John said, trying to keep his anger under control. He *had* granted permission for Richards to speak freely, after all. "I just see no other way to resolve this crisis, short of violence."

He couldn't blame Richards for being concerned. Captains were *not* meant to expose themselves to danger, not when they had expendable XOs under their command. But he couldn't trust Commander Watson to handle delicate negotiations, nor could he send Howard or Richards himself. The hostage-takers would probably regard sending a subordinate as a deliberate insult - or worse, a sign of fear or weakness.

"It has to be done," he said. He couldn't see any other alternative. "And don't fuck up, if you have to assume command."

He returned the salute, then walked down towards the shuttleport and climbed through the hatch. The pilot was already waiting for him, the engines powered up and ready to go. John sat back in his seat, buckled himself in and braced himself. The shuttle dropped away from *Warspite*, then plummeted through the atmosphere at terrifying speed. John forced himself to concentrate on the sensations, even though they were thoroughly unpleasant. It made a change from worrying about his fate, when he walked into Government House. The hostage-takers might simply shoot him on sight.

And that would cost them their lives, he thought, coldly. *The Admiralty would never let that pass, would it?*

The shuttle touched down with a deafening *bump*. John rubbed his ears, then got up and walked towards the hatch. The cool night air struck him in the face as he stepped outside, still smelling of brine and rotting wood. Major Hadfield was standing just outside the shuttle, waiting for him. He didn't look pleased.

"Captain," he said, stiffly. "The Deputy Governor insists on speaking with you."

"He can wait," John said. There was no time to reassure a corporate lackey. Besides, the Deputy Governor had declared martial law. The situation was in John's hands until he returned authority to the civilian government. "Has there been any change in the situation?"

"Not at Government House, sir," Hadfield said. "However, there have been movements around the various refugee sites. I think the hostage takers won't be alone for much longer, if they're alone now. Rumours are spreading rapidly."

He spat. "The Deputy Governor hasn't helped," he added. "He keeps going on and on about monies owed to the CDC. I don't think the rest of the colony will remain calm for much longer, sir. I've actually started plans to lift our personnel back into space. This place won't remain secure if they decide to attack it."

John nodded. There was only a single section - ten men - assigned to guard the spaceport. It was nowhere near enough men to do more than defend the shuttles as they fled, or die bravely if the attack was pushed hard enough. The thought of fleeing before a crowd of ill-armed civilians was galling, but it might be the only realistic option. He was damned if he was going to bombard the colony into submission.

"Act as you see fit," he said. He turned and looked towards the handful of lights in the gathering darkness, marking the location of the city. "Have you told them I'm coming?"

"Yes, sir," Hadfield said. "We called them on the telephone. They said they'd receive you."

"Then I need to go," John said. "Have two Marines escort me until we reach the edge of their defences, then I can go on alone."

Hadfield gave him a long sharp look, then saluted. "Hedrick and Abdul can escort you, sir," he said. He sounded reluctant to let John out of his sight. "And have a good one."

John felt his heart beating madly in his chest as he walked into the city, feeling darkness pressing around him as the last remnants of twilight faded away. Cromwell City looked eerie in the darkness; there were only a handful of lights, marking inhabited buildings. There should have been more, he was sure, but he had a feeling that much of the population was trying to hide. They'd probably seen countless movies showing assaults on terrorist strongholds in the Third World…and just how bloody they could become, if matters got out of hand. The fact that most of those movies were about as realistic as *Star Wars XXI* was neither here nor there.

They're propaganda, John thought wryly. It helped to distract himself. *They can't show British forces in a bad light, but they can paint the terrorists*

*as evil little shits. And, to be fair, most of them are evil little shits, or they
wouldn't have put their base in the middle of a city full of innocent people.*

He pushed the thought aside as a pair of figures loomed out of the
darkness. "The Captain goes in," one said. "The others remain outside."

"Wait here," John ordered the Marines, then stepped forward. "Take
me to your leader."

The two figures exchanged glances. Up close, John could see they were
desperately frightened, which could be either good or bad. Their clothes
looked to have been repaired once too many times, the original fabric
covered with patches and pieces of cloth from other garments. He would
have placed their ages at being in their mid-twenties, but they looked thin
enough to be much younger. It was quite possible their current diet didn't
include something important.

"This way," one of them said. He sounded like he was trying to be
firm, but he was too nervous to pull it off. "If you have a weapon, please
give it to me now."

"I came unarmed," John said.

His escorts weren't impressed. As soon as they reached Government
House, they pulled John into a sideroom and searched him thoroughly,
removing his wristcom and a small portable radio headset. They didn't
find any weapons, but they did insist on checking John's name and face
against the files in Government House, then carrying out an even more
intense and intimate search.

"You are planning to buy me dinner afterwards, I hope," John said.
"What sort of idiot would conceal a weapon down there?"

"I've seen weapons hidden there in the movies," one of his escorts
said. "Jackie Spring conceals a laser pistol in her cunt."

John rolled his eyes. "Jackie Spring is a fictional character," he said,
with heavy patience. He'd watched a couple of episodes with Colin, yet
once one got past the sex appeal there wasn't much else to attract him.
He could appreciate a female body, but he wasn't wired to find it attractive. "There isn't anything about her that is even remotely real, including
her breast size. They only show her hiding weapons up there so they can
attract the punters with full nudity. Or haven't you noticed just how often
she loses her clothes each episode?"

He snorted. "I would hate to sit down if I had a laser pistol crammed up my arse," he added, snidely. "It would be a very embarrassing way to go."

His other escort blinked in surprise. "You mean…naval crewmen don't lose their clothes on a regular basis?"

"*No*," John said, firmly. He tried to imagine his former commander's reaction to crewmen running through the ship, stark naked, then decided it would be safer to charge a terrorist encampment alone, without even a single pistol. "Nor do they have sex with everyone who shows the slightest bit of interest. Jackie Spring was created by someone who not only never served in the Royal Navy, but purposefully didn't learn a thing while they were writing porn with a bare hint of a plot."

"Oh," the escort said.

John straightened his uniform. "Now we have discovered that I have no weapons, and that Jackie Spring isn't actually real," he said, "take me to your leader."

CHAPTER

TWENTY ONE

John had had no time to skim through the CDC's files, so he had no idea who was facing him when he was shown into the Governor's office. One man, sitting behind the desk, looked to be in his late twenties, while another looked to be in his early forties. The former looked torn between determination and fear; the latter looked to have given up on all hope. Behind them, a handful of armed guards watched, equally torn between fighting and giving up.

Not hardened terrorists, then, John thought, in relief. It was impossible to negotiate with someone who had a Cause. *Just desperate men.*

"Thank you for seeing me," he said. "I'm Captain Naiser."

"Thank you for coming," the younger man said. His voice was a strange mixture of anticipation and fear. "At last someone is taking us seriously."

"You didn't give us much choice," John said. He made a show of looking around. "Are you going to give me a chair, or do I have to stand here like a boy facing the headmaster?"

The older man nodded, then motioned to one of the guards. He found a chair, then placed it in front of the desk. John sat down, then rested his hands on his knees and looked up. It was much easier to talk when he didn't have to stand to attention at the same time.

"So," he said, before either of the men could say a word. "What do you want?"

The younger man blinked. "What do you mean, what do we want?"

178

"You took Government House and seized hostages," John said, dryly. It was growing increasingly clear that *nothing* had been planned in advance. "I assume you didn't do it for shits and giggles, did you? What do you want?"

There was a long pause. "Several things," the older man said. "First, we want our debts cancelled. We didn't choose where the farms were built and it isn't fair that we should be plunged back into debt because of that poor choice."

"You did take out the debts with the intention of repaying them," John pointed out.

"Most of us were on the verge of repaying the debts before the flood," the older man said. "But if we have to start again, we won't be able to finish before we run out of time. Furthermore, we all invested heavily in equipment for our farms. Much of that has been lost or seriously damaged by the flood."

He had a point, John knew. And he wasn't unsympathetic to the farmers.

"I'll take that under consideration," he said. "Next?"

"We want the Deputy Governor gone," the younger man said. "This" - he waved a hand to indicate their surroundings - "wouldn't have happened without him."

"Probably not," John agreed. "You might have to put up with him until a ship arrives to claim him, though."

"Then at least he should be stripped of power," the older man said.

"Again, I will take that under consideration," John said. "Next?"

"Our wives," the younger man said. "We want them back."

John sighed. "I believe the ship left Earth prior to our departure," he said. "We do intend to search for them, once this crisis is resolved."

"The CDC is keeping them from us," the younger man insisted.

"I highly doubt it," John said, somehow keeping the sneer out of his voice. "They would have to be insane to even try. If the ship was reported lost in space, they'd have to pay compensation...and if they were caught trying to hide the women, they'd be torn apart in the streets. The Government wouldn't let them get away with it, not now."

He met the older man's eyes. "We will search," he promised. It was probably better not to discuss the odds of finding the missing ship, not now. "Next?"

"Full amnesty for everyone involved in this...protest," the older man said. "Things got out of hand, Captain; we understand that. But we insist on full amnesty before we stand down."

"And political freedom," the younger man added. "There are to be no attempts to break us up, disarm us or otherwise put the colony into lockdown."

That, John knew, wasn't possible. It would require hundreds of colonial marshals to keep the colony under tight control - and they simply wouldn't be provided. The CDC would have to offer enlistment bounties well above the norm just to raise a few dozen marshals, with shipping to Cromwell being what it was. It was quite possible the beancounters would refuse to pay, choosing instead to come to terms with the colonists.

But they might well try to interfere with the colony in other ways. Weapons had to be shipped from Earth, after all, while there was only a small ammunition plant on the planet's surface. There were plenty of ways to impede the colonials from stocking up on weapons without doing anything overt. Hell, it was hard enough getting export licences for anything heavier than a hunting rifle, even in the best of circumstances.

"I see," he said. "Are those all of your demands?"

"Yes, Captain," the older man said. "Can you grant them?"

John smiled. "The Deputy Governor declared martial law," he said. "I have wide authority to handle the crisis as I see fit."

He paused. "There's also the very real prospect of you being able to sue the CDC," he added, carefully. "It's quite clear that the local survey work was botched. We inspected the great lakes to the south and...well, the flood was an accident waiting to happen."

The older man snorted. "The CDC has money, lawyers and political connections," he said, darkly. "How could we file a lawsuit against them? We can't even get back to Earth!"

John smiled. "First, you could send the papers back with us, or another freighter," he said, flatly. "You would not need to rely on one of their ships. Second, the government is trying to get as many people away from Earth as it can. I don't think there would be any great enthusiasm for allowing the CDC to publically screw the first wave of colonists. And yes, that is what they'd be trying to do, if they fought."

He looked from one to the other, trying to gauge their thoughts. The older man was looking for a way out; the younger man, more stubborn, wanted to fight. He didn't trust John, or the Governor, or the CDC. And, John had to admit, it wasn't an unreasonable attitude.

"This is what I propose," John said, carefully putting the pieces together in his mind. "Your debts will be cancelled as compensation for the botched survey work. You will have first call on new farmland, but you will have to take out new loans if you want to purchase newer pieces of equipment from Earth. The CDC will not, I suspect, send them to you for free, even if you do have a valid claim."

The younger man frowned. "Then why should we take the deal?"

"Because the CDC would try to fight it through the courts," John said. "It might be years before the matter was resolved, with no guarantee it would be resolved in your favour."

"But you just said the government would not be happy with the CDC," the younger man objected. "Or were you lying to us?"

"The government would certainly bring pressure to bear against the CDC," John said. "But their pressure might not be effective. This way, both sides get to cut their losses and trade claim for claim. More to the point, you could take out new loans at once and have equipment shipped to you."

"I see your point," the older man said.

"Good," John said. "Second, as I said, we will search for the missing freighter. I can't promise anything, but we will definitely look."

"Aye, right," the younger man said.

John ignored him. "The issue of amnesty is likely to be a problem," he warned. "I do understand your situation, but you did step well over the line. I would therefore propose that each of you involved in this… protest…do a day's worth of community service every month for the next two years."

"Outrageous," the younger man thundered.

"It's more than generous," John said, coolly. "These are not the days of social decay, young man. Political protest is one thing, but committing crimes in the name of protest doesn't give you a free pass. On Earth, you would be looking at two to three years in a work gang, with only one day of rest a week. Like it or not, you took aim at the very foundations of society when you launched your protest. There has to be some form of punishment."

"And if we hadn't," the younger man snapped, "would we have attracted your attention?"

Probably not, John thought. *But now you have it, I have to think of a way to resolve this crisis without violence.*

"One question," the older man said. "Do you have the authority to grant all this?"

"Yes," John said, flatly.

The older man held up a hand before his companion could say a word. "We would like to discuss this in private," he said. "If you would wait in the next room…"

John rose, then allowed his escorts to take him into the next room. It was a barren storage compartment, completely empty. He leaned against the wall and waited, knowing that matters were now out of his hands. If the older man convinced the younger to give in, the crisis could be resolved peacefully…but if not, there would be no choice but to use deadly force. And that would leave a number of people dead in its wake. It was quite possible that John might be among the dead by the end of the day.

You knew the job was dangerous when you took it, he told himself, firmly. *And you knew you had very little choice.*

———

Hamish urged the rest of the guards out of the office, leaving him and Brian alone. "We need to take the offer," he said, once the door had slammed shut. "We're not going to get a better one."

"But…they might cheat us," Brian whined. He didn't sound willing to compromise. "Or stick a knife in our backs."

"Yes, they might," Hamish agreed. The problem with any agreement, as far as he could see, was that the colonists had no way to enforce it. He could follow the Captain's logic - the CDC would want the problem to go away as quickly as possible - but, at the same time, he knew they were giving up too many of their bargaining chips. "However, the only other option is to fight."

"We have weapons," Brian said. He tapped the rifle slung over his shoulder meaningfully. "We *can* fight."

Hamish sucked in his breath. "Brian, *listen* to me," he said. "We're trapped in this dumpster, with only a handful of entrances and exits. The Royal Marines can take us by force, if they want, or simply drop a KEW on our heads. There isn't much point in preserving the remains of the city, is there? Half of the buildings around us will have to be knocked down anyway in the very near future."

"They'd kill people," Brian protested. "British citizens. They wouldn't do that!"

"They could also evacuate the city under cover of darkness," Hamish said. He glanced at his watch, meaningfully. "It's night now, Brian, and we don't have any night-vision gear. They could be moving half the population now and we wouldn't know a thing about it. Tomorrow…perhaps the last thing we'll hear is the sound of a KEW falling through the atmosphere before it blows Government House into a crater. There is no way out."

"We could sneak out under cover of darkness," Brian said.

"The Marines *do* have night-vision gear," Hamish reminded him. He'd heard that the Marines had continued recovery work, even in the dead of night. "They'd see us crawling out and open fire. There's no way to escape, save coming to what terms we can."

He softened his voice, trying to reach the younger man. "We can't hope for better terms," he added. "If they break their word, then we can consider taking steps. Until then, perhaps we should be grateful it has worked out as well as it has."

Brian nodded, reluctantly. "Very well," he said. "But what can we do for community service?"

Hamish shrugged. "Dig ditches, perhaps," he said. The colony wasn't old enough to evolve a monetary economy. Tasks like barn-raising were shared among the men, who would assist their fellows in exchange for assistance for themselves. "It would be a great deal worse on Earth."

"I know," Brian said. "The Troubles saw to that, didn't they?"

The Troubles were a sore spot, Hamish knew. Academics and historians were ambient about the Troubles - and about how they'd ended. Was the heavy repression, a return to older values, justified? Or had it merely been the first step towards a home-grown tyranny that would have matched Hitler, Stalin or Perrine? But, whatever else the government of the day had done, they'd restored law and order to British streets.

But it came with a price, he thought. *Political protest became much more restrained. And so did freedom of thought.*

"Then we concede," Hamish said. "We'll speak to the others, then talk to the Captain. And end this before something goes badly wrong."

Brian snorted. "You mean it hasn't already?"

———

They'd taken his wristcom, but John had always been skilled at tracking the passage of time without one. It was nearly an hour before they opened the door and invited him out of the tiny room, then into the Governor's office. This time, the guards had been dismissed; he was facing only the two leaders. John nodded to them both, then sat down without waiting to ask for permission. His legs were cramping uncomfortably.

"We have decided to accept your terms," the older man said. "If you will tell your Marines to fall back, we will evacuate the dumpster and let you have the hostages."

"Thank you," John said, briskly. "I will ensure the Governor signs off on the deal."

"The Deputy Governor will be a pain in the arse about it," the younger man muttered, sullenly. "He won't sign anything."

"Yes, he will," John said. The colony was still under martial law. He could take the Deputy Governor off-world, if necessary. "I'll see to it."

"Right," the younger man said. He lowered his voice. "Is it really true?"

John frowned. "Is *what* true?"

"The war," the younger man said. He sounded as if he was afraid of being laughed at, as if he thought he was talking nonsense. "Was there really a war against an alien race?"

"Yes," John said. "I fought in it. My…my lover died fighting the enemy. Earth itself was bombarded and millions of people died. The universe changed forever."

"I didn't believe it," the younger man said. He shook his head in disbelief. "It still seems impossible to grasp."

"I can show you records," John said. "Everything from Vera Cruz and the Battle of Earth to the final battle at New Russia and the death of *Ark Royal*. Or reports on the Tadpoles and their biology, if you wish. I dare say you might even meet a Tadpole one day."

"And so our wives were held back," the older man said, sadly. "When do you plan to go in search of them?"

"Tomorrow," John said. "I'll get my crew back to the ship, then leave the system for Troyon, Spire and Boston. The Yanks will certainly be able to tell us if the transport ship passed through their system."

"They might have seized the ship," the younger man muttered.

"I doubt it," John said. He couldn't imagine the Americans bothering, not when there wouldn't have been any cause. Hell, the freighter would merely have slipped through their system without docking at the orbital station. "It would be an act of war."

He stood. "Bring in the hostages, then have your men ready to march out," he ordered. "And have my wristcom returned. I'll need to inform the Marines to expect them."

The two men exchanged glances, then hurried to do as he said. John inspected the hostages as they were brought into the room, looking for evidence of serious injuries or assault. The colonial marshals had some nasty bruises, but the remainder looked unharmed, at least physically. John knew they would have problems, in the future, coming to terms with the experience. It had turned their world upside down.

"Captain," the Governor said. " How can I thank you?"

"You can sign off on the agreement," John said, bluntly. The Deputy Governor couldn't override his superior, even if he did work directly for the CDC. Somehow, he doubted the British Government would overrule one of its own Governors. "And then you can make sure it is implemented."

"Of course," the Governor said, once John had outlined it for him. "It should solve the problem neatly."

John shrugged. "You should have done it just after the floods," he said. "I understand why you didn't, but you should have done. It would have saved a great deal of trouble."

He recovered his wristcom, then called Hadfield. The Marines would know about the agreement already, thanks to the bugs, but he knew Hadfield wouldn't move without orders. Once the vast majority of the hostage-takers were out of the dumpster, the Marines could move in and secure the building, then tend to the former hostages.

"Keep Gamble at the CP," he finished. The last thing he needed, right now, was for Gamble to start threatening to repudiate the agreement. It would only provoke another uprising at the worst possible time. "I'll wait for the medics here."

CHAPTER
TWENTY TWO

"Absolutely out of the question!"

John sighed as the Deputy Governor spun around to face his superior. "Governor, we are not obliged to accept agreements made under duress," he snapped. The Governor's office echoed with his voice. "There is no way this...*agreement* will be accepted by the consortium!"

"It will be," the Governor said. "I do not believe there is any other solution to our problem."

"They signed the contracts," the Deputy Governor thundered. He turned to glare at John. "Use force! Make the rabble obey!"

John somehow managed to keep his voice calm. "I have twenty-two Marines under my command," he said. "That is nowhere near enough Marines to keep control over a small town, let alone an entire colony. All I could do would be to apply punitive strikes, which would be of only limited value when the colonists could simply vanish into the undergrowth and hide indefinitely. The exercise would be pointless."

"You have other crew on your ship," the Deputy Governor insisted.

"If I stripped out every man who was qualified to fire a heavy weapon," John said evenly, "I would have only the bare-bones of a skeleton crew, while I still wouldn't have enough men on the ground to hold the colony. The only way to force them to go back to work, as you put it, would be to ship in a large garrison and, I assure you, there would be no political enthusiasm for such a deployment. There are too many calls on the army's manpower back home on Earth."

"Be reasonable," the Governor said. "Or do you want another riot just after the warship leaves?"

"This wouldn't have happened if you'd clamped down at the start," the Deputy Governor insisted. "I…"

John cut him off. "If the survey team had done a better job, the flooding could have been avoided," he said. "If the war hadn't broken out, their wives and children could have been shipped to them before they started to feel cheated and alone. If…but there's no point in focusing on what might have been. All we can do is deal with the situation as it stands."

He came to a decision and sighed, then looked at the Governor. "With your permission, sir, I would like to take Deputy Governor Gamble with me when I depart," he said. "I do not feel the peace of the colony would be enhanced by his presence."

The Deputy Governor stared at him. "You're…*arresting* me?"

"If you want to look at it like that," John said, evenly.

"This is outrageous," the Deputy Governor snapped. "You do not have the authority to drag me off this world!"

"But I have the authority to expel you," the Governor said. "I know, I know, you have stock options and interests that force you to take a hard line. You want that seat on the board and it will only come if you make Cromwell a success. But you've threatened any real chance of actual success, Murray, and I can't risk you doing any further damage."

He looked at John. "Captain, I would be pleased if you would take him with you when you go."

"Of course," John said.

He called one of the Marines and ordered him to escort the Deputy Governor to pack a small bag, then take him to the spaceport. If Gamble refrained from causing trouble, he could have one of the small cabins set aside for guests; if not, there was always the brig. John considered putting him in the brig anyway, without waiting for problems, but dismissed the thought. It was going to be hard enough convincing the Admiralty to support him without adding mistreatment of a semi-prisoner to the list of problems.

"Well," the Governor said, when they were alone. "It seems I have good reason to thank you."

"It's all in a day's work," John said. "And besides, we sorted out a problem that could have grown into a nightmare."

"So you did," the Governor agreed. "Is there anything we can do for you?"

"No, thank you," John said. Normally, they would have asked for fresh food and drink, but Cromwell was in no condition to provide anything. The Marines had shot some examples of the local wildlife for the mess and that would have to do. "Just make sure you support us when the CDC starts making a fuss."

"Of course," the Governor said. He smirked. "I've been thinking about retirement anyway."

They shook hands, then John walked back to the spaceport, followed by a couple of Marines. It might have been his imagination, he thought, but the city seemed more...optimistic somehow, now that the agreement between the Governor and the farmers was public knowledge. John only hoped it would last, once the hard work of repairing the damage began. Even without their old debts, the farmers were still having to redo their work...and their wives and children were still missing.

It might be time to start searching for replacements, John thought. There was no shortage of unmarried women who might accept passage to Cromwell, on the understanding that they would marry a farmer at the far end. Some of them wanted to be farmers themselves, others thought they had no hope of finding a proper job. *But they have their hearts set on the women they married.*

He laughed at himself, bitterly. *And if Colin was still alive*, his own thoughts mocked him, *would you want Colin or some random bloke off the street?*

Hadfield met him by the remains of the CP. "Everyone is either here or in orbit, sir," he said, with brisk efficiency. "No one seems to have deserted."

"Good," John said. Desertion was rare, but it did happen. "I don't think anyone would want to desert here."

"I don't know, sir," Hadfield said. "Several crewwomen got propositioned pretty damn badly while they were on duty. This place is *very* short of single women."

"As long as they don't try to leave before their contracts expire, I don't mind," John said, dryly. "I assume they all made it back without incident?"

"Yes, sir," Hadfield said. "There were no problems."

John nodded, then turned towards the shuttle. "Then let's go," he said. "And see if we can find the missing women and children."

He sobered as they walked into the shuttle. No matter how he looked at it, he knew the odds of actually finding the missing ship were terrifyingly low. Ships had vanished before, even warships; there was a whole string of missing ship reports that had never been satisfactorily explained. Some ships might have been jumped by the Tadpoles, in the opening days of the war, but others had vanished a long way from alien space. Maybe it had been a life support crash, he thought, or maybe something more sinister. But there was no way to know.

"Take us back to the ship," he ordered. He keyed his wristcom as the shuttle powered up its drives. "Mr. Richards, assemble the senior officers in the briefing room once I arrive. We have a search to plan."

———

"I can't say it is going to be very easy," Armstrong said, once Midshipwoman Powell had finished distributing mugs of tea and coffee. "We know *Vesper* passed through the Terra Nova System - we have it logged by the naval base - but after that, nothing. There are seven separate systems where something could have happened to her."

John nodded, studying the holographic starchart. In some ways, the task looked simple; *Vesper,* unable to transit alien-grade tramlines, couldn't have altered her planned course. But any spacer knew that each of the icons on the display marked an unimaginably huge area of space, with even the largest fleet carrier smaller than a needle in a haystack. If *Vesper* had drifted off her planned route, there was little hope of finding her.

We have to try, he thought, grimly. *I am damned if I am not making an effort, even if it is foredoomed to failure.*

"With that in mind," he said, "how do you propose we proceed?"

Armstrong swallowed, then looked at the chart. "I propose we attempt to hail her in both Troyon and Spire," he said, "but continue towards

Boston. The Americans will be able to tell us if *Vesper* passed through their system. If so, we know that whatever happened had to have happened in either of the empty systems."

"Good thinking," John said. He focused the display on Troyon and Spire. "Troyon has at least one tramline that has never been properly explored, while Spire has an unclaimed Mars-like world. There might well be a hidden colony there, one that snatched *Vesper* for breeding stock."

Hadfield looked doubtful. "Do you think that's possible, sir?"

"There were several attempts to set up hidden colonies during the war," John reminded him. "Spire might be a good candidate, if the colonists thought they were desperate. There's even less there to attract the Tadpoles than a human power."

"Dry and cold," Richards mused. "They would probably simply ignore the world, if they thought it was valueless."

John shrugged. Hadfield was right to doubt. It was unlikely that any survivalist colony would risk its privacy by snatching an entire freighter. But if they thought there was a desperate need for breeding stock - and there had been over two thousand women and children on *Vesper* - they might have taken the gamble. Given enough time and preparation, it wouldn't have been *that* hard to keep the captives under control.

But it was the most optimistic scenario, he knew. The worst was never knowing what had happened to the freighter and her crew, let alone her passengers. There would never be any closure for their husbands and fathers, just...an endless barren emptiness. John had known that Colin was dead; he'd come to terms with it, somehow. None of the fathers on Cromwell would ever be able to say the same.

We have to try, he reminded himself.

He looked at Hadfield. "I assume our unwelcome guest is stowed away?"

"He was complaining about the cabin when we left him, sir," Hadfield said. "Apparently, there isn't enough room to swing a cat."

John smiled. The only officer on the ship who had a larger cabin was himself. "Tell him that they're the best we can provide," he said. "And that he will be expected to take meals with the officers. Or starve."

"Aye, sir," Hadfield said.

"We will depart in two hours," John said, rising. "Mr. Armstrong, plot out a least-time course from here to Boston. We will transmit hails in both Troyon and Spire, but we need to check with Boston ASAP. You can also plot out a search pattern for both systems, as well as the unexplored tramline. If *Vesper* passed through Boston, we will need to double-back to Spire and start our search."

"The Americans may be able to help," Richards observed. "Do they have a ship on station?"

"Not according to the last intelligence report," Howard warned. "They're as concerned as we are with fortifying all the systems between Earth and Tadpole space. Smaller colonies like Boston will have been largely left to their own devices."

He shrugged. "It's a larger colony than Cromwell, sir, but it isn't *that* much larger," he added. "I don't think they have anything tramline-capable on permanent station."

"Wait until we have a miniature Puller Drive," Commander Watson said, suddenly. "It will allow us to deploy more courier boats in each settled system."

John blinked. Commander Watson was normally content to keep her mouth shut in staff briefings. Unlike almost any other officer he knew, she hadn't said a word about losing most of her responsibilities to Richards. He wished he knew if she was grateful someone else had taken them, which was possible, or if she hadn't realised she had them in the first place. Neither option was particularly reassuring…

"Dismissed," he said. "Commander Watson, remain behind."

He clicked off the holographic display as the compartment emptied, then swung round to face her. "I meant to ask," he said. "How are you coping with your current workload?"

"I am designing the next set of modified drive units," Commander Watson said. "The calibration shock we experienced the first time we used the drive can be prevented by creating a modified drive matrix that automatically adjusts itself to the tramline…"

"English, please," John said, hastily.

Commander Watson didn't smile. "Imagine each tramline as a lock," she said. "The pre-war drives used brute force to break through the lock, allowing access. But the alien drives have to be adapted to actually *fit* the lock or they have unpleasant side effects. My modified drive matrix will allow the key to automatically fit the lock, without the need for long calibration and recalibration."

"A skeleton key," John said, slowly.

"Basically, yes," Commander Watson said. "Indeed, I may have cracked the math that would allow us to form the key without the lock."

John stared at her, feeling his mouth hanging open. "Genuine FTL?"

"Yes," Commander Watson said. "However, the power requirements are staggering. I believe that even the *Theodore Smith*-class of carriers would be unable to handle the demands. We would probably need a carrier-sized starship that was almost all engine, rather than…well, everything else."

Starfighter launch bays, weapons, crew quarters, everything else, John thought. "We could always use it as a carrier, just scaled up," he said. "Use it as a carrier for smaller starships, rather than starfighters. Even attach a fleet carrier to the giant ship…"

"There would be issues," Commander Watson said. "Both kinds of Puller Drive rely on the tramlines to provide most of the motive force. Using a drive without a tramline would send the power requirements rising up to infinity - and the more mass one added, the greater the power requirements would be."

"So it's useless," John said.

"The first tramline-capable ships were huge brutes," Commander Watson reminded him. "It took ten years of careful experimentation to redesign the drives so smaller ships could use them. I dare say the more we poke around with the drive matrix, the more we will understand what we are doing, which will allow us to work out how to minimise the power requirements."

That, John knew, was all too true. Terra Nova might not have become such a disaster zone if the first tramline ships hadn't been so expensive. The world had thought there would only be one accessible planet and everyone had rushed to stake a claim to the surface. But instead, there had been hundreds of accessible worlds, once the drive had been improved. Terra Nova had largely been forgotten in the excitement.

"I hope you succeed in finding a way to jump without the tramlines," he said. Every naval officer born would share that hope. "Do the Tadpoles have a lead on us?"

"They developed the original theory, so I would assume so," Commander Watson said, thoughtfully. "But if they have actually cracked the problem, they haven't told us about it."

They wouldn't, John thought. The war might be over, but there was always the possibility of a rematch. Both sides would concentrate on building up their fleets and weapons technology as much as possible, hoping to have a few surprises to throw at the enemy if the war resumed. *If they could jump without the tramlines, the war would be over within a couple of weeks, before we even knew we were fighting once again.*

"I feel this is important," he added. "Would you like to hand the remainder of your duties to Mr. Richards and concentrate on your work?"

He couldn't help feeling a little embarrassed at his own words. Very few officers would willingly surrender any duties, no matter how over-worked they were, if only to avoid suggesting they were incapable of han-dling them. The Royal Navy could be merciless to officers who didn't feel they were worthy of promotion. After all, if *they* had no faith in them-selves, why should the Navy?

"That would be suitable," Commander Watson said. Her voice sounded warmer than he'd expected, for an officer who was being effec-tively demoted. "There is less for me to do in engineering, now the matrix is properly functional."

John felt another twinge of embarrassment at her ready acceptance. He cursed her patron under his breath, knowing it would probably cause problems when *Warspite* returned to Earth. Commander Watson would probably be quite happy remaining as a boffin, tinkering with her designs and offering suggestions to the engineers, while she wouldn't have to han-dle the XO's duties. And yet, he'd - technically - relieved an officer without due cause. There would an inquest when he returned home.

Of course there will be, he thought. *Admiral bloody Soskice will make damn sure of it.*

"You are free to remain in your quarters, of course," he added. He'd have to write something in the log, preferably an explanation that didn't implicate the First Space Lord. Admiral Soskice was going to ask a number of hard questions and the First Space Lord would have more leeway if he wasn't getting the blame. "And thank you."

"Thank you, Captain," Commander Watson said.

John watched her go, then called Richards and told him that he would be officially assuming the role of XO. If there were any problems, he added, they could be passed to him.

"Yes, sir," Richards said. "But I don't think there will be any I can't handle."

"Good," John said.

He rose and walked to the bridge. "Are we ready to depart?"

"Aye, sir," Armstrong said. "The course is laid in."

"Then take us out, Mr. Armstrong," John ordered. He sat down in his chair and nodded to Richards, who had already taken the XO's console. "And be ready to launch a pair of probes as soon as we cross the tramline."

CHAPTER
TWENTY THREE

"Dear Penny," Percy said. "It has been an interesting voyage."

He paused the recorder while he considered what to say next. Penny wouldn't be interested in any of the finer details of training with his men. She'd once told him that her sole interest in the Royal Marines centred around the cheesecake calendar they produced each year for charity. Percy had refused to take part in the event ever since.

"We did some relief and recovery work on Cromwell," he said, after a moment's thought. "It was very like the work I did at home, only easier. The colonists were more used to taking care of themselves than British citizens. Now, we're starting a search for missing women and children. The odds aren't good."

Better not say anything more, he thought, as he paused the recorder again. Penny *was* a reporter, after all. She might take what he told her and use it to build a story, which would be embarrassing for the Royal Marines. *Just...move on to the next step.*

"I hope you're well and enjoying your job," he concluded. "I'll hope to see you for Christmas, but there are no guarantees of anything out here."

He jumped as he heard the sound of clapping behind him. "Bravo," Peerce said, as Percy spun around. "A letter worthy of Charles Dickens himself."

"I could think of something else worthy of Dickens," Percy snarled. "How long have you been there?"

"Long enough," Peerce said. He looked past Percy and out through the porthole, watching the unmoving stars. "It's never easy to write a letter home, is it?"

"No," Percy said. "What should I say? Dear Family, today was another boring day of training, exercises and drills. I had my arse kicked around the boxing ring three times in quick succession, then the boss beasted me for not turning in my paperwork on time?"

"I don't think that would go down well," the Sergeant agreed, dryly. "Still, I didn't come to catch you committing the dreaded sin of letter-writing. Lieutenant Hadfield wants to see you in twenty minutes."

Percy hesitated, trying to think if he'd done anything that would warrant a lecture from the commanding officer. But he couldn't think of anything. There hadn't been much time to do anything, beyond a hand-ful of drills; they'd been tired after the deployment on Cromwell and the Lieutenant had decided to give the men some downtime. He certainly hadn't screwed up on Cromwell itself or he would have heard about it by now.

"I'm on my way, Sergeant," he said.

He wanted to ask if the *Sergeant* knew why he'd been summoned, but somehow he managed to hold his tongue. Instead, he saved the message, then moved it to the ship's outgoing message buffer. The messages would be relayed to Boston, whereupon they would be passed to the next British or American ship to be heading home. Eventually, probably in several months, Penny and Canella would get their letters.

The thought cost him a pang. They'd already been separated for two months - and he wasn't foolish enough to believe it would be less than another two months, at least, before he returned to Earth. Would Canella remain faithful or would she find someone else? They weren't married, they didn't even have a close relationship…and yet the thought of her leaving him hurt. Maybe it was just because of the shortage of women onboard ship, he told himself, as he stood. *Warspite's* crew was largely male and the handful of females were courted by almost all of the men.

But it wasn't something he wanted to talk about, not to the Sergeant. It was strange; normally, a corporal was not an officer, nor expected to act the part. But on *Warspite*, he had one peer - Corporal Thomas Hastings - and one superior…and Peerce, who seemed to move between being his superior and subordinate, depending on the situation. Percy had been trained to be adaptable, but he honestly couldn't understand why the system was so lax. But then, *Warspite* had been lucky to get *any* Royal Marines.

He followed Peerce back to Marine Country, where a pair of Marines stood guard outside the hatch. They were from 1 Section, Percy knew, and must have done something stupid to be punished with guard duty. *Warspite* simply didn't have enough Marines to spare any of them for ceremonial duty. He returned their nods, then stepped through the hatch and into the compartment. Peerce paused long enough to chat briefly with the guards, then followed Percy. The hatch slammed shut with a loud *bang*.

"Percy," Lieutenant Hadfield called, from his office. "Come in here, if you please."

I wasn't aware I had a choice, Percy thought, coldly. Corporal Thomas Hastings was already there, sitting in a field-issue chair and looking disgustingly sure of himself. A mug of coffee rested on the table in front of him, while two more waited beside the coffee machine. Percy found himself relaxing, slightly, as Hadfield motioned to the dispenser. The CO wouldn't be offering coffee if he was in a bad mood, or intended to beast someone from one end of the ship to the other.

"So far, our scans of the system have turned up nothing," Hadfield said, once Percy had poured himself a mug of coffee and sat down. Peerce stood behind him, leaning against the hatch. "I can't say I'm surprised."

Percy nodded. Troyon was practically useless, at least for human settlement. There were no planets and only a handful of asteroids, floating near the local star. The only thing that held any interest was the presence of three tramlines, one leading to an unknown destination. It was unlikely it led anywhere interesting, Percy knew, but he couldn't help feeling a flicker of excitement when he considered the possibilities. Perhaps he should have gone into the Survey Service after all.

But you always wanted to defend, rather than just see what lay over the next hill, he reminded himself. *And the Royal Marines made a man of you.*

"We need to consider possibilities for searching Spire," Hadfield continued. "There might well be a black settlement somewhere within the system."

"Then they will be very well hidden," Peerce said. "There may be only one planet, but…"

He gave a surprisingly Gallic shrug. "Planets are *big*."

Percy nodded. Spire I - the sole body of any size within the system - was roughly comparable to Mars. It wasn't as large as Earth, but on such a scale it hardly mattered. It would be impossible to search the entire world in anything resembling a reasonable length of time. An army consisting of every soldier and spacer in human service would have problems searching the entire world. Peerce was right. Planets were big.

"They will need some technological presence, if they are to survive there," Hadfield pointed out. "Spire isn't a world where they can go back to nature."

"True," Hastings agreed. "But sir, they may have dug far below the surface. If they wanted to avoid attention from the Tadpoles, they'd need to establish their colony well underground."

"I expect as much," Hadfield said. "They may well have left signs on the ground for us to see, though."

And we could be grasping at straws, Percy thought, grimly. There was no proof that *Vesper* had been anywhere near Spire, or that there was a hidden colony on the planet. But the odds of a hidden colony of survivalists were better than finding the ship, if something had happened to her in the depths of interstellar space. He honestly couldn't tell if his commander truly believed in a hidden colony or if he was just considering the most likely of a set of absurd possibilities.

He took a breath. "How long are we going to spend on the search, sir?"

"As long as the Captain says, Corporal," Hadfield said. "We may turn up nothing. But at least we have to try."

"Yes, sir," Percy said.

Hadfield keyed a switch and a holographic image of the planet appeared in front of them. "I don't think there's any point in deploying to the surface," he said. "We'll use drones and orbiting recon probes to sweep for any signs of intelligent life, then send scout teams down if necessary. There's nothing else we can do with the manpower on hand."

Percy nodded in agreement. There was no hope of searching the entire planet manually.

"If we don't find anything, we may try tactics designed to draw a reaction," Hadfield continued.

"Or there may be nothing there to find," Hastings injected.

"There might well be nothing," Hadfield said. "Do you have any counter-suggestions?"

Hastings considered it. "There's a handful of asteroids in Troyon," he said. "We could check them first. If I was building a survivalist colony, I'd want it in space, near the asteroids, so I could move if necessary."

"It would be harder to hide," Percy pointed out.

"But easier to move," Hastings countered. "Let's face it, Percy; if there's someone hiding on Spire and we find them, they're dead. There's nothing stopping us from dropping KEWs on their heads until they surrender or die. A handful of hits might even take out their life support, dooming them to an unpleasant death. That planet's atmosphere isn't even as thick as pre-terraforming Mars."

"Then it's a strange place for a survivalist colony," Percy said. "Why go there when they could have easily reached Cromwell? It was certainly listed on the pre-war starcharts and they could probably have landed without alerting the colonists."

"Cromwell would also attract the Tadpoles," Hastings said. "Even if the survivalists didn't know the Tadpoles liked to live underwater, they'd know a life-bearing world would attract attention. The Tadpoles would want it for themselves. They'd have to give up technology to avoid being killed...and what sort of idiot would want to live like that?"

Percy nodded. Years ago, a planet had been claimed by a group of religious settlers who'd wanted to make a life without modern technology, which they considered the root of all evil. But when they'd landed, they'd discovered that settling a world without technology was almost impossible. The colony had run into trouble from the beginning and, after twenty years, there had been a revolution and the technology-hating elders had been overthrown. It hadn't happened fast enough, though, to save lives.

He shuddered. *They didn't even have technology to make birthing easier*, he thought. *Too many of them died in childbirth, or caught something they couldn't cure.*

Hadfield tapped the table. "We are moving away from the issue at hand," he said. "We need to plan our search."

"Start with Troyon," Hastings advised. "If we find nothing here, we can always double-back to Spire."

———

"You wanted to see me?"

John looked up as Commander Watson entered his cabin. The younger women looked surprisingly relaxed for someone who had been effectively demoted, proving - if John had had any doubts - that she neither wanted nor asked for the rank. Something would have to be done about the shipyard crews, he told himself, as he motioned for her to take a seat in front of his desk. They had to be taught to listen to design crews, even ones who weren't in the formal chain of command.

It will be easier with the next ship, he thought. *We worked most of the bugs out of this one.*

"I did," he confirmed. She still wasn't calling him 'sir.' From anyone else, he might have taken it as passive-aggressive resistance, but he had a feeling she simply didn't understand why anyone would waste time on social niceties. "We need to discuss some matters."

She rested her hands in her lap, then looked at him expectantly.

John found himself considering precisely what to say. She wasn't a crewwoman who had screwed up by the numbers and was in desperate need of a chewing out. Nor was she a villain, or truly responsible for the position she'd been placed in, when the ship left Earth. It wasn't easy to decide how best to approach the subject, not when he knew she wouldn't understand half of what he had to say. And chewing her out would have felt too much like bullying a helpless child.

"Commander," he said, finally. "Would you allow someone inexperienced to work on your drive matrixes?"

"No," Commander Watson said, in horror. "They wouldn't know what they were doing."

"Of course not," John agreed. Engineering had the longest training period in the Royal Navy, with good reason. The engineers had to under-stand what they were doing, rather than simply installing components they didn't have the slightest idea how to fix, if they went wrong. No one could be allowed to do anything by rote. "But you were placed in the same position when you were made my XO."

He paused, wondering how she would react. He'd expected everything from angry denials to frank agreement. But all she did was tilt her head at him, owlishly, and wait for him to continue.

"An officer on the command track normally has at least ten years of experience in lower ranks before being promoted to Commander," John continued. "You didn't have *any* experience in the lower ranks."

He sighed, inwardly. The war had messed up the normal promotion schedules. John himself didn't have ten years of experience before being promoted to *Captain*, let alone *Commander*. Quite a few younger officers had stepped into dead men's shoes as the war raged on, no doubt causing long-term problems for the future.

But Juliet Watson had spent most of her career in the NGW Program, either at Nelson Base or one of the hidden complexes dotted around the Solar System. She'd never served on a starship before *Warspite*, let alone issued orders outside her chosen field. There was no disputing the simple fact she was a genius, but she was also socially inept and unprepared to issue orders to the lower ranks. And she wasn't remotely ready to lead away teams or anything else that the average XO might be required to do.

"You weren't suited for the post," John finished. "Do you understand it?"

"Yes," Commander Watson said, slowly. "I think I do."

Bet no one explained it to you like that before, John thought. *It would have been hard for Philip to say that, and he's normally no respecter of persons.*

"You were a potential liability right from the start," John said. "No, scratch that; you *were* a liability. It would have been awkward if I had been killed on Cromwell, leaving you in command of the ship. Matters would not have gone well. It would be like putting an unqualified midshipman in charge of recalibrating the drive matrix while the ship was under way."

"I understand," Commander Watson said. "My position was technical, not command-ranked."

"You will need to say that at the inquest," John said. He had no doubt there would *be* an inquest, no matter what he said in his report. "In fact, you could explain why your XO duties took you away from your *real* duties."

"I will," Commander Watson said.

John concealed his amusement with an effort. Commander Watson was many things, but she wasn't a dissembler...and she had no idea of the political firestorm surrounding her. But when she stood in front of the Board of Inquiry and explained, without any regard for the political niceties, just how awkward the whole issue had been, it might just end up buried before the explosion took out several careers.

"I will make a note in the log that you stepped down from your position voluntarily, as you no longer needed it," John said. It would destroy any other officer in the command track, but Commander Watson wouldn't care. She had the experience - and proved expertise - to get people to listen to her and that was all that mattered. "You will need to counter-sign it, of course, but I dare say it shouldn't be a problem."

"I will," Commander Watson said. Her voice showed no hint of any emotion, not even concern for the future. "If we do that now, I can return to work at once."

John nodded, then tapped his terminal and opened the ship's log. In theory, he was supposed to make a comprehensive entry every day, but in practice he rarely had the time. There would hopefully be more time in the future, as Richards could handle the XO's duties without needing to be supervised. He tapped out a brief entry, then swung the terminal around for Commander Watson to see. The former XO thumb-printed it without hesitation.

She needs a minder, John thought, shocked. Everyone was taught, during the first week of basic training, to read documents before they signed them. There had been no shortage of horror stories about loan sharks who had made loans to military personnel, knowing that the military would serve as their collection agent. *And maybe even a declaration that she isn't even competent to tie her shoelaces together without help.*

"Thank you," he said, instead. He'd have to speak to Johnston. The Chief Engineer could mind Commander Watson, when - if - she went on shore leave. There were few people who would cross him and none would do it twice. "And I'm sorry."

Commander Watson regarded him blankly. "For what?"

"Never mind," John said.

He watched her leave his office, then added a note into the log that she was still to receive Commander's wages. The beancounters would probably complain loudly, but he found it hard to care. Besides, someone like Commander Watson had to be treated properly, if only so she could remain productive. A mind like that didn't come along very often.

And if Richards and Howard refrain from killing each other, he thought, as he rose, *this ship might just run perfectly after all.*

CHAPTER
TWENTY FOUR

John had hoped - against all hope - that they would stumble across *something* in Spire, but the single-planet system seemed as deserted as Troyon. Reluctantly, he'd launched a handful of probes towards the planet, then ordered *Warspite* to proceed to Boston. The American-settled world had hailed them as soon as they'd approached, requesting permission to send an officer onboard. John had agreed, then fired off a request of his own.

"I'm afraid we saw your ship passing through," Commodore Andrew Sivula said, in a thick southern accent. "She looked fine to us, but she didn't stop."

"I'm not surprised," John said. They sat together in his cabin, drinking from a bottle Sivula had brought with him. "The crew was in something of a hurry."

"But they never made it to their destination," Sivula mused. "I do recall a report from a survey crew of a starship being detected in Troyon, but it wasn't very clear. It might well have been a sensor glitch."

John frowned, studying the American closely. Like every other intelligence service in the human sphere, MI6 had collected files on foreign military officers, both friendly and potential enemies. Sivula had served in the war, first as XO of USS *Enterprise* and then CO of USS *George Bush* during the Battle of Earth. After the end of the fighting, he'd been reassigned to Boston as the USN's local CO. John had the feeling it was actually something of a demotion. Boston didn't have any naval ships assigned to her, apart from a handful of cutters and shuttles. They couldn't hope to stand off any determined attack.

"I'll need the records, if possible," he said. "When was this?"

"A couple of months before your ship passed through," Sivula drawled. "I forwarded the records to Washington, but the Pentagon never got back to me. They might just have dismissed the reports as glitches and thought no more about them."

"Maybe," John said. "But the report will have to be checked."

"I'll have copies sent to you," Sivula promised. "And I understand you had problems on Cromwell?"

"Flooding," John said. "The Governor was asking if you had anything you could spare - he sent along a wishlist, just in case. If you can, the CDC will pay for it, once the accounts are presented on Earth."

"I'll see what we have," Sivula said. "I can't promise anything, though. We got cut off from Earth by the war and the local settlers aren't too fond of Washington right now. There's been quite a lot of angry muttering recently."

"Just like Cromwell," John said.

"Yeah, but the settlers here elect their government," Sivula said. "The next election may see them either demanding rights as a US state or outright independence. It won't be easy to resolve the crisis, if they choose to demand independence. There's a vast amount of money invested into the colony."

"George III didn't manage to square that circle," John observed. "I hope you *can*."

"Me too," Sivula said. "You'd also have to arrange transport for whatever we offered, Captain. We don't have a freighter to spare."

"I can call one from Pegasus, if necessary," John said. He sighed under his breath. It looked as though they would have to return to Pegasus, then Cromwell, then Troyon to commence the search for the missing ship. It would take nearly a week at best possible speed. "But let me know what you can offer first."

"Give us a couple of hours, once I return to the planet," Sivula said. "I'll let you know by then."

He cleared his throat. "This is a wonderful little ship you have here, Captain."

"Thank you," John said, blandly. He wasn't blind to Sivula's reasons for demanding a visit. The American would be missing life on a starship, but he would also want to evaluate the Royal Navy's latest designs. "We're quite proud of her."

"You must be," Sivula said. "Being out here, all alone, with no one to give you orders…it sounds like heaven."

"And also being the sole person to take the blame," John said, dryly. But he knew Sivula was right. There was something exhilarating about being in sole command, about operating far from the Admiralty. *Warspite* and her sisters had practically been *designed* for operating on their own. "We also have to solve a great many problems."

"I know," Sivula said. "Here, all I really have to do is sort out mining disputes. They didn't want a Commodore out here, Captain. The Department of Colonisation wanted a caretaker out here, with enough authority that starship commanders would listen to him."

"It may get more exciting soon," John mused.

"If the vote goes through," Sivula said. He shook his head, slowly. "They've been talking about shipping more colonists out here, refugees from the East Coast. But the first wave of settlers and their families are objecting to it. They don't want newcomers who will subsume them, not when they worked so hard to build a new world."

"Problems, problems," John said. "Is it a very real concern?"

"I think so," Sivula said. "There's only ten thousand settlers on the surface, Captain. It was meant to be more by now, but the war cut us off from our supplies. They've developed a culture of their own, based on an ideal of the American Wild West. A handful of newcomers can be assimilated, but a few hundred thousand will overwhelm the local population. They're not happy."

"The end of the war didn't bring peace," John said.

"No, it didn't," Sivula said. "And you know what else has been happening? The Indians and Turks have been visiting this system, just passing through. But they're not doing anything apart from passing through and that bugs the hell out of me. What are they doing?"

"Evading transit fees," John guessed.

"Maybe, but we're not in any state to collect them," Sivula said. "I know they have colonies not too far from here, yet there's no logical reason to visit Boston. There's something funny about it, Captain. I've tried to report it to the Pentagon, but they haven't bothered to reply."

John frowned. "They could be trying to create a precedent for free passage," he said. "Or…maybe they're aware of the tramlines from Pegasus to Earth."

He activated his terminal and called up a starchart. "They could cut two weeks off their passage if they went via Pegasus," he said, "but that would require an advanced Puller Drive. If they have one" - he knew they would have to assume the worst - "they could be trying to create a precedent now, which would force us to honour their rights even after the systems were fully developed."

"Bastards," Sivula said.

"Yeah," John said.

He cursed under his breath as he started to mentally compose another report to the Admiralty. The various treaties governing possession of star systems agreed that the owner of the system had the right to levy transit fees, but only if the fees were levelled consistently. If they had a precedent for free passage, the Turks and Indians - and anyone else, for that matter - could legally refuse to pay, even after the Royal Navy and the USN deployed warships to protect the system and enforce the rules. And the World Court might well decide in their favour.

It wouldn't have, five years ago. The major interstellar powers would have backed each other against the upstarts. Even the Russians or Chinese would have supported the British and Americans, while the French would probably have tried to stay out of it. But now, with the major interstellar powers badly weakened by the war, the decision could go either way. In the long term, wasting fuel by sending freighters through the newly-settled systems could pay off in a big way.

"I will bring this to the attention of the Admiralty," he said, firmly. "And I will be happy to forward your report too."

"Thank you," Sivula said, rising. "And thank you, also, for your hospitality. You can keep the rest of the bottle."

"It tastes better than moonshine," John said.

"That's probably because your crew are trying for quantity over quality," Sivula observed, snidely. "The moonshiners down on the planet below are trying to produce their own wines to compete with supplies from Earth."

"Typical," John said.

Sivula snorted.

John escorted him back to his shuttle, then returned to the bridge. Boston was a considerably more active star system than either Pegasus or Cromwell, with dozens of tiny asteroid colonies floating in the asteroid belt. Most of them would have only one or two inhabitants - asteroid miners tended to be an odd bunch - but given time they would provide a considerable supply of raw materials to the planet below. One ship, a converted freighter, was beaming transmissions all over the system, mainly VR programs ranging from historically inaccurate romances to outright porn. Another was moving from asteroid to asteroid, picking up rock ore and resupplying the miners with food and drink.

"I've been tracking the ships, sir," Howard said. "Most of them are primitive tech."

"Easier to fix," John reminded him. "They can build their own miners in a machine shop, if necessary, instead of shipping something all the way from Earth."

He smiled, remembering his first history classes. The real bottleneck had been getting large numbers of men and women out of Earth's gravity well. Once in orbit, they'd been halfway to anywhere within the Solar System. Asteroid miners could use technology that would be comprehensible to Stevenson or Brunel and never be any the worse for it.

And many of those miners were British, he thought, with a flicker of pride. *Space turned a decaying country into a powerhouse once again.*

"Yes, sir," Howard said. "But they would also be sitting ducks if the shit hit the fan."

"Not so," Richards said. "New Russia's asteroid miners largely managed to avoid detection from the system's fall to the end of the war. So did many others."

Forbes cleared her throat. "Captain, Commodore Sivula has just sent us a set of sensor records," she said. "They're dated three months ago."

"Copy them to tactical," John ordered. "Paul, see what you make of them."

There was a long pause as Howard examined the records. "They're vague, sir," he said, finally. "If we take them as read, the American freighter picked up a frigate-sized starship in Troyon at very long range. But there's little else and it could easily be a case of automated software trying to put together a picture and drawing the wrong one."

John stepped up to the console and peered over Howard's shoulder. "I see," he said, finally. "Do *you* think it was nothing more than a sensor glitch?"

"Impossible to be sure, sir," Howard said. "Commercial ships simply don't have military-grade sensors. The contact was so brief there was no time to firm up the sensor lock, if one could have been held at such range. But I don't *think* it was a glitch. Glitches don't tend to produce such perfect images."

"They're not perfect," Richards objected.

"They're perfect, sir, given the sheer range and poor quality of the sensors," Howard countered. "But that leaves us with a different question. Assuming the contact was real, sir, what *was* it?"

John felt a shiver running down his spine. "An alien ship?"

Richards blinked. "Sir?"

It was possible, John knew. There shouldn't have been any warships running through the region, not so soon after the war. As far as he knew, *Warspite* was the first warship to visit Troyon and Cromwell for months. None of the other interstellar powers had reasons to send warships so far from home either, unless the Indians and Turks were definitely up to something. But even if they were, why show themselves to a freighter?

But an *alien* ship? There *was* that unexplored tramline...

"I don't think so," Howard said, "although it would be impossible to be sure. The ship looked to have been built with human tech. Even the smallest Tadpole ship looks quite different to one of ours, even on long-range sensors."

"Which leaves us with another problem," John mused. "If that ship was real, what was it doing there? And if it was real, was it responsible for *Vesper's* disappearance?"

He puzzled over it for a long moment. No matter what the Turks and the Indians wanted, they would have to be insane to actually hijack or destroy a freighter crammed with colonists on their way to their new home. It would mean war, pitting the culprit against the might of Britain and America - and probably France and China too. There was no other word for it, but utter madness.

But if they captured the ship, then steered her into the sun, there would be nothing left for anyone to find, he thought. *They might consider it worth the risk...*

And yet, that didn't make sense either. There was nothing to be gained by destroying the ship, not when it brought so many risks in its wake. The best course of action would be to do nothing, unless they wanted to cripple Cromwell's development. But the colony world wouldn't be allowed to die...

"Captain," Forbes said. "A second message has just arrived for you."

John nodded, then walked back to the command chair and sat down, pulling his console towards him. Commodore Sivula had checked his records, then offered a small quantity of emergency supplies. They would be enough, John decided, to help Cromwell through the coming winter, before more help could arrive from Earth. He thanked the Commodore, then promised to send one of the freighters from Pegasus as quickly as possible. No doubt one of the captains would be delighted to leave Pegasus behind.

"Lieutenant Armstrong, plot us a course for Pegasus, best possible speed," John ordered. "Lieutenant Forbes, inform the locals that we intend to leave orbit in thirty minutes."

He rose. "Mr. Richards, you have the bridge."

"Aye, Captain," Richards said.

John stepped back into his cabin, then sat down and hastily started to draw up a report for the Admiralty, attaching the American sensor logs as evidence. The Admiralty would probably approve of making a search for *Vesper*, although the beancounters would also wonder if it was an effective use of the Royal Navy's time and resources. John contemplated their reaction for a moment, then shrugged in dismissal. Quite apart from the moral responsibility to do the right damned thing, it would be several weeks before they could order him not to do anything of the sort.

He smiled at the thought, then finished writing the report, ran an encryption program and transmitted it to the planet below. The Americans would forward it to the Admiralty, when a suitable ship arrived in the system to play messenger, without attempting to open it. Hopefully, the Admiralty would feel compelled to send additional ships out to Cromwell, while encouraging the Americans to do the same. Unless, of course, the Foreign Office managed to scupper the whole idea...

Bloody typical, he thought, sourly. *The Foreign Office would be more concerned about offending someone than helping us out.*

His intercom bleeped. "Captain," Richards said. "We have a course laid in for Pegasus."

"Understood," John said. "Inform the crew we will be departing in twenty minutes and, if they want to send any final messages, they have to do so before we leave orbit."

"Yes, sir," Richards said. "I believe they are already aware of our departure time."

John's lips twitched. Richards was reminding him, politely, that such matters were the XO's job. But then, he *had* been trying to do what he could to take some of the weight off Commander Watson...

"Good," he said. "I'll be on the bridge momentarily."

He rose, then glanced at his terminal. A private message had appeared, sent directly from the planet. Commodore Sivula had attached copies of long-range sensor logs charting the movements of non-American starships in the system, including - John was amused to see - *Warspite's* arrival. But he was right; there were an unusual number of foreign starships making their way through the system, heading further up the chain towards Cromwell.

They could be using the third tramline from Troyon, he thought. *There might be an unclaimed Earth-like world up there.*

He shrugged. That too made no sense. If the Indians or the Turks had stumbled across an inhabited world, logically they would have filed the discovery with the World Court in order to stake a claim. Or was there something about the world that made it unlikely their claim would be upheld? The only realistic excuse for not accepting their claim was the presence of an alien race, but they had treaty obligations to report the presence of another alien race to the Earth Defence Organisation. Who knew how dangerous the newcomers were likely to be?

And you're imagining things, he told himself, firmly. *All you really know is that* Vesper *disappeared somewhere between Boston and Cromwell. You have no proof of outside involvement in any of this, save for the Indians and Turks. And all they sent through Boston were freighters…*

Shaking his head, he stepped through the hatch and onto the bridge.

"Course laid in, sir," Armstrong chirped, as if Richards hadn't already told John. "We're ready to depart."

"Then take us out of orbit," John ordered. It would have been nice to spend a couple of days in orbit - the crew could do with some proper shore leave - but there was no time. "And take us right to Pegasus, best possible speed."

"Aye, sir," Armstrong said.

John settled back in his command chair and forced himself to think. Nothing about the whole affair made sense, which meant…what? A disaster, a misunderstanding…or a foreign plot?

You'll find out, he promised himself. *And then you will know what you are facing.*

CHAPTER
TWENTY FIVE

"We should be able to claim a record, sir," Armstrong said. "From Boston to Pegasus and then to Troyon, in less than a week."

"So we shall," John said. It *had* helped that they hadn't stayed at Pegasus any longer than it had taken to send orders to Captain Minion, but Armstrong was right. It *was* a record. "And now we're here, commence the search pattern."

He settled back in his command chair and reviewed, once again, the barren nothingness of Troyon. Part of him wanted to head directly to Spire, to start the search there, as it was possible there *was* a hidden colony on the rocky world. But Troyon *did* have the third, unexplored tramline... and it *was* where the mystery ship had been sighted. It was, he felt, the best place to start the search.

"Aye, sir," Armstrong said. "We're focusing on the asteroids first."

"Good," John said. If someone wanted to *hide* the missing ship, they could simply have depowered her, then left the hulk to drift among the asteroid cluster. There would be no way for someone to separate her from the asteroids unless they made a visual inspection. "Lieutenant Forbes?"

"Yes, sir?"

"Start broadcasting our IFF code and trigger signals," John ordered. "If there's an emergency beacon somewhere in this system, I want to find it."

"Aye, sir," Forbes said. She tapped a switch on her console. "Transmitting now."

John forced himself to relax, knowing it would be hours before they picked up a response…if, of course, there was an emergency beacon out there. Standard beacons didn't broadcast continually, knowing there was a risk of running out of power before a SAR team arrived, even in the Solar System. Instead, they waited for a signal from a rescue mission and then responded, summoning the rescuers to their precise location. Even a half-second transmission would be enough to draw *Warspite's* attention. The system had been tested and retested often enough, as well as proving effective in real life.

But they would have been lost for over a month, John thought, coldly. There were ways to freeze people until they could be rescued, but a freighter like *Vesper* wouldn't have carried the right equipment. He'd heard of a case where a stranded crew had tried to set up a makeshift cryogenic tank, but all four of the stricken miners had wound up with brain damage when they'd been recovered. It was hard to imagine a freighter crew running the same risk, even if they *had* had the tools on hand.

The asteroids grew closer on the display. John studied them carefully, noting the small collection of nickel-iron and water asteroids, enough to sustain a tiny population for years, if necessary. But none of the asteroids seemed to have been touched by human hands, let alone spun to produce gravity and turned into habitats. John hadn't expected to encounter survivalists here, not where there were only a few places they could hide, but it was still disappointing. It would have been nice to solve the mystery so quickly.

"Captain," Howard said. "I think you should see this. It's the live feed from Probe #4."

"Show me," John ordered.

The holographic display changed, showing a close-up image of a giant water-ice asteroid. It looked as random as any other such asteroid, until the probe focused on a relatively small area and revealed that human tools had been used to chip ice from the asteroid. There were contingency plans to mine water-ice asteroids for fuel - it would damage drives, John recalled, but it was doable - yet this was on a very small scale. It looked more like someone had wanted drinking water, but hadn't dared go to Cromwell or Boston for supplies.

"They could have come here for supplies," Forbes whispered. "If they cracked the water, they could produce oxygen to keep themselves alive."

"But if that's true," Richards said, "where are they?"

Good question, John thought. *Vesper* would have had enough supplies to get from Earth to Cromwell, but how much further could she have gone? Given the number of passengers, her life support had to be pushed to the limit even before she ran into trouble. *If she was still intact, here and now, wouldn't she have signalled us when we first entered the system?*

Howard put his concerns into words. "We passed through this system twice," he said, "both times screaming our IFF at the universe. If they were here, and still alive, wouldn't they have called us back?"

"They could have lost radio," Armstrong pointed out.

"There are plenty of ways to attract our attention, if they failed to rig up a radio transmitter," Forbes said, bitterly. "Even a drive flare would be detectable."

"But if they had lost their radios, they might not know we were here," Armstrong offered. "If they didn't hear our signal, they wouldn't have known to respond…"

"Save the speculation for later," John said, curtly. He keyed his terminal. "Major Hadfield, your evaluation please?"

"Someone took a reasonable amount of water, presumably to keep the crew alive," the Marine said. "There are ways to date the mining, sir."

"Use them," John ordered.

It was nearly an hour before they had their answer. The mining had taken place six months before the end of the war.

"It couldn't have been *Vesper*," John said, "although it does raise another question. Who mined the asteroid in the first place?"

"Humans," Hadfield said, bluntly. "We checked the tools. They were standard-issue mining tools, of the kind provided to almost all starship crews."

John swore under his breath. That proved nothing. The major interstellar powers had worked hard to standardise everything in the years before the war, apart from a handful of components that were considered highly classified. There was no way to know if the tools had originally been manufactured in Britain, America or Russia, at least not from the scars they'd left on the asteroid…or if they hadn't been traded to someone else after they'd been produced.

But who had it been? There hadn't been any major push towards the sector before the war; Cromwell was the only known colony past Boston, and the CDC hadn't had the resources to fund a major settlement program. Survivalists *might* have come out so far, during the war itself, but they had to have known there was little past Cromwell…unless the third tramline led somewhere interesting. His gaze swept back to the system display, showing the tramline marked in yellow for *unexplored*. They would have to survey it when - if - they located *Vesper* or declared her lost to causes unknown.

And see if the Turks or Indians found anything interesting, John thought. *But why wouldn't they tell us about it?*

A dull chime echoed through the compartment. "Captain," Forbes said, her voice high with sudden excitement. "I'm picking up *something*."

"Ah," Richards said, with heavy sarcasm. "Underling's Inability Descriptive Syndrome."

"As you were," John said, as Forbes flushed brightly. He hadn't known Richards watched Jackie Spring. But then, the joke had been old before Jackie Spring had been more than a gleam in a horny old producer's eye. "What are you picking up?"

"An emergency beacon," Forbes said. A blue light blinked to life on the system display, showing a location several million kilometres from the asteroid cluster. It was right along the projected least-time course from Tramline One to Tramline Two. "Her IFF reads out as *Vesper*!"

"Mr. Armstrong, take us there," John snapped. The Marines had returned to the ship, thankfully. "Flank speed!"

"Aye, sir," Armstrong said. A dull thrumming echoed through the hull as he yanked her away from the asteroids, then up to full speed. "ETA, thirty-seven minutes."

"I could try to trigger a core download," Forbes offered. "It would save time."

John considered it, then shook his head. There was no way to know just how *Vesper's* crew had set up their emergency beacons. A core dump might wipe the beacon completely, if they'd activated those settings, even though it was technically against regulations. And the beacon itself could have easily been damaged by whatever had disabled or destroyed its mothership. Better not to take chances, he told himself, when they would be ready to scoop the beacon out of space in less than an hour.

"We can wait," he said. He keyed his terminal. "Mr. Johnston, prepare for a beacon recovery operation. I want to know everything that beacon saw before it switched itself into sleep mode."

"Aye, sir," Johnston said. The Chief Engineer sounded relieved. "I'll have a team ready to pick it up once we're there."

———

Forty minutes after detection, once the beacon had been given a careful examination, the Chief Engineer and his team went EVA to inspect the beacon, then prepare to bring it onboard *Warspite*. To John's relief, the car-sized beacon showed no signs of tampering, let alone sabotage that might have caused it to explode, once it was onboard his ship. The Chief Engineer carefully inserted a lead into the databanks, then copied everything to a remote datacore., which was then flown back to *Warspite*. They left the beacon itself drifting in space.

"There's no sign of anything going wrong until they reach this system," the Chief Engineer said, once the datacore had been analysed. He'd brought it into the briefing room to show the senior crew. "Most of the entries are mind-numbingly boring; there's only one interesting note, a statement that Lieutenant Higgins was reprimanded by the Captain for spending too much time seducing the colonists. However, matters change rapidly once the starship enters the Troyon System. Shortly after leaving the tramline, she comes under attack."

John sucked in his breath. "Under attack? By whom?"

"Unknown," Johnston said. "The first hit took out her civilian-grade sensor nodes and disrupted the entire network. I don't think there's any hope of recovering anything more from the beacon, sir, although we will certainly try. However, the ship was ordered to surrender immediately afterwards and boarded. The Captain released the beacon with orders to continue receiving updates until the whole affair was over. Apparently, the boarding party never noticed the beacon was gone."

Or they did notice, too late, John thought. *And spaced the Captain when they discovered that he'd left clues behind for any searchers.*

"Pirates," Richards said, in disbelief. "Real fucking pirates."

"So it would seem," Johnston said, grimly. "But sir…how the hell can piracy be made economical?"

John shrugged. Maintaining a warship was costly. The beancounters had bitched and moaned about the cost of the pre-war Royal Navy, although *that* had stopped in short order when the Tadpoles attacked Vera Cruz. Even if someone had produced an armed freighter, it would be impossible to obtain supplies from tiny colonies like Cromwell, even if the crew was prepared to bombard the colony into submission. And it would definitely attract attention from genuine militaries, who would do whatever it took to take out the pirate ship.

"I think we may have to ask them," he said. Could the Turks or the Indians be supplying the pirates? It was possible, but it would be an act of war. And they couldn't keep their involvement a secret indefinitely. "Until then…"

He turned to look at the Chief Engineer. "Mike," he said, "where did they go?"

"The last signal the beacon recorded noted the ship was being taken towards Tramline Three," Johnston said. "And from there, into unexplored space."

"So we go after them," Howard said.

"We could be travelling along that tramline within an hour," Armstrong added, eagerly.

John thought quickly, weighing up the problem. Cold logic said he should report the whole affair to Pegasus and Boston, then send a message to the Admiralty. There was no way of knowing what was lurking at the far side of the tramline, from a single pirate ship - he was still having problems wrapping his head around that concept - to an entire rogue planet of survivalists. He had no idea if the pirates had *known* what *Vesper* had been carrying…

But those are British citizens in enemy hands, he thought. It was a rule that had been established during the Troubles, when it had become less important to appease public opinion by not launching punitive strikes against terrorist states. *We can't leave them there to their fate.*

He turned to Richards. "Have copies of our logs and the beacon records transferred to a drone, then prep it for departure," he ordered. "When the freighter comes through this system" - he briefly considered waiting, but he knew it would take too long - "the drone can upload its contents to the ship, which can take the files to Boston. The Americans can forward them to the Admiralty."

"Aye, sir," Richards said.

"Mr. Armstrong, I want you to plot us a course that will take us through the tramline and out at the edge of the unexplored star system," John continued. "I do not want to jump in on a predictable least-time course. We have no idea what we may be facing."

"Aye, sir," Armstrong said. If he was disappointed at not charging through the tramline, guns blazing, he didn't show it. "I'll plot the course now."

John nodded. "Mr. Howard, study the beacon logs as best as you can and try to determine what we may be facing," he continued. "Look for any clues as to the ship's origin, weapons load and anything else you may consider important. Run your conclusions past Mr. Richards, then be ready to brief me once we're underway."

"There may be little more from the beacon," Johnston warned. "I can try to model out the last moments of *Vesper*, but her internal network was badly damaged. Her final recordings may not be reliable."

"You can do the best you can," John said, addressing Howard. "I will understand if you find nothing useful."

He nodded to the younger man, then motioned to the datacore. Johnston was right; there might be little left to recover, but they had to try. Besides, it would keep Howard busy. He didn't need time to brood on women and children in pirate hands. They'd all seen the Jackie Spring movie where Jackie had infiltrated a pirate crew, slept her way to the top and then handed the pirates over to the authorities. The script had been appalling, the acting hideously over the top, but no one had watched it for the words. They'd been more interested in watching Jackie Spring - and a hundred supporting actresses - falling out of their clothes time and time again. Maybe it was exciting, when everyone was an actress and the deaths were staged, but there was nothing erotic about it in real life. How could there be?

Because some people will do anything for a thrill, he thought, sourly. Sin City had offered everything that a person might find exciting, ignoring foreign laws, common sense or even simple human decency. *You could rape a willing victim in Sin City, male or female, young or old, if you were prepared to pay for your fun.*

He shook his head. Perhaps it was a good thing, after all, that Sin City had been destroyed.

"Major Hadfield, prepare your Marines for a rescue mission," he continued. "I want them ready to board *Vesper*, assuming she is still intact."

"Yes, sir," Hadfield said. He didn't raise any objections. "I'll start running training drills immediately."

"I don't know who attacked *Vesper*," he said, addressing the entire compartment. "I don't know if the colonists are still alive. But I *do* know that we will find the people who kidnapped them, that we will hunt them down and bring them to book for their crimes. Dismissed."

He watched them file out, suddenly feeling very old and tired. He'd been a very junior pilot when Vera Cruz had been attacked, young enough to adapt without too many problems to a universe that suddenly included murderous aliens. There had still been some wonder in the universe, even though the aliens had been intent on smashing humanity into ground. But older officers, he'd heard, had had problems accepting the fact that aliens existed. He'd sneered at them at the time, muttering darkly to Colin about old fogies who should have shuffled into retirement years ago, but he understood now. The universe had been turned upside down.

It doesn't matter if there is only one ship, he thought. *The precedent has been set. There will be other pirates in future.*

He shook his head. They'd have to check the records, see if someone had lost a starship during or shortly after the war. But then, it might prove pointless. The war had caused so much disruption that quite a few ships, even Royal Navy vessels, remained unaccounted for. It had only been recently, he recalled, that one mystery had been solved. A frigate, reported lost to causes unknown, had rammed a Tadpole ship, destroying both vessels. Who knew what might have happened to other ships?

"Captain," Armstrong's voice said. "The course is now laid in. We will enter the tramline in five hours from departure."

"Far enough from our destination star to remain undetected," John said. There were ways, in theory, to monitor the tramlines to detect arriving starships, but they'd never been made to work in practice. However, most systems at least *tried* to monitor least-time emergence zones. "Get us underway once the drone is launched."

"Aye, sir," Armstrong said.

John looked at the final recordings from *Vesper*, then rose, feeling cold anger stirring in his breast. Whatever had happened, it was his job to deal with it. There was no one else he could ask for orders, no one to take the burden off his shoulders. All he could do was carry out his duty as best as he saw fit.

Calmly, he strode onto the bridge and prepared his ship for war.

CHAPTER
TWENTY SIX

"Transit complete, sir," Armstrong said.

John felt a shiver running down his spine. No one - at least no one British - had entered this system before, not until now. There could be anything in the new system, anything at all, from aliens to a hidden human colony. He kept his eyes fixed on the display as it slowly started to fill with data, cursing the survey teams under his breath. They should have at least jumped through the tramline once and scanned its destination before returning to Cromwell.

"There's little here," Howard said, in disappointment. "The star's a white dwarf, there are no planets and only a handful of comets."

"That we can see," Richards reminded him. "Comets wouldn't leave any traces on the star's gravity field."

Shit, John thought. "Are there any other tramlines?"

"Yes, sir," Howard said. A red line blinked into existence on the display. "Another human-grade tramline, heading into the unknown."

John studied the display, thinking hard. A comet could be turned into a base, if necessary; they tended to have all the elements for supporting a basic colony, although they were often lacking in raw materials. But he had a feeling that the mystery starship had continued down the other tramline, heading deeper into unexplored space. This system should have been swept by the survey team, he knew, and would be swept soon enough, as interest in the sector grew stronger. The further away they were from Cromwell and Boston, the easier it would be for the pirates - he still had difficulty accepting their existence - to hide.

"Take us towards the next tramline," he ordered. "But keep us in full stealth mode."

"Aye, sir," Armstrong said. "Least-time course?"

"No," John said. "Dog-leg us around the system. I want to remain undetected at the far end too."

"Aye, sir," Armstrong said.

John turned to Richards. "Continue to monitor the system," he ordered, as he rose. "And alert me at once if you detect any signs of a technological presence."

"Aye, sir," Richards said.

"You have the bridge," John said. There was far too much paperwork to do for him to justify remaining on the bridge. "I'll be in my cabin."

He stepped through the hatch, then called Midshipwoman Powell. "Please bring me coffee," he ordered, when she appeared. "And a ration bar or two."

"Aye, Captain," the young woman said.

John smiled at her, then sat down and activated his terminal. Richards had done a good job of sorting through the paperwork Commander Watson had left undone, but everything had to be checked and checked again. At least it provided gainful employment for the handful of junior officers, John considered, as he inspected the list of supplies, looking for discrepancies. It didn't take outright malice or theft to have something listed on the manifest that simply didn't exist.

"Thank you," he said, when Midshipwomen Powell returned. The ration bar looked thoroughly unappetizing, as always, but the coffee smelt heavenly. "I'll drop the mug off when I'm done."

She nodded and retreated. John watched her go, feeling a flicker of pity. Normally, the Captain's Steward would be an enlisted crewman, someone who hadn't gone through the full training program before boarding a starship. But *Warspite* was too small to carry a dedicated steward. Midshipwoman Powell hadn't signed up to tend his needs, serve food in the wardroom or anything other than start working her way towards command rank, but she had no choice. John made a mental note to ensure she had a good report, at the end of the voyage, and perhaps swap her with one of the other midshipmen. As it stood, she was gaining the least experience of her fellows.

It will look bad on her record, he thought. *And that will breed resentment.*

Shaking his head, he returned to his paperwork.

The intercom buzzed an hour later. "Captain," Richards said, "we have detected no traces of any technological activity. If there's anything hidden here, it's lying doggo, impossible to detect."

"Understood," John said. They wouldn't get any better sensor readings unless they moved closer to the star, which would waste time if the missing ship wasn't here. "Keep us on course for the tramline."

"Aye, sir," Richards said. He paused, just long enough to set alarm bells ringing at the back of John's mind. "The lads would like to name the system."

John snorted. It was tradition, backed up by the World Court, that whoever discovered the system got to name it. What was *also* tradition was arguing over who had actually done the hard work. The survey crews… or the country that had paid for their ship? There had been no shortage of arguments in the past, he knew, and they seemed unlikely to end in the future. But then, the only world that had been named by consensual agreement had been Terra Nova…and 'New Earth' was blindingly obvious.

"Tell them they can submit suggestions, which I will include in the report to the Admiralty," John said, finally. *He* had no interest in naming the system after himself or one of his family - the thought of a planet called John was darkly amusing - but he didn't mind if the rest of the crew had a few suggestions. "But the Admiralty might have other ideas."

"Aye, sir," Richards said. "I'll keep them from suggesting anything *too* unprintable."

John laughed. "Make sure you do," he said. "One planet called Hellhole is quite enough."

———

Percy crept down the darkened corridor, weapon in hand. The hatch ahead of him lay open, tempting him to slip into the sideroom. But he knew from grim experience it could easily be a trap…he unhooked a grenade from his belt, then held up three fingers to the fire team following him. They signalled their understanding as Percy counted to three, then hurled the stun grenade into the compartment. Blue-white flashes of light seemed to drive the darkness away.

He moved into the room and searched for potential threats, weapon held at the ready. But there was nothing even remotely dangerous. The compartment had clearly once been occupied, but the inhabitants had been moved away days ago. He checked the washroom - it was smaller than the one assigned to the Marines on *Warspite* - and then keyed his radio.

"Clear," he said.

"Clear," Peerce echoed. "Team Two is moving to the next compartment."

Percy and his fire team fell into backstop position as Team Two advanced, threw a grenade of their own into the next compartment and charged in, weapons raised. "Clear," Hardesty snapped, moments later. "All clear!"

Percy made a hand signal to his men, ordering them to follow him, then sprinted forward to the next compartment. The hatch was closed, locked solid. He motioned for Peerce to work on the hatch as the Marines took up defensive positions, sweat trickling down his back as he looked for threats. The enemy was somewhere on the giant ship, he knew, as he unhooked another grenade from his belt. But where?

The hatch hissed open. Percy threw the grenade into the compartment, then charged forward, into a madhouse. Women and children were screaming and falling to the deck, while, behind them, their captors were raising their own weapons. Percy barely had time to choose his targets; he aimed instinctively at anyone holding a weapon and opened fire. Two men dropped to the deck, dead, before the others returned fire. Fisherman stumbled backwards, then fell to the deck. Moments later, all of the pirates were dead.

"Medics," Percy snapped, keying his radio. Stun grenades could leave grown men twitching uncomfortably for hours on end. Worse, they could cause permanent damage to a child. But there had been no alternative. "Get the medics down here now!"

"They're on their way, Corporal," Hadfield said, calmly. "Secure the surrounding area, then start preparing to take the hostages back to the shuttle."

"Yes, sir," Percy said. "I…"

"Contact," Hardesty snapped. Gunfire broke out, further down the corridor. "Incoming enemy troops, wearing armour!"

"Hold the line," Percy said. The pirates had reacted quickly; they'd organised a counterattack, then thrown it right into the Marine position. But then, whatever they wanted the hostages for, they couldn't allow the Marines to liberate them. "We're coming."

The ship shook as someone threw an explosive grenade down the corridor. Percy dropped to the deck as he crawled out of the compartment, then fired a pair of rounds towards the enemy, who had taken up firing positions in two side compartments. There was almost no cover at all, he noted; the Marines couldn't advance, but nor could the enemy. Stalemate.

"Put a grenade through both of those hatches," he ordered, as an enemy soldier fired a burst towards him. "Explosive."

"Explosive, aye," Peerce said.

Percy braced himself. Stun grenades could be used indiscriminately, despite the risks; explosive grenades couldn't separate friend from foe. It was quite possible that he was about to cause a massacre. But he couldn't afford to let the enemy drive him back, or force the Marines out of the ship.

"Grenades away," Peerce said. He was an excellent cricketer, Percy noted. Both grenades went sailing through the target hatches and exploded with staggering force. "Go!"

Percy lunged forward, followed by Team One. He stepped into the compartment and hastily searched for enemies, but most of the pirates seemed to have been killed by the blast. There were no sign of civilian hostages, thankfully. The next cabin was equally clear; the only survivor was a stunned-looking pirate, his legs broken by the blast. Peerce bound his hands with a plastic tie, then left him for the medics.

"Incoming," Hardesty snapped. "Shit!"

Percy jumped out of the compartment and swore himself. Four naked women were walking towards them, their faces twisted with fear. Behind them, using the women as shields, were four pirates, holding weapons in their hands. The women themselves had metal collars around their necks, ready to explode if someone behind them pushed a button. It reminded Percy of the tracking collars used in some of the high security prisons. Escape was impossible. If the collars were taken out of the prison, they exploded - and if they were removed without the proper authorisation, they exploded. No one, as far as he knew, had ever managed to cheat the system.

"Hold position," he ordered. The pirates opened fire. He winced as the women howled in pain. "Target the pirates..."

For once, he wasn't sure *what* to do. If they stunned the women and their captors, someone could detonate their collars at a distance. The women would be dead instantly, while the explosions might prove deadly to the Marines as well. Normal collars were designed to only kill their bearer, but the pirates could easily have modified the design. God knew they weren't standard equipment on starships, after all.

But he couldn't let the pirates use human shields too.

They know they're dead anyway, he thought. Pirates were officially classed as 'enemies of humanity,' a classification that hadn't even been applied to the Tadpoles. Piracy in space was no different from piracy on the water, at least as far as the law was concerned. Captain Naiser and his crew could hang the pirates or space them and no one would give a damn. And even if they hadn't been, the ROE allowed them to hang anyone who tried to use innocent civilians as human shields. It had been deemed the only way to prevent such barbaric tactics.

But it also made them desperate, Percy thought.

He unhooked a stun grenade from his belt. "Stunner," he called, hurling it towards the women. Blue-white light flared, sending tingles down his spine; the women staggered, then collapsed to the deck. Suddenly unprotected, their captors were hastily gunned down, their bodies left to fall on top of their former shields. "Move!"

The Marines raced forward. "Here," Peerce snapped, as he stepped through an open hatch. "Drop that or you're dead!"

Percy followed him. Inside, a pirate was leaning against the far bulkhead, one trembling hand poised over a small terminal. Peerce flicked on his laser sight, allowing the beam to become visible as it passed through the dust in the air. Normally, the lasers were toned down to keep them invisible - they led any watchful eyes right back to the Marine holding the sight - but Percy had to admit they were hellishly intimidating. The pirate certainly seemed terrified.

He dropped the terminal. Percy stepped forward as the pirate raised his hands, careful not to wander into Peerce's line of fire, then picked up the terminal. It was simple, enough; he realised. They'd effectively downloaded an app for operating the collars. One button triggered the explosives, another made the collar tighten like Darth Vader torturing subordinates and a third released them. He tapped the third button, then checked the stunned women. Their collars had opened and fallen to the deck.

"Exercise terminated," Hadfield said. "I say again, exercise terminated."

Percy blinked in surprise, then hastily closed his eyes as the simulated starship faded out of existence. His head swam for a long moment, forcing him to swallow hard to keep his gorge from rising. VR sims were near-perfect - the user's mind tended to fill in any missing details - but disconnecting from them in a hurry always left him feeling sick. Civilian users were gently brought out of the semi-trance.

Which isn't really an option for us, Percy thought, dully. He removed his helmet, then blinked twice at the suddenly-dim compartment. *We might have to move from training for war to actually fighting in the blink of an eye.*

"Hey, Corporal," Hardesty said. "I could run a kick-ass sex tape in these things."

"And then the Sergeant would kick *your* arse," Percy said. "Bring your own private toy if you want to have VR sex."

He smiled, humourlessly. Marine VR sims were an order of magnitude ahead of civilian models, although the sex sims were catching up rapidly. What did it say about humanity, he wondered suddenly, that sex drove so much development? It was quite possible, one day, that no one would ever have real sex at all. And what would *that* do to the human race?

"It wouldn't be the same," Hardesty said. "If I wanted to be a wirehead, I wouldn't have joined the Marines."

"Probably not," Percy said. He stripped off the rest of the VR outfit, then placed it in a basket for cleaning and stepped naked into the shower compartment. Peerce and two of the others were already there, counting down the minutes until they had to get out of the water and go dress. "How do you think we did?"

"As best as we could," Peerce said. "Boarding a starship that hasn't surrendered is never easy."

Percy nodded. There had been a handful of boarding actions during the war, but only one real success. The Tadpoles had probably been so surprised at a force of Royal Marines swarming onto their ship that they hadn't had time to hit the self-destruct before they were overwhelmed. Later, they'd tried boarding human ships themselves, but they'd never taken one intact. But then, no one had surrendered during the war.

It didn't help that we couldn't talk to them, he thought, as they stepped out of the shower and dressed rapidly. *Even now, talking to a Tadpole is difficult. We may never understand them completely.*

"You all did well," Lieutenant Hadfield said. He looked pale, unsurprisingly. Several of the others looked as though they wanted to throw up. "We're only an hour away from the second tramline. We might be needed."

"Yes, sir," Peerce said. He turned to address the men. "You lot; get yourselves something to drink - and I mean water - and then catch forty winks. Sleep in your battledress; you may need to grab weapons in a hurry."

"The problem remains unsolved, though," Hadfield said. "How do we board and storm a starship the size of *Vesper* without them hitting the self-destruct or killing most of their captives before it's too late?"

"I don't know, sir," Percy admitted. "Does *Vesper* have a self-destruct?"

"The pirates could easily have rigged one up," Hadfield said. "A standard nuke wouldn't be that hard to produce, if they had the right tools."

"Shit," Percy said. If the pirates wanted to take out a few of the Marines, all they had to do was wait until the Marines had boarded the ship and then detonate the nuke. There would be no warning before it was far too late. "Who *are* they?"

"Unknown," Hadfield said.

"There's a betting pool in the mess," Peerce put in. "The current favourite is a renegade military ship. After that, either aliens or a converted civilian ship."

Hadfield snorted. "I trust you are not encouraging the lads to gamble?"

"They don't need the encouragement," Peerce said, stiffly. "I am merely monitoring the gambling to make sure it doesn't move out of acceptable levels."

Percy nodded. Gambling wasn't precisely forbidden by regulations, but there were rules. No Bootneck could gamble his future wages, or more than a third of his shipboard account balance. He wasn't sure he approved of the idea of gambling - he'd seen people lose everything because they kept assuming the *next* game would bring them victory - but it was better to have it under some form of supervision than drive it underground.

"I think it would be unwise for me to place a bet," Hadfield said. "Besides, there wouldn't be much to win if I bet on the favourite."

Peerce smiled. "No, sir," he said. "None of the favourites are good earners."

He shrugged. "That said, we all need some sleep," he added. "Who knows what will be waiting for us on the other side of the next tramline?"

"God," Percy said.

"That's a very low probability," Peerce said, deadpan. "But you can put a bet on it if you like."

CHAPTER
TWENTY SEVEN

"Jump complete, sir," Armstrong said.

John nodded, then watched the display. This time, the star was a G2, comparable to Sol and most of the other stars that had given birth to inhabitable planets. Another red line jumped into existence, marking yet another tramline heading into the unknown. Moments later, it was joined by a second, alien-grade tramline. John studied its projected destination and calculated that it headed back towards human space. There might be a shorter way to reach their current location, in the future.

"Good," he said. "Can you see any planets?"

"Aye, sir," Howard said. "There's one gas giant…gravity scans don't indicate any other large planetary bodies."

"Interesting," Richards mused. "A lone gas giant is unusual."

"It could have several moons, like Pegasus," John reminded him. A gas giant could supply an entire star system with enough HE3 to keep its economy going for centuries. "Helm, set course for the gas giant, but remain in stealth."

"Aye, sir," Armstrong said. *Warspite's* drives hummed louder as she got underway. "ETA seven hours, twenty minutes."

"Get some rest," John ordered, briskly. It was unlikely they would encounter anything threatening in interplanetary space. "The secondary crew can handle the voyage to the gas giant."

Armstrong looked rebellious, but he didn't try to argue. John wasn't too surprised; young officers rarely comprehended the true scale of any star system. There was no point in keeping Armstrong, or Howard, or any of the others on duty for seven hours, while they exhausted themselves. A tired crew would make mistakes. Richards summoned the secondary crew, then passed command to them. John rose, went to his cabin and climbed into bed without bothering to undress. It felt like no time at all had passed before the alarm started to bleep, informing him that they were now an hour away from the gas giant. John rubbed his eyes, then showered, changed his clothes and returned to the bridge. The gas giant was looming large on the holographic display.

"She's nearly a third again the size of Jupiter," Lieutenant Logan said, as she rose from the command chair. She headed the secondary bridge crew. "It's a mystery why she hasn't collapsed into a small star."

"Maybe she will, one day," John said, as he took his chair. "There was that plan for turning Jupiter into a star, wasn't there?"

He smiled. There were all sorts of crazy ideas out there, ranging from constructing Dyson Spheres and Ringworlds to turning gas giants into stars and using them to warm moons like Titan and Ganymede until they could support human life. But most of them tended to flounder on the limits of human technology, at least as they were now. Even the fastest brute-force terraforming program still took over a century to produce a liveable world.

"Yes, sir," Logan said. "But I don't know how we'd proceed."

John shrugged as the remainder of the primary crew returned to the bridge and took their posts, then turned back to the display. Nothing had been detected, beyond a handful of moons, none larger than Phoebes or Demos, Mars's tiny moons. None of them looked particularly habitable; indeed, John was starting to suspect that the reason there were no other planets in the system was because the gas giant had sucked in all the material that would have eventually produced other planets centuries ago. The astronomers would have fun dissecting the star system, he decided. He just hoped they showed more common sense than usual and refrained from getting too close to a particularly interesting event.

"Captain," Forbes said, suddenly. "I'm picking up a spurt of chatter on standard radio bands."

John leaned forward, feeling ice running down the back of his neck. "Aimed at us?"

"I don't think so," Forbes said. "It wasn't a focused radio or laser beam. I think it was just a burst of random chatter."

John exchanged glances with Richards. "Can you tell us what it said?"

"Negative, sir," Forbes said. "The chatter was encrypted. My systems cannot crack the coding in a hurry."

Shit, John thought. "Can you localise the source?"

"Yes, sir," Forbes said. A red icon blinked to life on the display. It seemed to be hanging in low orbit over the gas giant, rather than one of the moons. "It's coming from that location."

John looked at Armstrong. "Mr. Armstrong, take us on an intercept course," he ordered. It had to be a starship, if the transmission was coming from low orbit. "Best possible speed consummate with maintaining our stealth."

"Aye, sir," Armstrong said.

"Prepare to launch a probe," John added, addressing Howard. "But do *not* launch without my specific permission."

"Aye, sir," Howard said.

John thought rapidly. There was only one reason for a starship to come to a gas giant and lurk in low orbit; they had to be in desperate need of fuel. The pirates? There was nowhere else they could obtain fuel, not unless they wanted to take the risk of returning to a more settled star system, which would be defended by a national military force. It wasn't *easy* to mine a gas giant without a proper cloudscoop, but it could be done.

Red light washed over the display. "Contact," Howard snapped. "Sir, they just made us!"

"Red alert, all hands to battlestations," John ordered. He wasn't too surprised. The faster they moved, the harder it was to stealth their drive emissions. Clearly, the pirates had an alert sensor crew. "Launch the probe, then drop stealth and punch us up to flank speed."

"Aye, sir," Armstrong said.

"The probe is sending back a visual now," Howard added. It was considerably faster than any manned ship. "It has the enemy ship in its sights."

John leaned forward as an image appeared in front of him. Hanging against the gas giant was a mid-sized frigate, a pre-war design. A long tube hung down from the starship, dipping into the gas giant's atmosphere like a straw dipped into a glass of water. As he watched, the makeshift cloud-scoop was abandoned and left to plummet into the gas giant's atmosphere, where it would be lost forever. Judging by the leaking traces of atmosphere around it, the pirates wouldn't mourn the loss.

"That's a *Russian* frigate, sir," Howard said. "She's a modified *Kirov*-class or I'm a monkey's uncle. They built them to patrol New Russia after they laid claim to the system; I don't think they were ever deployed any-where else."

Richards checked his terminal. "They were all reported destroyed, as of the end of the war, sir," he said, softly. "The Russians lied to us?"

"Maybe," John said.

He gritted his teeth. One of the classified documents he'd had to read had been an order to consider the Russians potential enemies, at least outside the Sol System. It had puzzled him at the time - as far as he knew, the Russians were members of the Earth Defence Organisation in good standing - but perhaps the Admiralty had known something after all. And yet...it made little sense. Why not just consider the Russians universally hostile? And why issue the order in the first place?

Did the Russians attack the missing ship? He asked himself. *And, if they did, were their actions sanctioned by the Russian Government?*

It didn't seem likely, he considered. Russia had lost most of her off-world investment during the war, while the settlers on New Russia had shown their opinion of their distant masters by revolting against them. The Russians would have to be out of their minds to provoke a conflict with Britain, let alone the rest of the EDO. They had to know that human-ity remaining united in the face of a hostile universe was the only hope of long-term survival.

But if the pirates were renegades, they'd be more afraid of being caught by their fellow Russians than anyone else.

"Hail them," he said. "Order them to heave to and prepare to be boarded."

"Aye, sir," Forbes said.

"They're leaving orbit," Howard reported. "I think they're planning to make a run for it."

"Pursuit course, Mr. Armstrong," John ordered. The Russians wouldn't have been wrong to run, if they were facing a pre-war cruiser. *Warspite*, on the other hand, was faster than anything the Russians would have seen, at least anything *human*. "Lieutenant Forbes?"

"No response, sir," Forbes said. "I hailed them in English and Russian."

John shrugged. Almost everyone spoke English these days, certainly everyone living in space. It was the language of planetary datanets, two-thirds of human entertainment and work in space. Someone who didn't speak English would be lucky if they found a menial job, away from a habitable world. Their inability to talk to the patrons would be a major liability.

Unless they worked in Sin City, he thought, grimly. *There, not being able to talk to the guests might be a definite advantage.*

He shrugged. The Russians would definitely be able to speak English. They were just choosing not to reply.

"Repeat the hail," he ordered. The two ships were shaking down now. A stern chase was always a long one, but *Warspite* was slowly overhauling her quarry. "Inform them that if they do not cut their drives and prepare to be boarded, they will be stopped by deadly force."

There was a long pause. "Picking up a reply, sir," Forbes said. "They're protesting that any attempt to board their ship would be an act of war."

John smiled. "Then demand the current Russian IFF codes," he said. "And repeat the demand to heave to."

"No reply, sir," Forbes said, after a moment.

They couldn't have the current IFF codes, John thought. *If they fled New Russia, the last set of codes they'd have would date from before the war. They've been changed a dozen times since then.*

"Captain," Howard said. "They're locking weapons on our hull."

"Stand by point defence," John snapped. He couldn't help a flicker of nervousness. *Warspite* had never been in a real fight before - and he knew better than to underestimate his opponent, even if she was a smaller ship. "Prepare to engage!"

The Russian ship spat a salvo of missiles towards *Warspite*. John allowed himself a moment of relief - they were all pre-war designs, without any of the improvements that would have made them deadlier threats - and then watched grimly as they sliced into point defence range, closing in rapidly on their target. The Russians had an unfair advantage, part of his mind noted. *Warspite* was literally racing to impale herself on their weapons.

"Point defence ready to engage," Howard reported.

"Fire at will," John ordered.

Was it his imagination, he asked himself, or did the Russians *twitch* when *Warspite* opened fire with her plasma cannons? The pre-war point defence systems had been pathetic, compared to the point defence weapons humanity had copied from the Tadpoles, then rushed into mass production. Plasma cannons ran a very real risk of overheating and exploding, the Royal Navy knew from bitter experience, but they put out unbelievable amounts of fire. Five out of six missiles were destroyed before they had a chance to enter engagement range and explode. The sixth took a glancing hit, then exploded.

"Contact nuke, sir," Howard reported.

"No major damage," Johnston said, through the intercom. "Some of our sensors have been blinded, but they can be easily replaced."

"Good," John said. A laser head would have posed a far greater risk to the ship. "Mr. Howard, can you target their drives with a laser head?"

"Aye, sir," Howard said. "But I couldn't guarantee a perfect hit…"

"Don't worry about it," John said. "Fire!"

Warspite shuddered as she unleashed two missiles of her own. It rapidly became clear that the Russian ship hadn't seen any modifications, let alone a full-sized refit, since the start of the war. Their ECM and point defence systems were outdated by several years, while the *Warspite's* missiles were designed to penetrate much stronger layers of point defence. The Russian ship twitched to one side, then flipped over - John was marginally impressed - before reversing and charging back towards *Warspite*. One missile fell to its heavy lasers, the second to a standard-issue railgun.

"Both missiles down, sir," Howard reported. He sounded irked. "I…"

"Engage with lasers," John ordered. "Mr. Armstrong, keep us a safe distance from them at all times."

"Aye, sir," Armstrong said.

John braced himself as the Russians barrelled towards *Warspite*, closing the range with terrifying speed. They might have been playing chicken, he speculated, or they might have seriously intended to ram the British ship. It would destroy both ships if they did…he hesitated, then relaxed slightly as Armstrong altered course. Howard opened fire at the same moment, his lasers slicing into the enemy's hull.

"They've bolted armour to their hull, sir," Howard reported.

They saw the Tadpoles at work, John thought. Tadpole weapons had been designed to burn through thin-skinned human ships, wrecking havoc on their innards. They'd wiped out a whole fleet of carriers within moments, once they'd opened fire. *The Russians did what they could to adapt to a universe the aliens controlled.*

He wondered, suddenly, just what the Russians thought had happened, then dismissed the problem. He'd have his answers soon enough.

"Continue firing," he ordered, as the Russians lanced around again. They had to be pushing their drives to the limit to pull off such stunts, repeatedly, but the Russians had always favoured the brute force approach to starship construction. Their carriers and frigates carried enough fusion reactors for ships several times their size. And their compensators seemed to be built along the same lines. "Aim for their drives."

"They're launching missiles, sir," Howard snapped. "Point defence is primed to engage."

"Good," John said. The Russians grew closer, spitting deadly fire towards *Warspite*. If they'd faced a pre-war cruiser, John suspected, they might well have won. But *Warspite's* armour was enough to take the laser hits without significant damage to her inner hull. "Fire at will."

"Gotcha!" Howard said. He cleared his throat, embarrassed. "Sir; we have disabled their drive section."

"Put some distance between them and us," John snapped. He wanted to launch the Marines, but he knew better than to take the risk. If the Russians wanted to go down fighting, they could just self-destruct once the Marines were onboard. "Lieutenant Forbes; hail them. Inform them that if they surrender without further ado, they will not be returned to Moscow."

"Aye, sir," Lieutenant Forbes said.

John waited, studying the Russian ship on the display. Her drive section had been badly damaged; at a guess, she'd lost two of her fusion reactors and most of her internal power. It was unlikely, though, that she'd lost everything. *She* hadn't had a profiteering engineer sabotaging her drives. But then, he had to admit, her components were likely to need replacing in any case. There was no way they could beg, borrow or steal what they needed from Cromwell or Boston.

"They're responding," Lieutenant Forbes said. "They want to know what *will* happen to them?"

Good question, John thought.

"Tell them they won't be shot," he said. "If they surrender without further ado, they will be transferred to Cromwell, where they can serve as indents for a few years and then blend into the planetary population."

"Aye, sir," Lieutenant Forbes said.

Richards leaned close to John and whispered in his ear, too quietly for anyone else to hear. "The Admiralty won't like you offering such terms, sir."

"I know," John said. There was no tolerance for pirates on Earth, certainly not after the resurgence following the alien bombardment. "But we need that ship intact, along with her databases. It may be the only way to find the missing women and children."

He sighed. Governor Brown wouldn't be happy either. Indents were always blamed for anything that went wrong on colony worlds, which was at least partly why so few of them were dispatched from Earth in the first place. And it would be worse for the Russians, because they *had* kidnapped the colony's women and children.

And if they get murdered by the colonists, he asked himself, *should we really care?*

"They're responding, sir," Forbes said. "They want to be treated as prisoners of war."

John snorted. "And ask them where they want to be sent, when we get them home?"

The Geneva Conventions had been a joke long before the Troubles, but the major powers still attempted to honour them, at least when dealing with their peers. But the Russians wouldn't want to be returned to

Russia, which would be their fate once the war came to an end. And, as there wasn't a war, they would be returned almost at once. Unless, of course, they were found guilty of war crimes. In that case, they could be shot out of hand. It was unlikely the Russians would do more than lodge a muted protest.

We could send them home, he thought, with a flicker of dark humour. *They would be put in front of a wall and shot for desertion.*

"They say they're willing to accept your first terms," Forbes said, after a moment.

"Good," John said. "Inform them that any resistance to my Marines will result in the immediate destruction of their vessel."

He keyed his terminal. "Major Hadfield, you may launch your shuttles at will," he said. "Good hunting."

"Aye, sir," Hadfield said.

"Marines away, sir," Howard said.

John nodded. "Keep missiles locked on their hull," he ordered. He tapped his console, opening a link to Main Engineering. "Damage report?"

"Minor damage to our sensor blisters, sir," Johnston reported. "Our armour was scorched and pitted, but held. I'm drawing up a repair plan now."

"Good," John said. He looked at his bridge crew. "You all performed splendidly, all of you. This will be noted in my log."

"Thank you, sir," Richards said.

And Thank God I managed to steer Commander Watson out of her position, John thought. *Who knows what would have happened then?*

CHAPTER
TWENTY EIGHT

"Good God," Hardesty said. "What a fucking mess."

"As you were," Percy snapped, as the Russian ship came into view. Her hull showed the patchwork signs of too many makeshift repairs, even before *Warspite's* lasers had sliced her drive section into ribbons. "Remain alert at all times. They could be planning an ambush."

A dull clunk ran through the shuttle as it docked with the Russian ship. Percy picked up his rifle, ran a quick check on his light armour, then stepped up to the airlock. It hissed open, allowing a gust of foul-smelling air to billow into the shuttle. The Russians would know to replace their atmospheric filters regularly, he was sure, but they would be running short of supplies. He stepped through the hatch and into an airlock, which opened into a long corridor. If anything, the air was fouler inside the ship itself.

He looked up as a tall man stepped into view, his face lined and rugged, his hair starting to turn white. "Welcome onboard *Petrov*," he said, as if the Marines were just visiting. His English was oddly accented, as if he'd learned it in adulthood. "I am Captain Aleksandr Sergeyevich Nekrasov."

Percy was in no mood for games. "Assemble your men," he ordered, curtly. "I am obliged to warn you that, while provisional POW status has been granted to you prior to your arrival on Cromwell, any attempt to escape, harm or mislead my men will result in severe penalties."

Nekrasov gave him a long look, then keyed an outdated wristcom and issued orders in Russian. Slowly, a handful of crewmen appeared at one end of the corridor and walked towards the Marines, looking alternatively relieved and terrified. They were all male, Percy noted, save for a pair of pale-faced women at the back. The Russians had always been less willing to allow women to serve on their warships, he recalled, although he couldn't recall why. Not, in the end, that it mattered.

"If you are carrying any weapons, get rid of them," he ordered. "You will be searched, bound, then transferred to our ship."

He nodded to the Marines, who beckoned the first crewman forward and searched him, quickly and efficiently. Once he was clean, they bound his hands and pushed him into the shuttle, then moved to the next crewman. He was carrying a pair of knives, both of which were confiscated. Percy kept a sharp eye on proceedings, making a mental note to arrange for both of the women to be kept separate from the men. If their ship had been away from any bases for at least five years, chances were they would have been in danger from their male comrades if the Captain had lost his grip.

"Captain," he said. "Is this your entire crew?"

"The survivors," Captain Nekrasov said. "Seven of my crew are dead."

Percy ordered the Captain bound, then led his Marines on a quick search of the Russian starship. He'd never had the chance to visit *Ark Royal*, but he couldn't help wondering if the aging carrier had felt quite as old as the Russian vessel. It was clear, far too clear, that the Russians had been on their last legs, even before they'd run into *Warspite*. Their sensors were failing, their weapons decaying…even their life support was starting to collapse, despite the colossal over-engineering. In some ways, the captured crew were lucky. It wouldn't have taken more than a single catastrophic failure to leave them breathing vacuum, light years from any prospect of help.

"We've located the remaining bodies," he said, once they picked their way through the shattered drive section. "They're all here, sir."

"Very good," Hadfield said. He'd wanted to lead the mission in person, but Peerce had talked him out of it. Percy was more expendable. "And the ship's computers?"

"Powered down," Percy said, after a quick check. "I think the engineers will have to have a look at her, sir."

"I'll have them called, once we sweep the ship again," Hadfield said. "Good work, Percy."

"Thank you, sir," Percy said.

———

"I've had the male prisoners moved into Hold Two," Richards said, an hour later. "The Captain and the female prisoners have been placed in the brig, for the moment. They should be fairly secure."

"Good," John said. He turned to Doctor Stewart. "What can you tell us about our guests?"

"Very little," Stewart said. "I've taken DNA samples and compared them to our database, but none of the prisoners were included in any of the files the Russians shared with us, during the war. I suspect the Russians believe them to have been killed during the First Battle of New Russia."

"So they wouldn't have bothered to share any details," John mused.

"No, sir," Stewart said. "Health-wise, they're not in good shape. Their diet must have been pretty poor, because at least two of them are at risk of scurvy."

John shook his head in disbelief. "These aren't the days of Lord Nelson," he protested. "Their commander *must* have known the dangers."

"I imagine they had problems obtaining the foodstuffs they required," Stewart said. "I don't believe that ship was intended to operate alone, certainly not for five years."

"It didn't," Johnston said. The Chief Engineer looked grim. "There were at least two other ships with her, when she fled New Russia."

John looked at him. "I thought they'd purged their computer cores."

"They did," Johnston said. "But they didn't actually *destroy* them, Captain, and they underestimated our skill at recovering data. I think there are huge tracts of data still missing, well beyond recovery, but we managed to pull out quite a bit."

He took a breath. "As we surmised, sir, this ship and two of her consorts fled New Russia after the carriers were lost," he explained. "They must have believed the war to be utterly hopeless…which wasn't really a bad guess. I don't think they knew about *Ark Royal*. They spent the next six months working their way through the tramlines to Boston, and then up into unexplored space. I think they saw this whole sector as being least likely to attract the Tadpoles."

"They might have been right," John mused. "And then?"

"Good question," Johnston said. "The log entries get sparse after their arrival in this sector, Captain. There's some reference to a habitable world, a place to set up a new home, but nothing very clear. At some point, they must have realised that the war was over and the human race had won, which would have been a nasty shock. They couldn't hope to return home without being shot."

"They probably decided to set up a secret colony of their own," Hadfield put in. "Taking the women and children would allow them to make their colony self-sustaining."

John nodded, sickened. There had been two women on the ship, out of a thirty-strong crew. The Russians wouldn't have had a hope of setting up a long-term colony, not without more women or medical technology they didn't have. But by stumbling across *Vesper*, they'd found everything they wanted dropped into their lap. Had they known, he asked himself, just what *Vesper* was carrying? Or had it been a stroke of immensely good luck?

They could have made a link with someone in Boston, he thought. *Vesper's manifest might have been shared with the Americans before she went through the system.*

"And that leads to a different question," he said. "Where is *Vesper* now?"

"I think they took her through the human-grade tramline," Johnston said. "They didn't have any modifications to their drive, Captain. The alien tramlines would be inaccessible to them."

"We could ask," Hadfield pointed out. "They're effectively pirates. We owe them nothing, certainly not a chance to live the rest of their lives in relative safety. Enhanced interrogation is legally permitted."

John considered it, then shook his head. He'd always thought of himself as a pragmatist, and there was an argument in favour of using drugs, lie detectors or even torture, but he'd accepted their surrender on the promise of good treatment. The Russians could hardly do anything to stop him, if he decided to force them to talk, yet it would be disastrous in the long run. No one would surrender to the Royal Navy if they thought they would be tortured to death, then shoved out of the nearest airlock.

"No," he said. "We can search the next system without forcing them to tell us anything."

"I don't want to be the voice of caution, sir," Richards said, "but shouldn't we consider reporting back to Boston?"

"That would leave women and children in enemy hands," Hadfield snapped.

John held up a hand. It was Richards's *job* to point out the dangers in proceeding onwards, deeper into the unknown. Two more Russian frigates wouldn't be much more of a threat, not if they were in no better shape than *Petrov*, but a single mistake could cost them everything, including the evidence they'd gathered so far. Richards was right; there were advantages in turning and returning to Boston...

But Hadfield was also right. Turning back would mean leaving women and children in enemy hands. He hated to think of what the Russians must have done, to make the women submit to them, or what might have been done to the children. The Russians might even have started planning to raise them as their own, using them as the next generation of settlers. But how could they hope to set up a technological colony with only three frigates?

"We have to proceed," he said. "Mr. Johnston, is there any hope of learning much more from the hulk?"

"I don't believe so, sir," Johnston said. "The Russian crewmen do not seem to have written any journals or anything else we can use as a source of intelligence. We didn't even find any private terminals or datapads in their quarters and the only datachips we found were either games or porn."

"The Russians value information security," Hadfield commented. "Any of their officers who kept a private journal would be in deep shit when the FSB caught him. They'd string him up as a warning to the next fool who thought he could get away with it."

"We only allow them on the main datanet too," John said. Private terminals were permitted, grudgingly, but anyone who put classified material on them would be in trouble. "They would be purged along with the rest of the computer cores, if necessary."

He looked at Johnston. "Can the Russian ship be salvaged?"

"It would be cheaper to build a modern frigate from scratch, sir," Johnston said. "Right now, she is utterly incapable of generating a drive field, energising a beam or travelling down a tramline. We could tow her to Cromwell and use her as an orbiting base, sir, but I can't imagine any other use for her. She wouldn't even be worth more than a few thousand pounds if we tried to collect prize money for her."

John had to smile. The Royal Navy handed out prize money for 'interesting' captures, yet there simply weren't that many that qualified. He'd heard that half the crew of *Ark Royal* had become millionaires after they'd brought home an *alien* ship, but they'd been the exception.

"Then carry out one final sweep of her hull, then power her down and mark her location carefully," he ordered. "We can arrange for her to be towed back to Cromwell later."

"Aye, sir," Johnston said.

There wouldn't be much disappointment, John knew. A few thousand pounds shared among the crew, even if he refused his ten percent, wouldn't go very far. Salvaging *Vesper* and her passengers would be much more lucrative, once they managed to get the colonists to Cromwell. But it was better not to plan for what he would do with the money until he actually earned it.

"Good work, all of you," John said. He looked at Richards. "Can we sustain the prisoners?"

"There shouldn't be any problems feeding them on ration bars for the next few months," Richards said. "We might consider giving them ration bars to be cruel and unusual punishment, but based on what they were eating on the ship I dare say they'll be glad to get them. Their food processor had major problems. I think it was actually rejecting elements they needed to live."

"Ouch," John said. He'd never met anyone who liked the bland ration bars, even before they learned just *what* was reprocessed and used to produce them, but they did provide everything a human needed to live. If the Russians had been accidentally poisoning themselves, they might have *very* good reason to be grateful they'd been caught. "And security?"

"They're unarmed," Richards said. "I've sealed off the whole compartment and Major Hadfield has placed two Marines on guard duty outside. They shouldn't be able to break through the hatch, sir, let alone escape. If any of them do cause trouble, we can either handcuff them to the bulkhead or simply drug them into a stupor."

"I would prefer not to keep them drugged indefinitely," Stewart said, sharply. "We don't have the tools to freeze them safely, sir, and drugging someone for long periods can cause dangerous complications."

"As long as they're secure," John said. "And their commander?"

"He's in the brig, sir," Hadfield reminded him. "He can be held there without guard, although I do have someone watching him and the women. I have a feeling the women may crack and tell us something important, if we take care of them."

John felt his eyes narrowed. "How badly were they treated?"

Stewart shrugged. "Physically, they're in no worse state than the men," he said. "Mentally, they're in a very dark place. I don't think they were actually raped, sir, but they were certainly very aware of the possibility. I saw similar cases in some of the worse-run refugee camps after the bombardment."

"I see," John said. "Is there anything we can do for them?"

"I've assigned my nurse, Pomona Scott, to tend to them," Stewart said. "They would probably respond better to another woman right now. In the long term, we may be able to get them talking to Lieutenant Forbes or Lieutenant Logan. However, they are likely to be a screwed-up mess, thanks to the way they were treated. I would not count on getting anything useful out of them."

"Then we won't," John said. "Mike, how long will it take you to deal with the enemy ship?"

"An hour, no more," Johnston said. "We brought most of the useful material over with us, when we did the first sweep. If you don't mind, I'd prefer to vent the ship's atmosphere completely. There are rats and cockroaches breeding down in the depths of her hull."

"As you see fit," John said. The Russians had allowed themselves to go to pieces...he wondered, absently, if he would have done any better. If *Warspite* had been alone, with the certain knowledge that they would all be hung if they returned home, how would *he* have coped with the situation? "We'll depart in one hour. Mr. Armstrong?"

"Yes, sir?"

"I want you to plot out a course for the new tramline, but - again - I want to enter the system from the edge," John ordered. "If there are two prowling ships out there, I really do *not* want to be detected."

"Aye, sir," Armstrong said.

"I can plot out possible engagements, sir," Howard offered.

"Just remember that war is a democracy," John reminded him. It had been hammered into his head, time and time again, that no battle plan ever survived contact with the enemy. The Russians, desperate to escape detection and capture, might do something unpredictable. "The enemy gets a vote too."

He looked at Richards. "Ready a second beacon," he added. "Again, copy our logs and sensor records, then launch it here. If something happens to us, at least the next ship will have a trail of breadcrumbs to follow."

"Aye, sir," Richards said.

But the Russians will know they've been detected, John thought. They'd know when their frigate failed to report home, wherever 'home' happened to be. *What will they do then?*

He scowled. *Or will they assume that she merely ran out of luck and suffered a catastrophic disaster? Or is that wishful thinking?*

"Good work, everyone," he finished, putting the thought aside. It *had* been good work. *Warspite's* crew had faced their first real enemy and defeated him soundly. "Dismissed."

He rose as his crew filed out of the compartment, then tapped a switch. The holographic display changed to show the view from the ship's hull; the Russian frigate hanging in the foreground, the unmoving stars behind. It was astonishing just how well the Russian starship had held up, John couldn't help thinking. Five years without a shipyard, without even a new set of spare parts, and the vessel had still been reasonably functional. If she'd had a carrier accompanying her, John suspected, she could have kept going indefinitely.

The crew must have been on the verge of madness, he thought. There had been studies done on the effects of isolation in space, but apart from the early space travellers, there had been few cases of people being truly isolated, or being more than a week from safe harbour. But the Russians had not only been months from Earth, they'd known they couldn't go home again. Perhaps that was why they had turned to piracy. They'd not seen any other way to survive.

His intercom bleeped. "Captain," Armstrong said. "Our course is prepared and laid in."

"Wait for the engineers to return to the ship," John said, dryly. Hiding the Russian frigate might come in handy - at least, the ship's hull would be useful, if she were towed back to Cromwell. "And then we can set course for the next system."

And hope, he added silently, *that the rest of the pirates await us there.*

CHAPTER
TWENTY NINE

"The star's another G2, sir," Howard said.

John allowed himself a breath. "Planets?"

"Nine, sir," Howard said, after a moment. "Eight of them are definitely rocky worlds."

He sucked in a breath. "Captain," he said, sharply. "There are *seven* tramlines in the system!"

John looked up at the display, feeling a sudden shiver of excitement. Seven tramlines to seven potential destinations alone would be a worthwhile find, but combined with the presence of a life-bearing world - assuming there *was* a life-bearing world in the system - it would set the crew up for life. The British Crown would claim the system, set up a colony and charge transit fees for starships using the tramlines. It would do the economy a power of good.

"Impressive," he said, keeping his voice even. "Can you pick up any traces of technological presence?"

"Negative, sir," Howard said.

But that meant nothing, John knew. The Russian refugees presumably wouldn't want to call attention to their presence by emitting radio signals. They'd only stumbled across the captured frigate through luck. The only way to *confirm* the Russians weren't in the system was to search it, thoroughly. He leaned back in his command chair and waited as more and more data appeared in the holographic display. Two of the rocky worlds were well within the life-bearing zone, not too close and not too far from the local star.

That means nothing too, he reminded himself. *Titan and Clarke are both further from their primary stars and they have life, if not intelligent life.*

"Keep us in stealth, but take us towards the nearest planet," he ordered. "Best possible speed."

He contemplated the system's prospects as *Warspite* slowly slid further towards the star. There was no gas giant, which explained why the Russians had been mining in the nearest system, but there *was* an asteroid belt and eight presumably barren rocky worlds. It would give the system a hefty boost, once a colony had been established; it was possible, judging from the tramlines, that one of them ran back towards Pegasus. The British Crown would snatch all the worthwhile real estate in the sector before anyone else knew what had been discovered. He smiled at the thought, then contemplated the image of the rocky world. The ship's telescopes revealed that it had an oxygen-rich atmosphere, which almost certainly meant it was Earth-compatible. Britain's claim to the sector would be upheld by international law.

"Captain," Forbes said. "I just picked up a brief flicker of radio chatter."

John looked at her. "From the Russians?"

"I'm not sure," Forbes said. "The source was somewhere near the second planet, but the radio system seemed almost primitive."

John frowned. Were the Russians trying to set up a tech base of their own? They'd need one, if they wanted to establish a proper colony, but it would also run the risk of being detected by outside powers. If they truly wanted to hide, they'd set up the colony on the surface, then send their ships into the sun. But who would want to give up technology to live on the ground like savages?

People who happen to be desperate, he thought. *And perhaps people they want to keep under control.*

"Continue to monitor the system," he ordered. "Mr. Howard, launch a stealth probe towards the planet on a ballistic trajectory. I want to know what we're about to encounter."

"Aye, sir," Howard said. He keyed his console. Moments later, the probe shot away from *Warspite*, plunging further into the system. "Probe away, sir."

John nodded, then forced himself to relax. It would be hours before the probe got close enough to learn more about the planet, but he couldn't leave the bridge, not now. He checked the reports from Main Engineering - and Commander Watson's notes on the new tramline - in the hopes of diverting himself from his worries. But there was nothing special about the tramline, save for its destination. The drive matrix had barely needed to be recalibrated to allow them to make a safe transit, without the crew throwing up on the deck.

The seconds ticked slowly away, until the first report came back. "Captain," Howard said, "there are three starships orbiting the planet."

"Show me," John ordered.

The display changed to show the live feed from the probe, beamed back to *Warspite* through a laser beam. Two large starships hung in high orbit; a smaller ship, clearly a sister to the frigate *Warspite* had already captured, hung lower. John had no difficulty in recognising *Vesper*; he'd seen her outlines often enough while he'd been reviewing her files. The massive bulk freighter looked dead and cold, even her running lights deactivated. John hoped - prayed - that meant the Russians had shipped the colonists to the surface. *Vesper* couldn't have remained habitable for very long if her life support had been powered down.

"She's definitely *Vesper*, sir," Howard confirmed. "I have a visual on her hull."

"At least we know where they went," Richards muttered. "They have to be here."

"Probably," John agreed. The Russians would have problems shipping so many colonists elsewhere without the giant freighter. "And the other ship?"

"I'm not sure," Howard confessed. "Captain, the war book flags it as an assault transport, but it doesn't quite match the profile."

John leaned forward. The Russian ship was slightly smaller than *Vesper*, bristling with shuttles and sensor blisters. It looked to have been designed to insert troops on a planetary surface, without relying on bases already established on the ground. The Royal Navy would use a fleet carrier for the task, if it had to carry out an amphibious offensive from space, but the Russians tended to use cruder ships. They might have seen value in building a specialised design.

And it wouldn't have been expected to join the battleline at New Russia, he thought, grimly. *Her commander might have beaten feet out of the system as soon as the battle went badly.*

He keyed his terminal. "Major Hadfield, I need an assessment," he said. "How many troops might the Russians have under their command?"

"Unknown, sir," Hadfield said. "I would speculate, at most, a couple of thousand, but I can't see so many choosing to desert Mother Russia."

And the ship could have been empty when the battle began, John thought. *They wouldn't have risked so many troops, not when they might have been needed on the surface.*

He shook his head, then returned his attention to the display as more and more details popped up in front of him. The Russians seemed to be operating on very low power, which suggested their ships were reaching the end of their endurance, but he knew better than to take that for granted. A small team of workmen seemed to be swarming over *Vesper*, cannibalising the ship to help keep the other two going; he wondered, absently, just how long the Russians thought they had before something irreplaceable snapped. *Vesper* was a civilian ship, even if she had spent time in the RFA. She didn't carry many military-grade components that could be reused.

The second Russian frigate seemed to be in better condition, he decided. It was something of a mystery why the Russians hadn't sent *it* to mine for fuel, unless he was wrong and the Russian ship was incapable of leaving orbit. He considered the problem for a long moment, then dismissed it. There were more important matters at hand.

"Mr. Howard, they must have a colony on the surface," he said. He wouldn't have kept the prisoners in orbit, not if it could be avoided. There would be too great a chance of a successful uprising. "Can you locate it?"

"Aye, sir," Howard said. "The probe is entering orbit now..." He broke off. "*Fuck me!*"

"Mr. Howard," Richards snapped!

"Sorry, sir," Howard said. He sounded stunned. "Captain, I think you should take a look at this."

John leaned forward as images appeared in front of him. The planet was unusual, he noted; unlike Earth, there was more land than sea. A handful of giant lakes could be seen, but they weren't interconnected. There was no reason why a single land power couldn't rise to dominate the entire planet...his thoughts trailed away as Howard focused the feed from the probe. There were settlements dotted all *over* the planet. For a moment, John refused to grasp what he was seeing. Even Terra Nova, Washington or Britannia didn't have such a vast network of settlements. It would take *centuries* to build up such a vast population, even with the baby boom following the war.

And then it clicked.

"Jesus Christ," he whispered. "They're *aliens!*"

"Yes, sir," Howard said.

John felt his heart pounding in his chest. It wasn't impossible to believe, not after the Tadpoles, that a third world might develop intelligent life. There were quite a few worlds where, if evolution had taken a few more steps, it might have produced intelligent life before the human race arrived to foreclose the possibility. But somehow, coming face to face with the reality of a third intelligent race left him breathless. He'd never seriously expected to discover a non-human race on *Warspite's* first cruise.

"Pull as much data as you can from orbit," John ordered. His voice sounded strange in his ears, as if he was as stunned as his tactical officer. "And route it through the Marines as well as the tactical department."

Richards had another concern. "Do they pose a threat?"

"I don't think so," Howard said, after a moment. "There's no sign of steam power, let alone radio signals. I'd say this world is at roughly the same level as Britain, in the days of the Spanish Armada. But there's no way to be sure. The Russians had several years to work with the natives."

"Shit," Richards mused. "Captain, the Russians could have given the natives human technology."

John nodded in agreement. There were laws against sharing human technology with aliens, but it wasn't as if the Russian refugees could be hung more than once, no matter how many crimes they'd committed. For the first time, he found himself seriously considering backing off and sneaking back to Pegasus to whistle up help. Aliens placed a whole different gloss on the scene. *Warspite* was no survey ship, with a crew of sociologists who might be able to make contact with the aliens...

But Vesper and her colonists are here, he thought. *We can't abandon them, not now.*

The regulations might have been written before First Contact, but they still held force. A starship that encountered intelligent alien life, particularly *spacefaring* alien life, was to attempt to avoid contact and report home, placing the contact mission in the hands of professionals. In the event of contact being unavoidable, the starship was to ensure that the newcomers learned nothing about the human sphere; if necessary, the ship was to destroy itself rather than risk its databases falling into unfriendly hands. And nothing, absolutely nothing, was to be shared with the aliens without permission from Earth. If the Russians had made contact, if the Russians had given the aliens human technology, they'd broken one of the few rules shared by all spacefaring nations.

He shuddered. It hadn't really been a problem with the Tadpoles. If anything, the Tadpoles had been more advanced than the human race; they'd been equals, rather than a weaker race that could be overshadowed by humanity. But a primitive race…human history wasn't encouraging, when it came to weak or primitive societies making contact with stronger or more aggressive nations. Hundreds of societies had been overwhelmed, shattered or simply exterminated by the newcomers.

The Native Americans want a planet of their own, he thought, recalling the political debate that had consumed the United States, just prior to First Contact. *But is there enough of their society left to let them form something their pre-Columbus ancestors would recognise?*

But there was another issue, one that had bugged him when the 'Prime Directive' had been debated during his officer training. The primitive society might *want* to be contaminated. What sort of idiot would want to refuse medical treatments that might keep them alive for a few more decades or technology that would spare them years of backbreaking labour? And what sort of monster would *deny* them the technology, choosing instead to leave them to suffer and die in the mud? Just for the sake of preserving a primitive culture? It wasn't an argument he regarded as valid. How could he?

Howard cleared his throat. "The probe has spotted a section of prefabricated buildings here," he said, tapping his console. A red light appeared on the display. "The Russians have set up a base next to a large alien settlement."

"A city," Richards mused. He looked at John. "Captain, I think we must assume the Russians have broken the non-intercourse edict."

"It certainly looks that way," John said. The Russians couldn't have avoided being noticed by the aliens, not if they'd landed *there*. They had to have made contact with the locals and then…and then, what? What did the Russians gain from making contact? "But why?"

"They may wish to dominate the planet for their own safety," Richards speculated. "Or they may be merely playing games."

John shuddered. He'd heard stories about wealthy westerners who'd chosen to live in the Third World and done precisely that. Money talked, particularly if it came from the West; someone with enough money could set up a small army of their own, then set out to get their kicks by starting a war. In some ways, he thought, it was worse than sex tourism. It got thousands of locals killed for someone's sick amusement.

And the aliens would be completely incapable of resisting, he thought, as the alien city came into sharp focus. *They'd be unable even to appeal to us to do something about the rogues.*

"Mr. Howard," he ordered, slowly. "Show me the aliens."

Howard altered the display. An alien appeared in front of him, standing on top of a giant building. John had half-expected a Tadpole-like creature, but it was clear the alien bore a closer resemblance to humanity. His - or her - skin was scaly, suggesting reptilian ancestors; his head was covered in feathers, although John couldn't tell if it was a fancy piece of headgear or the alien version of hair. The body seemed to be largely humanoid, yet it flexed in odd ways. John had the impression that, if forced to run, the aliens were capable of moving faster than any human.

Armstrong coughed. "Is that a *he* or a *she*?"

"Unknown," Howard said. His voice sounded torn between amusement and disgust. "But would you want to take *that* to bed?"

"Gentlemen, please," John snapped.

The alien looked up, as if it could see the watching probe. His - John decided to assume the alien was male, at least until they learned how to tell the difference - eyes were beady, like a bird. Or a lizard, his own thoughts added; it was quite possible, he figured, that the alien could focus on two different objects at once. The nose was flattened against the scaly skull, the mouth was full of very sharp teeth. There was no sign of any ears.

Howard pulled back the camera, showing him a large section of the city. It looked primitive, as if it belonged to Imperial Rome or Greece, but it teemed with aliens. Some of them were clearly soldiers, carrying weapons that looked like blunderbusses; others looked like workers, or slaves. A shot outside the city showed a camp, crammed with aliens; John had no difficulty in recognising a slave pen. The aliens, it seemed, had yet to abolish slavery on their world.

"I don't know how much more we can pick up from orbit, sir," Howard admitted. "We really need a team of sociologists."

"I know," John said. He tried to imagine how the alien society might be governed, but drew a blank. Human history suggested kings or emperors; the aliens, though, might have come up with something new. "But it can wait."

He turned to look at Richards. "The pirates didn't breathe a word about the aliens, did they?"

"No, sir," Richards confirmed. "The only mention in their logs of something even remotely relating to non-human life was a note about a life-bearing world."

And they meant it too, John thought. He hadn't realised it referred to actual *aliens*. No one had.

"I have a focus on the Russian camp," Howard said.

John turned. The Russian settlement looked more like a fortress than a permanent home, a handful of prefabricated buildings surrounded by high walls and farmland. Only a handful of humans could be seen, most of them women. They looked as if they were prisoners, John noted; beyond the walls, chained aliens worked the fields. *They* were very definitely slaves.

And the women can't run, John thought. *If they did, they would be killed by the aliens themselves.*

"My God," Richards said.

"I don't think God wants anything to do with this," John said. He cleared his throat. "Mr. Howard, draw as much data as you can without alerting the Russians. Mr. Armstrong, hold us here. Mr. Richards, you have the bridge."

He keyed his console. "Major Hadfield, it's time we had a long chat with our guests," he said, shortly. "Bring Captain Nekrasov to my quarters, in chains."

"Aye, sir," Hadfield said.

John rose. The presence of alien life changed everything. There could be no half measures any longer. One way or the other, he would have answers. And then they would come up with a plan.

"Lieutenant Forbes, work on the Russian women," he added. "See if they could be convinced to tell us something too."

"Aye, sir," Forbes said.

John took one last look at the alien world, then turned and left the bridge.

CHAPTER
THIRTY

John looked up as Captain Nekrasov was escorted into his cabin by Lieutenant Hadfield and two burly Marines. They weren't really necessary - the Russian had his hands cuffed behind his back, while his legs were shackled - but it did help to remind the Russian that he was a helpless prisoner. John studied the man for a long moment, then motioned for the Marines to push him into a chair. The Russian looked old, old and worn. Life as a refugee, then a renegade must have been hard.

But John felt no sympathy. How could he?

"Captain," he said, shortly. "We found your camp - and the aliens you *forgot* to mention to us."

Nekrasov shrugged. "So what?"

John felt his temper fray. "You and your men not only fled the war, which wouldn't be our problem, but captured a British ship and its passengers," he said. "And, if that wasn't enough, you broke the non-interference edict by landing on an alien world and introducing human technology to the natives. I don't believe our original deal covered meddling in an alien society."

The Russian shrugged, again. "I don't believe it *didn't*," he said, dryly. "Or are you that keen to break your word?"

"The women and children you kidnapped were scheduled to go to Cromwell, where we planned to take you as prisoners," John pointed out. "All we'd have to do is tell the locals what you did and wait for them to butcher you and your men. If they were prepared to risk an uprising, they certainly wouldn't hesitate to kill you."

"I don't think my government would approve," the Russian said.

"No," John agreed. "They'd want to hang you themselves."

He met the Russian's eye. "Your nation is in deep shit," he said. "I don't know why, I admit, but they've been on the outs with the other spacefaring powers. Your government is struggling to regain control of New Russia, your economy is in the shitter and large numbers of skilled personnel are leaving. I don't think anyone in the Kremlin would seriously consider picking a fight with us over you. They're much more likely to thank us for hanging you from the nearest tree."

"You're talking nonsense," the Russian said.

"No," John said, although he knew the Russian had no way to know it. "And even if I was lying, what about the laws you've broken? Your government will set a new record for repudiating you when they find out what you've done to helpless natives. You'll be put on trial in front of the World Court, then hung. Whatever deal we made with you won't last when Earth finds out what you've done."

The Russian's eyes narrowed. "Can your authority be overridden so blatantly?"

"I would hate to have to find out," John said. "But it really doesn't matter. You and your men won't survive Cromwell unless you talk to us, now."

For a moment, he thought he'd won. But then the Russian set his face in stone and stared at him, defiantly. "Do your worst," he said. "We're dead anyway."

You overplayed your hand, John thought, crossly. *You can't threaten a man who knows he's dead whatever happens.*

"We shall see," he said, sharply. He looked up at the Marines. "Take him back to his cell."

"He doesn't have anything to lose," Hadfield said, when the prisoner had been marched through the hatch. "And he's been treated, sir. I don't think truth drugs will work on him."

"Crap," John said. He looked down at his desk, then back at the Marine. "Do you have any ideas?"

"I doubt his subordinates know *that* much," Hadfield said, "but it's hard to see how they can have avoided learning of the aliens. One of them might talk, if we offered a chance to escape punishment completely."

John considered it. In theory, he could make whatever deals he liked with the Russians and the Admiralty would accept it. They might be furious with him, when they found out about it, but they wouldn't want to cast doubt on a Captain's authority when his ship was light years from Earth. It might cost John his career - commanding officers had been quietly sidelined when they overstepped the bounds, even if they weren't formally punished - yet the deal would have been kept. But with aliens involved…

He shook his head. The Admiralty might back him, but the Prime Minister would be furious and the World Court would want to try the Russian pirates for blatant defiance of International Law. It would set off a major political catfight that might well tear the Earth Defence Organisation apart, perhaps even bringing down multiple governments. No one would thank him for bringing such a nightmare home.

But did he have a choice? There was no way he could *hide* what they'd found, or what the Russians had done. Captain Nekrasov had been right; no matter what he did, the Russians were dead anyway. They had nothing to lose by keeping their mouths shut…

"We might be able to get away with making a deal with a subordinate," John mused. "They could not be expected to disobey orders."

He sighed, inwardly. It was the old question of when obeying orders became, in itself, a crime. Soldiers and spacers were meant to obey orders, but what should they do when an illegal order was issued? Disobedience could mean death. And the whole issue of what was a war crime had never really been settled. John had been told, during his training, that the only way to *know* was to lose the war, in which case the victors would happily put the losers on trial for war crimes. It had never been anything other than a form of victor's justice.

"See if one will talk," he ordered. "And be ready to move him to the remaining brig cell if necessary."

His intercom bleeped. "Captain, this is Forbes," a voice said. "One of the Russians would like to talk."

"That's lucky," John commented, dryly. "Have her brought to my office, under escort."

"Aye, sir," Lieutenant Forbes said.

Five minutes later, Forbes and a Marine escorted a young woman into John's quarters. She looked as thin as her male counterparts, her face pale and worn. Long dark hair hung down around her face, suggesting that she was trying to hide behind her hair. She looked, very much, as if she was trying to project an attitude of helplessness, as if she was someone in need of protection. If John had been interested in women, he admitted privately, he had a nasty feeling it would have been effective.

"Captain, this is Tatyana Yevgeniyevna Bodrova," Lieutenant Forbes said. "She's a doctor - or she was, before her ship was captured."

John wasn't too surprised. The Russians tended to leave women out of combat roles, even though they had always been willing to use women as spies, assassins and support staff. It wasn't something he understood, although the near-catastrophic population decline Russia had suffered during the Age of Unrest had probably had something to do with it. The Russian Government had handed out bounties to each ethnic Russian woman who had at least three Russian children - there had been no room for mixed marriages in Russia - and used it to boost their population. Like so many of the other steps taken during the same period, by all manner of governments, no one was sure if it had been justified or not.

"Captain," Tatyana said. Her voice was low, almost seductive. "I…I need to know what will happen to me."

"If you tell us everything, without hesitation, you will be allowed to work as a doctor on Cromwell," John said. Doctors were in too short supply for one to be lynched, particularly if she happened to be young, fertile and beautiful. The cynic in him was sure it wouldn't be long before Tatyana picked up a husband. "Or, if you don't want to live there, we can take you back to Earth and determine your future there."

Tatyana lowered her eyes. "Would I be away from the others?"

"If you want," John said. He felt his patience grow thin. "But we need answers now."

"Very well," Tatyana said. She took a long breath. "General Rybak was in command, when the shit hit the fan at New Russia. He thought the aliens would be easy meat for the Multi-National Force and loaded a hundred soldiers onto the assault transport, ready to board the alien ships after the battle. Instead, the aliens cut the fleet to ribbons and the General ordered us to flee. So we jumped through the tramlines, heading as far from the aliens as we could."

She looked up at him, pleadingly. "The General said we would find a place to rebuild and then set out to recover our lost worlds," he said. "None of us thought Earth would last more than a month after New Russia. We all agreed that the only thing we could do was run and hide. We slipped through Boston and through a tramline listed as unexplored. And then we discovered the aliens."

Hadfield leaned forward. "Do they have a name?"

"We can't speak their language," Tatyana said. "There's something about the shape of their mouths that makes it impossible. We call them the Vesy."

"Scales, in Russian," Hadfield commented. "Why not Lizards? Or Reptiles?"

Tatyana eyed him. "Does it matter?"

John shrugged. "Carry on," he said. "So you found the Vesy and then…what?"

"We studied their world long enough to pick up the dominant language," Tatyana said, after a moment. "The General was quite happy to kidnap a handful of the aliens so we could study them. Once we had a grasp on their tongue, we landed the shuttle near one of the city-states and made contact. The God-King saw our arrival as a gift from the gods and welcomed us to his city. It wasn't long before he struck a deal with the General. We would help him unify his world in exchange for help and supplies."

She paused. "I think the General honestly thought we would need their help to rebuild our fleets," she added. "Given a century, we could help the Vesy to build their own spacecraft and shipyards, then take the war to the aliens. We would unite their world, then lead them to the rescue of the human race."

Hadfield leaned forward. "What sort of assistance did you give him?"

"Some troop support, orbital reconnaissance, that sort of thing," Tatyana admitted. "Most of our supplies were quite limited, but we were able to help his armies lunge out and conquer most of the surrounding city-states. Those that submitted quickly and accepted the God-King's right to rule were allowed to pay tribute, provide troops and suchlike. And those that didn't were crushed, their populations enslaved or sacrificed..."

Her voice trailed off. "They're monsters," she said. "And the General *encouraged* it."

"They sound very human," Hadfield observed, dryly.

John nodded in agreement. It was impossible to be sure, but the God-King's state sounded like something akin to the Aztec Empire. The smaller cities were permitted some degree of freedom, provided they bent the knee to the Aztecs, while anyone who dared resist was crushed mercilessly. But the Aztecs had always had limits on their military power, he recalled, vaguely. The Vesy had the advantage of human help and support. Even the introduction of Napoleonic-era human tech would change the balance of power, without turning the aliens into a threat to humanity.

"Maybe they were," Tatyana said.

She took a breath. "The General kept his two frigates watching the tramlines," she continued. "One day, a freighter came along the tramline from Boston and was snatched. The crew discovered that humanity had actually *won* the war. I thought the General would be delighted, that we could go home, but instead he grew madder. None of us could go home, he said, without being executed. And he was right."

John felt an odd flicker of sympathy. If the General had been right, the Russian refugees would have been the last survivors of the human race. There wouldn't have been any choice, but to use the aliens to build a new civilisation and eventually settle accounts with the Tadpoles. But he'd been wrong and his people were now trapped. The nightmare they'd unleashed on the aliens wouldn't be forgiven. They literally had nowhere to go.

"He took another ship," Tatyana said. "This one was crammed with women and children. He had them brought to Vesy, then shipped down to the surface and announced they would be the mothers of a whole new generation. Most of the women were shared out among his men, among those who supported him. The children were pushed aside to be raised by the soldiers, by the troops who still supported the General."

Vesper, John thought.

"He's going mad," Tatyana said. "Isolation combined with the grim awareness of total failure...it's enough to drive anyone insane. His command crews are loyalists; anyone he doubted was moved down to the surface years ago. I don't think he would have left me on the ship if the crew hadn't needed a doctor. And there's nothing any of us can do."

Hadfield snorted. "You don't think about relieving him?"

"And if we did," Tatyana asked, "what then? We'll all still be shot when we get home."

"We will see," John said. He had a nasty suspicion she was right. The Russians had committed so many crimes it would be hard to decide which one they were actually being executed for. "What's the current situation on the surface?"

"The God-King rules thousands of square miles," Tatyana said. "We've been giving him radios and other toys to help maintain his domain. And quite a few other ideas. They didn't have any concept of political commissioners until we introduced it to him. Given time, he will rule the entire world, while the General starts building his own tech base."

How long would it take, John asked himself silently, *for them to build up a spacefaring tech base of their own*?

But there was no way to know. Humanity had advanced in fits and starts; it had taken nearly eighty years to move from the early ballistic missiles to a working SSTO design, then another thirty to produce the first gravity drives. Going by humanity's experience, it would take at least five hundred years to put the Vesy in space to stay. But humanity hadn't had a roadmap to the stars, handed out by more advanced aliens. The Vesy might reach the stars in less than a century, if they avoided all the false starts.

And yet, they couldn't remain hidden for a century, he thought. *Even if we're lost too, other starships will probe along the tramlines. They will discover this world and take steps.*

The General had to know that, he thought. But he was desperate. Perhaps, if he managed to get the aliens into space before their world was discovered, he would be able to bargain with the human race. Cold logic suggested the scheme was unlikely to work, but what price logic when people were desperate? The General and his loyalists literally had nowhere else to go.

"Tell me about them," he said, instead. "How close are they to humanity?"

"They're nothing like us, internally," Tatyana said. "I dissected a couple of them, back when we were studying their world. They're basically egg-layers; they can mate at any time, like us, but when their females are in mating season they tend to lose control and submit to the first male they see. Their society is heavily patriarchal because of it. Mentally..."

She shrugged. "I would say they had the same baseline intelligence as humanity," she added, slowly. "In some ways, though, they are quite different. Their scents change, depending on emotions, and they pick up on this. I think they actually have problems lying to one another, although I can't be sure. They didn't seem to understand the concept when I asked."

John frowned. "Translation problems?"

"Perhaps," Tatyana said. "Their language is relatively simple, according to the computers, but impossible for humans to pronounce. They can speak Russian, though; by now, I would imagine that Russian is spreading with terrifying speed. Everyone in their hierarchy wants to be able to speak it."

"So we could talk to them," Hadfield said, slowly. "That's...interesting."

"They lack quite a number of concepts," Tatyana warned.

"I suppose they would," John said. "One final question, then. Are there people on the surface who might help us?"

"Human or alien?" Tatyana asked. "Humans...I don't know. Just about everyone is scared of the General, Captain. A couple of men defied him and he had them both impaled. Aliens? There's no shortage of resistance to the God-King, but it hasn't had much success. The bastard has been quite successful in keeping his boot firmly fixed on their necks."

"I see," John said. "I want you to tell us everything you can remember, no matter how unimportant, about the aliens and the remainder of your colony. Everything you tell us will be recorded, then studied."

He looked at Lieutenant Forbes. "Please escort her back to the brig, then record everything she says," he ordered. "I'll have questions forwarded to you from other departments."

"Aye, sir," Lieutenant Forbes said.

She helped Tatyana to her feet, then marched her through the hatch. John sighed inwardly, then turned to Hadfield. The Marine seemed as stunned as he felt.

"The General is likely to do something stupid if we sneak back and return with reinforcements," he said. Besides, he wasn't sure he *wanted* to pull *Canberra* away from Pegasus. The escort carrier would offer extra firepower, but it would leave the new colony exposed to potential enemies. "We have to deal with him now."

"Yes, sir," Hadfield said. "But getting him away from Vesy is not going to be easy."

CHAPTER
THIRTY ONE

John couldn't help feeling a certain sense of anticipation as he stepped into the briefing room and nodded to his senior officers, who had risen to their feet. It was childish, in a way, but *this* was a true challenge. Part of him just couldn't wait to get stuck into the pirates who had done so much harm, no matter what they thought they'd been doing. And the prospect of rescuing the kidnapped women and children was a valuable bonus.

"Be seated," he said, as he took his seat. A hologram of Vesy floated over the table, drawing his eye towards it. The world looked surprisingly normal, compared to Tadpole Prime, but it hardly mattered. Earth set the standard for *normal* and she had given birth to an intelligent race. "The situation is dire."

He took a breath. "We cannot afford to wait for reinforcements," he continued. "It will take at least three months to get reinforcements from Earth, assuming they were dispatched at once. By then, the Russians will have realised that they've lost a ship. They will probably assume the worst and do something stupid."

"Like butchering the womenfolk," Hadfield put in, quietly.

John nodded. "We have two separate problems," he said. "First, we have to disable or destroy the Russian ships. Our source" - Tatyana - "believes that none of the kidnapped women and children are kept onboard the ships, so we do not have to hold back. However, we also have no idea what weapons the assault transport carries. It may be a tougher customer than it seems.

"Second, we have to suppress the Russian base on the surface before they can give us another hostage situation," he added. "Or, for that matter, convince the God-King to rise up against us and attack, stabbing us in the rear. That too will be tricky."

He paused, inviting comment.

"The assault transport may be just a modified freighter, sir," Howard commented. "It shouldn't pose a serious threat."

"We don't know that," John said, although he privately agreed. There was little to be gained by wasting resources on an assault transport. The Russians would either control orbital space above the targeted planet or avoid the risk of launching an offensive. "We have to assume the worst."

He switched the display to show the star system, silently cursing the tyranny of physics under his breath. Timing would be everything…and he knew, all too well, that it wouldn't be on their side.

"This is my plan," he said. "We will arrive here" - he tapped a space along the tramline - "accompanied by a drone. The Russians will see us as a pair of private survey ships, here to survey the system for possible settlement. They will have no choice, but to come after us with both of their ships. It would be disastrous for them if a survey ship was to report back to Earth, detailing the presence of so many tramlines."

"They would have problems intercepting us, sir," Armstrong said. "We'd be too close to the tramline for their peace of mind."

"But they would assume they have a ship behind us," John pointed out. "We jump back through the tramline; they follow us, screaming a warning to their mining ship. We'd be caught between two fires."

He paused. "Or so they will assume," he said. "Instead, we are going to capture or destroy both ships. We'll throw everything at them, up to and including the kitchen sink. Whatever happens, those ships are going to die."

"Yes, sir," Richards said.

John nodded to Hadfield. "Prior to showing ourselves to them," he added, "we will slip the Marines into the planet's atmosphere. Once the Russian ships have been engaged, the Marines will attack the Russian settlement and overwhelm it. The objective will be to prevent the Russians either slaughtering the hostages or setting up another hostage crisis, one that will be a great deal harder to resolve. We must, again, assume the worst. The Russians have nowhere to go. If they think they're on the verge of being defeated, they will try and gore us as badly as they can before they go down."

"We could offer to accept surrender, sir," Richards suggested.

"We will try," John said. "But the Russians have no reason to expect anything other than a short march to the hangman. They will have no reason to surrender."

"The timing will be tricky," Armstrong said. "The offensive would have to be mounted once the Russian ships were too far from the planet to double back."

"We will launch the offensive once the Russian ships are engaged," Hadfield said. "The settlers will know about it at the same moment as ourselves, but they won't be ready. *We* will be."

Howard had another, more pressing concern. "What if the locals attempt to intervene?"

"We'll engage them, if necessary," Hadfield said. "However, it is unlikely they can react fast enough to prevent us from overwhelming the Russians."

John nodded. "We will head to orbit as quickly as possible, once the Russian ships have been dealt with," he said. "If the compound has been secured, we can strike local formations from orbit, should they attempt to attack our positions."

He shuddered, inwardly. It was unlikely the God-King would surrender his monopoly on Russian technology so calmly. Indeed, given what Tatyana had told him about the locals, Russian technology was all that kept him from overstretching himself and being slaughtered in an uprising. The slave pens didn't suggest a happy population. John shuddered, again, at what they'd seen from orbit. Something would have to be done about that, one day.

"The Russians have done a hell of a lot of damage, sir," Richards said. "Shouldn't we be considering how best to approach the aliens?"

"I think that's best left to the diplomats," John said. The Vesy weren't a spacefaring race. It wouldn't be hard to pull out of the system entirely, or make contact later, once tempers had cooled. "They may feel we shouldn't have any further contact with the Vesy…"

But their system wouldn't be left alone, John knew. Seven tramlines…like Terra Nova, dozens of nations and hundreds of corporations would descend on the system, establishing research bases and using the tramlines as they saw fit. Vesy itself was a biological treasure trove, as the third planet to produce an intelligent race; it was highly unlikely that the World Court would be able to prevent humans from making further contact with the natives. And the native culture would both fascinate and horrify human civilians. There would be demands for everything from armed intervention - for the native's own good, of course - to the forcible introduction of modern technology. It wouldn't be long before the native culture was worn to a nub.

And yet, would that be a bad thing? From what little they'd seen, the native culture was horrific. Like so many primitive human societies, their system was based on sexual, religious, racial and even intellectual apartheid. Destroying it could only be a good deed; introducing the aliens to a better way to live would be even better. The vast majority of *Vesy* might not even *want* to keep their culture, once they developed technology that would allow them to change it. And who could say they didn't have the right to live as they pleased?

And they will never rule their own system, he thought. *By the time they make it into space, their system will be legally free to anyone who wants to use it.*

He cleared his throat. "We will proceed to the tramline in seven hours," he said. "Get some rest, then ready yourselves. All hell is about to break loose. Dismissed."

"Inspirational, Captain," Richards said, once they were alone. "But are you sure this is the right thing to do?"

"Yes," John said, flatly. Commander Watson would never have questioned him. But then, she cared nothing for anything outside her sphere of interest. "We can't let this go on, Phil."

"I know," Richards said. "But you're taking one hell of a risk."

John nodded. *Warspite* could be lost, countless light years from home. Or the Marines could lose the fight on the surface, forcing him to negotiate with desperate Russians. Or the Russians might leave the system, or slaughter the entire population of Vesy in a desperate attempt to hide what they'd done. They could do it, too; a single asteroid, propelled with enough force, could wipe out the entire planet.

"It has to be done," he said, simply. "The traditions of the Royal Navy demand it."

He smiled, tiredly. Francis Drake or Sir Walter Raleigh would probably not have disapproved of slavery, as long as they were doing the enslaving. But Nelson, Cunningham and poor doomed Gannett would have pitted themselves against a notionally superior force, if that was what it took to uphold the navy's traditions. And Theodore Smith had died bravely, every weapon blazing to the last, to save the entire human race. *He* would not have backed down from such a challenge.

And that, John knew, was that.

———

"Dear Penny," Percy said. "I don't know when you'll get this letter, so I'll make it short and sweet. We've found the missing women and children, but we've also found another alien race. Yes, *another*. You may want to inform your editor, if the news hasn't already hit the datanets by the time you get this message."

He took a breath, then went on. "The Russians are holding their entire planet in bondage," he added. "It looks like the remains of North Africa, only worse. They're backing a madman, according to the prisoners, who is trying to enslave the entire world. And it falls to us to try and do something about it. In six hours time, I and the rest of the Marines will be launched on a do-or-die mission. For some of us, it will be do-*and*-die. They made me learn Russian during training, so I will be the point man. That's the poor bastard who normally gets shot at first. I may not come back.

"If I don't…"

He broke off, considering. Like all of the Marines, he'd written a will prior to leaving Earth; it had felt odd to write it, but he knew it needed to be done. Death came for everyone, in the end; a young soldier, part of the finest fighting force in the world, could still die in combat, or be so badly wounded he had to be invalidated out of the service. And if that happened, his family had to be cared for…

"If I don't come back," he said, "remember I love you."

It was a bitter thought. He'd fought with his sister for years. They'd battled each other over everything from toys to movies, to boyfriends and girlfriends…and yet, when the tidal waves had rolled over the west coast, they'd put their differences aside and struggled together to survive. He'd been protective of her and she, he understood now, had been protective of him. How much time had they wasted scrabbling like cats and dogs?

But we needed to grow up, he thought. *Our parents were gone.*

That, too, was a bitter thought. Their father had died on *Ark Royal*, but at least they *knew* he was dead. No one had ever found a trace of Molly Schneider. Percy knew the odds were against it, yet there were times when he wondered if she had found a sugar daddy and vanished to somewhere the floodwaters had never touched. His mother hadn't been a bad person, not really, but the influx of prize money from *Ark Royal* had ruined her. Percy wondered, sometimes, if it would have ruined him too.

"Tell Gina and Canella I love them too," he added. Gina had been their babysitter, to all intents and purposes, even though Percy and Penny had both been in their teens. It still galled him to remember what immature little bastards they'd been before the floods. "And give my regards to Martin. And everyone else."

He paused, then clicked off the recording and transferred it into the secure datacore. If something happened to him, and it might, the recording would be added to the collection of messages he had recorded for his sister. He wasn't sure if she would like to have them, after hearing her brother had died, but he knew she would hate him making the choice for her. Their father, after all, hadn't sent many messages home after Operation Nelson. Or, perhaps, they'd been preserved in secure storage until they were declassified. No one he'd asked had been willing to tell him.

"Corporal," Peerce said, as Percy stepped out of the recording compartment. "Can't sleep?"

"Yes, Sergeant," Percy said. He glanced at his watch; five hours until departure. "I couldn't sleep a wink, so I recorded a message instead."

"Not a bad thought," Peerce said. "But I advise you not to be caught by the Lieutenant. You need to be well-rested for when the shit hits the fan."

Percy nodded. They'd gone over the plan several times, but they knew so little for certain that they might well wind up having to improvise halfway through. It was good, in a way - the British military had developed a whole culture based on muddling through - yet he knew from exercises that muddling through could only take you so far, if one lacked the resources one needed. And, if the Russians had been careful, it was quite likely the shuttles would be spotted as they dropped into the planet's atmosphere. Things would *definitely* get hairy at that point.

But they won't be expecting anything more dangerous than a hot-air balloon, he thought, coldly. *Why would they bother to set up a radar station at their base? It would only draw attention if someone surveyed the system.*

Because they know they couldn't escape detection in any case, if someone surveyed the system, his own thoughts answered him. *This world has an intelligent alien race. That's going to bring the sociologists running from all over the human sphere. And the Tadpoles would probably want to examine the Vesy too.*

"You're awake too, Sergeant," he said, instead. He kept his voice as innocent as possible. "Can't *you* sleep?"

Peerce gave him a warning look. "Someone has to keep an eye on you lot," he growled, darkly. "And besides, I went four days without sleep on Alien-1."

"Doped up on something at the time," Percy said. "Why didn't you get any rest?"

"We were scouting for potential threats," Peerce said. "The Rhino - the American CO - wanted to verify the region was clear. One thing led to another and we ended up caught in the midst of their counteroffensive. It was not a pleasant time."

"It wouldn't have been," Percy agreed. He'd seen videos from Alien-1. The Tadpoles had been cumbersome on the land - they preferred the water, except when they needed to build factories on the surface - but they'd made up for it by throwing a vast amount of firepower at the human invaders. By the time Admiral Smith had returned to the planet, the humans had been in serious danger of being wiped out. "Is that where you got your medals?"

"Most of them," Peerce said. "The Yanks gave me a Purple Heart, as I forgot to duck when the aliens were hurling fire at us."

He shrugged, then blinked as the hatch opened. Percy straightened to attention as he saw the Captain, peering into Marine Country, and snapped a sharp salute. The Captain returned it, a moment later.

"Captain," Percy said. "Is there something we can do for you?"

"No, thank you," the Captain said. "I'm just touring the ship."

He nodded to both of them, then stepped back through the hatch.

"That's rarely a good sign," Peerce said, when the hatch had closed. "The Captain touring his ship before a battle."

Percy shrugged. "Perhaps he can't sleep too."

"Get some rest," Peerce suggested, firmly. "Both you and he need it."

"Yes, Sergeant," Percy said.

———

John had explored *Warspite* thoroughly after taking command, learning every nook and cranny of his ship. She *was* a remarkable design in many ways, he considered, even if the Royal Navy considered her a stopgap measure. There wouldn't be many like her, he'd been told…but even so, she'd done the Royal Navy proud. Now, though, she would face her harshest test.

He walked from deck to deck, inspecting the departments as he moved. The brig was still secure, the prisoners held firmly in their cells. Further down, the hold was locked and guarded by a pair of armed spacers; John made a mental note to ensure the prisoners were cuffed and shackled before the shit hit the fan. The last thing he needed was desperate prisoners loose on his ship when she was fighting for her life. He stepped into the tactical section and reviewed their work, then muttered a few words of praise. But there were too many unknowns for him to take their work for granted. The Russians might have a few surprises up their sleeves.

"Captain," Johnston said, when he stepped into Main Engineering. "Touring the ship?"

"Yes," John said, shortly. It was traditional for a commanding officer to tour his ship before a battle. Admiral Smith had done it, after all, and *that* made it tradition. "I trust Main Engineering is ready for a scrap?"

"As ready as we will ever be, sir," Johnston said. "I think we worked all the bugs out now."

"Good," John said. "And Commander Watson?"

"Still in her cabin, working hard," Johnston said.

John smiled at the note of wistfulness in his voice. "You can court her now, you know."

Johnston flushed. "Sir!"

"Better wait till we get home," John said, after a moment. "Tomorrow… we will have something to celebrate."

"We will, sir," Johnston said. "And thank you."

CHAPTER
THIRTY TWO

"Captain," Richards said. "The Marines are ready to depart."

John nodded. The Russian starships hadn't deployed any satellite network, knowing it would be a dead giveaway to any human ship that happened to stumble on the system. It wasn't an unwise precaution, but it did mean that their surveillance of the planet's surface was seriously limited. There were gaps in their coverage the Marines could exploit.

"Inform Major Hadfield he may depart on schedule," he said. "We will hold position until the Marines are on the ground."

He sucked in his breath as the two shuttles separated themselves from *Warspite*. Timing was everything…but if the Russians picked up a sniff of the shuttles as they dropped into the planet's atmosphere, the plan would have to be scrapped at once. *Warspite* would have to engage both Russian ships, in orbit, knowing that one or both of them could rain KEWs on the planet's surface or simply alert their fellows before they were taken out. He hated taking so many chances, not with a plan where everything had to go right for it to work perfectly, but he hadn't been able to come up with an alternative. All he could do now was watch, wait and play his cards as best as he could.

"Captain," Howard said. "The shuttles have slipped into stealth. They're very good; I know where they are and yet I can barely see them."

"Thank you, Mr. Howard," John said dryly. "And will that hold up when they enter the planet's atmosphere?"

"It would depend, sir," Howard said. "The Russians have no reason to watch closely for incoming shuttles."

But if they're feeling paranoid, John thought, *they might have set up a passive sensor net on the ground.*

He shook his head, then forced himself to relax. All he could do was wait. And pray.

———

Percy watched though the shuttle's sensors as Vesy slowly came into view. She was an impressive sight, not unlike the Earth he'd imagined before he'd looked at a few maps in school and realised the land didn't go on forever, after all. It was easy to imagine the Vesy building a global empire - Alexander the Great and the Romans had carved out vast empires on Earth with inferior technology - and then stagnating, not unlike Imperial China. But if what they'd been told was true, the Vesy had been divided up into smaller states before the Russians got involved.

I wonder how they maintain the balance of power, Percy thought. *And how they replenish their ammunition.*

The thought made him smile. He knew from experience that any major military power could march through the Middle East or Africa with impunity, at least as long as the ammunition held out. There had been a couple of near-disasters during the Age of Unrest when small outposts *had* almost run out of ammunition, under the pressure of constant attacks. The Russians would not have found it easy to replace the ammunition they wasted supporting their ally. But if they ran out, it wouldn't have been long before they were overwhelmed by their enemies. They had to have set up a small ammunition plant somewhere and started to churn out small rounds, if nothing else.

We keep most of our technology as primitive as possible to make it easy to repair, he thought, grimly. *The Russians might well have done the same.*

He looked back at the planet as the two enemy craft disappeared over the horizon. They shouldn't be able to see *anything* on the nearest side of the planet, which was slowly twisting into night. Only *Vesper* remained, a dead hulk in geostationary orbit over the enemy compound. Percy studied her through the shuttle's passive sensors, seeing nothing that indicated the Russians might have turned her into an observation platform. By now, he reasoned, they had probably stripped all the supplies that were meant for Cromwell out of her hull and shipped them down to the surface. They needed them to help maintain their settlement.

And feed themselves, he added, mentally. *This world must lack some trace elements the Russians need for their diet.*

"We are about to enter the atmosphere," the pilot said, softly. "Brace for turbulence; I say again, brace for turbulence."

The shuttle rocked wildly a bare second later. Percy heard whoops from some of the Marines as the shuttle shuddered, then plummeted into the planet's atmosphere, leaving his stomach hundreds of miles above him. The entire hull seemed to creak - he told himself frantically it was an illusion - then shuddered again. He closed his eyes and concentrated on remaining calm; the shuttle spun violently, then dropped once again. It felt almost as if the pilot was ducking down, then holding them long enough for the passengers to relax, then dropping them down again. Behind him, he heard the sound of someone retching. One of the Marines had been sick.

There was a final shudder, then the shuttle levelled out. Percy opened his eyes, then glanced at the screen. The shuttle was flying over the ocean - the great lake, he supposed - and heading south, towards the shore. They'd been told there were no alien settlements near the Landing Zone, but he knew better than to take that for granted. The aliens might have set up smaller villages that would have escaped notice, somewhere by the shores of the lake.

"Landing in five minutes," the pilot said.

"Grab your weapons and goggles," Peerce snapped. The shuttle rocked from side to side, then steadied. "I want a perimeter established as soon as we're on the ground."

A final dull crash echoed through the shuttle, then nothing. The hatches flew open, allowing the first troops to hurl themselves out onto the alien world. Percy scooped up his rifle and followed them, wishing they'd chosen to make a parachute or orbital jump entry instead. But there would have been too much risk of being seen by the enemy. Warm air, smelling vaguely of pollen, slapped at his face as he plunged through the hatch. They had landed in a small clearing, he noted, as they took up position around the shuttle, ready to repel attack. It was surrounded by plant life that looked almost Earth-like, save for the weird-looking flowers. He couldn't help a shiver as he looked at them.

"LZ is clear, sir," Peerce said, addressing Hadfield. The Lieutenant had landed in the other shuttle, which had landed next to them. "No sign of contacts, either human or alien."

"Good," Hadfield said. He raised his voice. "Break out the netting, then get these shuttles concealed. We don't have much time."

Percy nodded briskly - salutes were forbidden in combat zones - then scrambled to obey. The shuttles would stick out like sore thumbs if they weren't concealed by the time the Russian ships passed overhead. His section rapidly dug out the camouflage netting, then draped it over the shuttles and keyed it to match the surrounding rainforest. It was unlikely the Russians paid enough attention to the ground to notice any small discrepancies.

And if they're paranoid enough to notice, his thoughts added, *we're dead anyway.*

"1 Section, get unloading the shuttles," Hadfield ordered. "2 Section, secure a line of advance."

"Aye, sir," Percy said.

He led his section towards the trees, then under them. The scent of pollen grew stronger as they stepped onwards; the ground seemed to twitch with strange, spider-like animals. He caught sight of a lizard-like creature the size of a small cat, which eyed him beadily before twitching and vanishing so quickly he had the impression it had teleported. There was no proper road, which meant it was unlikely they would be able to make speedy progress, but at least they could pick their way towards the Russian base.

"Excellent," Hadfield said, when Percy reported back. "Finish unloading the supplies, then get suited up and ready to move."

Percy nodded. The Marines hadn't worn their combat suits in the shuttle, if only to keep them from getting in the way if they had to bail out in a hurry. He wasn't sure he approved of the decision, but it was Hadfield's call to make. He joined 1 Section in unloading the remaining boxes from the shuttle, then donned his suit. It was lighter than some of the heavy combat armour he'd used during basic training, but it had a reassuring sense of invulnerability that made him feel better about stepping into the darkness. In many ways, it was an illusion, but he clung to it anyway.

Besides, he thought ruefully, *heavy combat armour would only get in the way.*

The Marines scooped up boxes, then started to walk towards the trees, leaving the empty shuttles behind. There simply wasn't the manpower to leave the pilots with the craft. A warning message blinked up in his HUD, noting that the Russian ships would be overhead in ten minutes. He sucked in his breath, then kept walking. If the Russians saw the shuttles, they would probably drop KEWs over the area and then send in ground troops to finish the job. It was their standard pattern, after all.

Moments passed. No hammer fell from high overhead.

"I don't think they saw us," Hastings muttered. "They would have attacked, wouldn't they?"

"Yes," Hadfield answered. "Now, keep marching towards the enemy base. I want to get as close to them as possible before the sun rises."

Percy glanced at his HUD as they continued to march, spreading out into small fire teams. Vesy had a twenty-six hour day - he smiled at the thought of thirteen o'clock - with a predicted daytime of seventeen hours. The Vesy themselves, lacking any form of electrical power, were unlikely to go out in the night, unless they were forced to by their superiors. It wasn't an uncommon pattern in primitive societies, he reminded himself. People rose with the sun and went to bed with the moon.

But they might have perfect night vision, he reminded himself. The Tadpoles could certainly see in the dark like cats. Their eyes, designed for the darkness below the waves, had no trouble on land, no matter how dark it was. *We have to assume the worst.*

The key to marching, he'd been told, was not to concentrate on how long the march was. Even an objectively short match - he'd started by running a mile and a half in less than eight minutes, when he'd gone to the mandatory insight day - could seem to take forever, if one remained focused on the distance. Instead, he just needed to concentrate on putting one foot in front of another and keeping going, whatever happened. Lads he'd known who had wanted to join the SAS had been binned - sent back to their parent unit - for refusing to carry on, once they'd been told they had to do another eight miles...after completing the first thirty.

"Halt," Peerce called. "There's something up ahead."

Percy froze, then reached for his weapon as the alien building came into view. It was built from wood - no, it was built from *living* wood, as if the woodcarver had started to carve from the tree while it was still growing. He couldn't help being reminded of the 2106 remake of *Return of the Jedi*, when the furry teddy bears had been replaced by half-naked tribesmen who lived in homes in the treetops. It had been a great success, but his mother had refused to let him watch it and he'd had to sneak in a viewing at a friend's house. But he hadn't understood why she'd refused until he'd been old enough to start finding girls interesting.

"Tab west," Hadfield muttered, as the Marines slowly fell back. Detection by the aliens could be very good or very bad. "Keep low and avoid contact, if possible."

"Aye, sir," Hastings said.

Percy echoed him a moment later, his eyes scanning the trees for signs of movement. How well would the Vesy show up in his NVGs? They were cold-blooded creatures, the Russians had said; it was quite possible they would be invisible, at least in the darkness. But they had motion detectors too...he cursed, wishing they'd thought to ask the Russian doctor that question, as well as a dozen others. The Russians must have had *some* way to secure their compound against infiltration or they would have had a far harder time of it on the surface.

But they couldn't actually lose, Percy thought. *They could keep calling in fire from orbit until the enemy were stamped into the mud.*

He sighed, inwardly. Like all the Marines, he'd reviewed the testimony from the Russian doctor. If the Russians were serious about turning the Vesy into allies, they couldn't afford to hammer them too hard, could they? But the Vesy had a far smaller world, in some ways, than humanity. The Vesy the Russians hammered might believe in their existence, but what about the Vesy a few thousand miles from the Russian base? If there were *humans* who had refused to believe in the Tadpoles after Vera Cruz, why wouldn't there be Vesy who refused to believe in the *humans*?

"Contact - front!" Peerce hissed. "One Vesy; dead ahead of us."

Percy looked up, just in time to see the alien jump back into the darkness with terrifying speed. He'd seen soldiers perform all kinds of remarkable feats, but he had the feeling the alien was faster than any of the Royal Marines…or indeed anyone, save for an enhanced trooper. But it was impossible to be sure.

"Do *not* fire unless I give the order," Hadfield said, as the Marines halted. "We don't need more enemies."

"Sir," Percy said, "they won't know we're not Russians."

He shuddered. There had been times, during the Age of Unrest, when Chinese or Russian troops had been targeted by various factions who had mistaken them for British or Americans. And most of those factions lived in a world where telecommunications allowed anyone, no matter how isolated, to be aware of global politics and power shifts. The Vesy would be lucky if they knew of *humans*, let alone human factions. The thought of being attacked on suspicion of being Russian was horrifying. They would have to defend themselves, which would risk alerting the Russians to their presence.

And wouldn't that be ironic, he thought.

"Another contact," Peerce said. "And another."

Percy frowned as the alien stood in front of them, his head twitching from side to side in a remarkably bird-like manner. A chill ran down his spine as he took in the humanoid, yet very inhuman shape. The alien was tall, taller than the average human, with scaly green skin, dark and beady eyes and a flattened nose. He - Percy assumed he was a male - wore a loin cloth that covered his genitals, but little else. It was chillingly easy to realise, now, that he wasn't looking at a man in a suit. The proportions were all wrong.

The alien remained unmoving, save for his eyes. Percy had stood stag often enough to know that remaining completely still was difficult, at least for him. *He* would never stand guard in front of Buckingham Palace. And yet the alien seemed to make it look easy. Like lizards in the zoo, Percy realised slowly, the aliens had no involuntary movements. Only the head moved, allowing the alien to peer at them with both eyes.

Sneaking up on one of them won't be easy, Percy thought. *They have a far wider field of vision than us.*

"There are more of them," Hastings said, warningly. "They're closing in from all sides."

The alien took a step forward and held up its hands, palms extended outwards. Percy couldn't help noticing the claws, which could tear through human flesh like knives through butter, but he had to admit the alien wasn't making any hostile moves. Instead, the alien stood there long enough for the humans to see him, then opened his mouth, revealing very sharp and jagged teeth.

"Hello," he said, in Russian.

"Corporal," Hadfield said.

Percy nodded and took a step forward, then opened his helmet. It was sheer luck he spoke Russian; like all Royal Marines, he'd been encouraged to learn a foreign language during Basic Training and he'd chosen Russian. The incentives for mastering the tongue had seemed worthwhile, even when he'd found himself stumbling over the words. But then, it was easier than trying to learn to speak to the Tadpoles. No human could speak their language without a considerable amount of enhancement.

"Hello," he said. He wished, suddenly, that he'd had more chance to review his lessons since graduating. For all of the higher-up's interest in having soldiers speak Russian, he hadn't had much chance to practice. "I greet you."

"You are not them," the alien said, jerking a claw towards the Russian base. His voice was so thick Percy couldn't help flashing back to the times when his mother had told him not to talk with his mouth full. "You are trying to hide from them."

"Yes," Percy said, hoping desperately he hadn't just made a terrible mistake. "We are here to fight them."

"We are hiding from the God-King," the alien said. "The" - he made another gesture towards the Russians - "helped him to take our lands."

"They did, breaking our laws," Percy said.

"We will assist you," the alien said.

Percy held up a hand, then stepped backwards to where Hadfield was waiting, standing next to Peerce. "These guys want to help," he said. "I think they're refugees, hoping for a chance to fight back."

"Or it could be a trick," Peerce said. "Did you consider that, Corporal?"

Percy hesitated. "Sergeant," he said, "if they wanted to betray us, they could have done it by now. Or even attacked us themselves. I think we can work with them."

"Then we shall," Hadfield said. "I will inform the Captain. You start talking to our new friends and see if they can get us closer to the Russian base before dawn breaks."

"Yes, sir," Percy said.

CHAPTER
THIRTY THREE

"They're talking to the aliens?"

"Yes, sir," Forbes said. "The aliens speak Russian."

John scowled, then tapped his terminal. "Lieutenant Hadfield, report," he ordered. It was a breach of protocol to issue direct orders to the Marines on the ground, particularly when it ran into the dangers of micromanagement, but it had to be done. "What is the situation?"

"The aliens claim to have been driven from their lands by the God-King," Hadfield said. "They've offered to assist us in reaching the Russian compound, then launching the attack."

"I see," John said. He hadn't seriously considered the prospect of enlisting alien allies. On one hand, they could be very helpful; on the other, they might be dangerously unpredictable. "Do you think they can follow orders?"

"I don't know, sir," Hadfield admitted. "We're working on them now, but their Russian is limited and ours isn't much better."

"Then I leave the matter in your hands," John said, cursing himself. It would look, at the inevitable inquiry, as if he'd passed the buck to Hadfield. "Do you believe you can make it to the compound before daytime or do you want to hide for a day and attack at night?"

"We haven't been spotted, sir," Hadfield said. "I believe we would be better waiting, then launching the attack the following evening. It would give us more time to work with the aliens."

"Then we will delay the offensive," John said. "But we will have to head to the tramline in seventeen hours, if only to start our side of the operation."

"Understood, sir," Hadfield said. "We'll keep in touch."

John nodded as the link broke, then forced himself to relax. There was nothing else to do, but - once again - wait.

———

Percy couldn't help being charmed by the alien village, hidden under the canopy. It was remarkable, a blending of clearly artificial structures with hollowed-out trees and underground caves. The aliens were every-where, staring at the humans; their faces, utterly unreadable, remaining inhumanly still. Percy had driven through towns and villages where the womenfolk had been hastily shoved back into their homes, while the men hurled curses or even rocks towards the intruders and their vehicles. In some ways, the alien village was definitely an improvement.

But it's creepy too, he thought. It was the sort of place he would have loved, as a kid - he and Penny had always wanted a treehouse - but it was also crammed with aliens. *And who knows what they're really thinking?*

He sighed as he looked at the aliens, moving from place to place with an eerie loping gait. It was impossible to tell the males from the females; they all wore loincloths, all covering the same region. They might all be males, he thought, but if so…where were the females? But then, the orbital surveillance hadn't been enough to pick out the males from the females either. The aliens didn't seem to have breasts, let alone differences in build.

"They call me Ivan," the alien said. He was some kind of leader, Percy had been able to discover, although he wasn't sure just what *sort* of leader. His Russian wasn't good enough to sort out the difference between kings, priests and elected rulers. "They wanted me to serve as a slave, talking to us" - he spoke a word Percy suspected was their own name for themselves - "and passing on their orders. I deserted when I had a chance."

"Good for you," Percy said. The alien's hands twitched. "How did you enter their service?"

Ivan made a gesture that looked remarkably like a human shrug. "I was ruler of a city," he said, drolly. "The God-King overwhelmed the walls and took the city, bathing the streets in the blood of my people. I was spared and sold as a slave. They saw I had a gift for languages and taught me their tongue. Once I had learned all I could, I left them."

Percy looked up at the village. "Are all these your people?"

"No," the alien said. He spoke several words Percy didn't recognise. "They were...fleeing from the God-King, hiding in the sacred forest. I made myself their leader."

Percy wondered, absently, just how much of that was true. Ivan certainly *seemed* to be the undisputed leader of the resistance, but there was no way to be sure. He had been royalty...but would that really matter if his state was gone? Prince Henry was an impressive person, Percy had to admit, yet he wouldn't honour Princess Elizabeth if she lost her throne, her rank and her country. She'd never struck him as anything other than a bird in a gilded cage.

But it didn't matter, not right now. All that mattered was planning the attack on the Russians.

"Right," he said. "We need to start working on details."

Ivan, he discovered after an hour of talking backwards and forwards, was very far from stupid. Unlike some of the God-King's more slavish followers, he didn't seem to believe that the Russians - or the British - were supernatural beings. He might not understand their technology, but he didn't mistake it for magic. He'd already learned more about the Russians and their weaknesses than anyone had a right to expect.

But that shouldn't be a surprise, Percy reminded himself. He'd studied the wars in Afghanistan and Iraq that marked the start of the Age of Unrest. They'd both been fought against seemingly primitive people, but those people had been far from stupid and learned how to adapt themselves to take on the advanced militaries occupying their countries. *Once they got over the shock and awe, the God-King's enemies probably started doing the same.*

"So there are three hundred Russians on the ground, not counting the women and children," Percy said, after explaining how to tell the difference between male and female humans. "Some of them are with the

God-King at all times, assisting him; others stay at their complex, defending it from all intrusion?"

"Correct," Ivan said. "And you want them all alive?"

"If possible," Percy said. He shuddered. It was hard to blame the Vesy for wanting to butcher the Russians, but they would slaughter the kidnapped women and children too. "They are innocent victims."

"We will try," Ivan said, doubtfully. "But many of our fighters want revenge."

"Yeah," Percy said. The prospect of losing control was one of the reasons modern-day militaries preferred not to use local levies. "Tell them that they will be rewarded for every live captive, male or female, they turn over to us."

He smiled, although he still felt nervous. It would be so much easier to simply handle the mission themselves, but he knew that wasn't an option. Four hundred Russians...and a number of women who might have committed themselves completely to their kidnappers, once Stockholm Syndrome had a chance to set in. The Marines would be badly outnumbered.

But at least we have much to use as rewards, he thought. The God-King had bought allegiance by offering modern knives, flashlights and other items of human technology; items that were cheap and disposable for humanity, but priceless for the Vesy. *Let's just hope they don't stop fighting to take captives.*

He sighed. The Vesy hadn't had a tradition of total war until the God-King allied himself with the Russians. Normally, according to Ivan, two city-states would contest, then the weaker of the two would submit to the stronger, while still retaining some internal autonomy - and the prospect of a successful revolt, sometime in the future. It wasn't unlike the ancient Athenian or Spartan Empires, Peerce had pointed out, when Percy had shared what he'd discovered. City-states in uneasy alliances, sometimes switching sides at the drop of a hat.

It seemed small, Percy knew. And yet Athens and Sparta had fought for decades before Sparta finally won the war.

And even that didn't last, he thought. *The Macedonians and Alexander the Great - then Rome - saw to that.*

But the God-King had upset everything, Ivan had said. The first armies to confront him had marched out, expecting ritualistic combat, only to be brutally slaughtered by Russian weapons. Later armies had hidden behind their walls, assuming they were solid; missiles designed to blow holes in tanks had smashed right through them, allowing the God-King's forces to storm the cities. Males had been butchered, females had been raped; any survivors, once the bloodlust had faded, had been enslaved and marched off in chains. Percy had no idea how sustainable the new empire was - Alexander's empire hadn't lasted long, after his death - but it hardly mattered. The God-King would butcher or convert half the planet if he wasn't stopped.

"You will need to see the compound yourself," Ivan offered. They'd tried to draw out maps, but the Vesy didn't seem to be good with them. "I can take you there."

Percy shook his head. "I don't look like you," he said. There would be value in a reconnaissance mission, he was sure, but not one that ended with his capture. "They'd see me coming and snatch me."

He smirked. "We do have other ways to probe, though."

The interior of the buildings was surprisingly cool, despite the heat outside. Inside, Privates Hardesty and Fisherman had set up a passive sensor array, then a set of surveillance and medical gear. Some of the Vesy had already volunteered to be scanned by the doctor - the Russians, it seemed, had actually assisted some of the wounded, if they were useful - while others were studying the sensor nodes with rapt fascination. Fisherman explained, patiently, that some of them could carry the recorders up to the compound, then return to share what they'd seen. Ivan laughed, once he understood what he was being shown, then hurried to round up a set of volunteers.

"Be careful," Hadfield warned, while Percy was waiting for the volunteers to assemble. "You cannot afford to assume they think like us."

Percy nodded. Ivan was definitely more human than the Tadpoles, but some of his casual comments had been enough to worry Percy. He'd shown no sign of hesitation over the prospect of slaughtering *everyone* in the compound, even human women and children. Only the promise of reward had convinced him to agree to take prisoners. But then, human women and children were unlikely to be interesting to any of the Vesy. The Russians had argued, more than once, that nits bred lice…and the Vesy, it seemed, had been excellent students. It was clear the God-King had embraced religious genocide with enthusiasm.

"You need to carry one of these devices about your person," Percy said, when the volunteers had arrived. "Don't let them be seen by the Russians. They will suspect the worst."

He watched the volunteers go, then sighed and sat down. Most of the Marines were resting, catching forty winks while they had the chance, but he couldn't force himself to rest. Instead, he looked over towards the medical table, where one of the Vesy was being scanned. The medic seemed to be having fun, waving all kinds of sensors over the alien body. It wasn't so easy to tell what the alien made of it.

"She's pregnant," Seymour Chalmers said, when the scanning was complete. "With at least two healthy eggs."

Percy blinked. "That's a *she*?"

"Yes," Chalmers said. "That's very definitely a *she*."

The alien rose, then strode out of the room. Percy stared at her retreating back, still unable to tell the difference between a male and a female. Had he been wrong? Was Ivan actually a female? Or were the clues too subtle for human eyes to detect?

"I think the only major difference is between their legs," Chalmers said, when Percy finally asked. "The women have a vagina; men have a penis, but it's completely retractable. I think scent plays a major role in their mating, Percy. They may be able to have sex all the time, like us, but when they're ready to actually become pregnant their hormones drive them into bed again and again. Once they *are* pregnant, their scent changes again and becomes a turn-off. They don't get to have sex while pregnant."

"I see," Percy said. "Can they use birth control?"

"I don't think so," Chalmers said. "One of the escaped prisoners had been effectively castrated; from what they said, he is neither interested in women nor capable of attracting them. They may be able to block out the male scent and thus keep their hormones from triggering, but it would be unreliable."

He shrugged. "We could probably come up with something," he added. "There may be ways to prevent women from going into mating season. But that would definitely change their society in unpredictable ways."

Percy frowned. "Would that be a bad thing?"

Chalmers gave him an odd look. "Back in 2050, they developed a pill that would allow you to select the sex of your baby without any irritating medical procedures," he said. "If you happened to want a little boy, you took a course of blue pills before intercourse. Or pink, if you wanted a girl. It might not have been the smartest medical treatment to make available to everyone."

"I don't understand," Percy said. "Why?"

"Tell me something," Chalmers said. "In our society, how many positions are sex-specific?"

"The Royal Marines," Percy said. "A handful of elite military units. The Women Wardens."

"Precisely," Chalmers said. "Only a handful of positions are exclusively for one sex or the other. A brother and sister can join the Royal Navy, or any corporation, and climb to the very highest levels without being impeded by their sex. There is no advantage to being born male or female."

"Unless you want to be a Royal Marine," Percy said.

Chalmers ignored him. "But in other societies, having boys was considered better than having girls," he added. "A girl was considered inferior; at best, she was suitable only to cook, clean and have babies of her own. Men were the masters of the universe; their sisters were expected to stay in the shadows and do as they were told. And a father who had a small army of sons claimed lots of prestige. What do you think happened when those societies gained the ability to choose their children's sex?"

Percy flushed. "They chose boys," he said.

"Precisely," Chalmers said. "And, twenty or so years after the pills became available, very few of those young men could find wives. Even after they realised the problem, the cultural bias in favour of men was still overpowering. Each family told themselves that someone *else* would have the young women."

"And none of them did," Percy guessed.

"Quite," Chalmers said. "And it got worse. To us, homosexuality is just…another personal choice. If you're wired to fancy your own sex, well…you're wired to fancy your own sex and no one else really gives a damn. But to them, homosexuality was sinful and anyone who practiced it would burn in hell. Prostitution, too, was sinful…assuming they could find women willing to serve in the brothels. Those young men had no way of getting sexual release without committing one sin or another."

"Shit," Percy said.

"It tore their society apart," Chalmers said. "The Chinese had a similar problem, but they got it under control before the pill made matters worse. These people couldn't or wouldn't allow the government the power it needed to tackle the issue. I cannot help, but wonder just how many of the young idiots who impaled themselves on our guns were driven by sexual frustration. The promise of forty virgins in heaven after one dies must seem very tempting if there is no hope of getting married in life."

"And what will happen here, if we start meddling?"

Percy considered it. "The Russians have already started meddling," he said. "We'd just be putting things back the way they were."

"No, we wouldn't be," Chalmers said. "Even if there's no further direct contact between us and them, their society would have been changed forever."

"Maybe," Percy said. "But would that be a bad thing?"

"I wish I knew," Chalmers said.

He tapped the medical computer he'd carried from the shuttles to the village. "I could synthesise a counter-hormone that would prevent a female from coming into her season," he said. "Or one that would make any male who scented her think she was pregnant. There would no longer be any need to keep the young females separate from the young men. And what would *that* do to them?"

"A more equal society?" Percy guessed.

"Or a *less* equal one," Chalmers offered. "If women enter the local workforce as equals, what will that do to male job opportunities?"

He shrugged. "The people I talked about used that as a reason to keep women in the homes," he warned. "They said that if women acted like men, men would be emasculated. Young men wouldn't be able to find jobs if young women were taking them all…"

"That makes no sense," Percy said.

Chalmers pointed a finger at him. "You're using logic and reason," he said. "People are not logical, Corporal. *Fear* is rarely logical. If you're the one on top, you are automatically afraid of anything that might dislodge you, even though cold logic says otherwise.

"Imagine a slot opens for promotion up the ranks," he said. "There are five men, counting you, who want the job. All else being equal, what are your odds of getting it?"

"One in five," Percy said, automatically.

"Correct," Chalmers said. "Assume you now have five women added to the five men. What are the odds of you getting the job?"

"One in ten," Percy said.

"Exactly," Chalmers said. "Do you see their thinking now?"

He sighed, then sat down on the makeshift bed. "Every change in society has unpredictable consequences," he said. "And sometimes they have been disastrous. What will happen to the *Vesy* when the changes start reshaping their society? I have no answer. And nor will anyone else."

CHAPTER
THIRTY FOUR

"He looks odd," Gina said. "Are you sure that's a baby?"

Gillian McDougal glared at the younger woman. "Yes, I'm *sure* that's a baby," she said, as she moved the sensor over Gina's womb. She was sure Gina hadn't been *this* silly when she'd been training for the colony mission. "It sure as hell isn't a little alien."

Gina smiled, nervously. "Do you think Josef will like him?"

"I hope so," Gillian said, tartly. "I'm sure he will be delighted."

She helped the younger woman to her feet, then reminded her to drink plenty of water and take the supplements that were provided with all meals. Gina hugged her in delight, then headed out of the room, swinging her hips in a manner that would have shamed a younger and less reserved girl. But then, Gillian knew that Gina's mental stability was more than a little questionable. They were all slowly going insane.

None of them had expected to be taken prisoner by pirates. The whole concept had been thought insane, the stuff of bad movies written by lousy scriptwriters more intent on showing nude bodies than anything resembling a plot, but it had happened. *Vesper* had been boarded and the captain and his crew had been taken prisoner, then the ship had been steered through the tramlines to Vesy. And there, they had been told that they would be breeding stock for the next generation of human settlers. The Russians had been polite, but firm. They were prisoners now, the women had been told, and they had to learn to adapt.

Some *had* adapted, Gillian knew. Gina wasn't the only one to believe herself in love with her Russian…but then, love made it easier to endure the fact they were prisoners. It wouldn't have been *that* hard to get out of the compound, yet she knew just how many monsters lurked beyond the walls. The locals - aliens, of all things - would quite happily kill any human who showed her face without protection. They had good reason to hate the Russians by now.

She sighed, then reached into her desk drawer and produced the bottle of homemade vodka, then took a long swig. It tasted foul, as always, but it helped to keep her from losing herself in depression. The Russians had done their best, she had to admit, to build a medical centre, yet it was terrifyingly primitive compared to the facilities on Cromwell, let alone Earth. She had a suspicion that, when the first babies started to be born, she was going to get very rapidly overwhelmed. A number of women were training as midwives, but they were completely unpractised. They would have to learn by doing.

Bastards, she thought, as she put the bottle back in the drawer. The Russians knew she was too valuable to lose, which meant she risked nothing more than a beating for being drunk on duty, but she might very well kill someone if she tried to operate on them while drunk. *Dirty filthy fucking bastards.*

The words echoed in her head as she rose to her feet, then stepped into the makeshift medical ward. Aliens had built it to her specifications, but she still knew it was far from perfect. Two beds held Russians, both injured in the line on duty; she contemplated an accident, despite her oaths, before reminding herself that the Russians would take it out on the children. A third bed held a young woman, sleeping off the results of a brutal beating. Her 'husband' was a drunkard, a coward and a brute, Gillian knew. But none of the other Russians seemed to give a damn about how he treated the girl.

Or anyone else, for that matter, she thought, as she stepped out of the medical compound and looked towards the fence. *They're all starting to crack under the strain.*

She groaned inwardly at the thought. The Russians spoke English, after all, and they used it to speak with their 'wives'. Gillian had urged the women to learn as much as they could from their 'husbands,' even though the Russians had little patience for backtalk. It hadn't painted a pretty picture. The Russians had thought they were the last survivors of the human race, then they'd discovered they were nothing more than deserters. They couldn't go home again, she knew, which made them desperate. And increasingly prone to savage violence.

A sound caught her attention and she looked towards the source. A handful of children - all girls - were playing a complicated game that seemed to be a mixture of dodgeball and football, watched by a single grim-faced Russian. Gillian didn't know what had happened to the male children; they'd been taken from their mothers the day after they'd all been shipped down to the planet's surface, then moved into a different compound. She wasn't sure if they had been executed, or started training to serve the Russians, but it hardly mattered. There was no way to get to them, even for her.

She fought down the urge to collapse into despair as she walked away from the compound, catching sight of a handful of alien slaves working on the next building. The Russians weren't kind to the kidnapped women, but they were positively *savage* to the slaves. Their bodies were laced with scars, left behind by whippings that would have killed any humans; their faces were torn and broken where they'd been hit and kicked repeatedly. It was as if their despair, their certain knowledge they were doomed, had freed the Russians from all civilised restraints. The overseers saw the aliens as nothing more than cattle. To her horror, the aliens seemed to agree.

"Mother," a voice said. "What are you doing here?"

Gillian sighed, inwardly, as one of the guards came up behind her and smiled. They all called her Mother, for reasons she had never been able to discover. But then, their leader *had* told them that a trained doctor was firmly off limits. She would have been surprised if anyone had dared to question, let alone disobey, the General's orders. She'd watched him strip the skin from a man's back for daring to lay a finger on one of the children.

"Wandering," she said. The guard - she had never troubled herself to learn his name - wasn't a bad man, not compared to some of the others. But she wasn't about to share anything of herself with him. "And yourself?"

"Just back from Petrograd," the Russian said. He smirked. The God-King's city had an unpronounceable name, so the Russians had promptly declared it Petrograd. No one knew or cared what the Vesy thought of it. "We're going to be moving again in a week, heading to Warsaw."

"Oh," Gillian said. She didn't know how many Vesy had died since the Russians had arrived, but she would have guessed it was well over a million. They'd died in their thousands on the battlefields, then in their tens of thousands as their cities were stormed in a manner that would have horrified Genghis Khan. "I'm sure you will have fun."

"I'm sure I will too," the guard leered.

Gillian shuddered. The Russians had fallen far, too far. They knew they were doomed, so why *not* indulge themselves with every manner of depravity known to man? And it helped that the Vesy weren't human. Basic empathy was something the Russians seemed to lack, at least for alien lives. Some of the Russians, she had to admit, had been quite kind to their wives, even if they *had* been forced into marriage.

"I could give you fun too," the guard offered. Compared to some of the chat-up lines she'd heard, it was positively subtle. "I could be at your bedroom at nightfall…"

"Go to the devil," Gillian said.

She regretted it the moment the words left her mouth. The Russian wouldn't dare touch her, she was sure. His commander had made quite sure of that, when he'd issued his edict and dared them to disobey. But he could find one of the other women, the ones the Russians had deemed useless, and take his fury out on her…

Instead, he laughed. "You don't know what you're missing," he said. "Sally said I was the best she'd ever had. She begged me to do it again and again."

Or didn't want to provoke you into beating her again, Gillian thought. Sally, like so many others, had cracked under the strain. *Would you have stopped if she said no?*

The guard snorted, then jogged past her, heading for the small fortress at the centre of the compound. Calling it a fortress was generous, perhaps, but nothing the natives had could get through prefabricated walls. Gillian wondered, as she watched him go, if the Russians were right to be paranoid. By now, the Vesy had to hate humanity - all humanity - with a burning passion. Maybe they would attack, accepting the death of thousands of warriors in exchange for destroying the humans, once and for all.

But the rocks will fall and the Vesy will die, she thought. *And that will be the end.*

She shuddered, feeling suddenly sick. She hated this world, she hated the omnipresent heat, she hated knowing she was helpless, that one day the Russians would turn on her or the aliens would rise up against humanity, not knowing or caring that two-thirds of the humans were actually slaves. And she hated watching so many of the girls give up, surrendering themselves to the Russians who pretended to be their husbands. What manner of person, she asked herself, falls in love with her rapist?

It was Stockholm Syndrome, she knew. The human mind adapted. Whatever happened, no matter how intolerable the situation, the human mind adapted. And if that meant believing a lie, believing that sex and violence were love…

She wanted to cry. No matter how she tried, she could barely recall her husband's face.

But instead, she walked back to the medical compound. There was work to do.

And a beating waiting for her, she knew, if she didn't do as she was told.

———

"This is the compound," Peerce said, as the Marines gathered round the chart he'd drawn on the floor. "We have gathered a considerable amount of data from our local sources, much of which has been verified by the remote sensor nodes."

Percy squatted next to him and watched as the Sergeant pointed to the markings outside the Russian wall.

"The Russians are surrounded by a large number of fields," Peerce said. "I believe the Russians cleared the space deliberately, to make it harder for an enemy force to sneak up on their walls. Since then, they have allowed their slaves to start planting various food crops in the cleared soil, both to introduce the natives to human water-feeding techniques and to provide another barrier. The natives frown on destroying cropland."

He paused. "They have also produced roads," he added. "I don't think I need to tell you that the roads are carefully watched."

Percy nodded. The God-King might not be as impressed by the roads as he was with the weapons, but he might change his mind soon. Good roads were the key to binding an empire together, particularly once the natives started using cars, lorries and tanks. Hell, even a marching army could cover more ground if it was travelling a road. The Romans had proved *that* centuries before the first automobile had been developed and put into mass production.

"There are a handful of outer buildings here, here and here," Peerce continued. "Buildings Alpha and Beta are slave pens, hosting three hundred slaves each. At night, the slaves are locked in their pens and fed a tiny ration of seeds and water. They are not only locked in, but left in chains. I don't think they will be able to either escape or join in the fighting on either side."

He paused. "Building Charlie is a small army barracks," he warned. "The Russians have been training a small number of locals in human-style military tactics. We don't know how loyal these soldiers will be, but we have to assume the worst."

"They're not allowed inside the wall," Fisherman commented. There was a faint sneer on his face as he spoke. "The Russians must not trust them very much."

"They'd be fools if they did," Peerce agreed. He cleared his throat. "The wall itself" - he tapped the map with his stick - "is built from brick and clay, rather than anything prefabricated. A single antitank missile will blow a hole in it. You will notice that there are watchtowers along the wall, spaced evenly along the perimeter, as well as roving patrols outside the wall. Our friends" - he nodded to Ivan - "inform us that anyone moving close to the compound at night does so at risk of his life. The Russians shoot first and ask questions later. However, their timing is always predictable."

Percy had to smile. They'd been taught to vary the timing of their patrols, just to prevent the enemy taking advantage of an opportunity to sneak through the guards and into the compound. The Russians might be faking it - their watchtowers presumably had night-vision gear - or they might be overconfident. It was unlikely that anyone would dare to attack their compound.

"We will check this ourselves, of course," Peerce said.

He moved his pointer to the interior of the compound. "The complex has seemingly expanded several times," he said. "You will note there are actually several internal walls that have been left in place, legacies of previous expansion. Internally, there are twenty-nine large buildings, ranging from the Russian barracks to storage dumps and a small prisoner compound. The kidnapped women, as far as we can tell, are largely kept in these two barracks here, but we cannot assume they're *all* being held there. We were unable to get anyone close enough to be sure."

"Crap," Percy commented.

"The centre of the compound is *here*," Peerce said. "The building is a prefabricated design, presumably taken from *Vesper*. It seems to serve as the linchpin of the Russian compound, with radio connections to the God-King and the orbiting starships. We believe the General, their commander, resides there. Again, however, we don't know for sure. There are limits to how closely we can probe the compound without alerting the enemy."

"Thank you, Sergeant," Hadfield said, after a moment. He turned to address the men. "We have two priorities. First, save as many of the women and children as possible; second, convince the Russians to surrender. That will not be easy. They expect to be hung when taken prisoner."

Percy frowned. Hanging was the standard punishment for any captured insurgent, terrorist or enemy combatant who openly flouted the laws of war, but it sometimes backfired. In this case, the Russians would have no reason to surrender if they thought they were going to die anyway. Why not go down fighting?

"We will be telling them that if they surrender, they will live," Hadfield continued. "The Captain intends to push for this, even though it will cause a great many problems for his career. However, the Russians may not believe him."

He looked from face to face. "Therefore, we have to assume the worst," he warned. "I want any armed Russian taken down with maximum force.

If they surrender, they are to be bound for later collection. You are to do the same to the women and children, no matter how harmless they seem. We do not know where their loyalties lie."

"Yes, sir," Percy said.

It wasn't a pleasant thought. He would have preferred a simple battle, but engagements in the Shooting House on Earth had taught him that civilians could switch sides after being held hostage for long enough. The women had to be treated as potential enemies until the battle was over and there was time to sort the good from the bad.

He shivered. And, in quite a few of those exercises in the Shooting House, far too many of the hostages had died in the crossfire.

"This is how we're going to do it," Hadfield said. He started to sketch out lines on the ground with a stick. "1 Section will assault from the north; 2 Section will assault from the east. I want mortar fire on the barracks, both Russian and slave-soldier, as soon as the offensive commences, taking them out before they can join the fight. Our allies will attack from the south and west, liberating the slaves as they move."

And hopefully keeping them out of the complex itself, Percy thought. Promises of plunder or not, the aliens would be hard to control when they saw their tormentors losing their grip on power. *There will be a slaughter if they decide to have a go at everyone.*

"We will also deploy drones and other support weapons," Hadfield added. "Call on them if you need their assistance."

"Aye, sir," Percy said. He had no idea if the Russians had any antiaircraft weapons positioned around their complex, but if they didn't a drone would be very useful. "And mortars on-call for fire?"

"They will be ready," Hadfield assured him.

"Pity we don't have any gliders," Hastings commented. "We could drop in on them from high above."

"But we don't," Peerce snapped. "We have to make do with what we have."

"True," Hadfield agreed. "Are we all clear on the basics of the plan? Corporals?"

"Yes, sir," Percy said. Hastings echoed him.

"It's an hour from here to the edge of their compound," Peerce said. "We will rest up for the day, then move out when it gets dark. By then, the starships should be on their way towards the tramline. If not...if not, the plan may have to be revised."

He took a breath. "Get some rest," he ordered. "It may be the last chance you have."

CHAPTER
THIRTY FIVE

"We're in position, sir," Armstrong said.

John nodded. The delay had gnawed at him, even though it had given the Marines a chance to gather intelligence and plan their assault. If the Russians had detected them…

They didn't, he reminded himself, firmly. *And now it's time to carry out our share of the plan.*

"Deploy the drones," he ordered.

"Aye, sir," Howard said. There was a long pause as he worked his console. "Both drones are now deployed."

"Activate the drones," John ordered.

"Drones online," Howard said.

John took a breath. The tramline was seven light minutes from the planet; it would take seven minutes for the Russians to detect the drones, then another seven minutes before John and his crew would know if the Russians had taken the bait. They had to act, John was sure; they had to stop the prospective survey ships before they retreated back to Boston to report the existence of a system with seven tramlines and a life-bearing world. *No one* would miss a chance to claim Vesy.

But they can't stay hidden indefinitely, John thought. *They could disappear a pair of scouts, yet sooner or later someone would notice the system had become a black hole and send a fleet to investigate. Or would they assume the tramline actually* did *lead to a black hole and then place the entire system off-limits?*

He shook his head. It was hard to calculate the destination of an alien-grade tramline, but the tramlines the Russians used - the only tramlines they knew existed - could be projected by any competent gravimetric engineer. There would be no *reason* for anyone to assume the system was full of natural hazards capable of destroying every ship that jumped through the tramline. These days, it was much more likely that the Admiralty would conclude there was a hostile alien race on the other side and take steps to investigate the threat.

The timer bleeped. "Sir," Howard said. "They should have detected the drones."

"Good," John said. Not for the first time, he cursed the time delay under his breath. FTL sensors would be another useful thing for the boffins to invent. "Let me know the moment they leave orbit."

He forced himself to wait, despite the tension. It had been easier, he told himself, when he'd been a starfighter pilot, even though there'd been a war on. Then, he'd waited in his cockpit until the higher-ups had launched him out to do or die. He'd never had to worry about anyone, but his wingmen. Now, he was responsible for the entire ship and her crew…

And you have a job to do, he reminded himself, sharply. *So shut the fuck up and do it.*

———

General Vasiliy Alekseyevich Rybak hated Vesy. He hated the heat, he hated the smell and, worst of all, he hated the natives. The world was uncomfortable, every breath he took reminded him that he would never see Earth again and the natives, the disgustingly primitive natives, were nearly useless. He'd hoped, once, to use them as janissaries to recover Earth from her alien masters. Now, all he could do was hope to forge a united government, a government the human race would recognise, that could legally justify everything they'd done when Vesy was discovered by human explorers.

He sat upright, feeling sweat tickling down his brow. Something had woken him, but what? The goddamned air conditioning had failed again, he realised, as he pushed his blankets away from his body. It was hot and humid and very unlike Mother Russia. Beside him, Mary twitched uncomfortably, but didn't show her face. He'd trained her well.

The intercom beeped, again. "General," a voice said.

"Report," Rybak growled.

He wanted to go back to sleep, but he knew better. No one would have dared disturb him unless it was important. It had taken weeks of patient effort to impose discipline on his men, but there had been no choice. Their only hope was unity, first to survive in an alien-dominated universe and then to forge something that would allow them to keep their lives when they were rediscovered. He'd done terrible things to dissidents in order to keep the rest of the bastards under control.

"General, long-range sensors are picking up a pair of starships exiting Tramline Alpha," the voice said. "They're currently seven light minutes from Vesy."

But they'll come look at us soon, the General thought, rubbing his aching head. He needed a drink, but he didn't dare pour himself a glass of anything stronger than water or sweet tea. *If they see the tramlines, they will know they've stumbled across a system worth claiming. And once they see Vesy itself…*

He sighed, inwardly. "Order the ships to investigate and…detain the intruders," he said. "I want them brought back here in chains."

"Yes, General," the voice said.

Rybak closed the connection, then glanced at his watch. It was the middle of the afternoon, when all humans needed to rest and escape the heat, but the coming night wouldn't bring any relief. Vesy remained inhumanly hot; he'd need to get a team to repair the air conditioning before he could get any actual work done. But he needed to speak with the God-King, to encourage him to take the next two cities on the target list. If the God-King controlled even a majority of the planet, the human race would recognise him as the supreme ruler…

He shook his head, bitterly. It was his only hope, he knew, of saving his life. If he forged a united world, he could present the Vesy to Mother Russia as allies…and force his government to back his actions and take him back into the fold. He had no illusions. If he returned home without something to offer, he would be shot for deserting his comrades during the Battle of New Russia. And yet, the more he did to ensure the colony's success, the harder it would be to convince his government to let bygones be bygones.

They'll want this system, he thought, once again. Legally, whoever owned the life-bearing world owned the system. The Vesy would have clear title to their own system and the God-King, his ally, would rule the Vesy. *They have to want this system.*

He shrugged, then pulled back the covers to reveal the naked girl. Mary stared up at him, then lowered her gaze rapidly. Rybak leered at her, noting how she no longer made any effort to cover herself. He'd beaten obedience into her until she'd surrendered completely to him. It had been a stroke of luck to capture the colonist women, but it had definitely been worth it. His men had been delighted to finally have women of their own...

The girl cringed back from his smile. Rybak smirked, then stood and walked towards the shower. There was no time to enjoy himself, as much as he might have wished to indulge. Instead, he would need to watch as the newcomers were captured...and then determine the best course of action, if there were more ships on the way. Perhaps it was time to arrange for a few 'accidents' that would obliterate anyone standing in the God-King's path. There might no longer be time for a slow, deliberate conquest.

He stepped into the shower and cursed under his breath as foul-smelling water cascaded from high overhead. Cooling and cleaning the water required energy they didn't have, not when they were so short on everything from generators to filters. It made him want to sleep, not remain awake. But there was no choice. All he could do was press on and hope he completed his plan before it was too late.

Or we will never be able to return to Russia, he thought. *And that would be the end.*

———

"Captain," Howard said. "The two Russian ships have left orbit."

"Good," John said. "Both of them?"

"Yes, sir," Howard confirmed. "There's no hint they've deployed drones of their own."

But they might have done, John thought. He pushed the concern aside with an effort. The Russians had no reason to assume a trap...and every reason to commit both of their remaining ships to the operation. They dared not allow one of the supposed survey ships to duck back into the tramline and vanish. Given a few minutes of leeway, the survey ships would not only manage to hide, but start the long path back to human space.

"Good," he said, again. "ETA?"

"Five hours," Howard said. "They're taking it easy."

John considered it - the Russians could have been on them sooner, if they'd pushed their drives - then decided the Russians probably didn't want to spook the survey ships. If he'd been a survey officer who'd seen two warships barrelling at him like a bat out of hell, he would have sent one of his ships back home at once, just in case. Survey officers were known for being curious, but the Royal Navy didn't allow them to take risks. One ship could be sent back at once, while the other could wait and see if the newcomers were friendly or inclined to open fire without bothering to communicate.

"Then we shall wait," he said.

He forced himself, once again, to wait. It was never easy to tell what one side knew - and thought the *other* side knew. John wondered, absently, if the Russians thought they were being stealthy, then dismissed the thought. Even by pre-war standards, the Russians weren't trying to hide their ships. It would have been hard for them to sneak up on a pre-war survey ship in any case - their hulls were practically crammed with sensor gear - but they weren't even trying to mask their drive emissions. They must intend to send a message at some point, he reasoned, one that would convince the survey ships to remain where they were. But what could they say that wouldn't set alarm bells ringing in the CO's head?

This system is officially unclaimed, John reminded himself. *Do they plan to actually claim it was only recently discovered?*

Or did the Russians have something else in mind. They knew - or thought they knew - that they had a ship in the last system, the frigate *Warspite* had captured. Did they think the frigate would be in position to capture a runaway? John keyed his console, bringing up the system display and running through the calculations in his head. No naval officer would rely on such a plan - it required far too many things to go right - but a ground-pounder might consider it workable. It wouldn't be the first insane concept to be put forward, in all seriousness, by a ground-pounder who couldn't grasp the realities of ship-to-ship combat.

The survey ships would go into stealth mode as soon as they knew the system was occupied, John thought, coldly. *They would evade all prospective threats in the next system as they made their way home, taking every precaution to avoid being detected. The frigate wouldn't even know they were there, if they managed to sneak past the ship on their way into the system…*

"Captain," Forbes said. "I'm picking up a message from the Russian ships, aimed at the drones. They're identifying themselves as Indian ships, sir, and are requesting the survey ships make contact."

John blinked, then nodded. The Russians - or at least their leadership - clearly knew more about current affairs than he'd assumed. Using Indian IDs wasn't unbelievable; John would have believed it, if he hadn't seen the hulls. The Indian Navy wouldn't want to spend money on ex-Russian craft when it could build more modern ships for itself. Besides, the frigate *Warspite* had captured was Russian, the troops on the ground were Russian, they'd taught the aliens to *speak* Russian…the evidence was overwhelming.

He smiled. *But they don't know that we know*, he thought. *They think we're just a bunch of survey officers following the tramlines.*

"Feed them some comforting lies," he said. "Tell them we would be happy to recognise their claim to the system and we look forward to comparing notes on the tramlines."

"Aye, sir," Forbes said.

John smiled to himself. If the ships in the system had *really* been Indian, there wouldn't have been much room to dispute their settlement rights - if, of course, the Vesy hadn't existed. They would have beaten anyone else to the system, after all; the World Court would uphold their rights, if it came down to an open dispute. But the presence of the aliens complicated matters. They, not the human interlopers, would have title…

He dismissed the thought. The Russians had to be stopped. After that, they could deal with the Vesy.

"They will be on us in thirty minutes," Howard warned.

"Then prepare to engage," John said.

———

The command centre was a joke, Rybak knew. It was nothing more than a small room at the heart of a prefabricated building, originally intended to serve as a storage compartment. But he'd had a handful of computers and radios moved into the chamber, then trained his staff until they could use them to assist the God-King in directing his forces. The locals thought radio was magic - they had no concept of radio waves or how they worked - but they had been able to learn how to use radios, once they had managed to overcome the shock. It was easy, now, for the God-King to coordinate his armies over multiple fronts, giving him a decisive advantage over his enemies.

The studied ruthlessness helps, Rybak thought, as his officers turned and saluted. *The Vesy know they have no choice, but to submit to his rule - or die.*

He had no intention of allowing the God-King to repeat the mistakes of Mother Russia. All other religions were to be crushed, without mercy. The priests were killed, the temples were torn down and attendance at sermons of the one true religion was compulsory. None of the Vesy had ever considered the value of a bureaucracy when it came to controlling people; they hadn't realised, until it was too late, that a slip of paper could make the difference between life or death. These days, a priest had to stamp a bearer's passport before that bearer could leave the temple...and, if the stamp was lacking, the bearer would be in serious trouble with the religious police. He would probably be castrated, then sent to the slave pens. Only one willing to rat out his fellow unbelievers would be spared.

The Tsars were fools to allow countries and religions to survive, he reminded himself. How much trouble might Mother Russia have saved itself if it had crushed the Poles, Ukrainians, Turks, Central Asians and Jews? *In ten years, there will be only one society on this world - ours, the one we shaped.*

The weapons were the easy option, he knew. It was the other changes that would make the God-King unbeatable. Roads for armies; radios for coordination; propaganda to make the unconquered grow weak at the knees; bureaucracies for population control; secret policemen to root out heresy as well as traitors…it would not be long before no one dared cough, without permission in triplicate. And the purges removed all elements of previous command structures. There would be no one left to organise resistance any longer…

"The ships are closing in on the newcomers," an officer said. "They're ready to engage."

"Then tell them to fire at will," Rybak said. There was no time to waste. He dared not allow either of the newcomers to make their escape. "And then keep me informed."

———

"They're inviting us to dinner, sir," Forbes reported. "They want to compare notes."

"How nice," John murmured. "Tell them we will be honoured to accept their invitation."

The thought made him smirk. He liked to think that even the most single-minded survey officer, with a curiosity bump the size of a planet, would be feeling uneasy by now. The Russians were still coming towards the supposed ships, rather than reducing speed and trying to look harmless. But then, if he'd been in command of the Russian ships, he might have wondered why the survey ships were just sitting there. Surely, one of them would have seen fit to move back through the tramlines by now.

Survey officers aren't primarily military officers, he thought. *Or they weren't, before the war. The Russians might not have realised that's changed.*

He looked at Howard. "Do we have a lock on the assault transport?"

"Yes, sir," Howard said. "Our main gun is locked and loaded, but not powered up."

John cursed under his breath. It took a minute, according to their live-fire tests at Pegasus, to charge up the plasma gun. The Russians would have plenty of time to detect the emissions and sheer off, if they realised what they were. And then…he'd been torn between firing at the transport and the frigate, before realising the assault transport had to be taken out first. If the worst happened, the frigate wouldn't be able to intervene so decisively against the forces on the ground. The Russians might see sense and surrender to the Marines.

"Then commence power-up sequence," he ordered. The Russians would know, as soon as they detected the emissions, that *Warspite* was no survey ship. "And prepare to engage."

"Aye, sir," Howard said.

John looked at Forbes. "If they ask what we're doing, hit them with some technobabble," he added. "See if they can be convinced we're not doing anything dangerous."

"Aye, sir," Forbes said.

"The Russians are altering course," Howard said. Alarm rang through his voice. "They're bringing tactical sensors online!"

Rumbled, John thought. A single radar sweep would reveal that one of the ships was an illusion created by two drones and the other a warship. There was no longer any point in trying to hide.

"Fire," he ordered.

CHAPTER
THIRTY SIX

The lights dimmed, just for a second, as the plasma cannon fired.

"Direct hit, sir," Howard reported. "The assault transport is crippled."

They must have bolted on additional armour, John thought. The plasma cannon should have burned through any pre-war hull, save for *Ark Royal* and the handful of frigates with solid-state armour plating. *Bollocks.*

Or maybe not, he realised, a second later. The transport's hull might have remained largely intact, but it was so badly damaged it was unlikely that anyone had survived.

"The frigate is opening fire," Howard added. "They're launching missiles."

"Return fire," John snapped. "Bring point defence online, then take us in pursuit."

"Aye, sir," Howard said.

"Hail them," John added. "Order them to surrender. Pledge good treatment if they give up now."

"Aye, sir," Forbes said.

John sucked in his breath as the Russian ship altered course, swinging from side to side as if her helmsman was drunk. They'd just seen one of their fellows crippled with a single shot, John knew; they had to know they were in deep trouble. But they also thought they were dead anyway, if they surrendered or not. The only thing they saw as a realistic response was to keep fighting.

Not that we could hit them with the plasma gun again, he thought. *That was very much a sucker punch.*

"Point defence going active now, sir," Howard said.

"Good," John said, quietly. On the display, plasma bolts lanced out towards their targets and, one by one, swatted the missiles out of space. None survived long enough to get close to the target and detonate. "Continue firing."

"They haven't responded to our messages, sir," Forbes said.

"Then send the *go* order to the Marines," John ordered.

He ran through the calculations, once again. It would take seven minutes for the order to reach its destination, then a few more minutes for the Marines to start their attack on the compound. Would the Russians have time to get their defences into place before the shit hit the fan? There was certainly no indication the Russians knew the Marines were already on the planet. But the Russians would certainly know that all hell had broken loose near the tramline.

"The Russians are trying to break off, sir," Howard reported.

"Take us in pursuit," John snapped. He was *damned* if he was going to let the Russians evade justice, not now. "Continue firing!"

The Russian ship kept weaving from side to side, as if they feared another plasma shot. John allowed himself a tight smile, then watched as Howard launched another spread of missiles towards the Russian ship. This ship's point defence was better than the last ship's, he acknowledged, but not good enough to hold out indefinitely. A laser head exploded close to the ship, sending a ravening beam stabbing deep into its vitals. The Russian ship seemed to stagger, then lost speed rapidly.

"I think we damaged the drives, sir," Howard reported. "I'm picking up a great many signs of internal distress…"

He broke off as new red icons appeared on the display. "They launched another salvo of missiles," he warned. "They're still fighting."

John shook his head in disbelief. No one could blame the Russians for giving up, not now. Even if they managed, by some dark miracle, to win the battle, they were doomed. Their ship was crippled, unlikely to make it back to the planet before it was too late; their comrade was completely smashed, half-melted by the plasma strike. But they were still trying to fight…

He considered his options, rapidly. Boarding the ship was impossible, not without the Marines. He could ask for volunteers from the crew, if necessary, but they weren't trained to board and storm enemy vessels. Even if they had been, the Russians might just blow up their own ship as soon as they were boarded, purely out of spite. And leaving them in space, crippled and helpless, meant condemning their crew to a lingering death.

They deserve to suffer, part of his mind insisted. It was true, he knew; the Russians had brutalised a helpless race, as well as kidnapped civilians. But the rest of him disagreed. *They don't deserve to suffer that much.*

"Take them out," he ordered, quietly.

"Aye, sir," Howard said. He launched a final missile straight into the Russian ship's hull, where it detonated. The Russian ship exploded into a fireball of expanding plasma. "Target destroyed."

John nodded. "Mr. Armstrong, take us back to the planet," he ordered. "Best possible speed."

"Aye, sir," Armstrong said.

"And get me a damage report," John added. "Did we take *any* damage?"

"No, sir," Johnston said. "We took them out before they could do us any real harm."

"Good," John said. He reminded himself, sharply, not to get overconfident. *Warspite* was the product of five years of additional research and development, including ideas borrowed from the Tadpoles. The Russian ships had been old before the war. Their next opponent might be equal, or superior, to the cruiser. "Prepare to deploy KEWs."

But he knew, all too well, that matters on the planet's surface might be settled, one way or the other, before *Warspite* reached orbit.

———

Percy couldn't help feeling a chill running down his spine as he crawled towards the Russian compound, feeling remarkably like the narrator from the VR version of *The War of the Worlds*. The Russian compound was a brooding fortress, lined with watchtowers and floodlights, watching warily for any signs of incoming attack. Every so often, a searchlight would sweep the surrounding fields, with machine guns and armed guards ready to engage any enemy troops. Percy had wondered, at first, why the Russians even bothered with the searchlights, but the more he thought about it, the more he realised the Vesy would be impressed by the lights. They were more intimidating than unseen night-vision gear.

He held up a hand as the Marines reached the edge of the field, then buried themselves beside a giant haystack. The Russian guards walked around the walls every twenty minutes, a predicable patrol that didn't seem to be altered, even though experienced soldiers should know the dangers. Percy wasn't sure if the Russians were too worn out to care or if it was part of a cunning plan to lure in the enemy, should they wish to engage. Instead, all he could do was prepare himself for the offensive.

Peerce tapped him on the shoulder, then held up his hands to signal that the section was ready to move. Percy nodded back, then resumed his survey of the Russian walls. It galled him to have to give up two of his men, but there was no choice. They were needed to man both the mortar tubes and the antitank weapons. He hoped the Russians didn't have any-one in armour, or carrying their own antitank weapons. They wouldn't need them, he told himself, to defend their compound. It wasn't as if they were about to be attacked by tanks.

Mark your targets, he signalled, as the guards came back into view. *Get ready to move.*

His suit automatically zoomed in on the guards; the Russians wore combat battledress, not armour of their own. They didn't look enthusiastic about being outside the walls, something Percy found entirely understandable. Vesy had plenty of wildlife that had devel-oped a taste for human flesh, even if the natives knew better than to touch a Russian near the compound. The guards slouched - he could think of no better word for it - around the compound, then returned to the gates. They didn't seem too concerned about the possibility of being attacked.

But they know the enemy cannot get too close without being detected, he thought. The Vesy did show up on night-vision gear, after all, and *they* couldn't hide from the sensors. *They don't know we're here.*

He braced himself as an alert flashed up in his HUD. *Warspite* should have engaged her targets by now and, win or lose, the Marines were going to assault the complex. There was no other choice; if they managed to capture the Russians, they might manage to convince the ships to surrender even if they did manage to escape *Warspite*. The last few seconds were ticking away…

Behind him, he heard the sound of a mortar being fired. *Warspite* must have sent the *go* order, he realised, as he knew the crews wouldn't have fired without orders. The first shell arced high over the complex, then came down on top of the alien barracks. A thunderous explosion echoed through the air, followed by the sound of shooting as snipers targeted the visible guards and watchtowers. Antitank missiles screamed through the air and slammed right into the walls; Percy saw one of the watchtowers explode, then a wall start crumpling inwards as a missile struck home. A second volley of mortar shells came pealing through the air, hammering the other side of the compound. The Russians would have to be dead to miss the fact they were under attack, particularly now. And they would start planning to launch a counterattack…

He smirked, then jumped to his feet and started to run.

———

General Rybak grabbed for his pistol before his mind caught up with his body and realised that the complex was under attack. He had the weapon half-drawn before he realised that they were under attack by *modern* weapons, rather than the primitive cannons and blunderbusses the Vesy had developed for themselves. The sound of mortars was quite distinctive, as were the antitank missiles.

"General," his aide snapped. "We're under attack!"

"You don't say," Rybak snarled. He cursed savagely, then started considering his options. "Have the reserve forces deployed now, then moved to seal the walls. Get the sleeping troops up, then into combat armour. And contact the God-King. Tell him I want an army dispatched to support us."

"Yes, sir," the aide said.

Rybak glared at his retreating back, then forced himself to think. The warships had been lured away…and then a ground attack had been mounted, using modern weapons. That could *not* be a coincidence. He'd been tricked, he saw now; somehow, the enemy had managed to get troops down to the surface, without being detected. In hindsight, not deploying a satellite network had been a major mistake.

It can't be helped, he told himself. *Bad rolls of the dice are a fact of life. You just need to roll with the mistakes and learn from them.*

"And call the ships," he added. He already knew it would be too late, that the ships might already have been destroyed, but he had to try. "I want them back here ASAP."

"Yes, sir," his aide said.

The sound of shooting grew louder as the enemy, whoever they were, pressed their offensive against the walls. Rybak had to admire their cunning, even though they seemed reluctant to actually fire into the complex itself. He couldn't understand why, but it gave him an opportunity to mass his troops and launch a counterattack. And the God-King's army would be on the way, soon enough. Teaching the natives the concept of a rapid reaction force had been nothing less than a stroke of brilliance.

He has to support us, Rybak thought, as the seconds ticked away. *Without us, his empire will be torn to shreds.*

"The walls are down, north and east," a voice snapped. "Mortar shells are hitting the walls, west and south!"

"I have two platoons ready to go," another voice called back. "They're armed, but not armoured."

"Get them to the east wall," Rybak ordered, sharply. The attackers might not know it, but by breaking through the east wall they were alarmingly close to his barracks. They had a chance to catch and slaughter some of his men before they were issued ammunition and deployed to fight back. "I want a line held there until we have armoured troops ready to go."

"Yes, sir," the voice snapped.

"General, I'm picking up a message," a third officer said. "They're offering to treat us fairly if we surrender."

"Don't be stupid," Rybak said. He had no illusions. Success would force the Russian government to back him, but failure would see him left in the cold to die. He and his men would be executed, if they survived long enough to be taken prisoner. "And don't bother to reply."

The ground shook as something detonated, alarmingly close to the building. "But sir…"

Rybak lifted his pistol. "Do as I fucking tell you or I'll fucking shoot you right fucking now," he shouted, angrily. He was damned if he was tolerating disobedience and backtalk, particularly when the future of his entire plan lay in the balance. Why couldn't his men do as they were told without the need for savage punishment? Their only hope was remaining united until the Vesy were united, then asking for support from Russia. "*Do not* send any reply!"

"Yes, sir," the officer said.

"They're coming up to the east wall," another officer called. "Men in armour!"

"Get the antitank weapons out there," Rybak ordered. "And get those goddamned shuttles in the air!"

He gritted his teeth as a thought struck him. The shuttles were invincible, by the standards of native technology. There wasn't a damn thing they could do to the craft, which could rain death on their armies and cities from high overhead. In some ways, they were far more intimidating than KEWs, which were invisible until they fell out of the sky and struck their targets. But the attackers, whoever they were, might have antiaircraft weapons as well as everything else. And the shuttles would be easy prey for modern weapons.

"General," yet another officer said. "I have a mortar team ready to go!"

"Then start some damned counterbattery fire," Rybak ordered. The enemy mortar teams were good, he had to admit. They'd taken out the slave-soldiers before the natives even knew they were under attack. Not that Rybak had much regard for them, but they could have soaked up a few bullets before being brushed aside. "Now!"

He swore, vilely, as sweat trickled down his back. Did he have to order everything personally? Did none of his men know how to think for themselves?

"I have a message from the God-King," the communications officer said. "He's dispatching a sizable force now."

"At least someone knows how to think," Rybak snapped.

He allowed himself a tight smile. The Vesy hadn't known how to react quickly before the Russians had arrived. They'd simply lacked the communications technology to respond instantly to a potential problem. But they'd learned their lessons well. The God-King's army would take shattering losses - it hadn't learned *that* much - but it hardly mattered. All that mattered was that their sheer numbers would tell against their enemies.

We can always rebuild, he told himself. Another chain of explosions shook the compound, sending dust drifting down from high overhead. *And hope to God that we manage to survive.*

———

Gillian had never found it easy to sleep on Vesy. It wasn't just the heat, or the awareness that many of the Russians considered her forbidden fruit, but some combination of the two that left her snapping awake at the slightest sound. She had often considered simply drugging herself, in hope of a good night's sleep, yet she'd never dared. It would have left her horrifyingly vulnerable if the guards had decided to try their luck, that night.

The sound of shooting snapped her awake. For a moment, she didn't know what she was hearing…and then, when her mind grasped the truth, she threw herself out of bed and down to the floor. The noise was growing louder - she could hear the Russians outside, shouting in their own language - suggesting that this was no drill. Someone was actually attacking the complex!

She crawled on hands and knees towards the door, then opened it and slipped into the medical ward. Her patients were awake, looking towards her; she could see fear in their eyes, even the two Russian patients. Gillian hesitated, then started to help the patients out of their beds and down to the ground. They'd be safer there, she told herself. But she was damned if she knew what else to do.

"Those aren't our guns," one of the Russians said. His voice was raspy, weak. "Not our weapons."

Gillian frowned. She had no illusions. The Vesy could not hope to mount an attack without help, not when the Russians could literally see in the dark, like cats. Any attackers would be torn to ribbons before they reached the walls. Had someone *else* stumbled across Vesy? A British ship, perhaps, or the Americans? She would even have welcomed a Russian or Chinese ship. They couldn't be worse than the rogues who had taught the Vesy the concept of religious genocide.

But what would the General do, she asked herself, when faced with total defeat?

She knew the General, knew him too well. He liked to think of himself as a pragmatist, but Gillian knew there was a darkness in his soul. The madness that had infected so many of the Russians had infected him too, driving him onwards in a desperate bid for…not for redemption, she was sure. He wanted *validation*. If he saw his last hope of success being destroyed, he might blow up the entire compound as a final gesture of spite.

But what could she do about it?

"Stay down," she said. She couldn't think of anything else to do. There were no weapons in the medical compound, nothing she could use to defend herself or her patients. A single hail of bullets would go through the walls like knives through butter. All she could do was wait…and pray that the newcomers weren't bent on slaughter. "Just keep your heads down."

The ground shook violently, once again. She gritted her teeth as one of her patients started to whimper, then crawled over and gave the beaten woman a hug. It was the only thing she could do.

God help us, she thought. *No one else can.*

CHAPTER
THIRTY SEVEN

"The enemy have started counterbattery fire," the mortar team reported.

"Then launch counterbattery fire of your own," Hadfield ordered. There were two forces engaging the enemy - four, if one counted the two Vesy armies making their way towards the walls - and coordinating them both was pure hell. "Take them out before they take *you* out."

He cursed under his breath. The drones weren't able to pick out *much* detail - the situation was too fluid for that - but it was enough to tell him that the Russians were starting to solidify their lines. Worse, perhaps, the locals had dispatched a massive army up the road towards the compound. It would take at least three hours for it to get there, he figured, but when the army did the Marines would have another problem. It wasn't going to be easy to solve.

I should be down there, he thought. It was a bitter thought. He should be leading his men in combat, not watching from a safe distance. *But I need to coordinate.*

He'd proven his bravery time and time again. No one would think any less of him for doing his duty. But it still rankled.

———

Percy swore under his breath as he reached the ruins of the wall, then peered inwards. The Russians had been taken by surprise, but they'd still managed to put together a makeshift defence. There were Russians shooting towards his men, forcing them to keep their heads down, while others were arming themselves with antitank weapons. *They* would take out a light combat suit without difficulty, killing the Marine inside.

There was no time for delay. He snapped out a series of orders, launching a set of grenades towards the Russian positions, then led the charge into the explosions. The Russians recoiled under the impact, then broke. Percy saw several of them fall to his men, then two more shot in the back as they tried to run. Only one tried to surrender and *he* was shot by one of his fellows, just before Percy killed him. The Russians, it seemed, were torn between giving up and fighting to the finish.

He led the way into the first set of buildings, which turned out to be crammed with supplies looted from *Vesper*. The Marines verified that the buildings weren't occupied, then pressed onwards, taking out a pair of snipers on the rooftops as they moved. Percy saw a handful of Russians pop up, fire off a handful of shots and vanish again, ducking before the Marines could take them out. A rocket flashed past him - he ducked, a second too late - and struck one of the Marines, blowing a hole in his suit. Percy swore as a red icon flashed in front of his face, then killed the launcher before he could reload and fire again. One of his Marines was dead.

"Incoming," Peerce snapped, as a line of armoured Russians made their appearance, ducking and dodging as they closed in on the humans. "Use plasma weapons; take them out."

Percy nodded, then selected his inbuilt plasma weapon and opened fire. Two Russians died before the remainder leapt for cover, suddenly aware that the British had weapons that could burn through suits as if they were made of tissue. They wouldn't have faced handheld plasma weapons in the past, Percy was sure. The Russians hadn't stayed in New Russia long enough to witness the fall of the system, let alone the occupation. Nothing daunted, they shot back with rockets, forcing his men to keep their distance. The advance seemed to have stalled.

"This is 2-lead," Percy said, keying his radio. It took him a moment to designate targets with his laser pointer. "I need shells here, here and here."

There was a long pause, then a hail of mortar rounds landed on top of the enemy positions. The ground shook violently; the Russians might have been armoured, and protected from anything short of a direct hit, but Percy was sure as hell they'd *felt* the impact. He snapped out an order, then lunged forward, hunting for targets. Three more Russians died before the remainder fell backwards, shooting frantically to cover their retreat. One turned, boosted his suit, and ran out into the countryside. Percy noted his departure in passing, then turned his attention to the rest of the compound. There would be time to handle the stragglers later.

Keep going, he told himself, as they broke into another complex. This one held children, all girls. They were crying and screaming, panicking helplessly. Percy had a sudden flashback to the first night he'd spent in the refugee camp, before he'd been press-ganged to help tackle the floods. The children had been crying then too, despite the best efforts of their parents.

"Get on the ground," he bellowed, but most of the girls were too far gone to hear him, let alone obey. "Get down and stay down!"

He cursed under his breath, then called in the building. The mortar teams had to be warned to exclude it from future firing patterns. He looked back at the girls, then shuddered. God alone knew what the Russians had done to them. He wanted to think they hadn't been abused, but the Russians had dropped so many civilised customs in the past six months...he still shuddered with horror when he recalled some of the scenes from the disaster zones in Britain. The girls would need years of therapy before they were recovered, therapy they probably wouldn't get. There weren't enough therapists in Britain to tackle all the trauma cases, he knew, and there were no therapists on Cromwell.

A terrible oversight, he thought, morbidly.

Gritting his teeth, he led his men back to the war.

———

"The savages are attacking the south and west," his aide snapped. "They're coming right through the fields."

"Order the guns to target them," Rybak ordered. How the hell had the intruders, whoever they were, made contact with the locals right under his nose? Had the God-King decided to sell the Russians out, after all? "And bring down mortar fire on their heads."

"Aye, sir," his aide said.

Rybak cursed out loud. The compound was under attack from all four sides, making it hard to tell which one was the *real* attack. Human forces seemed to be spearheading the attacks on the north and east, which suggest they were the most serious threat, but the natives were a major problem. He'd calculated that the God-King's forces could soak up bullets, if necessary, yet the equation also worked in reverse. His men didn't have unlimited ammunition, but they were being forced to spend it like water.

He looked at the map, trying to understand what was happening. The east attack had stalled, for a moment, then resumed. Several buildings had already fallen, while others were under threat or completely defenceless. The medical centre was about to fall, he saw, unless a miracle happened. It was utterly unsuited to serve as a strong point.

"Get those shuttles in the air," he repeated. "Now, damn it!"

———

"Corporal," Peerce snapped. "They're launching shuttles!"

Percy swore as red icons flared up in front of him. The enemy would be able to rain fire on them from high overhead, if they were given a chance. There were three shuttles, one a modified heavy-lift vehicle; he could guess, easily, just what it was carrying. A weapons pod wouldn't be too difficult to fit, he was sure. The Royal Marines had done it often enough.

"Take them out as soon as they come into engagement range," he ordered. It was a risk - a shuttle might crash on top of the advancing Marines - but it had to be done. "Hurry!"

Two of the Marines paused, then opened fire with plasma weapons as the shuttles made their first attack run. One exploded in midair, raining flaming debris onto the fighters below, while the other two, badly damaged, staggered away from the compound. Percy saw one of them, trailing fire, crash somewhere in the nearby forest; the other one made a forced landing just outside the complex. The Vesy would deal with her crew, he figured; the pilots had landed right in front of the advancing rebels. He just hoped they remembered to take prisoners.

He paused outside a building, then kicked open the door.

———

Gillian jumped as the door smashed inwards, then a hulking figure - clad in powered combat armour - pushed his way inside. She held herself very still as the figure peered at her, holding up her hands in surrender. For a long moment, everything seemed to freeze, then she caught sight of the flag on the figure's shoulder.

"You're British," she said.

"Yeah," the figure said. He raised his voice. "Lie down on the ground, face down, and put your hands behind your backs. Now."

Gillian hesitated, then obeyed reluctantly. The British troops checked the Russians first, then secured their hands and feet with plastic ties. Two of the patients objected, but most of them submitted without protest. Gillian wanted to fight as her hands were bound, yet she knew it was a wise precaution. Too many of the kidnapped women had fallen in love - or deluded themselves that they had fallen in love - with the Russians.

"You have to listen to me," she said, once the soldiers had secured the patients and searched the compound. "The Russians are going mad."

The soldier turned to face her. "We know," he said. "But all we can do is press onwards."

Gillian looked at him, then started to tell him everything she knew.

———

Percy listened, opening a channel so Hadfield and Peerce could hear her too. The woman - his records identified her as Doctor Gillian McDougal - was a good observer, better than some of the Royal Marines he'd known. She understood what the Russians were going through and had attempted to learn as much as she could about them. Her intelligence was useful…

…But it didn't change the fact that they had to push the offensive as hard as they could.

"Someone will be along to help you," he promised, when Gillian finally stopped speaking. He wasn't sure it was a promise he could keep.

There were no support troops, no reinforcements that could get the girls and their mothers out of the complex before the madman blew it up. All the Marines could do was press onwards and hope for the best. "Wait here until then."

Gillian gave him a sardonic look, but said nothing.

Percy exchanged a few brief words with Peerce as the Royal Marines stepped outside, then led his men towards the prefabricated building at the heart of the complex. The remaining armoured Russians had set up a new defensive line, he realised, but they were ill-prepared to stop his men. Their barracks might have served as decent positions against the Vesy, he decided as the Marines called down mortar shells on their enemies, yet they weren't designed to stand up to modern weapons. Armoured suits were best deployed in mobile combat, not fixed defence.

The building exploded into fire as three shells punched through the roof and detonated. Percy waited for a long second, then led the charge forward, pushing the remaining Russians out of the way. The next building was crammed full of women, all screaming in panic. Percy hesitated - some of the women were clearly threatening his men - and then threw a stun grenade into the building. It would keep the women out of trouble long enough for the Marines to either secure the compound or die trying.

He heard war-whoops from the west as they paused long enough to regroup, then step up to the very heart of the enemy base. The prefabricated buildings were larger than anything the Vesy slaves had built for their human masters, he noted; the doorways were heavily defended, as if the Russians had feared attack even in the centre of their power. It wasn't an ideal situation - the Marines would have to punch their way through the doorways, which would make their path predictable - but there was no choice.

"Go," Hadfield ordered, when Percy filled him in. "Hastings has been bogged down by the enemy."

Percy cursed under his breath. In an exercise, beating 1 Section to the prize would have pleased him enormously - and made 1 Section buy the drinks, afterwards. But, in the midst of a real battle, he would have liked to have their support. The Russians were still holding out, after all, and they'd had time to prepare a whole series of surprises.

But there was no choice. Bracing himself, he issued the order to attack.

———

The building shook, once again. This time, the blast was much closer.

"General," his aide said. "They're attacking the gates."

Rybak nodded in bitter understanding. "Pull back all available forces," he ordered. He had only two cards left to play, now the shuttles were gone. There hadn't been any response to the message he'd sent to the ships, which convinced him that they had both been destroyed. "We're going to barricade ourselves inside the building until the God-King arrives."

He saw two of his officers exchange worried glances and clutched his pistol, tightly. The God-King believed the crap he sprouted about being a living god - it helped that Russian technology could perform miracles, by local standards - but what would he make of the Russians if he saw them cowering, waiting desperately for support? Even the most hardened fanatic would have second thoughts if he saw the Russians on the verge of defeat. But there was only one other card and he was damned if he was using it unless all was lost.

"Yes, sir," the aide said.

———

"1 Section is gaining ground," Hastings reported. "They're falling back."

"I can see that," Hadfield said. The Russians, for whatever reason, hadn't tried to shoot down the drones. He had a bird's eye view of the compound and, now the Marines were pushing the Russians back, it was easier to sort out what was going on. "The mortar crews will deal with them."

He barked orders, then watched as more rounds slammed down among the Russian soldiers. Caught in the open, they were easy targets. A handful survived, long enough to be taken prisoner by Hastings and his men, but the majority were killed before they even knew they were under attack. Few surrendered willingly. Hadfield sighed, inwardly. The Russians believed they were doomed, so they were fighting to the bitter end. What else could they do?

"Push onwards," he ordered.

But he knew matters were moving out of his hands.

———

"The troops have been hammered," his aide said. "There won't be any reinforcements."

"Sir," another officer said. "We should consider their offer."

Rybak shot him. "No," he snarled, as the officer fell to the ground. "We will fight to the finish."

Another officer started to draw his pistol. Rybak shot him too, then turned, glaring from face to face until they all looked cowed. "I will see to it that they do not live to enjoy their victory," he said. "Keep fighting until the bitter end."

He turned and strode out of the compartment, sealing the hatch behind him. His quarters were just down the corridor; inside, Mary was lying on the floor, her entire body shaking with fear. Rybak snarled in contempt - how weak she was - and opened the sealed box he'd placed against the far wall. Inside, there was a single tactical nuclear warhead, one he'd had brought down from the assault transport once they'd set up the colony. It was easily powerful enough to wipe out the settlement, the attacking force and all hard evidence of who had founded it in the first place.

Opening the lid, he peered down at the keypad, then started to key in the first 16-digit code that would activate the warhead. It wasn't designed to be easy to trigger, unfortunately; he'd never bothered to have the engineers remove the standard verification system and replace it with a big red button. He smirked at the thought, then paused. Behind him, he could hear the sound of whimpering.

"You're about to die," he said, cheerfully. The warhead clicked once, then demanded the second code. In the distance, the sound of shooting and grenades was growing louder. The enemy, whoever they were, had forced their way into the building. They would be sweeping their way from room to room, looking for the command centre and happily unaware that it no longer mattered. "We're all about to die."

He heard a sound behind him and turned, too late. The knife appeared in his chest and he realised, dully, that Mary had stabbed him in the back. He hadn't thought she had the nerve to do *anything*! But if the fear of certain pain, of certain death, had kept her in his bed, the certainty of death had spurred her to fight. He spun, then crumpled to the floor, unable even to stand upright any longer. By the time the intruders broke into his quarters, it was far too late.

———

"They tried to detonate a *nuke*?"

"Yes, sir," Percy said. He looked at the sobbing girl, then at the dead Russian. "It's a tactical nuke. They must have thought they would need it at New Russia."

There was a pause. "Understood," Hadfield said. "Take as many surrenders as you can, Corporal, then help us start rigging defences. The God-King is still on his way."

Percy cursed. "The ship?"

"Still at least three hours away," Hadfield warned. "I don't think she can move much faster."

"Understood, sir," Percy said. He took one last look at the nuke, then helped the girl to her feet. She wouldn't be safe until all the Russians were either prisoners or dead. "I'm on my way."

CHAPTER
THIRTY EIGHT

"They were abusing the young men, sir," Hastings said. "Not physically, but they were preparing them to be soldiers."

Percy winced as Hastings gave his report. 2 Section might have secured the women, but 1 Section had overrun the barracks housing nearly a hundred male children, ranging from twelve to sixteen years old. The Russians had turned it into a demented scout camp, alternatively beasting the boys into shape and rewarding them lavishly. Thankfully, the Russians in charge of the lads had refrained from arming the kids and pointing them at the advancing Marines. Far too many of them would have been killed if they had.

"Keep them secure for now," Hadfield said. "And the Russians themselves?"

"We have around three hundred prisoners," Percy reported. "Save for the wounded, they're all held in the barracks, for the moment. The Russian commander himself is dead."

"Pity," Hadfield observed. He glanced down at his terminal. "The God-King's forces are still on the way."

"Yes, sir," Percy said.

"Get your men into defensive positions, then prepare to hold the line," Hadfield continued. "We'll have to pull the rest of the troops into the compound itself."

Percy cursed under his breath. Having ripped a number of holes in the colony's defences, the Marines would then have to *defend* it themselves.

The Royal Marines themselves could break contact easily - the God-King's forces couldn't hope to match their speed - and retreat back to the shuttles, but there was no way to move the women and children so quickly. And none of the Bootnecks would have willingly abandoned them to their fate.

"Aye, sir," he said. The Royal Marines had made last stands before. They might as well make one now, if the ship didn't return in time. "What about the shuttles?"

"I'm sending one of the pilots back," Hadfield said. "We need the others to work the mortars."

"Aye, sir," Percy said.

The Marines worked frantically as the God-King's army grew closer and closer. Percy coordinated with Ivan - the native allies would be needed, while Hadfield and Hastings placed men in position to intercept the natives when they arrived. He wished they had the material to place mines or improvised explosive devices around the compound, but the Russians hadn't stockpiled enough makeshift explosive to make it worthwhile. Ivan grew more and more reluctant to cooperate as the God-King's army approached, pointing out - time and time again - that the God-King's army had slaughtered its way through all resistance. Percy countered by reminding Ivan that the Marines had a *lot* of firepower and help was on the way.

But if they figured they could retreat, he thought, *they would have done it by now.*

He watched the advancing army through the live feed from the drones. It looked horrifically irregular, by human standards; it was a strange cross between Roman, Aztec and Russian military practices. The natives marched in unison, carrying standards that ranged from the skulls of their enemies to paintings showing the names and faces of their gods. Each of them carried a blunderbuss and a short sword, presumably made from iron. The Russians might have introduced steel, Percy reasoned, but it was unlikely they would have been able to produce it in any great quantities.

"They have catapults and cannon bringing up the rear," Hadfield observed. "I don't think I've seen anything like that outside a bad cartoon."

"Aye, sir," Percy said. The catapult looked like something he'd designed and built as a Boy Scout. However, it was no laughing matter. The aliens could easily bombard the compound with rocks…and, if they threw gunpowder instead, the results would be explosive. "I suggest we deploy the suits to take out their heavy weapons."

"Mortars can see to that," Hadfield said, shaking his head. "I don't want to weaken the defences still further."

Percy nodded, reluctantly. "Aye, sir," he said.

———

Gillian rubbed her wrists as she surveyed the wounded women and children. There were fewer than she'd expected; the Royal Marines, it seemed, had been careful about where they fired their weapons, unlike the Russians themselves. Giving them medical attention helped keep her from worrying about the short-term future, let alone the future any of the women could expect when they finally reached Cromwell. Who knew *what* would happen to them?

"I killed him," Mary said, quietly.

"Good for you," Gillian said. She'd thought Mary had broken, that she'd given up all hope of resistance…and then Mary had stabbed the General in the back, saving everyone. "Help me deal with these patients."

Mary nodded, then got to work. Gillian watched her for a long moment, then opened one of the medical packs the Marines had given her and dug out the painkillers. There was nothing she could do for some of the wounded, save issue them painkillers and hope they could be moved to a proper hospital soon. The Russians hadn't left her enough supplies to help the patients - or, for that matter, the Russians themselves.

"Gillian," Gina said. "What will happen to Alexander?"

"I don't know," Gillian said.

She couldn't help feeling a flicker of sympathy. The pregnant girl had just seen her life turned upside down, once again. Her Russian was either dead or a captive, while her husband might not welcome her back when she was carrying another man's child. And it wasn't as if she had been raped. Her husband might reason it wasn't her fault…or he might see it as a betrayal of her wedding vows. And he'd waited over five years for her…

And what looked like a reasonable survival tactic becomes something else, now we are free, she thought, morbidly. Gina wouldn't be the only one who would have to deal with the situation. *God alone knows what this is going to do to us.*

She shook her head. It was possible the natives would break the walls, then kill everyone in the compound. And if that happened, her concerns about the future would become immaterial.

"Shit," Mary said.

Gillian nodded. In the distance, she could hear the sound of the approaching army.

———

"I think they're trying to scare us, sir."

"So it would seem, Sergeant," Hadfield said. He looked at Percy, then grinned. "Are you feeling scared?"

Percy shook his head. The sound of trumpets was echoing across the fields as the aliens slowly came into view. Their movements were slow, deliberate. It was a good intimidation tactic, he had to admit, but the Royal Marines were taught to move fast, hit hard and never be where the enemy expected them to be. Besides, the looming mass of alien soldiers would make easy targets for the mortars. He smiled suddenly as he saw a horse-like creature - he couldn't help comparing it to a small dinosaur - canter into view, carrying an alien decked out in a surprising amount of plumage. That was a commanding officer, he decided, or he'd eat his hat.

"Good," Hadfield said.

"Lieutenant," Peerce said, quietly. He pointed towards a mounted rider, who was cantering towards the ruined gatehouse. "I think that's a messenger."

Hadfield nodded. "Percy?"

Percy nodded, then walked down towards the gatehouse, where three Marines were hastily setting up another line of barricades. They wouldn't stop a determined opponent for very long, Percy knew, but they would force them to mass in one place, easy prey for the mortar teams. He stepped through the gate and nodded to the alien. The alien nodded back, a gesture he had to have picked up from the Russians, then started to speak.

"In the name of" - several words in the alien tongue - "I call on you to surrender," the alien said. "To place yourself at the mercy of the gods and their one true spokesman. To submit yourself before us and bow your head in wonder at our majesty. To serve us as you would serve the elect of the gods..."

He went on for quite some time, bragging of the power and might of the God-King. Percy listened, recording the entire speech for the benefit of future historians, although as it dragged on and on he found himself growing increasingly irritated. But it was a delay in proceedings...the longer the aliens held back from attacking, the sooner the ship would arrive to save them all. When the alien finally came to a stop, having demanded their surrender no less than thirty times, Percy was ready with an answer.

"No," he said.

The alien seemed surprised, although it was hard to tell. Combat challenges were ritualistic among the natives, from what Ivan had said, and he'd no doubt expected Percy to respond in kind. He could have read a list of Royal Marine battle honours, Percy supposed, but they wouldn't have meant anything to the aliens. All that mattered was that the Royal Marines had no intention of surrendering to them.

He watched as the alien turned and cantered back towards the army. As soon as he reached the line, the trumpets blew once again and the entire mass of the army surged forward. Percy stared in horror - a mass charge would be utterly futile against emplaced machine guns - then darted back to the human lines. Hadfield issued an order, a second later, and the Marines opened fire. Hundreds of aliens fell in the first few seconds, but hundreds more kept coming, jumping over the dead or dying bodies as they advanced. Red blood, disturbingly human, splashed across the land.

Oh, you poor bastards, he thought, as the aliens kept coming. Hundreds upon hundreds died every time the machine guns raked their lines. *Whatever did you do to deserve such commanders?*

"Snipers," Hadfield said. "Take out their leaders."

But the aliens kept coming. The mortar teams opened fire, raining shells amidst the rear of the enemy lines, where they'd set up their cannons and catapults. A terrifyingly large explosion suggested that the aliens had also been stockpiling their gunpowder near the cannons, a mistake that had cost them dearly. They must not have faced any form of counterbattery fire before, Percy decided, although it was impossible to be sure. The Russians wouldn't have made *that* mistake.

Maybe they left some weaknesses when they taught the aliens how to fight, he thought, as he lifted his weapon. The aliens were still running over their dead bodies, almost reaching the shattered walls. *Or maybe they just didn't want the aliens thinking for themselves.*

The aliens howled as they crossed the wall, then opened fire. Pellets raced past the marine positions, bouncing off prefabricated buildings. Even the wooden buildings seemed to stand up well to alien fire, Percy noted, as he opened fire himself. The alien weapons didn't seem to have much kick, not compared to human designs. Had the Russians deliberately limited what the aliens could do, he asked himself, or had they simply run into problems making the aliens better weapons? There was no way to know.

He gritted his teeth as he saw an alien fall, right in front of him; there were always more, pushing forward despite the fire. The aliens howled and chanted - he assumed they were prayers - as they closed in, seeking revenge for what the Marines had done. Percy shot alien after alien, but the pressure was slowly forcing the Marines back. Why weren't they breaking? Were they so fanatical they could soak up thousands of casualties and just keep going?

"Pull back to the inner line," Hadfield ordered. "The mortars will cover your retreat."

"Aye, sir," Percy said. The ground shook as mortar shells landed amidst the aliens, blowing them into bloody chunks. But there were always more aliens, while he knew all too well that they were running short of mortar rounds. And everything else. They could slice the aliens apart…until they ran out of ammunition. "We're on our way."

A pause seemed to descend on the battlefield as the Marines fell back. Percy allowed himself a moment to hope that the aliens had had enough, that thousands - tens of thousands - of deaths had been enough to convince them to back off, or turn on their leaders. But a quick glance at the live feed from the drones killed his hope before it could fully blossom into life. The aliens were merely regrouping, despite the persistent sniper fire that killed their commanders and priests as they identified themselves. It dawned on Percy, suddenly, that the God-King had hurled the expendable units into battle first. He'd wanted them purged and the Marines had done it for him.

He must be out of his mind, Percy thought, darkly. *How many of his loyal followers are going to die today?*

But perhaps that was what the God-King wanted, he added, in the privacy of his own mind. The empire the God-King had built wouldn't last long, not without the Russians backing it up. Ivan had made that clear; the God-King was powerful, but it was the Russians who had given him a decisive advantage. His conquests would rise up against him, once they realised the Russians were gone. But if the God-King crushed the British, even at staggering cost, he might be able to keep his subjects too afraid to rebel.

"We have only a handful of mortar shells left," Peerce said, when the Marines regrouped at the inner defence line. "And not much Russian crap to put into battle either."

"Shit," Percy said. The Russians hadn't had enough weapons to make a real difference, much to his surprise, although they'd spent quite a bit trying to keep the Royal Marines out of their compound. They had always relied upon orbital fire to keep the natives in line. It was the same pattern they'd used on Earth, but they'd always had more ground troops on Earth too.

He took a breath. "The shuttles?"

"Not going to be here in time," Hadfield said. "And we don't have enough bullets left to keep fighting for long."

Percy nodded. Vesy was a strange place to fight and die, he figured, but there was no alternative. Besides, his father had died fighting to protect humanity from the Tadpoles. His son could do no less. He thought briefly of Penny, who would be left all alone on Earth, then remembered his girlfriend. Maybe she would find someone else, after he was gone. He hoped she would be happy...

"Make sure you hold the line as long as you can," Hadfield added. "I want to make sure we gore the God-King badly, if we die here. Let one of his enemies overthrow him once his forces are gone."

"Yes, sir," Percy said.

The trumpets blared. Percy turned to watch as the aliens began their second advance. This time, their tactics were better; one group rushed forward, while another covered their advance, then waited for the first group to cover them before advancing themselves. The God-King must have sent in his best men, Percy decided, as the Marines opened fire. They were spread out too, making it harder for the mortars to make a serious impact. Maybe *these* were the ones the Russians had trained personally.

"Hold the line as long as you can," Hadfield said, quietly.

The aliens kept coming, hurling makeshift grenades towards the human lines as they advanced. Percy opened fire with the rest of his section, knowing there just weren't enough humans to hold the line for very long. He briefly considered suggesting rearming the Russians, but dismissed that thought in an instant. The Russians couldn't be trusted not to shoot the Marines in the back, while the women had no time to learn how to shoot. Instead, all he could do was hold the line as best as he could.

A line of aliens charged forward, covered by their comrades. Percy muttered a curse, then led the fire team forward and lashed into the aliens with his armoured fists. Blood and gore went flying as he smashed through the aliens, then he cursed as the next group of aliens started hurling makeshift grenades. A red light flashed up in his HUD as Private Willis died; an alien had caught him, then detonated all the grenades on his body at once, causing an explosion powerful enough to tear through the suit. Another Marine followed him into death, while a third was wounded. His suit sealed itself automatically, but it was clear - far too clear - that he would need medical attention immediately. It wouldn't be forthcoming.

A final hail of explosions tore through the advancing enemy, then stopped. "The mortars are dry," Peerce said. "I say again, the mortars are dry."

Percy cursed as the aliens redoubled their efforts, forcing the Marines back. There would no longer be anything impeding the aliens from sending their men into combat…he braced himself, preparing to issue orders for a final stand. New icons popped up in front of him, warning that almost all of his remaining men were running out of ammunition. 1 Section wasn't in any better state, even if they'd had time to borrow ammunition from them. They were about to die...

And then the ground shook violently as fire descended from heaven. The entire compound heaved - he saw a building cave in on itself - as brilliant flashes of light rose up from outside the shattered walls. Suddenly, the alien advanced faltered, then stopped. The ground shook again and again as the final aliens were wiped out. Percy stared, only slowly realising what had happened. The ship had returned!

"Secure the area," Hadfield ordered. Outside, great plumes of smoke were rising up from the fields. "We'll have more ammunition sent down momentarily."

"Aye, sir," Percy said. Hastings said nothing. It took him a moment to realise that Hastings was dead. "I'll see to it at once."

The only thing costlier than a battle lost, the Duke of Wellington had said years ago, *is a battle won.*

Percy had never understood what he'd meant. The saying had always seemed odd to him. But now, looking at the devastated battleground, he thought he understood perfectly. They'd won, yet they'd still taken hideous losses...

...And it might not be over yet.

CHAPTER
THIRTY NINE

"What a mess," John muttered, as the shuttle dropped down towards the remains of the Russian compound. "What a fucking mess."

He braced himself as the shuttle touched down, then breathed in alien air as the hatch hissed open. Doctor Stewart and his assistants scrambled out at once, carrying pallets of supplies with them as they made their way towards the makeshift infirmary; John followed them at a more sedate pace. The scene that greeted him was one of utter devastation. Hundreds of wooden buildings had collapsed, while dozens of craters had formed around the compound, where the KEWs had landed. And there were thousands of alien bodies, lying everywhere.

My God, he thought. The natives had been completely unprepared for human weapons and technology. They couldn't have anticipated the sheer level of slaughter the Russians, and then the British, had unleashed. *What have we done?*

"Captain," Lieutenant Hadfield said. The Marine looked tired and worn, but confident. "I bid you welcome to Fort Knight."

John was too tired himself to smile. He should have rested - and Richards had urged him to rest - but he'd refused to sleep until he'd had a chance to assess the situation on the ground for himself. The desperate race back from the tramline, pushing *Warspite* to the limit, had almost been lost. An alien race so primitive that it had barely begun to work iron had almost wiped out his entire complement of Marines, as well as several hundred civilians and Russian captives. And now…now he had a hell of a mess to sort out.

"This place is largely indefensible now," Hadfield said, as they walked into the compound. "I had the natives take the bodies away - they're going to bury them all in a pit - but we don't have time to rebuild the walls or the other defences. The Russians made so many enemies that we can expect someone else to have a go at us, soon enough."

John nodded. "Can we move the civilians to a safer location?"

"I think we don't have much choice, sir," Hadfield said. "*Vesper*, according to the Russians, is beyond salvation. They were going to launch her into the sun, once they'd finished stripping her of anything useful. We'd need a transport to move everyone from Vesy to Cromwell."

"Shit," John said. In order to keep the humans safe, *Warspite* would have to remain in orbit; in order to move the humans to another location, *Warspite* would have to return to Pegasus and summon one of the freighters to Vesy. Catch-22. "We can deploy some automated KEW systems, but not much else."

"We've located a number of uninhabited islands," Hadfield said. "I was thinking we could use the shuttles to move the civilians there, then *Warspite* can return to Pegasus and borrow a freighter at leisure. However, we've run into something of a problem."

John *looked* at him. "A problem? Another problem?"

"Yes, sir," Hadfield said. "The Vesy have captured a number of Russians. They don't want to give them up and…well, they want the rest of the Russians too."

"I see," John said. "What for?"

"Technological help, I think," Hadfield said. "And perhaps to put them on trial."

John rubbed his tired forehead. There would be enough people with a claim on the Russians, by the time the World Court considered the case, to make it hard to determine just who got the right to execute them. The Vesy, at least, had a very good claim - and a reason to keep some Russians alive, if they were willing to work. And he wasn't sure he wanted to risk transporting the remaining Russians back to Earth. They would have to remain on Vesy anyway, at least until more ships arrived.

"I'll have to think about it," he said.

It wasn't going to be easy. He *did* have authority to make deals with aliens, but it was limited. No one had envisaged having to make an agreement with a primitive race. The assumption had always been that humanity would run into a peer power - a *second* peer power, he supposed. In hindsight, it was understandable. A primitive race could not have posed a threat to *Warspite*, even if they had been aware of her. But the Russians had made contact, leaving an awful mess in their wake.

"Their leader would also like to speak with you," Hadfield said. "I believe he wishes to negotiate with our commanding officer personally."

"Very well," John said. "Take me to their leader."

Hadfield smiled, then led him to one of the few surviving buildings. A number of Russians, their hands and feet shackled, were helping to clear up the mess, watched by a pair of armed and armoured Marines. They looked torn between fear and relief, John noted; the doom they'd feared had finally overwhelmed them, yet they were also free of their leader. The General had come alarmingly close to blowing up the whole compound. And wouldn't *that* have put the reporter among the politicians?

Inside, an alien was standing near the door, studying a mural one of the Russians had painted on the wall. John sucked in his breath sharply as he saw the alien - he'd met Tadpoles, in the past, but this alien was close enough to humanity to be considerably more disconcerting - and then nodded politely. He had no idea just what the aliens considered polite, he realised, as he sat down at the table, beside one of the Marines. He'd never had to handle a diplomatic meeting before, yet if he had, he knew he wouldn't have been better prepared.

"This is the leader of a Vesy faction," the Marine said. "The Russians called him Ivan."

"I thank you, in the name of my people, for your assistance," Ivan said. The Marine translated from Russian to English. "It is of the future I wish to speak to you now."

John nodded, again. "I thank you for your assistance," he said. He cursed mentally as he realised he didn't know what to say. "I look forward to a long and fruitful relationship between your people and mine."

The alien, thankfully, didn't beat around the bush. "We have a number of the...*Russians*...prisoner," Ivan said. "They have volunteered to remain with us. We would like the remainder of the Russians to be handed over to us too."

John frowned. If humans had trouble telling the aliens apart, it was quite likely the aliens had the same trouble with humanity. It was easy to imagine that they'd captured some of the missing women and children, in the honest belief they'd caught a handful of Russians. And the captives would be too fearful to hint they wanted to escape...

"We came to recover some of our missing people," he said. "We will want to see your captives first, just so we know who you have."

"That would be understandable," the alien said. "And the other Russians?"

John looked down at his hands. The Russians were doomed if they returned to Earth, he knew - and they would know it too. *Someone* would win the right to execute them, probably their own government. Maybe, just maybe, they could start to make up for what they'd done on Vesy.

"We will offer the remaining Russians the choice between remaining with you or returning home," John said. It would have a major effect on the planet's stability, he was sure, but secrets like gunpowder had already leaked. For better or worse, no one would be able to put the genie back in the bottle. "If they wish to join you, they will be allowed to do so."

"That would be acceptable," Ivan said. "And their mates?"

"They will be offered the same deal," John said. God alone knew what would happen to the women, the ones who had fallen in love with the Russians. If they wanted to stay behind, did he have the legal right to remove them by force? "But if they refuse to stay, we won't force them to stay."

"That would also be acceptable," Ivan stated. "Now, there is also the issue of military support against the God-King."

John groaned, inwardly. He had legal authority to take whatever steps were necessary to safeguard British lives and property, but none what-soever to intervene in local affairs. It was possible he could justify it as a defensive measure, after the God-King had attacked the Marines, yet the Admiralty might not buy his explanation. There were going to be enough problems after news of the whole affair reached Earth, no matter what else happened. It was quite possible he'd find himself facing a Court Martial for breaching the Non-Interference Edict. In politics, *someone* had to take the blame…and the Russian CO was dead.

But, at the same time, didn't they have a moral obligation to help Ivan?

And by the time I get orders from Earth, he thought, *the whole issue would be settled, one way or the other.*

"There is a limit to what we can provide," he said, slowly. "What sort of assistance would you require?"

"The Russians provided hammers from heaven," Ivan said. It took John a moment to realise he meant KEWs. "Can you provide the same?"

"For a while," John said. "But not for long."

They fell to haggling. After nearly an hour of heated discussion, John agreed to provide KEW support for a week, which would also give him time to set up a small settlement well away from the Vesy. Their great lakes held any number of isolated islands that could serve as a base, at least for the moment. Once the remaining humans were moved there, *Warspite* could return to Pegasus.

"Very well," Ivan said, afterwards. "I thank you."

"I thank you too," John said. He wondered how long that would remain true. There was a very good chance of a Court Martial in his future. "And I wish you the very best of luck in the future."

He wondered, absently, just what would happen to Ivan. The alien could regain his throne, then…then, what? Set up links with human traders and attempt to boost his people forward? Or try to ban human technology, in the hopes of avoiding social change? But it was unlikely to work. Gunpowder was far from the only genie that could never be stuffed back into the bottle. The Russians had tried to introduce so many ideas that the Vesy would be able to start moving forward in leaps and bounds, once they had a chance to relax and assimilate what they'd been told.

But, in the end, he knew he would just have to wait and see.

———

"Are you serious about this, Corporal?"

"Yes, sir," Percy said.

"You're requesting a transfer to Vesy," Hadfield said. "Never mind that you're effectively the First Corporal. Never mind that there will be promotion in your immediate future. Never mind...you're requesting a transfer."

"Yes, sir," Percy said, again.

Hadfield leaned back in his chair. "Stand at ease, Corporal, and talk frankly," he ordered. "Why?"

Percy took a breath. "Sir, with all due respect, I am one of the few people on this ship who speaks Russian," he said. "There isn't time to teach the Vesy English, even if we were inclined to do it. And there will *have* to be a number of Marines assigned to the settlement anyway, sir. I am the most qualified Marine to remain behind."

"That is true," Hadfield agreed. He paused. "You may not have realised this, Percy, but you've effectively requested an independent command."

"Sir?"

Hadfield smiled, rather ruefully. "I cannot desert my post," he said. "If I put you down on Vesy, with a handful of Marines, you would be the senior Marine. It wouldn't last."

"No, sir," Percy said. "I imagine it won't be long before a full company of Marines - or squaddies - is assigned to Vesy. However, I don't think we can afford to leave the Vesy without British contact even for a few short months."

"And it would do your career a power of good," Hadfield said, slowly. "Or are you going to try to convince me you never thought of that?"

"No, sir," Percy said.

"Very wise," Hadfield said. He met Percy's eyes for a long moment. "The Captain will have to be consulted, of course. I believe he will wish to leave a number of other personnel on the ground, at least for a few weeks. If he agrees, you will be left here until formal contact is opened and a proper garrison is dispatched. After that...you may be sent back to Earth and reassigned to the personnel pool. It could put a hitch in your career."

"I know, sir," Percy said.

"And I advise you to be very careful," Hadfield added. "These are not humans, Percy, even though they are humanoid. They may have moments

345

when they are completely unpredictable. You would be wise to bear that in mind at all times."

"Yes, sir," Percy said.

"Dismissed," Hadfield said. "You may want to write a new will."

Percy somehow managed to keep his smile off his face until he left the makeshift office. It wouldn't be pleasant, remaining on the planet once the ship had departed, but *someone* would have to remain…and why not him? Hadfield was right; if he established himself as one of the leading translators, as well as an expert in the alien culture, it *would* give his career a colossal boost. Yes, it would be risky. But if he hadn't wanted a risky life, he would have gone into accounting and spent his days helping wealthy businessmen to escape paying taxes.

Penny would be surprised, he knew, and so would his girlfriend. They'd expect to see him back on Earth, when *Warspite* returned. But he knew Penny, at least, would understand…

…And besides, she would probably be one of the first reporters demanding a pass to visit Vesy. He'd see her again soon.

———

"So you do want to return to Cromwell," John said.

"Yes, Captain," Gillian McDougal said. She sat in John's office, sipping a mug of tea. "My husband is there, waiting for me."

Your husband is in some trouble, John thought. It hadn't taken him long to realise that Gillian McDougal's husband was Hamish McDougal, one of the rebels from Cromwell. *But at least he's alive.*

"Then we will take you back, once we have a transport," John said. He knew there would be complaints - a doctor would be invaluable on Vesy - but he didn't want to hold her against her will. "What about the others?"

Gillian frowned. "Most of them want to go to Cromwell too," she said. "But some…some are scared of what they will face, soon."

John nodded, slowly. There had been a campaign, in the latter half of the war, targeting partners who cheated while their other halves were at the front. It had been a persistent problem, he knew; officers and crewmen received 'dear john' letters while they were serving, which tended to destroy their morale. Husbands and wives who did cheat had been hounded by the mob, some even being tarred and feathered. The war might be over, but its legacy remained.

And most of the settlers waited for years for their wives, John thought. He knew how *he* would have felt, if he had waited so long only to be disappointed, and he doubted it was any different for straight men. *They won't react well when some of their wives return, pregnant with another man's child.*

He cursed, inwardly. On Earth, the whole ghastly affair could be sorted out without violence; on Cromwell, it might not be so easy.

"We can take messages from the women to their husbands," he said. "And then...well, maybe they can see what sort of reaction they get."

"It might work," Gillian said. "But none of them had much of a choice."

"I know," John said.

He sighed. A man could accept an adopted child, either by marrying a widow or adopting a new child, because he *knew* the child was adopted. But it was harder to accept a cuckoo in the nest, even if the woman hadn't had a choice. There would be suspicion, which would rapidly harden into paranoia, about just what had happened...and nagging from well-meaning people would only make it worse.

We won, he thought. *And now we have to clear up the mess.*

"We will see," he said. "I..."

His intercom bleeped. "Captain, this is Armstrong," Armstrong said. "Can I report to you?"

John's eyes narrowed. "Yes, you can," he said. He gave Gillian an apologetic look, then keyed a switch. "Midshipwoman, please escort Doctor McDougal to the shuttlebay."

Armstrong stepped into the cabin as Gillian was escorted out. "Captain," he said. "You know I have been studying the tramlines in this system."

"Yes, I *know*," John said, tartly.

Armstrong ignored his tone. "It's not so easy to predict the destination of an alien-grade tramline," he said. "The gravity fluxes can be harder follow unless..."

"Get to the point," John ordered.

"Sir," Armstrong said. "One of the tramlines leads to Pegasus."

John stared at him. "Are you sure?"

"As sure as I can be without actually jumping down the tramline," Armstrong said. "The computers give it a 90% chance of leading to Pegasus."

John fought down the urge to bang his head against the table. If they'd known…he could have whistled up an escort carrier, or a freighter, right away. But it was useful, at least; there would be a new way to reach Vesy, shaving several weeks off the journey. Pegasus was about to become considerably more important. And who knew what would happen then?

"We'll test it," he said. If Armstrong was right, they could get a transport from Pegasus, then move the women and children to Cromwell directly. "And then we will finally head home."

CHAPTER
FORTY

"This is a very interesting report, Captain."

"Yes, sir," John said. It had taken a month to get back to Earth, after shipping the colonists to Cromwell and having an urgent discussion with Governor Baxter. At least Gamble had remained in the brig until they finally reached Earth. "It changes everything."

"*That* is an understatement," the First Space Lord said. He'd come to Nelson Base to meet John personally, something that worried John more than he cared to admit. "You do realise that it has already leaked out?"

"Yes, sir," John said.

"It's hard to tell what the media is most agitated about," Admiral Finnegan said. "The problems faced by Cromwell, the Indians and Turks expanding their influence, the Russian pirates, the existence of a whole new alien race, you...*bending* the Non-Interference Edict...there will have to be a Board of Inquiry, you know."

"Yes, sir," John said again.

"The Russians are outraged, of course," Admiral Finnegan continued. "I believe the early reports didn't manage to *quite* get across the concept of Russian renegades, so the Russians got a great deal of stick for violating the Edict themselves. By now, things have cooled down a little, but the Russians are still demanding an inquiry. They may want to blame you and your crew personally."

John frowned. "For what?"

"The Russians are in a delicate place at the moment," Admiral Finnegan said. "They may have good reason to be pissed at you."

He shrugged. "The World Court will debate the issue of just who gets custody of the remaining prisoners in the next few months," he added. "They'll be held in custody until then, Captain. The Russians have already filed a motion to have them handed over to Moscow as deserters, in line with the EDO Treaty, but I don't think that will get them anywhere."

"Yes, sir," John said.

He frowned. "Sir, can I ask a question?"

The First Space Lord lifted his eyebrows, but said nothing.

"Why...why are the Russians playing games?" John asked. "This situation wasn't *Moscow's* fault."

"Tell me, Captain," Admiral Finnegan said. "Do you know what a super secret is?"

"No, sir," John said.

"Most government secrets are boring or useless," Admiral Finnegan said. "A great many classified files have merely been classified out of habit. Or hidden away to keep embarrassing truths buried under a mountain of bullshit. But a super secret, Captain, is one that could have the most horrific effects if it got out. A super secret could bring down a government or start a war."

He met John's eyes. "The answer to the question you asked is a super secret, Captain," he warned. "I believe that only a handful of people know just what's driving the Russians, but it cannot be allowed to become public knowledge. The results would not be pleasant."

"Yes, sir," John said. He knew there was no point in probing further. "I understand."

"Good," Admiral Finnegan said. He pressed his fingers together as he sat back in his chair. "News of another alien race has already excited everyone, as you know. There are dozens of plans being put together to send diplomatic or trading missions to the Vesy. We won't be the only ones, I'm afraid; there isn't anyone who can legally claim their system, not even the Russians. But then, that too would start a war."

"Because Moscow would be accepting responsibility for the pirates," John said.

"Precisely," Admiral Finnegan said. "I think there will also be some additional colonists heading to Cromwell, which may help to smooth out matters in that direction. The CDC has reluctantly agreed to uphold the deal you made, helped by some arm-twisting from the Admiralty. And Pegasus, too, will get extra support. I predict a bright future for the system."

"Yes, sir," John said.

"You will probably get a medal, once the Board of Inquiry has finished tearing you to shreds," Admiral Finnegan said. "I don't think everyone is happy with you leaving a small garrison on the planet."

"I know, sir," John said. "But it had to be done."

"It raises political implications," Admiral Finnegan said. "The World Court has already stressed that we *cannot* claim the system."

"I wasn't *trying* to claim the system," John reminded him.

"I know," Admiral Finnegan said. "But not everyone believes it."

He shrugged. "You did well, Captain," he said. "And you handled it as well as it could be handled. But there is another issue that should be raised."

John nodded. He knew what was coming.

"Commander Watson," the First Space Lord said. "You do realise that relieving her of her position will have made you enemies?"

"Yes, sir," John said.

"Good," the First Space Lord said. "So tell me. Why did you do it?"

John took a long breath. "Sir, Commander Watson is a genius, but with all due respect to her and her patrons, she is not remotely suited to serve as an XO. Any inquiry into her conduct while serving on *Warspite* will lead to unpleasant conclusions, starting with dereliction of duty. For example, she tolerated junior officers handling tasks she should have handled herself. If I had had a completely free hand, I would have relieved her of duty long ago.

"I do not believe, sir, that she actually *intended* to avoid doing her job, but an inquest will assume the worst. She will have to prove her innocence, sir… and it's impossible to prove a negative. Her career will be blighted for nothing."

"I will grant you that," Admiral Finnegan said. "But why didn't you relieve her earlier?"

"I believed I could compensate for her," John said. He resisted the temptation to point out that it had been Admiral Finnegan who had warned him about the political issues. "I had been an XO myself, sir, while Lieutenant-Commander Richards could be slotted into place to pick up her work. However, the formal position would still rest with her. If I had died on Cromwell, she would either have assumed command or been pushed aside by Richards and Howard. Both would have caused major problems when *Warspite* returned home.

"Those weren't the only issues. She was charged with supervising the crews, but she gave them so little supervision that one of them started to steal military-grade components, while falsifying the logs. This very nearly proved fatal to the entire ship, Admiral. It could have killed us all, including her."

"And you had a man executed for it," Admiral Finnegan observed. "The Board of Inquiry will dissect that decision too."

"Yes, sir," John said. "I expect as much."

He frowned. "After Cromwell, I knew I could no longer take the risk of Commander Watson succeeding me," he said. "As I noted in my log, she was excused from her rank to concentrate on her speciality."

"Yes," the First Space Lord said. "You covered that nicely, Captain."

"Thank you, sir," John said. "I believe she will come up with something that will revolutionise interstellar travel."

"It would certainly make it harder for your new enemies to have a go at you," Admiral Finnegan agreed. "For the moment, the decision is confirmed. It helps that *Warspite* shook down nicely and there is no longer an argument for keeping Commander Watson on the ship."

He shrugged. "You and your crew will remain here for several months, I believe," he said. "I've arranged matters for you to have a few days of leave before the inevitable inquest starts, Captain. I expect the World Court will wish you to testify as well. They may also wish to charge you with breaking the Edict yourself, although I have it on good authority that the Prime Minister has no intention of allowing the charges to stand. The media is on your side."

John smiled. "Thank you, sir."

"It wasn't my fault," Admiral Finnegan said. He shrugged. "Off the record, I would suggest you don't go down to Earth. Whatever the media may be saying, there's no shortage of lunatics ready to accuse you of mass murder. Or of disturbing the noble savages with human ideas. I suspect revisionist historians may wind up painting you as the villain of the piece."

"I see," John said.

"The world is full of idiots," Admiral Finnegan pointed out. "There are already people talking about plans to send shipments of teaching aids to the Vesy...and plans to collect all the Russian technology from the natives, just to save them from being contaminated any further. I doubt it will calm down anytime soon."

"Yes, sir," John said. "If I may ask, what does the government have in mind?"

"His Majesty's Government has yet to determine a policy," Admiral Finnegan admitted. "I have a feeling you may be called to testify in front of the Parliamentary Committee on Human-Alien Relations. Dealing with the Tadpoles is hard enough, Captain, but at least we have a broad consensus among the spacefaring powers. Here...it's possible that each and every government will develop its own policy. Some will seek greater engagement and influence with the Vesy; others, I fear, will wish to leave them completely alone."

"Yes, sir," John said.

Admiral Finnegan studied him. "What would you suggest, if you had the ability to decide?"

John considered it. "I don't think we can prevent the knowledge the Russians introduced from spreading, sir," he said. "Even if we pulled back and quarantined the entire star system, their society would still change. If we wanted to help, we should at least seek to guide them around the pitfalls we encountered when we were developing technology. But, at the same time, we and they might both wind up making new and horrific mistakes."

"True," Admiral Finnegan agreed. "What would you suggest?"

"Careful engagement," John said. "Besides, the Russians might have been on to something, when they saw the Vesy as future allies."

"And until then," Admiral Finnegan said dryly, "we also need to keep them from being exploited. And what happens if they *want* to be exploited?"

He rose. "Return to your ship, then enjoy a few days of rest," he added, as John stood. "You'll need it. The Board of Inquiry will give you no peace until it has dissected each and every decision you made. After that, we will find a new mission for *Warspite*. You may be sent right back to Vesy."

"Yes, sir," John said.

He saluted, then left the office and walked down to the shuttlebay. Nelson Base was secure, he reminded himself, as he boarded his craft. There would be no protesters in front of the gates, no crowds of civilians demanding answers or the head of someone who had been made a scapegoat. He nodded to the pilot, then sat down and keyed his console. A BBC news report appeared in front of him. Someone, somehow, had obtained footage recorded by the Marines during the battle.

"Well," the presenter said, when the clip had finished. Rumour had it that she was an artificial composite, rather than a flesh and blood human being. Her breasts were too big, her chest was too thin and her figure was a perfect hourglass shape. She was just too inhumanly sexy to be real. "What do you make of that?"

"It proves that the Royal Marines are still the toughest soldiers in the human sphere," one of her guests said. "They held out against overwhelming odds."

"It proves that mankind, once again, has exported her problems to the stars," the other guest said. "These aliens were no doubt civilised before humanity made contact with them."

"The aliens were fighting amongst themselves before the Russians landed," the first guest said. A pop-up note hastily clarified that the Russians had been renegades, rather than an official contact mission from Russia. "All the Russians did was introduce human weapons."

"Which made the fighting worse," the second guest said. "And then we slaughtered hundreds of them."

More like thousands, John said, although he had to admit she had a point. Human weapons and ideas had made the struggle for power on Vesy much - much -worse. *And it hasn't ended yet.*

He shook his head, then clicked off the channel. There would be a few days of shore leave, then the Board of Inquiry…and, if he survived that, he would return to his ship. And then…Admiral Finnegan *had* talked about a return to Vesy, after all. It would be exciting, perhaps, to see what had happened on the planet since their departure.

Colin would have loved it, he thought, as the shuttle docked with *Warspite. And I think he would have approved.*

The End

Warspite and her crew will return.
Soon.

APPENDIX
GLOSSARY OF UK TERMS AND SLANG

[Author's Note: I've tried to define every incident of specifically UK slang in this glossary, but I can't promise to have spotted everything. If you spot something I've missed, please let me know and it will be included.]

Beasting/Beasted - military slang for anything from a chewing out by one's commander to outright corporal punishment or hazing. The latter two are now officially banned.

Binned - SAS slang for a prospective recruit being kicked from the course, then returned to unit (RTU).

Bootnecks - slang for Royal Marines. Loosely comparable to 'Jarhead.'

'Get stuck into' - 'start fighting.'

'I should coco' - 'you're damned right.'

Levies - native troops. The Ghurkhas are the last remnants of native troops from British India.

Lorries - trucks.

Rumbled - discovered/spotted.

Squaddies - slang for British soldiers.

Stag - guard duty.

TAB (tab/tabbing) - Tactical Advance to Battle.

Walt - Poser, i.e. someone who claims to have served in the military and/ or a very famous regiment. There's a joke about 22 SAS being the largest regiment in the British Army - it must be, because of all the people who claim to have served in it.

Wanker - Masturbator (jerk-off). Commonly used as an insult.

Wanking - Masturbating.

16254713R00210

Printed in Poland
by Amazon Fulfillment
Poland Sp. z o.o., Wrocław